Susan ... g up an ac ... con- sultar ... , and has ta ... anthropology.

She is the creator of the Matthew Bartholomew series of mysteries set in medieval Cambridge and the Thomas Chaloner adventures in Restoration London, and now lives in Wales with her husband, who is also a writer.

Praise for Susanna Gregory

'A lively and intelligent tale set vividly in turbulent medieval England'   *Publishers Weekly* on *An Unholy Alliance*

'A good, serious and satisfying read'
                              Irish Times on *A Masterly Murder*

'Excellent . . . the historical research is first rate. All in all, great entertainment for cold winter days'
                              Eurocrime on *To Kill or Cure*

'Once again Susanna Gregory has combined historical accuracy, amusing characterisation and a corking good plot to present a section of British history that is often overlooked: the emergence from the Dark Ages to Renaissance in the field of education and medicine'
                    Historical Novel Society on *A Poisonous Plot*

'Carefully researched, imaginative and evocative . . . this is a gritty but humorous period mystery'
                         Good Book Guide on *The Cheapside Corpse*

'Gregory never fails to impress with her immaculate research, creating an exciting and vivid historical, social and political backdrop and embellishing her stories with authentic detail and thrilling atmosphere'
                    Lancashire Evening Post on *The Chelsea Strangler*

Also by Susanna Gregory

The Matthew Bartholomew series

A Plague on Both Your Houses
An Unholy Alliance
A Bone of Contention
A Deadly Brew
A Wicked Deed
A Masterly Murder
An Order for Death
A Summer of Discontent
A Killer in Winter
The Hand of Justice
The Mark of a Murderer
The Tarnished Chalice
To Kill or Cure
The Devil's Disciples
A Vein of Deceit
The Killer of Pilgrims
Mystery in the Minster
Murder by the Book
The Lost Abbot
Death of a Scholar
A Poisonous Plot
A Grave Concern
The Habit of Murder

The Thomas Chaloner series

A Conspiracy of Violence
Blood on the Strand
The Butcher of Smithfield
The Westminster Poisoner
A Murder on London Bridge
The Body in the Thames
The Piccadilly Plot
Death in St James's Park
Murder on High Holborn
The Cheapside Corpse
The Chelsea Strangler
The Executioner of St Paul's

SUSANNA GREGORY

THE DEVIL'S DISCIPLES

THE FOURTEENTH CHRONICLE OF
MATTHEW BARTHOLOMEW

sphere

SPHERE

First published in Great Britain in 2008 by Sphere
Paperback edition published in 2009 by Sphere
This edition reissued in 2018 by Sphere

1 3 5 7 9 10 8 6 4 2

ISBN 978-0-7515-6954-4

Papers used by Sphere are from well-managed forests
and other responsible sources.

MIX
Paper from
responsible sources
FSC® C104740

Typeset in Baskerville MT by Palimpsest Book Production Limited,
Falkirk, Stirlingshire
Printed and bound in Great Britain by
Clays Ltd, St Ives plc

Sphere
An imprint of
Little, Brown Book Group
Carmelite House
50 Victoria Embankment
London EC4Y 0DZ

An Hachette UK Company
www.hachette.co.uk

www.littlebrown.co.uk

For Bill Kirkman

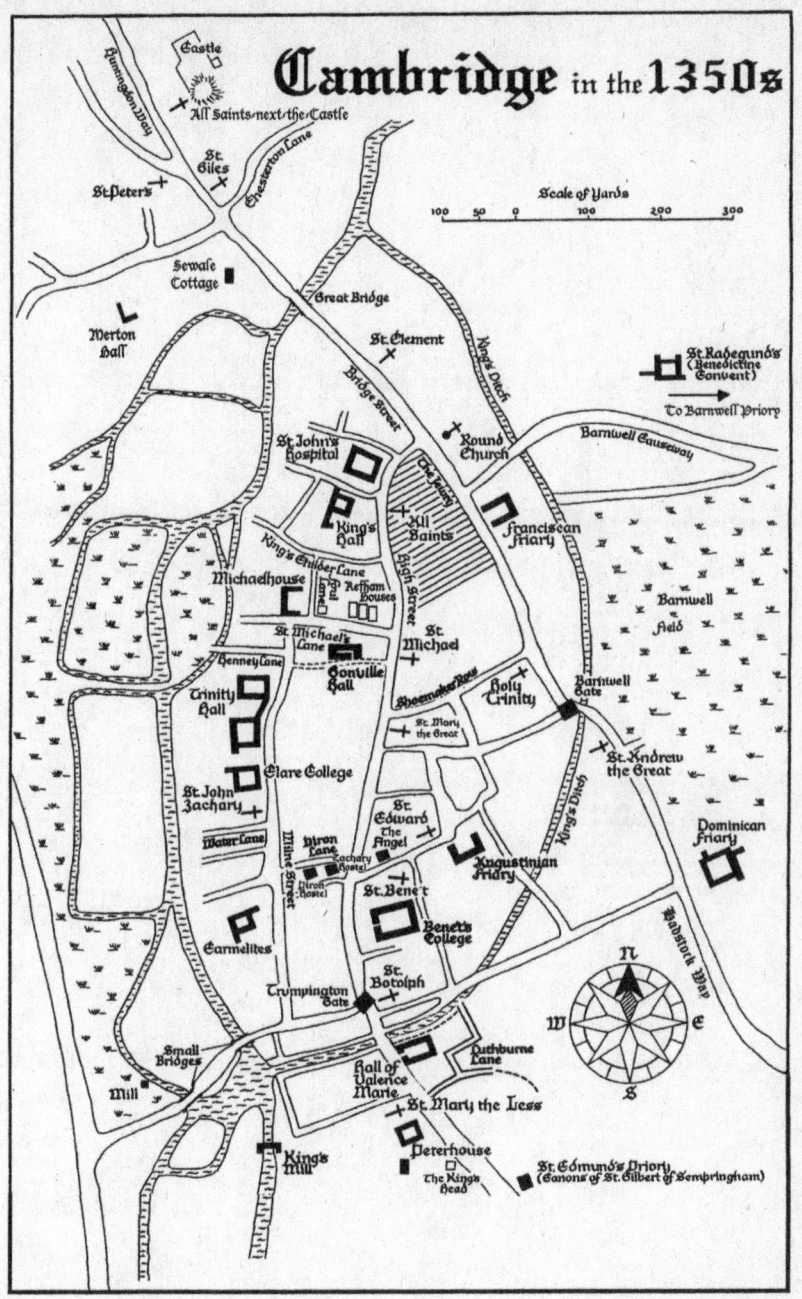

Cambridge in the 1350s

Castle
All Saints next the Castle
Huntingdon Way
St. Giles
Chesterton Lane
St. Peters

Sewale Cottage

Great Bridge

Merton Hall

St. Clement

Bridge Street

King's Ditch

St. Radegund's
(Benedictine Convent)
To Barnwell Priory

St. John's Hospital

Round Church

Barnwell Causeway

The Priory

King's Hall

All Saints

Franciscan Friary

Barnwell Field

King's Childer Lane

Michaelhouse

Astham Houses

St. Michael's Lane

Henney Lane

St. Michael

Gonville Hall

Shoemaker Row

Trinity Hall

Holy Trinity

Barnwell Gate

St. Mary the Great

St. Andrew the Great

Clare College

St. John Zachary

Water Lane

St. Edward The Angel

Augustinian Friary

Dominican Friary

Milne Street

Diron Lane

Zachary Hostel

Diron Hostel

St. Bene't

Bene't's College

Carmelites

St. Botolph

Trumpington Gate

Luthburne Lane

Babraham Way

N
W E
S

Small Bridges

Mill

Hall of Valence Marie

St. Mary the Less

King's Mill

Peterhouse

The King's Head

St. Edmund's Priory
(Canons of St. Gilbert of Sempringham)

Scale of Yards
100 50 0 100 200 300

Prologue

Cambridge, Ascension Day Eve (early June) 1357

It was almost a decade since the plague had swept across the country, snatching the lives of rich and poor, young and old, good folk and bad. Father Thomas would never forget the terror of not knowing who might be struck next, or of watching his fellow Franciscans die, one after the other. At first, the friars had believed they would be spared, because the Great Pestilence would only punish the wicked, but they could not have been more wrong. Indeed, a greater proportion of priests had died than laymen, a fact that had not been lost on the general populace. More than half of Cambridge's clerics had perished in those awful months.

But Thomas had survived. Unlike many of his brethren, he took his priestly vows seriously, and never let himself stray from the straight and narrow. When they bought themselves warm cloaks and good boots, he embraced poverty. When they pampered themselves with fine food, wine and even women, he piously declared that he had sworn to live a life of chastity and obedience. And when the plague had

1

descended on Cambridge, he had gone among the sick and dying, giving aid where he could. He had been spared, which he put down to the fact that he was an upright, God-fearing man, and when the disease had finally relinquished its hold on the little Fen-edge town, he made sure everyone knew it.

In the years that followed, he preached fervently about the dangers of sin. People had listened at first, but as time rolled on and the hideous memories began to fade, they slowly slid back into their old ways. Thomas was on the verge of giving up – let the Devil have their rotten souls, if that was what they wanted – but then he had met a fellow Franciscan named Edmund Mildenale. Mildenale had a single message: unless people repented, the Death would return, sweeping away evildoers so only the righteous would be left. Thomas was delighted. Mildenale's warnings matched exactly what *he* had been saying for the past nine years, and he spoke with a fiery conviction that was wonderful to hear. Thomas immediately joined ranks with him.

Mildenale liked to hold forth in the open air, rather than the more formal setting of a church, and encouraged his friends to do likewise. So, that morning Thomas was standing on a water-trough behind St Mary the Great, regaling passers-by with a description of what they would suffer in Hell unless they renounced evil. No one was taking much notice, which was annoying. Why could they not see that his message was important? Were they really so stupid? Then David and Joan Refham began to heckle him. Thomas loathed the Refhams – a coven of witches met in the abandoned church of All Saints-next-the-Castle on Sunday nights, and he was sure they were members.

'God did not help the faithful when the plague came last time,' Joan shouted challengingly. 'So why should we waste our time in churches now? Besides, sinning is a lot more fun than praying.'

'The Sorcerer will save us if the pestilence comes again, anyway,' declared Refham. 'He told us so himself, and I trust him a lot more than I trust your fickle God.'

Thomas was horrified by the number of passers-by who seemed to be nodding agreement. 'But the Sorcerer is a warlock,' he cried, aghast. 'He draws his strength from Satan.'

'Well, at least Satan listens,' countered Refham, beginning to walk away, bored with the debate. 'Which is more than can be said for God and His so-called saints.'

The exchange shocked Thomas, and he stopped sermonising to reflect on the growing popularity of the man everyone was calling the Sorcerer. At first, there had been nothing to distinguish him from the many other black-hearted rogues who convened sordid little gatherings in the depths of the night. All claimed they were better than the Church, and that their gods were stronger. But then tales began to circulate that the Sorcerer could heal the sick, provide protection against bad luck, and even grant wishes. Thomas grimaced. He and Mildenale had tried hard to find out the villain's real name, but the fellow was a master at keeping his identity secret – he wore a mask when he presided at his unholy gatherings, and he seemed to vanish into thin air the moment they were over. And it was difficult to fight a man who declined to show himself.

'Witchery is popular in the town at the moment, Father,' said Prior Pechem, seeing Thomas's disconsolate expression as he strolled past. Pechem was head of the

3

Cambridge Franciscans, although Thomas did not respect him. How could he, when Pechem declined to take a firm stance against sin? 'The Sorcerer is good at curing warts, and people admire him for that alone. But his star will fade – his kind always does – and the Church will be there to round up those who have strayed. Do not fret.'

But Thomas did fret, and thought Pechem a fool for underestimating the risk the Sorcerer posed. 'It may be too late by then,' he snapped. 'The Devil will—'

'I wrote to our Franciscan brethren in London, as you asked,' said Pechem, interrupting hastily before Thomas could work himself into a frenzy. 'As soon as I receive the answer to your question, I shall let you know. Of course, I am sure you are mistaken.'

'So you have said before, but I want to be certain.' Thomas began to speak more loudly, eager to make sure Pechem understood. 'Satan is all around us, and we must do everything to—'

'Quite so, quite so,' mumbled Pechem. 'Good morning to you.'

And then he was gone, reluctant to stand around when Thomas resumed his harangue, lest people thought he condoned the sentiments expressed in it. Thomas glared at his retreating back, then decided to abandon his efforts for the day. Refham's mention of the Sorcerer had un-settled him, and he found he was not in the mood for an impassioned tirade. He began to make his way home.

As he passed St Michael's Church, a solemn proces-sion emerged. The scholars of Michaelhouse had been praying for Margery Sewale, dead after a long illness. The College was the sole beneficiary of her will, and the Master was going to bury her the following morning. She had chosen an auspicious time to die, because the morrow was Ascension Day, and everyone knew that folk put in the ground on Ascension tended to spend less time in Purgatory than folk buried on other days.

Michaelhouse was Mildenale's College, so Thomas looked for him among the mourners. He saw him walking at the back of the procession, talking to two more Franciscans – Father William and Roger Carton. Thomas nodded amiably to Mildenale and Carton, although he greeted William rather more coolly. William had argued violently with him the previous evening, and hurtful remarks had been made on both sides.

He had not gone much further along the High Street when he felt a sudden, searing pain in his head. Then something struck his cheek, and he realised he had fallen face-down on the ground. Panicky voices rattled around him, echoing and distorted, but he recognised William's strident tones and Mildenale's softer ones. Then another joined in, this one calm, authoritative and reassuring. It was Doctor Bartholomew, Michaelhouse's physician, saying something about a thrown stone. Thomas raised a hand to his aching temple and felt a cut. Someone had lobbed a missile at him!

'It was a Dominican,' declared Father William furiously. William hated Dominicans, and blamed them for everything that went wrong, from bringing the plague to curdling his milk.

'Yes, one might well try to kill him for speaking out against sin,' agreed Mildenale. He made the sign of the cross. 'If so, then God forgive them for their wickedness.'

'Actually, I suspect it fell from a roof,' said Bartholomew with quiet reason. Thomas saw him glance up at the nearest houses, trying to see whether a tile had slipped.

But Thomas knew exactly what had happened. 'It came by magic,' he said, surprised to hear his voice sound so weak. 'A curse. The Sorcerer has set his poison on me.'

'Poison?' bellowed William, cocking his head as he strained to hear the whispered words. 'The Dominicans have poisoned you?'

'No, he said the Sorcerer did it,' corrected Carton. He sounded fearful. 'He did not mention Dominicans – and for all their faults, I do not think they go around cursing people.'

'Yes, they do,' countered William dogmatically. 'And they have murdered Thomas because he had the courage to stand against them. They—'

'He is not going to die,' interrupted Bartholomew firmly. 'The wound is superficial, and he will be perfectly well again soon. Help me carry him to the College.'

It was not long before Thomas was comfortably installed in the room Michaelhouse kept for visitors. It was a pleasant place, with clean blankets, polished wood and bunches of lavender hanging from the rafters. But Thomas was too agitated to appreciate the décor. He could not stop thinking about the Sorcerer – he was *sure* the man had caused the stone to fly through the air by some vile magic. The fellow wanted him dead, because he was prepared to make a stand against him. How long would it be before he tried it again? Why not that very day, while he was wounded and vulnerable? He tried to stand, but found himself frail and dizzy.

'Lie still,' said Bartholomew gently. He held out a cup that was brimming with a pleasant-smelling liquid. 'And drink this. It will help you sleep.'

'I cannot sleep,' Thomas objected, trying to shove it away. 'The Sorcerer has poisoned me with a curse. I must remain vigilant, to fight him when he comes.'

'You were hit by a stone,' said Bartholomew practically. 'Curses had nothing to do with it.'

Thomas did not believe him. 'The Sorcerer will kill me if I stay here, and then the Devil will have my soul. I must go home . . .'

'You are safe here,' said Bartholomew comfortingly. 'And you will feel better after a good night's sleep. By this time tomorrow, you will be strong enough to do battle with a dozen sorcerers.'

He had a convincing manner, and Thomas *was* tired. Moreover, Michaelhouse had sturdy gates, and porters to guard them. The Sorcerer could not come in. So Thomas snatched the proffered cup and downed the contents in a series of noisy gulps, ignoring the physician's pleas for him to drink more slowly. But there was no point in pussyfooting around: he had made the decision to swallow the remedy and recoup his strength, so he might as well get on with it. He lay down and closed his eyes, waiting for sleep to come. He would resume his war with the Sorcerer tomorrow.

But by the following morning, Thomas was dead.

'What happened?' cried Mildenale, looking at the body of his fellow Franciscan in dismay. More practical, Carton pushed past him, and began to intone prayers for the dead.

'I do not know.' Bartholomew was shocked. 'He should have slept soundly all night, and woken feeling rested this morning. I do not understand.'

'Was it the medicine?' demanded Mildenale, fighting back tears. 'Could that have killed him?'

'It was just a sleeping draught,' replied Bartholomew, dazed. 'It cannot have been—'

'Is it usual to provide sleeping draughts to patients with grievous head wounds?' Mildenale was working himself into a frenzy of grief. 'I have always understood from other physicians that it is better to keep them awake, so you can monitor their wits.'

'His injury was not that serious,' objected Bartholomew. 'And he was agitated, so I decided rest was the best remedy—'

'But you were wrong,' said Mildenale, his face white with anguish. 'You misjudged the situation. And in so doing, you have brought about the death of a friend and a fellow Franciscan.'

John Danyell stood on Bridge Street and felt fear wash through him. It was the darkest part of the night, and the shadows on Bridge Street were thick and black, yet he knew someone was watching him. What should he do? Run to the castle, where there would be soldiers to protect him? Hide in one of the dank, sordid little alleys that led down to the river? He was exhausted, not only from the effort of completing what he had had to do that evening, but from weeks of uncertainty and terror. He was not sure if he had the strength to run or to hide.

It was all the Bishop's fault, of course. If de Lisle had not been such an evil, ruthless tyrant, then Danyell would not have had to make the journey to London in the first place. He could have stayed at home in Norfolk, teaching his sons the masonry skills he had acquired over the years. He closed his eyes and wished with all his heart that he had never quarrelled with de Lisle. What had started as a minor spat had fast degenerated into a deadly feud, which culminated in the Bishop sending henchmen to besiege Danyell in his own home. Danyell shuddered at the memory; he had been sure they were going to murder him. Later, his friend Richard Spynk – another of de Lisle's victims – suggested they go to London together, to tell the King what his Bishop did in his spare time. Danyell had agreed without hesitation, full of righteous indignation at the way he had been treated by the malevolent prelate.

In London, he and Spynk had met others who had suffered at de Lisle's hands, and together they had presented a compelling case to His Majesty. Unfortunately, the wily Bishop had promptly fled to Avignon, where he skulked behind the Pope's skirts, although his henchmen had been forced to stand trial. Danyell had been delighted when the King imprisoned some and fined others: de Lisle's reign of terror was coming to an end. However, it was not quite over yet.

A second flicker of movement caught Danyell's eye, and he backed deeper into the shadows surrounding Margery Sewale's cottage. He had never met Margery, being just a visitor to the town, but he had heard she was to be buried the following day. Her house was empty, but the scholars of Michaelhouse – who now owned it – had left a lamp burning in her window. Or rather their servants had. Danyell had overheard one telling his cronies that a light would prevent her ghost from causing mischief, as ghosts were wont to do on the eve of their funerals. The scholars would not have approved of leaving an unattended flame in a valuable piece of property, so the book-bearer had only indulged his superstition after the academics had gone home.

Danyell's heart pounded when he heard the scrape of

a shoe on cobbles. Someone was definitely there. He reached for the amulet that hung around his neck, and gripped it hard. He did not know if it could protect him from whoever lurked in the darkness, but the witch who had sold it to him swore it was the most powerful charm she had ever made. He hoped she had been telling the truth.

There was another footfall, nearer this time. A figure emerged from the shadows and stopped. It seemed to be staring right at him. Danyell felt sick with fear. When the figure took a step towards him, his legs wobbled and he struggled to keep them from buckling. The figure advanced slowly, and Danyell thought he could detect a malicious grin in the faint light from Margery's lantern. Then he felt something grab him around the chest. In sudden agony, he dropped to his knees. Was it over? Had the Bishop won after all?

Chapter 1

Three scholars and a book-bearer stood in mute shock around the open grave. Margery Sewale had been hoisted from what should have been her final resting place and flung to one side like a sack of grain. Matthew Bartholomew, physician and doctor of medicine at the College of Michaelhouse, bent down and covered the sorry remains with a blanket, wondering what sort of person would stoop to such a despicable act. He glanced up at the sky. Dawn was not far off, although it was still too dark to see without a lantern, and the shadows in St Michael's churchyard remained thick and impenetrable. He jumped when an owl hooted in a nearby tree, then spun around in alarm when something rustled in the undergrowth behind him.

'Whoever did this is long gone,' said Cynric, his book-bearer, watching him. 'I imagine the villain went to work around midnight, when he knew he was least likely to be disturbed.'

Bartholomew nodded, trying to calm his jangling

nerves. Cynric had told him as much when he had broken the news of his grim discovery, along with the fact that the culprit had left nothing behind to incriminate himself – no easily identifiable shovel or trademark item of clothing. Nothing, in fact, except the result of his grisly handiwork.

'How did you come to find her?' the physician asked, wondering what Cynric had been doing in the graveyard at such an hour in the first place.

'You were gone a long time with the patient who summoned you earlier, and I was getting worried. Besides, it is too hot for sleeping. I was coming to find you, when I stumbled across her.'

He glanced at Margery and crossed himself. Then the same hand went to his neck, around which hung several charms against evil. The wiry Welsh ex-soldier, who had been with Bartholomew since his student days in Oxford, was deeply superstitious, and saw nothing contradictory in attending church on Sundays and consulting witches on Mondays.

'And you saw nothing else?' Bartholomew asked, rubbing his eyes tiredly. He could not recall the last time he had slept. The town was currently plagued by an outbreak of the flux – a virulent digestive ailment – and patients were clamouring for his services day and night. 'Just Margery?'

Cynric grasped his amulet a little more tightly. 'She was quite enough, thank you very much! Is anything missing?'

'There is nothing to steal,' replied Bartholomew, a little bemused by the question. 'She left Michaelhouse all her jewellery, so none was buried with her. And her shroud is a poor quality—'

12

'I do not mean ornaments, boy,' said Cynric impatiently. 'I mean body parts.'

Bartholomew gaped at him. 'What a horrible notion! Why do you ask such a thing?'

'Because it would not be the first time,' said Cynric, a little defensive in the face of his master's revulsion. 'You found the corpse of that Norfolk mason on Ascension Day, and what was missing from him? A hand! We said then that it was probably stolen by witches.'

That was true, although Ascension Day was more than a week ago – a long time in the physician's hectic life – and he had all but forgotten trudging home after visiting patients, and spotting the body in the wasteland opposite Margery's house. The mason had probably died of natural causes, and had almost certainly been dead when someone had relieved him of his fingers. However, the incident was disturbing when viewed in conjunction with what had happened to Margery.

'The town is full of witchery at the moment,' said Ralph de Langelee, Master of Michaelhouse, speaking for the first time since he had been dragged from his bed to witness what Cynric had found. He was a great, barrel-chested man, who looked more like a soldier than the philosopher he claimed to be, and most of his colleagues thought he acted like one, too. He was not noted for his intellectual contributions to University life, but he was an able administrator, and his Fellows were well satisfied with his just and competent rule.

Bartholomew was staring at the body. 'And you think Margery was excavated for . . .'

'For satanic rites,' finished the third scholar Cynric had called. Brother Michael was a Benedictine monk who taught theology. He was also the University's Senior

Proctor, responsible for maintaining law and order among the hundreds of high-spirited young men who flocked to the little Fen-edge town for their education. His duties included investigating any crimes committed on University property, too, so it would be his unenviable task to track down whoever had exhumed Margery.

'A lot of folk are refusing to attend church at the moment,' elaborated Langelee, when he saw the physician's blank expression. 'And they are joining covens instead. So I suppose it is not surprising that this sort of thing is on the increase.'

'Well?' asked Michael, when Bartholomew made no move to see whether Margery's body had suffered the same fate as the mason's. The physician was his official Corpse Examiner, which meant it was his job to assess anyone whose death the monk deemed suspicious. 'Has Margery been pruned?'

Bartholomew winced at his choice of words. 'I gave you a verdict when she died two weeks ago – of a long-term weakness of the lungs. You cannot ask me to look at her again.'

'I can, and I do,' said Michael firmly. 'I need to know why this outrage was perpetrated. Besides, Margery was your patient *and* your friend. You cannot refuse her this last service.'

Bartholomew regarded the body unhappily. He *had* been fond of Margery, and wanted to see the maniac who had despoiled her behind bars, but he had never been comfortable inspecting corpses that had already been laid to rest. He did not mind examining fresh ones; indeed, he welcomed the opportunity, because they allowed him to further his limited knowledge of anatomy, an art that was forbidden in England. He did not even

14

object to examining ones past their best, although he did not find it pleasant. However, when he was forced to look at bodies that had been buried, he invariably found himself overwhelmed by the unsettling notion that they were watching him with ghostly disapproval. He knew it was rank superstition, but he could not help it.

'Hurry up,' urged Langelee, when the physician hesitated still. 'I need to return to the College soon, to lead the procession to morning mass.'

Taking a deep breath to steady himself, Bartholomew pulled off the blanket, and counted Margery's fingers and toes. All were present and correct, and so were her nose and ears. Her hair was matted and stained from its time in the ground, but he did not think any had been hacked off, and her shroud also seemed intact. He was aware of the others moving back as he worked, and did not blame them. The weather was unseasonably warm, even before sunrise, and Margery had been dead too long. Flies were already buzzing, and he knew she would have to be reburied as soon as possible, lest she became a hazard to health.

'Nothing is missing,' he reported, sitting back on his heels and wiping his hands on the grass. It did little to clean them, and he would have to scour them in the first available bucket of water. His colleagues mocked him for his peculiar obsession with hygiene, but he considered it one of the most important lessons he had learned from the talented Arab *medicus* who had taught him his trade.

'Then why was she dragged from her tomb?' demanded Langelee.

'Perhaps the culprit heard me coming, and fled before he could sever anything,' suggested Cynric rather ghoulishly.

But Bartholomew disagreed. 'If he had wanted a body part, he could have taken one when she was still in the grave – he did not have to haul her all the way out to slice pieces off.'

'And I dug her an especially deep pit, because it has been so hot,' said Cynric, nodding acceptance of his master's point. 'I did not want her bubbling out, see. It cannot have been easy to pull her all the way up.'

'Then why?' asked Langelee, regarding the gaping hole with worried eyes. 'I do not understand.'

'Perhaps it is enough that she is exhumed.' Michael wiped his sweaty face with his sleeve. 'Some of the covens that have sprung up of late have devised some very sinister rites. I shall have to order my beadles to pay additional attention to graveyards from now on.'

'It must be the weather,' said Langelee. 'I have never known such heat in June, and it is sending folk mad – encouraging them to leave the Church, join cadres, despoil graves at midnight . . .'

'What shall we do with her?' asked Cynric, indicating Margery with a nod of his head. 'Shall we have another grand requiem, and lay her to rest a second time?'

'That would cost a fortune,' said Langelee. 'And the College cannot afford it. Besides, the fewer people who see her like this, the better. We shall rebury her now, and say a mass later. I do not suppose you know any incantations to keep her in the ground this time, do you, Brother?'

'I do,' said Cynric brightly. 'Or rather, Mother Valeria does. Shall I buy one for you? She is a very powerful witch, so I hope you appreciate my courage in offering to step into her lair.'

16

Langelee handed him some coins, ignoring the monk's grimace of disapproval. 'Make sure she provides you with a good one, then. We do not want to be doing this again tomorrow.'

When Margery was back in the earth, Bartholomew followed Michael into the church, leaving Cynric to pat the grave-soil into place and Langelee to return to the College. It was still not fully light, so the building was dark and shadowy. It was also pleasantly cool, and Bartholomew breathed in deeply, relishing the familiar scent of incense, old plaster and dry rot. Then he made for the south porch, where a bucket of water was always kept. He grabbed the brush that was used for scouring flagstones, and began to scrub his hands, wondering whether they would ever feel clean again.

'Did you notice the door was unlocked when we came in?' asked Michael irritably. 'How many more times must I tell everyone to be careful? Do they *want* our church burgled?'

'I am sorry, Brother,' said Bartholomew, glancing up at him. 'That was me. Clippesby offered to say another mass for Father Thomas, and afterwards, I must have forgotten . . .'

'It is time you stopped feeling guilty about Thomas's death,' said Michael firmly. 'We all make mistakes, and you cannot be expected to save every patient. He was not a—'

He stopped speaking when the door clanked, and someone walked in. It was their colleague, Father William, a burly friar with unruly brown hair that sprouted around a badly maintained tonsure, and a habit so deeply engrained with filth that his students swore it was the vilest garment in Christendom. William nodded to Michael, but ignored the physician, making the point that *he* was not yet ready to forgive or forget what had happened to his fellow Franciscan. He busied himself about the church, while Bartholomew finished washing his hands and Michael went to prepare for the mass. After a while, Bartholomew went outside, uncomfortable with the reproachful looks being aimed in his direction by the dour friar.

He sat on a tombstone, feeling sweat trickle down his back, and wondered why the weather had turned so hot. Did it presage another wave of the plague? He sincerely hoped not, recalling how useless traditional medicine had proved to be. There had been some survivors – himself among them – but their recovery had had nothing to do with anything he had done. His failures made him think of Thomas again, and he wondered whether he would ever be able to forgive himself for prescribing a 'remedy' that had killed the man. He closed his eyes, feeling weariness wash over him, but they snapped open when a howl echoed from the church.

He leapt to his feet and raced inside. William was standing over the baptismal font, pointing a finger that shook with rage and indignation. Flies buzzed in the air around him. Bartholomew ran towards him, then wrinkled his nose in disgust when he saw what had agitated the friar. There was a pool of congealing blood in the font.

Quickly, before their colleagues arrived for morning prayers, Bartholomew washed the font, while William scattered holy water around the desecrated area. The friar was livid, not just about the sacrilege, but about the fact that he had risen early to say prayers for Thomas,

18

and resented being diverted from his original purpose. Bartholomew tuned out his diatribe, not wanting to hear yet more recriminations about the man he had killed. Fortunately, it was not long before Langelee arrived, bringing with him the remaining Fellows, a gaggle of commoners – men who were granted bed and board in exchange for light teaching duties – and the College's students.

William gabbled through the mass at a furious lick that had the students grinning in appreciation. Their delight did not last long, however: it soon became apparent that he was rushing because he was scheduled to give the Saturday Sermon, and wanted as much time as possible in which to hold forth. Langelee had inaugurated the Saturday Sermons for two reasons. First, they provided the student-priests in his College with an opportunity to hone their preaching skills before they were assigned parishes of their own, and second, they allowed him to keep an eye on the fifty or so lively young men under his care on a day when they should have had a lot of free time.

Unfortunately, the Sermons were deeply unpopular with everyone. The students detested being cooped up inside, while the senior scholars objected to having the mumbled speeches of novices inflicted on them. And there was another problem, too. Michaelhouse had seven Fellows, five of whom were in religious Orders. The clerics also demanded a chance to pontificate in front of an audience that could not escape or interrupt, and Langelee could only refuse them for so long. And that Saturday, with the sun beginning to blaze down from a cloudless sky and the streets baked as hard as fired clay, it was William's turn. When the mass was over, the Master stepped forward with a marked lack of enthusiasm, made

19

a few ambiguous remarks about the quality of the day's speaker, and indicated with a nod that William could begin.

Flattered by the Master's introduction – although Bartholomew would not have been pleased to hear himself described as 'a man of probable wisdom' – William took a deep breath and drew himself up to his full height. His colleagues braced themselves. The Franciscan had always held strong opinions, but they had grown even more radical over the past few weeks, and he had become obsessed by the belief that the University was full of heretics – and by 'heretic' he meant anyone who disagreed with him. Because few scholars shared his dogmatic views, he was convinced the *studium generale* in the Fens was bursting at the seams with heathens, and considered it his personal duty to roust them all out.

'Heretics,' he boomed. The volume of his yell made several Fellows jump, which led to an outbreak of sniggering among the students. Michael silenced them with a glare; and when the Senior Proctor glared, wise lads hastened to behave themselves.

'Not heretics *again*,' groaned Langelee. 'He ranted about them last time, too.'

'It is all he talks about these days,' agreed Michael. 'And the town's current fascination with witchery is not helping, either – it is making him worse than ever.'

'The familiars of Satan swagger in our midst, and today I shall tell you about them,' promised William, a little threateningly.

'Here we go,' sighed Langelee. He spoke loudly enough to be audible to most of the gathering, although William was too engrossed in his own tirade to notice.

'They call themselves *Dominicans*,' William declared,

delivering the last word in a sibilant hiss that gave it a distinctly sinister timbre. He wagged his forefinger at the assembled scholars. 'And do you know why we know them as *Black* Friars? Because black is the Devil's favourite colour, and they wear it to honour him.'

'I thought Satan had a penchant for red, actually,' said Rob Deynman, newly installed as College Librarian. He was infamously slow witted and had no business holding a University post, but his father was rich and the College was prepared to overlook a great deal for money. A puzzled frown creased his normally affable face. 'At least, he is wearing scarlet in all our wall-paintings.'

'Yet another tirade against the poor Dominicans,' Langelee went on wearily. 'We are lucky they treat his remarks with the contempt they deserve, by ignoring them. They would be perfectly within their rights to take umbrage, you know. I would, if I were a Black Friar.'

'No one takes any notice of William's warped theories,' said Michael. Then his eye lit on Deynman. 'Well, no one with sense, that is.'

'I wish that were true.' Langelee pointed at two scholars who wore Franciscan habits. They were not exactly nodding agreement with William's harangue, but they were looking interested enough to encourage him to continue. 'Mildenale and Carton are sensible men, but they are listening to him. Perhaps it is because all three belong to the same Order.'

Michael's expression immediately became troubled. 'I wish Mildenale had not come to live with us twelve months ago. I know he taught here for a few years before going to become a parish priest in Norfolk and he was one of Michaelhouse's very first Fellows – so we are obliged to house him when he asks, but he worries me. Did you know our students call him *Mildenalus Sanctus* because of his extreme religious views?'

'Yes, "Mildenale the Holy" indeed. It is most alarming. I do not want my College populated by fanatics.'

'Fortunately, his converts are down to two now Thomas is dead. I understand why William thinks he is worth following – William is stupid and gullible, and has always fostered radical opinions – but I am disappointed in Carton. I thought *he* was more intelligent.'

'So did I. Why do you think he does it?'

Michael shrugged. 'It cannot be because he is a fellow Franciscan; no other Grey Friar has joined their little cabal. Personally, I think the Sorcerer is responsible for drawing Mildenale, William and Carton together. They are afraid of him, and feel there is safety in numbers.'

'The Sorcerer?' asked Langelee. 'What sorcerer?'

Michael raised his eyebrows. 'You have not heard the rumours? One of the heathen cadres that has sprung into being of late has an especially powerful leader who calls himself the Sorcerer.'

'I doubt Mildenale will be afraid of some self-appointed diabolist,' said Langelee doubtfully. 'He will see him as an enemy of God, and will itch to destroy him. You know how intolerant he, William and Carton are of anything even remotely pagan.'

'Unfortunately, the Sorcerer has a huge following, and that makes him dangerous. Father Thomas was convinced he was a Dominican, and may have persuaded Mildenale to his point of view.'

'And is the Sorcerer a Dominican?'

'Of course not! He will not be a friar of any description. However, I have no idea who he is.'

Langelee was thoughtful. 'Do you think this Sorcerer

has anything to do with the blood in the font? Or what happened to Margery?'

'William certainly believes so, but I shall reserve judgement until I have more information. Unfortunately, I am not sure how to proceed. I have been trying to infiltrate the Sorcerer's coven for weeks, but to no avail.'

Langelee clapped an encouraging hand on his shoulder. 'Do not fret, Brother. We have only just started the half-term break, so you now have eight lecture-free days to find answers.'

The monk regarded him balefully. It was true that teaching was suspended for the few days between the great festivals of Pentecost and Trinity Sunday, but Langelee did not want his students with too much time on their hands, lest they caused trouble in the town. To keep them out of mischief, he had organised a number of events, all of which the Fellows were obliged to supervise.

'I shall not have a moment to think,' he grumbled, 'let alone hunt grave- and font-despoilers.'

'You are excused, then,' declared Langelee promptly. 'Margery left our College all her worldly goods, so it is only right that we find out why she was desecrated.'

The monk looked crafty. 'I shall require help. Excuse Matt his College duties, too.'

'Are you sure?' asked Langelee doubtfully. 'He has not been himself since he killed Father Thomas, and might be more hindrance than help.'

Michael shrugged. 'Then it will do him good to think about something else.'

'You should challenge William's nasty insinuations, Matt,' said Michael, as he and his colleagues strolled home an hour later. It was sooner than anyone had anticipated,

23

because Langelee had grown steadily more appalled by the bigoted tirade, especially when William began to declare that Bartholomew's medical practices were prime examples of witchery in action, and had interrupted to announce it was time for something to eat. William had been incensed, declaring he was not halfway through what he wanted to say, but everyone else had applauded the Master's actions, even the Franciscans. 'Your refusal to defend yourself makes it look as though he might have a point.'

Bartholomew did not reply. His ears still rang from the discourse – not only from its poisonous content, but from its sheer volume – and he could not remember a time when he had been more exhausted. If William's voice had not been so loud, he might have fallen asleep where he stood. He took a deep breath, to clear his wits, but the air was hot and dry and not in the least bit refreshing. Next to him, Michael wiped his face with a piece of linen that was already soaked with sweat.

'I am sure you have a perfectly legitimate reason for visiting Mother Valeria the witch,' the monk went on. 'But declining to tell William what it is will see you in trouble.'

'It is none of his business,' said Bartholomew shortly. 'Besides, I shall have no patients left if I bray details of their ailments to anyone who asks, and the College would not like that.'

Michaelhouse derived a good deal of kudos from the fact that its resident physician was willing to doctor the town's poor – and that he invariably forgot to charge for his services. His absent-minded generosity meant his College was attacked far less often than other academic institutions, and the free consultations and medicines he dispensed to the needy saved it a fortune in riot damage.

'Mother Valeria is your *patient*?' asked Michael. He

24

watched his friend grimace, disgusted at the inadvertent slip. 'Do not worry; I will not tell anyone. But why did she come to you? She is a healer, and should know enough cures, spells and incantations to make herself better. She, of all people, should not need a physician.'

'Well, she did this time.'

Bartholomew was not usually brusque with his friends, and the monk found it disconcerting. 'You need an early night, my friend,' he said. 'Or are your dreams troubled by what happened with Thomas?'

Bartholomew winced. 'I have not managed to sleep much since —'

'You must put it from your mind. Dwelling on the matter will help no one.'

Bartholomew gave a rueful smile. 'I was going to say that I have not slept much because there has been no opportunity. There are only three physicians to serve the whole town, and the hot weather seems to have precip-itated this outbreak of the flux. I spend most nights with patients, so dreaming – about Thomas or anything else – has not really been possible.'

'And napping during the day is out, because of teaching. Langelee was wrong to have enrolled so many new students last Easter, because none of us can really manage, what with Clippesby still on leave. I never thought I would miss Clippesby – he is insane, after all – but I wish he was home.'

'I do not – not as long as Mildenale and William persist in their claims that all Dominicans are Satan-worshipping heretics. Clippesby is a Black Friar, and even his gentle temper would baulk at putting up with that kind of nonsense day after day.'

'William has always hated Dominicans,' said Michael.

'And having someone else who thinks the same way must be enormously satisfying for him. He is alone in his bigotry no longer.'

'But he has not always hated me, and I am not a Dominican, anyway. Yet these days, he attacks me at every opportunity. Is it just because of Thomas, or have I done something else to annoy him?'

'It is just because of Thomas. They quarrelled bitterly the night before he died, and William said things of which he is now ashamed; it is easier to be angry with you than to admit he behaved badly. Of course, you are not his only target at the moment. He seems ready to condemn the religious beliefs of virtually everyone in Cambridge these days.'

'He may have a point this time. Superstition is more rife than I have ever known it, and several of my patients say they regularly consult witches for charms and spells.'

'It is a pity the Church's most vocal supporter is *Mildenalus Sanctus*,' said Michael unhappily. 'He does more harm than good with his diatribes. Indeed, *I* feel like applying for membership of a cadre when I hear what he thinks the Church represents.'

Both scholars glanced behind them, to where the man in question was walking with Carton and William. Mildenale, a commoner, was in his late fifties, but still sported a head of lank black hair. He was in the habit of looking skywards when he spoke, as though addressing Heaven, although Bartholomew was sure the angelic hosts would not be impressed with some of the vitriol that spouted from his mouth. Like most people, the physician was uncomfortable with Mildenale's unbending piety, and he was certainly disturbed by the man's uncompromising views on 'heretics'.

Carton, on the other hand, was a Fellow, and he taught law. He was short, serious and something of an enigma. Although Bartholomew liked him well enough, he found he never knew what the friar was really thinking, and there was something reserved and distant about him that would prevent them from ever becoming real friends.

'I was just telling Langelee that I think the Sorcerer is to blame for our Franciscans joining forces,' Michael went on. 'He is becoming increasingly popular in the town, seducing people away from the Church. It was only when Mildenale realised how serious a threat the Sorcerer posed that he started recruiting the likes of William, Carton and Thomas.'

'And now Thomas is dead,' said Bartholomew, forcing himself to discuss a topic that was still painful for him. 'When I tended his wound, he told me the Sorcerer is a Dominican.'

'William and Mildenale agree. Of course, I have no idea what Carton thinks, given that I have never met a man more difficult to read. But the preaching of all three is a distraction I could do without. Monitoring them will impede my two investigations.'

'What two investigations?'

Michael's grin was rather crafty. 'I am glad you asked, because I need your help. The first is the blood that was left in our font; we must find out who put it there, because we cannot have it happening again. The second is learning who desecrated Margery Sewale's grave.'

Bartholomew held up his hands and began to back away. 'I cannot, Brother. I need the half-term break to prepare next term's teaching, or my students will not learn the—'

'You are my Corpse Examiner,' said Michael firmly.

27

'You cannot refuse. Besides, Langelee said you can be excused College duties if you assist me.'

Bartholomew thought about the cycle of disputations and lectures Langelee had organised. The timetable was so full that there would be very little time for preparing lessons; helping Michael meant the situation might be a good deal more flexible. 'Very well,' he said. 'But it does not set a precedent for the future.'

Michael smiled serenely, thinking a precedent had been set the first time they had ever investigated a murder together, some nine years before. Bartholomew just did not appreciate it.

Unfortunately for the monk, Bartholomew did not make it as far as the College before he received a summons from a patient. It was Isnard the bargeman, who lived in a cottage near the river. As usual, Isnard had spent his Friday night at the King's Head tavern, and had awoken that morning to find himself with a deep cut on his foot. He could not remember how it had happened, but it was an inconvenient injury, because it was the only foot he had; Bartholomew had been forced to amputate the other after an accident two years before.

'Someone must have done it during the night,' declared Isnard, when Bartholomew arrived and he saw that Michael had accompanied him. The bargeman was desperate to make a good impression on the monk, and did not want to be seen as a drunkard. 'It could not have happened at the King's Head, not with me drinking watered ale all night.'

He adopted a pious expression, and Bartholomew laughed. 'I heard the taverner broached a new cask of claret last night.'

Isnard's face was all innocence. 'Really? I did not notice. And I would not have swallowed claret anyway, because it might damage my voice. I have been keeping it honed, you see, for when I am allowed back in the Michaelhouse Choir.'

'My choir is full at the moment,' said Michael coldly. 'I have all the basses I need.'

'But none are as loud as me,' objected Isnard. His expression was piteous. 'Please let me rejoin, Brother. Singing in the King's Head is not nearly as much fun as singing with you, and we do not get free bread and ale after practices, either.'

Michael was unmoved, and turned his attention to the physician. 'Have you finished, Matt? My tenors are coming to see me this morning. We are going to discuss arrangements for the Feast of Corpus Christi, at which they will perform.'

'Will they?' asked Bartholomew unhappily. The choir was not the College's greatest asset, and Isnard had summed up its abilities rather neatly when he had boasted about the loudness of his voice. What the ensemble lacked in talent it made up for in volume, and took pride in the fact that once it got going, it could be heard up to two miles away, if the wind was blowing in the right direction.

'We are doing Tunstead's *Jubilate*,' added Michael as he sailed out, head in the air. It was a cruel thrust, because the *Jubilate* was one of Isnard's favourite pieces. The bargeman made a strangled sound that might have been a sob, and Bartholomew hastened to finish his bandaging, reluctant to witness the man's misery. Isnard caught his hand before he could leave.

'You must help me, Doctor! I have apologised for

saying rude things about you earlier this year, and you have forgiven me, so why does *he* continue to be offended? I cannot bear hearing the choir sing and not be allowed to join in. Please talk to him. If you do, I will give you a spade.'

'A spade?' echoed Bartholomew, startled. It was not an item guaranteed to appeal to the acquisitive instincts of most physicians.

'For digging up dead bodies,' whispered Isnard, tapping his nose confidentially. 'We all know it was a *medicus* who took Margery from her grave – for anatomy. And since Paxtone refuses to touch corpses, and Rougham condemns anatomy as a pagan rite, you are the only one left.'

'I did not exhume Margery,' cried Bartholomew, appalled that anyone should think he had.

Isnard looked sheepish. 'I see. Well, perhaps you will accept something else as a bribe then. A jar for storing urine, perhaps. I could get you a nice one. Will you talk to Brother Michael for me?'

Bartholomew mumbled something noncommittal, still shaken to learn he was seen as the kind of man who went around digging up the graves of his patients, and headed for the door. Michael was waiting outside, and shot him a sidelong glance as they began to walk along the towpath together.

'I suppose he asked you to put in a good word for him,' he said coolly. 'Well, you can save your breath. He harmed you with his accusations about your medical skills earlier this year, and it will be a long time – if ever – before people forget the lies he told. You may not bear him a grudge, but I do. I do not want him in Michaelhouse.'

'None of your other choristers are angels,' Bartholomew pointed out, thinking of the disreputable crowd that was attracted by the prospect of free victuals and enjoyable evenings spent bawling at the tops of their voices. 'It is no coincidence that the Sheriff knows most of them by name.'

Michael's expression was haughty. 'That may well be true, but I prefer thieves and vagrants to villains who attack my Corpse Examiner with unfounded, vicious allegations.'

'Isnard promised me a spade if I convinced you to let him back in.' Bartholomew did not tell the monk what Isnard thought he might do with it. 'Michaelhouse could do with some new tools.'

Michael began to laugh. 'A spade? Is that all he could think of to offer? You should hold out for a hoe, at the very least.' They walked in silence for a while. 'What do you make of Carton?'

Bartholomew was taken aback by the question. 'He is a good teacher. Why?'

'His students would disagree. He was a better educator when he was a commoner – before we elected him a Fellow. Since then, he has grown aloof and preoccupied, and seldom gives lectures his full attention. He is a fine example of someone who has been promoted above his abilities.'

Bartholomew's first instinct was to defend Carton, who was a colleague when all was said and done, but then it occurred to him that Michael was right. He recalled how the Franciscan had come to Michaelhouse in the first place. 'Clippesby recommended him to us.'

'And Clippesby is insane, so we were stupid to have accepted Carton on his word. You were the one who advocated Carton's promotion to Fellow, though, and it is not the wisest suggestion you have ever made. I thought he was just shy at first, but now I know him better, I realise timidity has nothing to do with it. He is actually rather sinister.'

Bartholomew was uncomfortable with the conversation. 'I would not go that far . . .'

Michael raised his eyebrows. 'All the Fellows – except William – are wary of him. None of us like the fact that he went so suddenly from quiet nonentity to a man with strongly controversial opinions.'

'I suppose it *is* odd,' conceded Bartholomew reluctantly. 'Perhaps he will be better when Mildenale leaves to found his hostel. That will not be long now, a few weeks at the most.'

'I doubt that will help – they will still see enough of each other to be dangerous. I thought Thomas's sermons were bad enough – driving listeners into the Sorcerer's eager arms – but Carton, Mildenale and William are much worse.' Michael grimaced when he saw the physician's stricken expression. 'Thomas's death was *not* your fault, Matt. How many more times must I say it?'

'Actually, it was. Thomas was fretful, so I gave him a sedative, hoping rest would speed his recovery. But it sent him into too deep a sleep – with fatal consequences. Even my rawest recruit knows never to sedate patients with serious head wounds.'

Michael frowned, puzzled. 'Then why did you do it?'

'Because I thought the injury was superficial; he exhibited none of the usual symptoms that indicate harm to the brain. But I was wrong. William's anger with me is wholly justified.'

'Why was Thomas fretful?' asked Michael curiously.

'He thought the Sorcerer had sent the stone flying through the air by dark magic. I do not believe in the power of curses, but he did, and I should have taken that into account. I have seen other perfectly healthy patients die because they have convinced themselves there is no hope.'

Michael raised his eyebrows. 'So, did Thomas die because you gave him the wrong medicine, or because he believed his time was up? You cannot have it both ways.'

'It was probably a combination.'

Michael was dismissive. 'You are taking too much on yourself. However, the guilt you feel should not prevent you from telling William the truth about Mother Valeria. What is the harm in saying you are treating her for an ailment, not learning how to be a witch yourself?'

'William cannot be trusted to keep a confidence, and what would happen to Valeria once it became known that she is obliged to consult physicians? Customers would lose faith in her cures, and she would starve. Besides, he should know I would never dabble with witchcraft.'

Michael gave a short bark of laughter. 'You might, if you thought it would help a patient. No, do not deny it. You are too open-minded for your own good where healing is concerned, and your medical colleagues are always chastising you for using unorthodox treatments.'

'I would never resort to witchcraft,' insisted Bartholomew firmly. 'Never.'

'You just said you should have listened to Thomas's belief that he was cursed,' Michael pounced.

Bartholomew rubbed his eyes, struggling to think logically. It occurred to him that he might not have prescribed the sedative had he not been so exhausted, and knew tiredness was beginning to affect his teaching, too. Still, at least he had not fallen asleep in the middle of his own lecture, as Michael had done the previous week.

'Lord!' he groaned, when he saw a familiar figure striding towards them. 'Here comes Spaldynge from Clare College. Every time he meets me, he makes some barbed remark about physicians being useless during the plague. I know we failed to cure people, but it was almost a decade ago, and I am tired of him goading me about it.'

'Ignore him. He makes the same comments to anyone involved in medicine – physicians, surgeons, witches, and even midwives. Personally, I think he is losing his wits.'

'Greetings, murderer,' hissed Spaldynge, as he passed. 'Killed any patients recently? Other than Father Thomas and Margery Sewale, that is. Her long illness should have given you plenty of time to devise a cure, but you let her die. You are inept, like all your colleagues.'

'It is difficult to ignore him when he makes remarks like that,' said Bartholomew, when the man had gone. 'He knows how to hurt.'

Michael's expression hardened. 'It is Isnard's fault. He was the one who first questioned your abilities. Now do you see why I am not keen on having him back in my choir?'

The College of Michaelhouse – or the Society of the Scholars of the Holy and Undivided Trinity, the Blessed Virgin Mary, and St Michael the Archangel, to give it its proper name – was located just off one of the town's major thoroughfares. It comprised an attractive hall, two accommodation wings, and a range of stables and storerooms, all of which stood around a central yard. Sturdy

34

walls protected it from attack – even when there was peace between the University and the town, there were disputes between rival foundations to take into account.

The yard had been baked rock hard by an unrelenting sun, so even the hardiest weeds were now withered stumps. Hens blunted their claws as they scratched for seeds, and the College cat lay under a tree, too hot to chase the sparrows that dust-bathed provocatively close. The porter's pet peacock had been provided with a basin of water, and it sat in it disconsolately, trying to cool itself down. Cracks had appeared in the supporting timbers of the building where Bartholomew lived, and he hoped the roof would not leak all winter as a result. The vegetables planted by Agatha the laundress were ailing or dead, and none of the trees in the orchard would bear much fruit. Cambridge's oldest inhabitants said they had never known summer to come so early and so fiercely.

'Dinner has finished,' said Michael in disgust, seeing scholars stream from the hall, laughing and chatting with each other. Last out were William, Mildenale and Carton. Mildenale was holding forth and William was nodding vigorously, although Carton's face wore its usual impassive mask.

Bartholomew did not think missing a meal was much of a tragedy. The College was not noted for the quality of its cooking, and the weather was not helping. Supplies were going rancid, rotten or sour much faster than usual, and Michaelhouse scholars had been provided with some dangerously tainted foods since the heatwave had started. This was a cause for concern, because Bartholomew was sure spoiled meat was responsible for the flux that was currently raging in the town.

'My head aches,' complained Michael. 'Yesterday, you

35

said it was because I did not drink enough wine. Do you have any claret left?'

'I said you needed more fluids, not wine,' corrected Bartholomew, leading the way to his quarters. 'Claret will make your head worse. Watered ale is best in this weather.'

He lived in a ground-floor room, which he shared with four students. It was a tight squeeze at night, and there was only just enough space to unroll the requisite number of mattresses. The cramped conditions had arisen because the Master had enrolled an additional twenty scholars in an effort to generate more income. Bartholomew might have objected to the resulting crush, if he had not been so busy: his days were spent struggling with classes too large for a single master to manage, while evenings and nights were given over to his many patients.

He supposed he should not grumble about the size of his practice. It was only two months since a healer named Magister Arderne had arrived in the town, declaring magical cures were better than anything physicians could provide. Arderne had left eventually, but folk had been wary of *medici* ever since – Bartholomew's colleagues were still undersubscribed, because many folk now preferred to consult lay-healers, such as Mother Valeria or the Sorcerer. Bartholomew's own practice, however, comprised mainly people who could not afford witches, and they came to him in droves. He appreciated their loyalty, and knew he should not complain when they needed him.

When he opened the door to his room, he found Cynric waiting. 'Arblaster needs you,' said the book-bearer, standing and stretching in a way that suggested he had been asleep.

36

'Arblaster?' asked Bartholomew, trying to place him. He was better with ailments than names, and invariably remembered people by what was wrong with them.

'The dung-merchant who lives near Barnwell Priory,' supplied Cynric, adding sourly, 'Perhaps his fingers are stiff from counting all his money. Manure has made him very rich.'

He and Bartholomew had spent the previous year on a sabbatical leave of absence, and during it, Cynric had changed. He had expressed a desire to learn Latin, had grown more confident of his own abilities, and less impressed by those who ruled by dint of their birth or wealth. He had also developed a disconcerting habit of speaking his mind, and was rarely deferential.

'He is rich,' agreed Michael. 'But I am told he is a decent soul, even so.'

Cynric pulled the kind of face that said he thought otherwise. 'And when you have finished with him, Bukenham is waiting.'

'Bukenham?' asked Michael in alarm. 'My Junior Proctor? What is wrong with him?'

'Doctor Bartholomew has forbidden me to talk about his patients' problems,' replied Cynric, shooting his master a reproachful glance for putting such an unfair restraint in place. 'He says they expect confidentiality. But, since you ask, it is the flux.'

'Thank you, Cynric,' said Bartholomew, too tired to remonstrate.

'It is a long way to Barnwell,' said Michael, sitting on a stool. 'And then an equally long way to Bukenham's lodgings near the Small Bridges. I am glad *I* do not have to race about in this heat.'

'He has no choice,' said Cynric, watching Bartholomew

37

pack his medical bag with fresh supplies. 'Everyone knows this particular flux can be deadly unless it is treated promptly. If he declined to tend Arblaster and Bukenham, they might die.'

As he gathered what he needed, Bartholomew supposed word must have spread regarding his success in combating the disease, because neither the dung-master nor the Junior Proctor had ever summoned him before. The remedy he had devised involved boiling angelica and barley in water, and making his patients drink as much of it as they could. A few had refused, on the grounds that it sounded too mild a potion to combat such a virulent illness, and they were still unwell. All the others had recovered, with the exception of two who had succumbed before he had developed the cure. They were dead.

'You should buy a horse,' said Cynric, not for the first time during their long association. 'The Prince of Wales gave you a small fortune when you tended the wounded after the Battle of Poitiers last year, so you can afford it. Arriving at a patient's house on horseback better befits your status than traipsing about on foot.'

Bartholomew did not like to tell him that the 'small fortune' was almost gone, and that most of it had been spent on medicines for his patients. Besides, he was not a good rider, and horses tended to know who was in charge when he was on them. And so would anyone he was trying to impress.

He went to the jug of ale that stood on the windowsill, supposing he had better follow the advice he had given to Michael and drink something before he went, then recoiled in revulsion when the smell told him it was already spoiled, even though he had only bought it the day before. He tipped it out of the window, along with some milk his students had left. He heard the milk dropping to the ground in clots, and did not like to imagine what it looked like. Cynric offered to fetch ale from the kitchen, and while he waited, Bartholomew collected powdered barley from the little room next door, where he kept his medical supplies. Michael followed, griping about how busy he was.

'Not only do I have Margery's disinterment and the blood in the font to investigate, but there are Bene't College's damned goats to consider, too.'

'What do the goats want you to do?'

Michael glared at him, not in the mood for humour. 'Seven of them have been stolen, and Master Heltisle asks whether I have caught the thief every time we meet. Does he think the Senior Proctor has nothing more important to do than look for missing livestock?'

'Goats are expensive. I do not blame Heltisle for wanting them back.'

'They will be in someone's cook-pot by now, and I doubt we will ever know who took them. What in God's name is that?'

He pointed to a complex piece of apparatus that stood on a bench. It comprised a series of flasks, some of which were connected by pipes. A candle burned under one. Bartholomew checked it carefully, then added water.

'An experiment. Carton found some powder in Thomas's room, and wants to know if it is poison.'

Michael regarded him in alarm. 'Poison? You mean William might have been right when he claimed Thomas was dispatched by Dominicans? Lord knows, he gave them enough cause with his spiteful speeches. However, I was happier thinking you had killed him with the wrong medicine.'

39

Bartholomew recoiled. 'That is an unpleasant thing to say.'

'I am sorry, but it would be disastrous to learn Thomas was murdered. William, Mildenale and Carton will certainly accuse the Dominicans, and the Dominicans will object. And it will not be an easy case to solve after more than a week – Thomas was buried on Ascension Day. Do you remember Mildenale insisting he go in the ground then, because it might mean less time in Purgatory?'

'Do you believe that?' asked Bartholomew. 'Margery did, and so did Goldynham the silversmith, because they and Thomas were all interred on the same day.'

'Superstition and religion are often difficult to separate,' replied Michael, a little patronisingly. 'But I do not believe a particular day is more or less auspicious for going into the ground. It is what you do in life that counts, not when you happen to be buried. However, I am more concerned with this poison than in discussing theology. What can you tell me?'

'That I doubt you will be adding Thomas to your list of investigations. I do not think this powder is poison. It smells of violets, which are used in cures for quinsy, and Thomas often suffered from sore throats. And even if it does transpire to be toxic, there is nothing to say Thomas swallowed it. I told you – he died because I gave him the wrong medicine. I wish it were otherwise, but it is not.'

Michael rubbed his chin. 'Carton does not share your beliefs, if he asked you to test this powder. He sees something suspicious in what happened to his friend.'

'Immediately after the stone hit him, Thomas claimed the Sorcerer "poisoned" him with a curse. I suspect it was his odd choice of words that has encouraged Carton to look for alternative explanations – and the reason why he refuses to accept my culpability.'

'Could it be true? Thomas did preach very violently against the Sorcerer.'

'The Sorcerer may have lobbed the rock that caused the initial injury, I suppose. Thomas thought it was propelled magically, although I do not believe—'

'So he *was* murdered?' interrupted Michael uneasily.

'Stones fall from roofs, they are flicked up by carts, they are thrown around by careless children. I doubt you will learn what really happened after all this time.'

But Michael was unwilling to let the matter lie. 'I do not suppose you looked for evidence of poison when you inspected his body in your capacity as Corpse Examiner, did you?'

'Rougham acted as Corpse Examiner for Thomas. It would have been unethical for me to do it, given that Mildenale and William had accused me of malpractice. But even if I had inspected him, I could not have told you whether he was poisoned. Most toxic substances are undetectable.'

Michael nodded at the experiment. 'Then why bother with that?'

Bartholomew looked tired. 'Because Carton said Thomas would have appreciated it. It is the least I can do.'

Bartholomew stepped out of the comparative cool of his room moments after Cynric had delivered the promised ale. The yard was a furnace, and he could feel the sun burning through his shirt and tabard. Michael started to follow, intending to visit the proctors' office in St Mary the Great, but had second thoughts when he saw the heat rising in shimmering waves from the ground. Langelee spotted his Fellows, and beckoned them to stand with him in the meagre shade of a cherry tree.

'Do you think William made a valid point in his Sermon?' he asked uneasily. 'Not about the Dominicans being responsible for desecrating Margery, obviously, but about there being fiends in our town – the Devil's disciples? It would explain some of the odd things that have been happening: the blood in our font, Bene't College's disappearing goats . . .'

'Stolen livestock is not odd,' said Bartholomew, surprised Langelee should think it was. 'Cattle go missing all the time, especially now, when meat spoils quickly. Goats are good to steal, because they are small, easily hidden, and can be butchered and eaten with a minimum of fuss.'

'Yes, but goats also feature in satanic rites,' said Langelee darkly. 'Everyone knows that, and these were seven *black* ones. William said they are going to be sacrificed, to appease demons.'

Michael grinned. 'Cynric told me they are only temporarily missing, and will return to Bene't as soon as they have finished having their beards combed by the Devil. Unsurprisingly, Master Heltisle was not very happy with that particular explanation.'

Langelee winced as he looked over at the book-bearer. Cynric had been waylaid by Agatha, who was demanding to know who had been at the new ale; he was spinning her a yarn that would see William blamed for the crime. 'Neither am I. Cynric knows far too much about that kind of thing. It makes me wonder how he comes by this intimate knowledge.'

42

'Cynric is not a witch,' stated Bartholomew firmly, keen to knock that notion on the head before it became dangerous. He ignored the nagging voice in his head that told him his book-bearer *was* rather more interested in unholy matters than was decent.

'No, but he is not wholly Christian, either,' countered Langelee. 'He attends church, but he also retains his other beliefs. In other words, he hedges his bets, lest one side should prove lacking. Unfortunately, it does not look good for a senior member of the University to keep such a servant.'

'I cannot be held responsible for what Cynric believes,' objected Bartholomew. 'Besides, he has always been superstitious, and no one has ever held it against me before.'

'It is not just Cynric.' Langelee began to count off points on thick fingers. 'You killed Thomas, a vocal opponent of the Sorcerer. You make regular visits to Mother Valeria, a witch. The exhumed Margery was your patient. And it was you who discovered the mutilated body of the Norfolk mason.'

'His name was Danyell,' supplied Michael. 'Fortunately, the deaths of visiting craftsmen are for the Sheriff to investigate, so at least I am spared looking into *that* nasty incident.'

'Finding a body does not make me suspect,' protested Bartholomew. 'And it was hardly my fault Margery was excavated, either.'

Langelee regarded him uncomfortably. 'Danyell was missing a hand. Why would anyone lay claim to such a thing, except perhaps someone interested in the evil art of anatomy?'

Bartholomew regarded him in horror. 'You think I took it?'

Langelee studied him carefully, arms folded across his broad chest. 'No,' he said, after what felt like far too long. 'You would not be so rash – not after that trouble with Magister Arderne earlier in the year. And there is the other rumour to consider, of course.'

'What other rumour?' asked Bartholomew uneasily.

'The one that says Doctor Rougham made off with Danyell's hand,' replied Langelee. 'He denies it, but his arrogance has made him unpopular, and people do not believe him. As a consequence, he has decided to visit his family in Norfolk before he is accused of witchery. He left you a message, asking you to mind his patients.'

Bartholomew was aghast. 'How am I supposed to do that? I am overwhelmed already.'

'Especially as you have promised to help me find out who pulled Margery from her tomb and put blood in our font,' added Michael.

'Then the sooner you catch the culprit, the sooner people will see you had nothing to do with these unsavoury incidents,' said Langelee. 'So, you have a vested interest in making sure Michael solves these mysteries. Do not look horrified. It is the best – perhaps the only – way to quell the rumours that are circulating about Cambridge's dubious physicians.'

Chapter 2

Bartholomew was troubled by Langelee's contention that half the town thought he was a warlock, but was to be granted no time to answer the accusations. A second message arrived from Arblaster, urging him to make haste. Although he would have preferred to go alone, he found himself accompanied not only by Cynric, but by Carton, too. The newest Michaelhouse Fellow did not often seek out the company of his colleagues – other than William and Mildenale – and the physician was surprised when Carton expressed a desire to join him.

'I have business at Barnwell Priory, which you will pass *en route* to Arblaster's home,' Carton explained. 'As you know, they are interested in buying one of Michaelhouse's properties, and Langelee has asked me to clarify a few details. Do you mind me coming with you?'

'No,' replied Bartholomew warily, wondering if the friar wanted him alone so he could accuse him of heresy. Or perhaps his intention was to persuade him to take major orders. It would not be the first time a Franciscan had tried to recruit him; the Order was notoriously aggressive in grabbing new members. Unfortunately for them, Bartholomew was in love with a woman called Matilde, and had not quite given up hope that she might return to Cambridge one day and agree to become his wife. Although he had not seen her in almost two years, his feelings had not diminished, and he could hardly marry her if he became a priest.

Carton smiled his strange smile, and gestured that the physician was to precede him through the College's front gate. 'Good. This term has been so busy that we have had no time to talk.'

'Right,' said Bartholomew. He thought fast, trying to come up with a subject that would discourage Carton from interrogating him about the points William had raised in his Sermon: his association with Mother Valeria, and his willingness to consider medical theories that had not been derived from the teachings of ancient Greeks. 'Actually, I did not know Barnwell wanted one of our houses. Which one?'

Carton looked amused. 'It was the main topic of discussion at the last Statutory Fellows' Meeting. Were you not listening? I suppose it explains why you were so quiet.'

The conclave had been called shortly after Thomas's death, and Bartholomew had spent the time silently agonising over what had happened. 'I must have been thinking about something else,' he mumbled uncomfortably.

'Barnwell wants the house Margery Sewale left us. There has been a lot of interest in it, and Langelee needs a complete list of potential buyers.'

'He cannot go himself?'

Carton smiled again. 'I volunteered. I like the canons – they always invite me to join their prayers when I visit. In fact, I would rather we sold Sewale Cottage to them instead of to any of the laymen who are after it.'

46

Bartholomew led the way through the tangle of alleys called the Old Jewry, passing the cottage in which Matilde had lived. He let memories of her wash over him, barely hearing Carton's monologue on Barnwell Priory's beautiful chapels. He remembered her pale skin, and the scent of her hair. He was still thinking about her when they passed through the town gate, and stepped on to the raised road known as the Barnwell Causeway. The Causeway was prone to floods during wet weather, and there were many tales of travellers wandering off it and drowning in the adjacent bogs. That summer, however, it stood proud of the surrounding countryside, and the marshes were bone dry. It wound ahead of them like a dusty serpent, wavering and shimmering in the heat.

As they walked, Carton began talking about a text he had read on Blood Relics, while Cynric lagged behind, bored. Bartholomew was not gripped by the complex theology surrounding the Blood Relic debate, either, but was content to let Carton hold forth. The Franciscan became animated as he spoke, and his eyes shone; Bartholomew was reminded yet again that he was a deeply religious man. Then he frowned as the friar's words sunk in.

'You think the blood of the Passion is *not* separate from Christ's divinity?' he asked, unsure if he had heard correctly. 'That is the Dominicans' basic thesis.'

Carton looked flustered. 'Yes, I know. I was just following a line of argument, to see where it led. I was not propounding it as an accurate viewpoint. Of course Christ's blood is separate from His divinity. Every decent Franciscan knows that.'

Immediately he began to talk about something else, but the excitement was lost from his voice. Bartholomew

47

wondered what was wrong with him. Then it occurred to him that Carton was a good scholar, clever enough to make up his own mind about the Blood Relic debate, so perhaps he did not agree with his Order's stance on the issues involved. Of course, if that were true, then he was wise to keep his opinions to himself, because William and Mildenale would not approve of dissenters.

Not long after, Bartholomew looked up to see Spaldynge sauntering towards them. A servant staggered along behind him, laden down with pots; the Clare man had gone to the priory to buy honey for his College. There was no way to avoid him on the narrow path and, with weary resignation, Bartholomew braced himself for another barrage of accusations. Sure enough, Spaldynge opened his mouth when he was close enough to be heard, but Carton spoke first.

'I have been meaning to talk to you, Spaldynge,' he said. 'It seems we have a mutual acquaintance – Mother Kirbee and I hail from the same village. She told me she still mourns her son.'

The blood drained from Spaldynge's face. 'What?'

'Mother Kirbee,' repeated Carton. Bartholomew glanced at him, and was unsettled to note that the expression on his face was cold and hard. 'Her boy was called James.'

Spaldynge stared at Carton, his jaw working soundlessly. Then he pushed past the Michaelhouse men without another word and began striding towards the town, head lowered. He moved too fast for his servant, who abandoned his efforts to keep up when one of the jars slipped from his hands and smashed. Spaldynge glanced around at the noise, but did not reduce his speed.

Bartholomew watched in surprise, then turned to Carton. 'What was all that about?'

48

'I do not care for him.' Carton's voice was icy, and there was a glint in his eye that the physician did not like. 'He rails against *medici* for failing to cure his family, but does not consider the possibility that *he* was to blame. Perhaps he was being punished for past sins.'

Bartholomew regarded him uneasily. He had heard other clerics say plague victims had got what they deserved, but he had not expected to hear it from a colleague – a man of education and reason.

'Fifteen years ago, Spaldynge was accused of stabbing James Kirbee,' said Carton, when he made no reply. 'The charge was dropped on the grounds of insufficient evidence, but that does not mean he was innocent. I suspect Spaldynge's family paid the price for his crime when the plague took them.'

Bartholomew frowned. 'Are you sure? About the murder, I mean. I have never heard this tale—'

'Of course I am sure,' said Carton irritably. 'How can you even ask such a question, when you saw for yourself how he took to his heels when I confronted him with his misdeed?'

'He did look guilty,' acknowledged Bartholomew cautiously. 'But—'

'Sinners!' interrupted Carton bitterly. 'They brought the Death down on us the first time, and they will do it again. And Spaldynge is one of the worst.'

Bartholomew was not sure how to respond. He was stunned – not only to learn what Spaldynge had done, but by the fact that Carton was ready to use it against him.

'Did you test that powder from Thomas's room?' Carton asked, changing the subject before the physician could take issue with him. Bartholomew supposed it was just as well, given that neither would be willing to concede the other's point of view and the discussion might end up being acrimonious. 'Was it poison?'

'The experiment is still running. Where did you find it again?'

'In a chest under his bed. I thought it might explain why he died so suddenly, because I still do not believe you killed him. No one should blame you, and it is time you stopped feeling guilty about it.'

Bartholomew blinked, baffled by the man and his whirlwind of contradictions – from spiteful bigot to sympathetic friend in the space of a sentence. Then they arrived at Barnwell Priory, and Carton left to knock on the gate, relieving the physician of the need to think of a response. Once he had gone, Cynric came to walk at Bartholomew's side. The book-bearer squinted at the sun.

'The Devil is responsible for all this hot weather. Father William said so.'

There was something comfortingly predictable about Cynric's superstitions – far more so than Carton's bewildering remarks. Bartholomew smiled, relieved to be back in more familiar territory.

'William told me the Devil is getting ready to unleash the next bout of plague on us, too,' he said. 'So he must be very busy.'

Irony was lost on Cynric, who nodded sagely. 'The Devil is powerful enough to do both *and* comb the beards of Bene't's goats. Carton is a strange fellow, do you not think? He is not the man he was. In fact, he has changed so much that there is talk about him in the town.'

'I do not want to hear it, Cynric,' warned Bartholomew. He had never approved of gossip.

50

'You should, because it affects Michaelhouse. It is his stance on sin – he condemns it too loudly.'

Bartholomew did not understand what his book-bearer was saying. 'I should hope so. He is a priest, and that is what they are supposed to do. If he spoke *for* it, I would be worried.'

'You are missing my point. He condemns it *too* loudly – and it makes me think it is a ruse.'

Bartholomew regarded him blankly, still not sure what he was trying to say. So much for being in familiar territory. 'A ruse?'

'For what he really thinks,' elaborated Cynric. 'Because it is said in the town that Carton is the Sorcerer.'

Bartholomew was used to his book-bearer drawing wild conclusions from half-understood facts, but this was a record, even for him. He regarded Cynric in astonishment, not knowing how to begin disabusing him of the notion, but aware that unless the belief was nipped in the bud fairly smartly, it would flower into something permanent.

'No,' he managed eventually. 'Carton is not a heretic, and you cannot say—'

'He has always been interested in witchery,' interrupted Cynric. 'We used to spy on the covens together, the ones that meet in St John Zachary or All Saints-next-the-Castle – I have been keeping an eye on them since the Death, as you know. Then he stopped coming, just like that. It was because he joined one, see. And he was so good at it that they made him their master. It is true!'

'It is not,' said Bartholomew, appalled that Cynric should have devised such a monstrous theory on such a fragile thread of 'evidence'.

51

'Think about it logically,' persisted Cynric. 'All the Fellows were asleep when Margery was hauled from her grave and the blood was left in our font – except Carton. I happened to notice his bed was empty as I walked past his room.'

'I was not asleep then, either,' Bartholomew pointed out. 'And it was very hot last night. I am sure Carton was not the only one who got up in search of cooler air.'

'He was,' declared Cynric, with absolute certainty. 'Similarly, you were all teaching when Bene't's goats went missing, but Carton was busy elsewhere – alone. And who was the only man to go out on the night Danyell died and his hand was chopped off – *other* than you? Carton!'

'Coincidence,' said Bartholomew. 'There will be perfectly rational explanations for all this.'

'There will,' agreed Cynric. 'And they are that he is the Sorcerer – the man whose dark power grows stronger every day, and who aims to seduce decent, God-fearing men away from the Church.'

'Is that the Sorcerer's intention, then?' asked Bartholomew, changing the tack of the discussion. He knew from past debates that Cynric would never accept that his 'logic' might be flawed, and did not want to argue with him. 'To promote his coven at the expense of the Church?'

The book-bearer nodded with great seriousness, then pointed to a small blemish on the palm of his hand. 'Along with banishing warts. I had one myself, so I bought one of his remedies, and you can see it worked. He is not all bad, I suppose.'

'Lord!' muttered Bartholomew, at a loss for words. He was beginning to wish he had made the journey alone, and wondered whether the heatwave was responsible for some of the peculiar thinking that was afflicting his Michaelhouse cronies.

'Here is Arblaster's house,' said Cynric, regarding it with disapproval. 'It is recently painted, which tells you he has money to squander while decent folk must eke a living in the fields.'

'He probably paid someone to do the work,' countered Bartholomew, getting a bit tired of the book-bearer's flamboyant opinions. 'Which means he provided employment for—'

'Great wealth is all wrong,' interrupted Cynric firmly. 'And against God's proper order.'

Bartholomew was tempted to point out that if Cynric felt so strongly about 'God's proper order', he should not be wearing pagan amulets around his neck. But he said nothing, and instead studied the cottage that so offended the Welshman's sense of social justice. It was larger than he expected, with a neat thatch and fat chickens scratching in the garden. Tall hedges surrounded a field that released a foul smell; he supposed it was where Arblaster composted the commodity that had brought him his fortune. Seven black goats were tethered under a tree by the river. While they waited for the door to be answered, Cynric jabbed the physician with his elbow and pointed at them.

'Bene't College lost seven black goats,' he said meaningfully.

Bartholomew rubbed a hand over his eyes. 'So Carton is the Sorcerer, and Arblaster – a respectable merchant – steals the University's livestock? What other tales can you concoct? That Master Langelee has a penchant for wearing our laundress's clothes?'

'No, but your colleague Wynewyk does,' replied Cynric,

without the merest hint that he was jesting. 'They are too large for him, but he makes do.'

Bartholomew was relieved when the door opened, saving him from more of Cynric's unsettling conversation. A woman stood there, small and pretty. She wore a red kirtle – a long gown – with a close-fitting bodice that accentuated her slender figure. Her white-gold hair was gathered in plaits at the side of her face, held in place with an elegant silver net called a fret. Her dark blue eyes were slightly swollen, showing she had been crying.

'Doctor Bartholomew,' she said with a wan smile. 'I recognise you from the public debates in St Mary the Great. It is good of you to come, especially as we are Doctor Rougham's patients, not your own. I am Jodoca, Paul Arblaster's wife.'

Bartholomew recognised her, too, because even scholars in love with women they had not seen for two years could not fail to notice such pale loveliness. His students talked about Jodoca in reverent tones, and had voted her the town's most attractive lady. He nodded a friendly greeting and stepped inside, grateful to be out of the sun at last.

The house smelled of honey-scented wax, and a servant was on her knees in the hearth, polishing the stones. Silken cloths covered the table and there were books on a shelf above the window. Bartholomew could see by the embossing on the covers that they were philosophical tracts, indicating that someone was interested in honing his mind. The house and its contents told him the Arblasters were wealthy folk who paid heed to the finer points of life. It told Cynric so, too, and he looked around him disparagingly.

'I have been so worried about Paul,' Jodoca went on. 'I am at my wits' end.'

'What is wrong with him?' asked Bartholomew. 'The flux?'

She nodded miserably, then turned to Cynric. 'There is new ale in the pantry, and it must have been an unpleasantly hot walk for you. My maid will show you where it is kept.'

Cynric beamed in surprise, and Bartholomew was under the impression that the book-bearer might be prepared to overlook her disgusting wealth if polite consideration was shown to servants.

'I have been watching for you from the upstairs window,' said Jodoca, looking back at Bartholomew. 'For one awful moment, I thought you were going to see the canons at Barnwell first. I saw one of you go in, and was afraid I might have to run over and drag you out again.'

'That was Carton,' provided Cynric, willing to be helpful in return for his ale. 'Michaelhouse is selling a cottage, and he has gone to discuss terms with the Prior. But we came straight here, because your summons sounded so urgent.'

'It is urgent,' said Jodoca, fighting back tears. 'I am frightened for Paul. We are used to dung, being in the business and all, but this flux is too horrible, even for us.'

'I will be in the pantry, then,' said Cynric, evidently thinking this was more detail than he needed. He had disappeared before Jodoca could add anything else.

Bartholomew allowed Jodoca to haul him along a corridor to a pleasant chamber at the back of the house. Here, the odour was rather less pleasant. The patient was sitting in bed, surrounded by buckets. He was pale and feverish, but not so ill that he could not do some writing. A ledger was on his knees, and he was recording figures in it. He smiled when Bartholomew was shown in.

'At last! I was beginning to think you might not come. It is a long way from town, and I understand you do not own a horse. It is a pity. Nags are good sources of dung.'

Arblaster was a large, powerful man with thick yellow hair that sprouted from his head in unruly clumps. He was a burgess, and Bartholomew had seen him taking part in various civic ceremonies, when the hair had been carefully wetted down in an attempt to make it lie flat. It usually popped up again as soon as it was dry, showing that attempts to tame it were a waste of time. Bartholomew knew little about him, other than the fact that he purchased large quantities of aromatic herbs to prevent the odour of his wares from entering his home: the apothecary claimed Arblaster was a bigger customer than all three of the town's physicians put together.

'I thought he was going to Barnwell Priory first,' said Jodoca, plumping up his pillows. 'But that was Carton, going to discuss house business with Prior Norton.'

'I suppose Barnwell is interested in Sewale Cottage,' said Arblaster. 'Greedy devils! They will own the entire town soon.'

Bartholomew went to feel the speed of the dung-merchant's pulse, already sure Arblaster was not as ill as his wife seemed to think. 'When did you first start to feel unwell?'

'Last night. It was probably the goat we had for dinner. I told Jodoca it was off.'

'And I told you to leave it, if you thought it was tainted,'

Jodoca replied, sitting on the bed and stroking her husband's hair affectionately. 'I have a summer cold, and could not taste it.'

'Goat manure is not as good as horse,' said Arblaster, smiling genially at the physician. 'Does your College own cows? If so, I will give you a good price for their muck.'

Bartholomew regarded him askance. He was not used to patients touting for dung in the middle of consultations. 'I think we send it to our manor in Ickleton,' he said, to bring the discussion to an end. 'What else did you eat yesterday?'

'Nothing. People despise dung, but it is the stuff on which our country is built. Without it, there would be no crops, which means no food and no people. We owe a lot to muck.'

Bartholomew did not find it easy to acquire the information he needed to make an accurate diagnosis, and by the time he had finished, he had learned more about manure and its various properties than was pleasant. The stream of information came to a merciful end when Arblaster was seized with a sudden need to make use of one of the buckets. The exercise left him exhausted.

'Two inmates from Barnwell hospital died of this flux last week,' he said breathlessly. 'I do not want Jodoca to join them in their graves – I have heard how fast it can pass from person to person.'

'There is no reason she should become sick,' said Bartholomew. He was tempted to explain his theory that rotten meat was responsible for the illness, but the brisk walk in the searing sun and the taxing discussions with Cynric and Carton had sapped his energy; he did not feel like embarking on a lengthy medical debate. 'And besides, the hospital inmates are old men. Jodoca is a young woman, and so is less likely to succumb.'

'You mean *I* will die, then?' asked Arblaster in an appalled whisper. 'Because I am a man who is approaching forty years of age?'

Bartholomew was aware that tiredness was robbing him of his wits; he should have known better than to make remarks that might be misinterpreted. 'Of course not. I can give you medicine that will make you feel better by morning. It contains—'

'My sickness is the Devil's work,' interrupted Arblaster, fear in his eyes now. 'I had an argument with Mother Valeria a week ago – she tried to overcharge me for a spell and I refused to pay. She must have cursed me. That is why I lie dying.'

'You are not dying,' said Bartholomew firmly. 'And Valeria does not put curses on people.'

'She does, boy,' countered Cynric, who was watching from the doorway, a jug of ale in his hand. 'She is very good at it, which is why you should never annoy her. She likes you now, but that could change in an instant. It would be safer if you had nothing to do with her, as I have told you before.'

'God's teeth!' muttered Bartholomew, wondering how Cynric came by his information. He did not have the energy for it, regardless. He turned back to the business in hand, removing angelica and barley from his bag, and dropping them into a pot of water that was bubbling on the hearth. 'Mistress Jodoca, your husband needs to drink as much of this as—'

'She is not staying,' said Arblaster. His expression was grimly determined. 'When I die, Mother Valeria will

58

come for my soul, and I do not want Jodoca here when that happens.'

'I cannot leave you,' protested Jodoca, aghast at the notion. 'I am your wife!'

'You are not going to die,' repeated Bartholomew. 'You are strong, and this is not a serious—'

'Please do as I ask, Jodoca,' interrupted Arblaster. 'Leave now, and go to stay with your brother. No woman should see her man's spirit ripped bloodily from his corpse.'

'That will not happen,' insisted Bartholomew although he could see Arblaster did not believe him. 'And someone needs to be here, to administer this cure. There is no need to send her—'

'Jodoca, go,' ordered Arblaster. 'If you love me, you will not argue.'

Tears flowing, Jodoca backed out of the room. Her footsteps tapped along the corridor and across the yard, then all was silent again. Bartholomew asked Cynric to fetch the maid, so she could be shown how to do the honours with the remedy, but she had apparently over-heard the discussion and fled, for she was nowhere to be found. The house was deserted.

'We cannot leave him alone,' said Bartholomew to his book-bearer. 'He is not as ill as he believes, but he still needs nursing. Will you wait here, while I walk to Barnwell and ask one of the canons to sit with him? It will not take long.'

He fully expected Cynric to refuse, knowing perfectly well that witches in search of souls was exactly the kind of tale the book-bearer took very seriously. Therefore he was startled when Cynric nodded assent. He was not surprised for long, however.

'Arblaster is wrong to think Valeria will come for him this afternoon,' said Cynric, sniffing in disdain. 'She will not do that until he has been dead for three nights. Of course, it would not worry me if she did break with tradition and come today, because I am wearing an amulet.'

'What kind of amulet?' asked Arblaster, overhearing.

Cynric fingered something brown and furry that hung around his neck. 'A powerful one, quite able to protect us both.'

Arblaster sagged in relief. He sipped Bartholomew's doctored water, complained that it did not taste of much, then sank into a feverish doze. The physician gave Cynric instructions about what to do if he woke, and made for the door.

'Do not stay in the convent too long,' advised Cynric. 'None of the canons are witches, but a couple turn into wolves on occasion. Luckily, I happen to have a counter-charm against wolves.'

Bartholomew felt his head spinning, and decided he should spend as little time with Cynric as possible until the Sorcerer had either been exposed as a fraud or had faded into oblivion, as all such prodigies were wont to do. He tried to dodge the proffered parcel, but the book-bearer managed to press it into his hand anyway. He smiled weakly, and shoved it in his bag, determined to throw it away later. He did not want to be caught with such an item in his possession, not after William's accusations regarding his association with Mother Valeria.

It was not far to Barnwell Priory, but seemed further because the road was so fiercely hot. Bartholomew felt the energy drain from him at every step. His senses swam, and he wondered if he was in line for a bout of the flux himself. He hoped not, because it would leave Paxtone alone to physic the entire town. After what seemed an age, he arrived at Barnwell's sturdy front gate. He leaned against the gatepost for a moment, standing in its shade and squinting against the sun's brightness.

The convent was owned by the Augustinian Order, and comprised a refectory, guest hall, infirmary, almonry, brewery, granary, stables and bake-house, all surrounded by protective walls and gates. In addition, there was a church and three chapels – one for the infirmary, one attached to the almonry and the other dedicated to St Lucy and St Edmund. As Arblaster had mentioned, the convent also owned a substantial amount of property in the town: houses, shops, churches and manors. Bartholomew could not imagine why Prior Norton should want to purchase yet more of it in the form of Sewale Cottage. Not being an acquisitive man himself, he failed to understand the bent in others, and was grateful Langelee had not given *him* the task of negotiating details with Prior Norton.

He knocked on the gate, thinking about what he knew of the Augustinians. Despite the convent's opulence, Norton had just twenty canons. There was, however, an army of servants and labourers who performed the menial tasks the brethren liked to avoid. The canons' lives were not all meals and prayers, however. They ran a school for boys, and the infirmary housed a dozen old men who were living out their lives at the priory's expense. They summoned Bartholomew not infrequently, because the infirmarian was not very good at his job, and tended to shy away from anything more complex than cuts and bruises. As a result, the physician should have known the canons reasonably well, but because they were mainly middle-aged, portly men who were going bald, he found it difficult to tell them apart. The infirmarian and his assistant were distinctive, but the rest were indistinguishable as far as Bartholomew was concerned, and he was glad Norton possessed a pair of unusually protuberant eyes, or he would have been hard pressed to identify him, too.

He was surprised when his rap was answered not by a lay-brother, but by Norton himself. The Prior's expression was one of extreme agitation, and the thought went through Bartholomew's mind that if he opened his eyes any wider, they might drop out.

'Why have you arrived so quickly?' Norton demanded, uncharacteristically brusque. 'We have only just sent for you.'

'Is something wrong?' Bartholomew was concerned. Arblaster had mentioned two men dead of the flux, and it occurred to him that the priory might be suffering from a more virulent outbreak than the one in the town.

'Yes,' replied Norton shortly. He turned, and Bartholomew saw his brethren ranged behind him, an uneasy cluster in their light-coloured robes. They murmured greetings, and some sketched benedictions. Bartholomew nodded back, noting they were as nervous and unhappy as their head.

Henry Fencotes, the infirmarian's assistant, stepped forward. Unlike his fellows, he possessed a full head of white hair, and he was thin. His skin was as pale as parchment, so his veins showed blue through it. He had consulted Bartholomew on several occasions because his hands and feet were always cold, even in the height of summer. Older than the others, he had come late to the priesthood, and it was said that he had lived a very wild life before his vows.

'Where is Brother Michael?' Fencotes asked, grabbing the physician's arm. His hand felt icy, like that of a corpse. 'We asked him to come, too. Did you leave him behind, because he is too fat to run? Will he be here soon?'

'I have no idea,' replied Bartholomew, growing steadily more uneasy. 'Is someone ill?'

'You could say that,' said Norton. 'Will you see Carton now, or wait until Michael arrives?'

Bartholomew felt alarm grip his stomach. 'Carton? What is wrong with him?'

'We told you in the message we sent.' Norton's face was grim. 'He has been murdered.'

Carton was in one of the convent's chapels, a handsome building with a lead roof. It was a peaceful, silent place, with thick stone walls and tiny lancet windows that made it dark and intimate. It was also cool, and Bartholomew welcomed the respite from the heat. He tried to ask Norton what had happened as he was ushered into the porch, but the goggle-eyed Augustinian was not of a mind to answer questions, preferring to give a detailed explanation of why he believed this was the first unlawful killing ever to take place in the convent he ruled.

Bartholomew bit back his impatience. 'A hundred and fifty murder-free years is an impressive record, Father Prior, but where is Carton?'

'In the chancel,' replied Fencotes. 'Podiolo is with him. Come, I will show you.'

'Podiolo came the moment I discovered . . .' Norton trailed off uncomfortably, gesticulating with his hand. 'But he said there was nothing he could do.'

Matteo di Podiolo was the infirmarian, and hailed from Florence. He had yellow eyes, a pointed nose and a mouth

63

full of long, sharp teeth; Cynric had once told Bartholomew that his mother was a wolf. He knew virtually nothing about medicine, and did not seem inclined to learn, either, preferring to concentrate on his life's ambition: to turn base metal into gold. He had built a laboratory in the infirmary chapel, and spent far more time there than ministering to his elderly charges. Perhaps, Bartholomew thought uncharitably, his lack of dedication was why two of them had died of flux.

'There was nothing *anyone* could do,' Podiolo said, emerging suddenly from the gloom of the nave and making them all jump. His curious amber eyes gleamed in the semi-darkness.

Bartholomew ducked around him and hurried after Fencotes, but the abrupt plunge from bright sunlight had rendered him blind, and he could not see where he was going. He could not even see Fencotes, although he could hear his footsteps a short distance ahead. He slowed, recalling that the flagstones in that particular chapel were treacherously uneven. Unfortunately, Podiolo was too close behind him, and failed to adjust his speed. He collided with the physician then stumbled into one of the plump, balding canons, who gave a shriek as he lost his balance and fell. Something clattered to the floor with him, and there was a collective gasp of horror.

'The stoup!' cried Fencotes, dropping to his knees with his hands clasped in front of him. 'You have spilled the holy water!'

The other canons began to babble their horror, and Podiolo yelled something about a bad omen. Bartholomew glanced at the chancel, itching to run to Carton's side but loath to do so while his sunlight-dazzled eyes could not see where the holy water had splattered.

'No one move,' ordered Norton, his commanding voice stilling the clamour of alarm. 'Use your hood to mop it up, Fencotes. Then we shall leave it on the altar until it dries. No harm is done – at least, as long as no one treads in it.'

With shaking hands, Fencotes dabbed at the mess, while Bartholomew started to ease around him, aiming for the chancel. It would not be the first time death had been misdiagnosed – he had no faith in Podiolo's dubious skills – and he might yet save Carton's life. He stopped abruptly when he became aware that the canons were regarding him with rather naked hostility. It was unsettling, and for the first time in weeks, he shivered.

'Prior Norton instructed you to wait,' said Podiolo coldly. 'There is nothing you can do for your friend. He is quite dead. I may not be the best infirmarian, but I know a corpse when I see one.'

'Please,' said Bartholomew quietly. 'Carton is my colleague, and I may be able to—'

'He is also a devout Franciscan, who will not appreciate you defiling holy water to reach him,' said Fencotes firmly. 'Be still, Doctor. I am going as fast as I can.'

'And I shall tell you what happened, to occupy your mind,' said Norton. 'Carton came to discuss the house your College is going to sell – Margery Sewale's place. A number of people are interested in purchasing it, and he came to find out how much we are willing to pay. He was going to tell us what others have offered, too, so we can decide whether we want to put in a higher bid. It was good of Langelee to send him.'

'Yes and no,' said Podiolo. 'It is in Michaelhouse's interests to secure the best price, and Carton was just facilitating that process. Langelee did not send him out of the goodness of his heart.'

'I have no love of earthly wealth,' said Fencotes, not looking up from his duties on the floor. 'But do not condemn Carton and Langelee for trying their best for Michaelhouse. It is not as if they are going to keep the money for themselves.'

'True,' acknowledged Norton. He opened his eyes further than Bartholomew would have believed possible. 'Anyway, I invited Carton to talk here, in the chapel, because it is the coolest place in the priory, and thus the most comfortable. Given the heat, I thought he might appreciate some refreshment, too, so I left him alone for a few moments while I went to fetch a jug of wine.'

'A few moments?' asked Bartholomew.

Norton's face was almost as pale as Fencotes's. 'Just the time it took me to hurry across the yard, tell Podiolo which claret to bring, and hurry back again. When I arrived, I found Carton . . .'

Bartholomew shot an agitated glance at the chancel. 'Found Carton what?'

'In the state he is in now,' finished Norton unhelpfully. 'I ran outside and yelled for Podiolo, who came to see what could be done.'

'But nothing could,' added Podiolo, flashing his wolfish smile, rather inappropriately.

'You said Carton has been murdered,' said Bartholomew. 'That means someone else must have been in here with him. Who was it?'

'The chapel was empty when Carton and I arrived,' replied Norton. 'And you can see it is too small for anyone to hide here without being spotted.'

Now Bartholomew's eyes had become accustomed to

66

the gloom, he could see Norton was right. The chapel comprised a nave, which was empty of anything except six round pillars, and a chancel. He could just make out a dark form lying behind the altar rail. There was no furniture of any description, and the only way in was through the door. The windows were narrow, no wider than the length of a man's hand, and it would be impossible for anyone to squeeze through them.

'So someone must have come in while you were away fetching the wine,' he said to Norton.

'Then whoever it was must have been very fast,' said Norton. 'I was not gone long. But it is possible, I suppose. However, I sincerely hope you do not suspect one of us of this dreadful crime.'

'Who has access to your grounds, other than canons and lay-brethren?' asked Bartholomew. He glanced at Fencotes, who seemed to be taking far too long with his mopping.

'The inmates at the hospital and the boys in the school,' replied the Prior. 'Plus the folk who come to buy our honey. Then the lay-brothers often invite their kinsman to visit. In fact, we tend not to exclude anyone who wants to come in.'

'You keep your gate locked,' Bartholomew pointed out, recalling how he had knocked and waited for an answer.

'That is to deter the casual highway robber,' replied Podiolo. 'But we keep a back door open for anyone who might be in need. We are not Michaelhouse, which requires tight security to avoid being burned to the ground.'

The holy water wiped away, Norton led the way to the chancel, where Carton lay on his face in front of the altar. The Franciscan's arms were stretched to either side, and his legs were straight and pressed together in a grotesque parody of a crucifix. And in the middle of his back was a knife.

Podiolo had been right when he said there was nothing Bartholomew could do for his colleague. The dagger wound looked as though it would have been almost instantly fatal, and Carton was already beginning to cool in the chill of the church. Bartholomew inspected the body by the light of a candle, but there was nothing else to see. Carton had been in good health when he was stabbed, and there were no other injuries or inexplicable marks.

Michael arrived eventually, gasping from what had been an unpleasantly fast hike along the baking Causeway. His eyes were huge and sad as he stared down at the dead Franciscan. After a moment, he dropped to his knees and began to intone last rites. The canons were silent, bowing their heads as he chanted his prayers. Bartholomew stepped away and began to prowl, looking for anything that might provide him with some explanation as to why someone should have felt the need to stab Carton and arrange his body in so unsettling a manner. He only confirmed what he already knew: that a killer must have taken advantage of Prior Norton's brief absence to walk through the door, kill Carton and leave the same way. When Michael finished his devotions, Norton, Podiolo and Fencotes repeated what they had told Bartholomew.

'So what you are telling me is that virtually anyone could have murdered him,' said the monk. He sounded disgusted. 'You have no idea who might be in your convent at any given time. Moreover, the knife is one of those cheap things that can be bought for a few pennies in the Market Square, and we are unlikely to trace its owner.'

'Yes,' replied Norton unhappily. 'I suppose we are telling you that.'

'I will have to mount an investigation,' said Michael, rather threateningly. 'Carton was a scholar of Michaelhouse, and I am duty bound to discover what happened to him.'

'I welcome it,' said Norton. 'The taint of death will hang over us, otherwise. Obviously, a canon had nothing to do with this, and we want an independent enquiry to prove it.'

'Right,' said Michael, making it clear he would make up his own mind about whether the canons should be exonerated. 'Was this the only time Carton visited you? Or has he been before?'

'He has never been,' said Podiolo, rather quickly. 'I would have seen him.'

'That is not what he told me,' countered Bartholomew. 'As we walked here together, he gave the impression that he liked coming, because you invited him to join your prayers.'

'He may have dropped in once or twice,' admitted Norton cautiously. 'But I would not have said it was a regular occurrence. Podiolo was probably unaware of it, though.'

'I was unaware,' agreed Podiolo immediately. 'I never saw him here before, although I knew who he was, because I have heard him preaching in the town. He said the people who died during the plague did so as a punishment for their sins, which cannot have made him popular. I suspect you will find the killer is a townsman who finds that sort of sentiment objectionable.'

'People do not break God's commandments for so paltry a reason,' objected Fencotes, shocked.

'They do,' said Norton shortly. 'And you are too good for this world, if you think otherwise.'

Podiolo's expression was sly. 'Let us not forget the tales that say Carton was the Sorcerer. He—'

'He was no such thing,' interrupted Michael angrily. 'He was a Franciscan friar who preached hotly against sin. I doubt the Sorcerer would be doing *that*.'

'Just because I mention the rumour does not mean I accept it as truth,' said Podiolo, raising a defensive hand. 'Besides, the Sorcerer is said to own considerable skill in curing warts, and Carton never made any such claim. Perhaps that fact alone is enough to exonerate him. Or perhaps it is not. After all, his speeches showed he was inexplicably familiar with the subject of sin – far more so than his fellow Franciscans. And one of them – Thomas – is dead.'

'So?' demanded Michael, struggling to keep his temper. 'What is your point?'

'My point is that Thomas's death may not have been all it seemed,' replied Podiolo, fixing the monk with his yellow eyes. 'I know the official explanation is that he was struck by a stone, and died after imbibing overly strong medicine prescribed by Bartholomew. But I am unconvinced.'

'Why?' asked Bartholomew tiredly. 'It is what happened.'

'I doubt a physician of your experience would make such a basic mistake,' replied Podiolo. 'And Thomas himself thought the Sorcerer had felled him with a curse, while I heard Carton suspected poison. Do not overlook the possibility that the deaths of these two friends might be connected. After all, both were Franciscans with outspoken opinions.'

'I am sure Wolf-Face would like us to think so,' murmured Michael in Bartholomew's ear. 'But perhaps he makes that comment to throw us off the real scent – *his* scent.'

'You think Podiolo is the killer?' whispered Bartholomew, alarmed. He had always been wary of Podiolo, but he did not see the infirmarian as a man who murdered friars in chapels.

'Why not?' asked Michael. 'I have the distinct feeling he is not telling us the whole truth.' He raised his voice and addressed the assembled brethren. 'I want to speak to each of you separately, to ascertain your whereabouts when Carton was dispatched.'

'Of course, Brother,' said Norton with a pained smile. 'We have nothing to hide.'

Establishing alibis transpired to be easier than Michael expected, because most of the canons had been in their dormitory, which faced north and so was cool. They were in the process of having it redecorated, and as they all had strong views about colours and themes, they had gathered to harass the artist. The only ones who had not been so engaged were Podiolo, Norton and Fencotes.

'Egg-Eyes, the Wolf and the Walking Corpse,' muttered Michael to Bartholomew. 'What a trio!'

'I was in the infirmary with the old men,' offered Fencotes helpfully. 'They like me to read to them of an afternoon. However, half were asleep while the rest have lost their wits, so I doubt they will confirm my tale to your satisfaction. You will just have to trust me, I am afraid.'

Michael turned to the infirmarian. 'Podiolo? You were

not in the hospital, or you and Fencotes would have used each other as alibis.'

'I was in my cell,' replied Podiolo. 'Studying a scroll that explains how to make gold from a mixture of sulphur and silver. I can show you the pages I read, if you like.'

'I am sure you can,' said Michael. 'And I am also sure you know this text backwards.'

'Well, yes,' admitted Podiolo. 'But that does not mean I am lying.'

'I have already told you where I was: fetching wine,' said Norton. He rolled his eyes. 'Lord, but this is a black day for Barnwell! How could God let such wickedness loose in our haven of peace?'

'How indeed?' muttered Michael.

When the monk had finished interviewing the canons, Bartholomew took Podiolo to Arblaster's house, where the dung-merchant already seemed better. Cynric had persuaded him to drink more of the boiled water than Bartholomew would have expected, given its uninspiring taste, although he was not pleased to learn that the patient had been told it contained magical properties – Arblaster was swallowing as much as he could in the belief that it would protect him from Mother Valeria.

'But it will,' objected Cynric, when Bartholomew remonstrated with him. 'If he drinks your potion and lives, she will not have his soul. So, it will protect him from her, albeit indirectly.'

Bartholomew was too tired to argue, and Carton's death had upset him more than he would have imagined. He had not been particularly close to the Franciscan, but Carton was a colleague, and it had not been pleasant to see him with the knife in his back. When he told Cynric what had happened, the book-bearer did not seem as surprised as Bartholomew thought he should have been.

'He preached a violent message,' said Cynric with a shrug. 'He accused people of killing their loved ones during the plague because they were steeped in sin. Of course folk are going to take exception to that. He distressed a lot of people with his opinions. Men like Spaldynge, for example.'

'You think Spaldynge killed him?' asked Bartholomew, recalling the spat Carton had engineered when they had met the scholar from Clare. Spaldynge was hot-headed and spiteful, and might well take action against a man who knew an unsavoury secret about him. And if he really had murdered someone in the past, then killing was no stranger to him.

'He might have done. And do not forget that Carton's friends were Thomas, Mildenale and William – all men who waged war on those hapless Dominicans.'

'God's teeth!' muttered Bartholomew, daunted. There were at least sixty Black Friars in Cambridge, both in the friary and holding town appointments as priests, teachers and chaplains, and he realised that any one of them might have taken exception to Michaelhouse's Franciscans. Then he reconsidered. 'But Carton was not especially damning of Dominicans. He agreed with the others if they pressed him, but he never made derogatory remarks of his own volition.'

Cynric shrugged again. 'This will not be an easy nut to crack, because virtually anyone could have slipped into Barnwell and shoved a knife between his ribs. After all, he walked through crowded streets to come here, and lots of people saw him set off along the Causeway with you.'

Podiolo was annoyingly inattentive when Bartholomew told him how to administer the barley water to Arblaster, and the physician was concerned when he saw him pull a book from his robes, clearly intending to pass the time by reading. Fortunately, though, Cynric's claim about the remedy's magical powers meant Arblaster was eager to down as much of it as he could possibly manage, and did not need an infirmarian to coax him to swallow more.

Bartholomew returned to the convent, to see if Michael was ready to go home, and was about to enter when he saw a man named William Eyton walking along the Causeway towards him. Eyton was the vicar of St Bene't's Church, an affable Franciscan who laughed a lot. He was friends with William, and had a reputation for preaching inordinately long sermons. Bartholomew had attended one once, and had come away with his head spinning from the leaps of logic and false assumptions. William had been with him, and had fallen asleep somewhere near the beginning, awaking much later to applaud loudly and claim it was one of the best discourses he had ever heard.

'I have come to purchase honey,' said Eyton cheerily, standing with Bartholomew while they waited for a lay-brother to open the gate. Knocking felt foolish, since the physician now knew he could walk unchallenged through the back door, or even scramble over a wall. 'I love honey, although it makes my teeth ache if I consume more than one pot in a single sitting.'

'You eat it by the pot?' asked Bartholomew, stunned. The canons sold their wares in very large vessels. 'Does it not make you sick?'

'Well, yes, it does, but it is said to keep witches at bay, so I do not mind a little nausea in a good cause. You should try it: William tells me you are more familiar with some of them than is safe.'

Bartholomew sighed, and wished William would keep his opinions to himself.

It was an unhappy gathering that prepared to travel from Barnwell Priory to St Michael's Church. Carton rested on a makeshift bier, and Norton provided two lay-brothers to help carry it. The men did not voice their objections aloud, but it was clear that they disliked being given such an assignment, and their surliness persisted even after the monk offered them money for their trouble. Bartholomew did not blame them. It was an unpleasant task to be doing at any time, but the heat made it worse. It was still intense, even though the sun was setting.

Eyton was one of a dozen men who watched Bartholomew cover his colleague with a blanket, his normally smiling face sombre. 'Carton took a courageous stand against those who lead sinful lives, and I am sorry someone has murdered him because of it,' he said.

'You think that is why he was stabbed?' asked Michael. He sounded weary, and Bartholomew suspected he had been regaled with a number of unfounded theories as to why the friar should have been killed. 'Someone took exception to his views about what constitutes a decent lifestyle?'

Eyton nodded sadly. 'I doubt the Sorcerer appreciated Carton telling folk that joining his cadre was a sure way to Hell. He or a minion must have decided to silence him. Poor Carton. His views were a little radical for my taste – and I fear he was a bad influence on my dear friend William, who tends to listen rather too readily to anyone who decries heresy – but he was a good man at heart.'

Michael indicated that the two lay-brothers were to take the back of the bier, while he and Bartholomew lifted the front. Normally, Cynric would have helped, but he had offered to stay and talk to the priory servants, who were more likely to confide in him than in the Senior Proctor.

'William and Mildenale are sure to insist on a stately requiem for Carton,' said Michael to the physician, as they set off towards home. 'But it is an expense the College cannot afford at the moment. Our coffers are all but empty.'

'Are they? I thought Margery Sewale's benefaction meant we were financially secure.'

'We will be, but only when her house has been exchanged for ready cash. Until then, we are worse off than ever, because we have had to pay certain taxes in advance. Why do you think there has been such a rush to sell the place? All the Fellows – except you, because you are hopeless at such matters – have been busy trying to drum up interest in the cottage among potential buyers.'

Bartholomew was not sure whether to be offended because his colleagues did not trust him, or relieved that he had not been asked to squander his time on such a matter. 'That was why Carton came to Barnwell,' he said. 'He was going to ask Norton how much he was willing to pay.'

They walked in silence for a while. Ahead of them, the town was a silhouette of pinnacles, thatches and towers against the red-gold blaze of the evening sky. Each was lost in his own thoughts, Michael processing the mass of mostly useless information he had gleaned from interviewing the canons, and Bartholomew thinking about Carton's unfathomable character.

'This is a sorry business,' said Michael eventually. He spoke softly, so the lay-brothers could not hear him. 'And I fear it will prove difficult to solve. Why do *you* think Carton was killed?'

Bartholomew tried to organise his chaotic thoughts. 'There seem to be several possible motives. First, there is the rumour that he was the Sorcerer. If that is true, the Church will see him as an enemy, and you can include virtually every priest in Cambridge on your list of suspects, as well as religious laymen who dislike what the Sorcerer is trying to do.'

Michael sighed unhappily. 'And Barnwell's twenty or so canons head that list, including their Prior. The only exception is Podiolo, who strikes me as the kind of man who might dabble in sorcery himself. He is definitely sinister.'

'He is, a little,' agreed Bartholomew. 'The second motive for killing Carton was his belief that people brought their plague losses on themselves. Such a stance is bound to attract angry indignation.'

'Such as from Spaldynge?' asked Michael. 'He has always blamed physicians for the calamity, and will not like being told it is his own fault that his family died.'

'Carton said Spaldynge killed someone called James Kirbee. Do you know if it is true?'

Michael was thoughtful. 'I had forgotten about that case. It was years ago, and was dropped for lack of evidence, although I recall thinking Spaldynge was probably guilty anyway. If Carton was going around reminding people about that, then it may well have led to murder.'

Bartholomew resumed his list of reasons why Carton might have been stabbed. 'And finally, there is his association with a group of very vociferous Franciscans who hate Dominicans.'

'And one of that group died last week,' mused Michael. 'Carton was not convinced that Thomas's death was all it seemed, and asked you to run an experiment to assess whether he was poisoned. Perhaps he was right, and your sedative really did have nothing to do with Thomas's demise.'

Bartholomew was not sure what to think. On the one hand, it would be good to be free of the burden of guilt, but on the other he did not like the notion that there was another suspicious death to explore. He said nothing, so Michael abandoned theories and began to think about evidence.

'Tell me what you were able to deduce from Carton's body,' he ordered.

Bartholomew disliked the way the monk always assumed he could produce clues from corpses as a conjuror might pull ribbons from a hat. And with stabbings, the chances of learning anything useful were slim. Yet he always felt he was letting Michael – and the victim – down when he said there was nothing to help solve the case.

'It is not easy to knife yourself in the back, so I think we can safely conclude that someone else was responsible,' he began, trying his best anyway. 'The dagger was cheap and unremarkable, so we stand no chance of identifying its owner. It does not sound as though Norton took long to fetch the wine, so the killer must have been fairly sprightly – to run to the chapel, stab Carton, and escape before Norton returned.'

'That does not help,' said Michael acidly. 'Most killers are sprightly. If they were not, they would not be contemplating murder in the first place, lest their victim turn on them.'

Bartholomew ignored him. 'The only blood was that which had pooled beneath Carton. So, I think he died quickly – he did not stagger around, and there is no evidence of a struggle. Perhaps he knew his killer, and did not feel the need to run away when he appeared.'

'Obviously, it was someone he knew,' snapped Michael irritably. 'And that is the problem. He knew a lot of people – through his teaching and the College, through his association with Mildenale's band of zealots, and possibly even through his denunciation of the Sorcerer.'

Bartholomew ignored him again, knowing frustration was making the monk sharp-tongued. 'The wound is high and angled downwards. I suppose that might mean it was inflicted by someone tall.'

Michael's green eyes gleamed. 'Now we are getting somewhere! Fencotes is tall.'

'He is also a devout man, who is not a Dominican, who has probably never heard Carton preach, and who does not own a fanatical dislike of witches. What would be his motive?'

'He was not always a canon; Cynric tells me he has lived a life that would make your hair curl. Norton and Podiolo are taller than Carton too. And so is Spaldynge.'

Bartholomew began to wish he had kept this particular piece of 'evidence' to himself. 'On reflection, most people are taller than Carton. I do not think it is much of a clue.'

'What do you think of the way Carton's body was laid out? Was the killer mocking his vocation?'

'Perhaps the culprit felt guilty about what he had done, and the crucifix pose was some bizarre way of trying to make amends. Or conversely, the body may have been arranged that way to taunt you.'

Michael's expression hardened. 'Then I will solve this crime, Matt. I vow it on Carton's corpse. No one mocks the Senior Proctor.'

Langelee was shocked to learn he had lost a Fellow, and although violent death was by no means a stranger to the University's scholars – or to a man who owned a dubious past as 'agent' for the Archbishop of York – he was still appalled when Michael broke the news. He stood next to the monk in St Michael's Church, watching Bartholomew manhandle the body into the parish coffin.

'He has only been a Fellow since Easter,' he said hoarsely. 'And I was just getting used to his oddities. Now I shall have to start again, with someone else.'

'Which oddities in particular?' asked Michael.

Langelee shrugged. 'His inexplicable readiness to associate with William for a start. No one has done that before, because most of us find his zeal tiresome. Then there was his strange interest in witchery. Did you know he used to spy on covens with Cynric? I assumed that, as a friar, he was simply trying to ascertain the nature of the opposition, but now I am beginning to wonder.'

'Wonder about what?' demanded Michael.

Langelee glanced furtively behind him. 'Not here, Brother. Have you finished, Bartholomew? Then come to my quarters. We should talk somewhere more private.'

They followed him down the lane, across the yard and into the pair of rooms that had been the Master's suite since the College had been founded, some thirty years before. They were spartan for a head of house, not much more spacious than those of his Fellows. He had a sleeping chamber that he shared with two students – after he had enrolled additional undergraduates earlier that year, no one was exempt from crowded conditions – and a tiny room he used as an office. It was packed with accounts, deeds and records, and there was only just space for the desk and chair he needed to conduct his business. Bartholomew wedged himself in a corner, while Michael stood in the middle of the room, parchments and scrolls cascading to the floor all around him as his voluminous habit swept them from their teetering piles each time he moved.

Langelee squeezed his bulk behind the desk, his expression grim. 'Carton's murder is bad for the College, because it comes too soon on the heels of Thomas's death.'

'Thomas was not a member of Michaelhouse,' said Bartholomew, puzzled by the comment.

'No,' agreed Langelee, 'but his fellow zealots are, and so is the physician whose medicine killed him. He is intimately connected with us, whether we like it or not. So, you must catch Carton's killer without delay, Brother. What have you done so far?'

'Interviewed Barnwell's canons,' replied Michael. 'But they had nothing of relevance to report, while Matt's examination of the body revealed little in the way of clues, either.'

'What about the lay-brothers?' asked Langelee. 'The servants. Barnwell has dozens of them.'

'I have been talking to them,' came a soft lilting voice from behind them. All three scholars jumped; none of them had noticed Cynric arrive.

'I wish you would not do that,' snapped Langelee. 'Well? What did you learn?'

'That not many layfolk were actually working when Carton was killed,' replied the Welshman, grinning when he saw how much he had startled them; he was proud of his stealthy entrances. 'All the canons were busy, so there was no one to supervise them. Most took the opportunity to abscond, to escape the heat by dicing in the cellars or sleeping under trees. And *that* is why the killer found it so easy to strike: the convent was essentially deserted.'

Michael rubbed his chin. 'This helps us understand how the crime was committed, but not in ascertaining the identity of the culprit. It still might be anyone, including Norton, Podiolo or Fencotes, who have no convincing alibis. Or Spaldynge, who just happened to meet Carton on the Barnwell Causeway. He might have decided to turn around and follow him.'

'Perhaps it was the Devil,' suggested Cynric matter-of-factly. 'There have been so many other unnatural happenings of late, what with the goats, Danyell's hand, Margery Sewale's grave, and the blood in the font, that perhaps Carton's murder is just another—'

'No,' said Michael forcefully. 'I smell a human hand in this, and I mean to see he faces justice.'

'Michael is right,' said Bartholomew, seeing Cynric was not in the least bit convinced. He did not want the book-bearer to start rumours that would be difficult to quell. 'The Devil would not have used a cheap knife to stab Carton.'

'You think he would use an expensive one, then?' asked Cynric keenly. 'Or are you saying he would employ his claws or teeth?'

Bartholomew tried to think of an answer that would not imply he had intimate knowledge of Satan's personal arsenal. 'It was a person,' he settled for at last. 'Not the Devil.'

Langelee scratched his jaw, fingernails rasping on bristle. 'Carton was more interested in witchcraft than was decent for a friar; Cynric will tell you that they watched covens together. Then he stopped. This happened at about the same time that *Mildenalus Sanctus* took to preaching against sin and the Sorcerer began to attract more followers.'

'Yes, it did,' agreed Cynric. 'Carton started preaching against sin, too, and anyone listening to his sermons was impressed by how much he knew about it.'

'And all this coincided with a sharp increase in heathen practices throughout the town,' continued Langelee. 'So, in a short space of time, we have Carton abruptly losing interest in the covens he was monitoring, an upsurge in radical and unpopular preaching by our Franciscans, a greater liking for witchery among the populace, and a more active Sorcerer. And now two of Mildenale's cronies are dead.'

'You think all these events are connected?' asked Bartholomew, puzzled. He could not see how.

Langelee shrugged. 'That is for you to decide. I am merely reminding you of facts that might have a bearing on Carton's death. I do not like the town's sudden interest in dark magic, though. It is causing a rift between those who are loyal to the Church and those who think there might be something better on offer.'

Michael sighed. 'We have eight days until term resumes. Let us hope that is enough time to work out what is happening.'

'Very well, but I am sending our students home in the meantime,' said Langelee. 'Cambridge feels dangerous at the moment, what with religious zealots threatening sinners with hellfire, and the Devil's disciples retaliating with spells and curses. I want our lads safely away.'

'That is a good idea,' said Michael, pleased. 'And if Carton really was embroiled in something odd, then they will not be here to take umbrage at any rumours. We do not want them defending his reputation with their fists.'

'Quite,' said Langelee. 'I do not want them joining covens, either, because they think they might be more fun than church. Hopefully, you will have evicted this Sorcerer by the time they return, and the danger will be over.'

Michael looked unhappy at the pressure that was being heaped on him, but knew the Master was right – students were always interested in anything forbidden to them. He turned to Bartholomew. 'It is too late to do anything tonight, and you have patients to see, anyway. We shall start our enquiries in earnest tomorrow.'

'Where?' asked Bartholomew.

'Here, in Michaelhouse,' said Michael grimly. 'With Carton's friends: William and Mildenale.'

Chapter 3

In Michaelhouse's hall the following morning, Langelee stood on the dais and cleared his throat, indicating he wanted to speak. The sun was slanting through the windows, painting bright parallelograms on the wooden floor. The servants were setting tables and benches ready for a lecture he was to give on fleas. No one was quite sure why he had selected this topic, and Bartholomew could only suppose he had been low on ideas. The scullions stopped hauling furniture when they saw that the Master was going to make an announcement first.

'There will be no analysis of fleas today,' he said, folding his beefy arms across his chest. 'The College is closed until next Monday, so you must all go home. Oh, and Carton is murdered.'

'That was an ill-considered juxtaposition of statements,' muttered Michael, disgusted. 'It looks as though he is shutting the College because a Fellow has been killed, which is not the case.'

He and Bartholomew were standing at the front of the hall, because he had wanted to gauge his colleagues' reactions when told the news. Bartholomew watched

William and *Mildenalus Sanctus* intently, but their response to Langelee's proclamation was exactly what he would have expected: a mixture of shock, disbelief and horror. Similar sentiments were written on the faces of everyone else, too, but Carton had not been the most popular member of the foundation, so few tears were shed.

'Do you think one of us might be next?' demanded William, voicing the question that was in everyone's mind, given Langelee's careless choice of words. 'Is some fiend intent on destroying Michaelhouse? A Dominican, for example?'

Mildenale was standing next to him. 'The Black Friars have nothing against us,' he said. But his voice lacked conviction, which frightened some of the younger students. Bartholomew was glad Clippesby was not in residence, sure he would be hurt by the unwarranted attacks on his Order.

'No, but they have something against me,' said William. 'And against you, Thomas and Carton, too, because we tell the truth about sin. They hate anyone who preaches against wickedness, because they are rather partial to it.'

A small, neat Fellow who taught law came to stand next to Bartholomew. His name was Wynewyk, and one of Langelee's most astute moves had been to delegate the financial running of the College to him. He excelled at it, and Michaelhouse was finally beginning to prosper.

'If someone had wanted to remove a zealot,' he said in a low voice, 'surely he would have chosen William or Mildenale? They are far more odious than Carton could ever be.'

'But William and Mildenale did not go to Barnwell yesterday,' Bartholomew pointed out, 'and thus present a killer with an opportunity to strike.'

'No, but they were both alone for a large part of the day, which amounts to the same thing.' Wynewyk sighed, and shook his head sadly. 'I am terribly sorry about Carton. Aside from his rigid stance on sin, he was a decent enough fellow. A little distant, perhaps, but not unpleasant. Who would want to hurt him?'

'That is what I intend to find out,' vowed Michael, overhearing.

'I hope it is no one here,' said Wynewyk. He waved a hand at the scholars in the body of the hall. 'Langelee enrolled twenty new students at Easter, and we have been too busy teaching to get to know them properly. I still feel our College is full of strangers.'

'I want everyone gone by dawn tomorrow,' Langelee was saying. 'I *know* Lincolnshire is a long way, Suttone, but you will just have to hire a horse.'

'You cannot order Fellows to leave,' declared William, outraged. 'I will *not* be ousted. So there.'

'Why not?' asked Langelee archly. 'Is it because you have nowhere else to go?'

'I have dozens of folk clamouring for my company,' snapped William, although smirks from his students suggested Langelee's brutal enquiry was probably near the truth. 'But I do not choose to see them at the moment. Besides, the College is at a crucial stage in the buying and selling of properties, and you cannot make those sorts of decisions without the Fellowship. You need us here.'

'That is true,' acknowledged Langelee with a grimace. 'Very well, the Fellows can stay.'

'What about me?' asked Mildenale. His eyes drifted heavenwards. 'God came to me in a vision at Easter, and ordered me to found a new hostel. I am on the brink of doing so, and it would be inconvenient to leave now. I should stay, too, working for the greater glory of God.'

'All right,' agreed Langelee tiredly, aware that to refuse would almost certainly result in accusations that he was taking the Devil's side. 'But everyone else must begin packing immediately.'

'Lord!' groaned Michael, as the Master stepped down from the dais and the students swooped towards him, full of questions and objections. 'He handled that badly. Now rumours will start that Michaelhouse has been targeted by a vengeful killer, and the other Colleges and hostels will assume we have done something to warrant the attack.'

'Not necessarily,' said Cynric, appearing suddenly at Bartholomew's side. 'Carton's murder is more likely to be seen as part of the battle between the Church and the Sorcerer. Unusually for Cambridge, it is not a town –University division this time, because there are scholars and laymen in both factions. Unfortunately, it means no one knows who is on whose side. Like a civil war.'

'He can be a gloomy fellow sometimes,' said Michael, watching him walk away to help the other servants move the tables. 'I wonder you put up with him, Matt.'

'He has saved my life – and yours – more times than I care to remember.'

'Well, there is that, I suppose,' acknowledged Michael. 'But which side will he choose in this looming battle between good and evil?'

'It is not a battle between good and evil,' argued Wynewyk. 'It is a battle between two belief systems, each with its own merits and failings. The Sorcerer will not see himself as wicked, but as someone who offers a viable alternative to the Church.'

'Wynewyk is right,' said Bartholomew, seeing the monk was about to take issue. 'And the Church can be repressive and dogmatic, so choosing between them may not be as simple as you think. It has adherents like William and Mildenale for a start, which does not render it attractive.'

Michael regarded him with round eyes. 'That is a contentious stance; perhaps William is right to say you dance too closely with heresy. However, while I might – *might* – concede your point, please do not express that opinion to anyone else. I do not want to see you on a pyre in the Market Square.'

Langelee had barely quit the dais before William was in full preaching mode, declaring loudly that no one would die if he put his trust in God and stayed away from Dominicans. Mildenale stood behind him, whispering in his ear, and Bartholomew noted unhappily that William's booming voice and Mildenale's sharp intelligence were a formidable combination. Michael watched in horror as the students began to be swayed by the tirade and, not wanting the Black Friars banging on the gate and demanding apologies for such undeserved slander, he stepped forward hastily.

'You interrupted the Master before he had time to explain himself!' he shouted, banging on the high table with a pewter plate in order to still the clamour and make himself heard. 'The reason you are being asked to leave has nothing to do with Carton, and nothing to do with Dominicans being in league with the Sorcerer, either. It is because of the latrines.'

A startled silence met his claim. Langelee tried to look as though he knew what the monk was talking about, but failed dismally. Fortunately, everyone else was too intent on gaping at Michael to notice the Master's feeble attempt to appear knowledgeable.

'What about them?' asked William eventually.

'The trenches are almost full, and Matt thinks the miasma that hangs around them in this ungodly heat will give everyone the flux,' elaborated Michael. It was the physician's turn to conceal his surprise, although he hoped he managed it better than Langelee. 'New ones will be dug, but until they are ready, it is safer for you all to go home.'

'But the Fellows will be here,' said Deynman the librarian. 'They still need to—'

'We will use the smaller pit by the stables,' replied Michael smoothly. 'It can cope with Fellows, but not with students and commoners, too, which is why you must all disappear for a week.'

'Why did the Master not say this straight away?' asked Mildenale, not unreasonably.

'Because heads of Colleges do not air such unsavoury topics in public,' supplied Deynman before Michael could think of a reply that Mildenale would believe. 'It is undignified, and they leave that sort of thing to senior proctors, who are less refined.'

'Thank you, Deynman,' said Michael, a pained expression on his face. 'Now, unless the Master has any more to add, I suggest you all go and make ready for an early departure tomorrow.'

Bartholomew was obliged to field a welter of enquiries about the relationship between latrines and miasmas, and it was difficult to answer without contradicting what the monk had said. While he believed that dirty latrines could and did harbour diseases, he was becoming increasingly convinced that the current flux had its origins in heat-spoiled meat. However, he supposed some good would come out of Michael's lie, because Langelee would have no choice but to order new pits dug now, which was something the physician had been requesting for months.

'They were more interested in your theories about hygiene than distressed over Carton,' observed Michael, coming to talk to him when most of the students had left and only the Fellows and commoners remained. 'What an indictment of his popularity.'

'I am sorry he is dead,' said Deynman, coming to stand with them while they waited for Mildenale and William to finish talking to the Master. 'He always returned his library books on time, which cannot be said for everyone. You two, for example.'

Bartholomew smiled sheepishly. 'Bradwardine's *Proportiones Breves*. I will bring it tomorrow.'

'You said that yesterday,' replied Deynman, unappeased.

'Is that the only tribute you can pay Carton?' asked Michael, hoping to sidetrack him. He was still using Lombard's *Sentences*, and did not want to give it back. 'That he was good at remembering when his library books were due?'

Deynman frowned, and Bartholomew could see him desperately trying to think of something nice to say. A naturally affable, positive soul, Deynman was always willing to look for the good in people, even when there was not much to find, and the fact that he was struggling said a lot about Carton. The Fellow had not been unpleasant, surly or rude; he had just not been very friendly, and had done little to make his colleagues like him.

'He donated three medical books to the library,' said Deynman eventually, looking pleased with himself for having thought of something. Then his face fell. 'Damn! I was not supposed to tell you about those. He said they are heretical and should be burned, but could not bring himself to do it, so he gave them to me to look after instead. The only condition was that I never let you or your students read them, lest you become infected with the poisonous theories they propound.'

'What books?' demanded Bartholomew keenly. Texts were hideously expensive, and the College did not own many, especially on medicine. The notion of three more was an exciting prospect.

Deynman opened his mouth to reply, then snapped it shut again when he realised he could not remember. So he led them to his 'library' – a corner of the hall with shelves, two chests and a table. Michaelhouse's precious tomes were either locked in the boxes or chained to the walls, depending on their value and popularity.

'Brother Michael can inspect them,' he said, kneeling to unlock the larger and stronger of the two chests. 'But not you, Doctor Bartholomew. Carton made me promise.'

He presented three rather tatty items to Michael, who opened them and shrugged. 'You are already familiar with these, Matt. They are by Arab practitioners, and Carton was a bit of a bigot regarding foreign learning. However, I doubt Ibn Sina's *Canon* will set the world on fire.'

'I hope not,' replied Bartholomew dryly. 'It has been an established part of the curriculum for decades.' He saw the librarian's blank look, and wondered if any of the lectures the lad had attended over the last five years had stuck in his ponderous mind. 'Ibn Sina is more commonly known as Avicenna, Deynman. You should know that, even if Carton did not, because you attended a whole series of debates on his writings last year.'

Deynman frowned, then shrugged carelessly. 'Did I? I do not recall. Incidentally, Mildenale told me Carton had collected a lot of texts on witchery, and said he was keeping them for a massive bonfire. He was going to have it in the Market Square, so everyone could enjoy it.'

'Why would he do that?' asked Bartholomew in distaste. Book-burning was deeply repellent to most scholars, regardless of what the tomes might contain, and the fact that Bartholomew was only learning now that Carton was the kind of person to do it underlined yet again how little he had known the man. The discovery did not make him wish he had made more of an effort.

'Because he thought people should be aware of the huge volume of material that contains dangerous ideas, or is written by infidels,' explained Deynman. He brightened. 'Now he is dead, can I have them for the library? We do not own any books on the occult.'

'I am glad to hear it – and I think we had better keep it that way,' said Michael, amused. 'However, Matt and I will sort through his belongings today, and the library shall have anything appropriate. I happen to know the College is the sole beneficiary of his will, so they will come to us anyway.'

'Good,' said Deynman. 'But make sure you get to them before *Mildenalus Sanctus* does. He disapproved of Carton's collection. I heard them arguing about it several times. He thought Carton should give them to him for destruction, but Carton refused. A couple of the rows were quite heated.'

'I see,' said Michael, exchanging a significant glance with Bartholomew. 'This is interesting. We shall have to ask him about it.'

'He will probably deny it,' said Deynman. 'He and Carton pretended they were the best of friends when I asked them to squabble somewhere other than around my books, but I know what I heard. But I am a busy man, and have no time to waste chatting. I want my books back today, and if you forget, I shall fine you. I can, because I am *librarian*.' He turned on his heel and swaggered away.

'Sometimes, I think promoting him to that post was not a very good idea,' said Michael, watching him go. 'He has turned into a despot.'

While Michael lingered, waiting to catch Mildenale and William as they left the hall, Bartholomew went to Carton's room in search of the books. Normally, he would have been uneasy rifling through a colleague's possessions, especially one so recently dead, but the fact that Carton had owned medical texts – albeit ones with which he was already familiar – made him hope that the Franciscan might have a few even more interesting items secreted away.

But he was to be disappointed. There was indeed a collection of texts locked in a chest at the bottom of Carton's bed – his students showed him where he hid the key – but it contained nothing to excite the curiosity of a *medicus*. There were several essays on Blood Relics, all of which supported the Dominican side of the debate, and a series of tracts scribed by Jewish and Arabic philosophers that the Franciscan had evidently deemed unfit for English eyes. Then there were three scrolls that told their readers how to make magic charms, while a large, heavy book, carefully wrapped in black cloth, proudly declared itself to be a practical manual for witches.

'He was going to burn them,' said one of Carton's room-mates, watching Bartholomew flick through the manual. It was not comfortable reading, even for a man who had encountered similar texts at the universities of Padua and Montpellier. 'And he kept them locked away in the meantime, so no one would inadvertently see one and become contaminated.'

'But you knew where he kept the key,' Bartholomew pointed out, knowing that locked chests in Colleges were regarded as challenges, not barriers, and room-mates expected to be familiar with their friends' intimate possessions. 'You could have read these texts any time he was not here.'

'We would not have dared,' replied the student grimly. 'He would have known, and we did not want to annoy him. He took his privacy far more seriously than you other Fellows.'

Bartholomew carried the theological and philosophical texts to Deynman, and handed the ones on the occult to Langelee. The Master started to peruse the guide to witchcraft, but soon became bored with its arcane language and secret symbols. He shoved it on a high shelf in his office, where Bartholomew imagined it would languish until it was forgotten.

The physician returned to the hall, to find Michael had been talking to Agatha the laundress. Agatha had exempted herself from the rule that no women were allowed inside University buildings, and ran the domestic side of the College with a fierce efficiency; scholars crossed her at their peril. She was, however, a valuable source of information, and Bartholomew was not surprised the monk had picked her brains about the various matters he was obliged to investigate.

'So, I know nothing about any of it,' she was saying. She sounded sorry; she liked to help the monk with his investigations, because it made her feel powerful. 'Not about Carton, the desecration of Margery and Danyell, the blood in the font, or Bene't's missing goats. However, I can tell you one thing you should know: the meat is spoiled for tonight's supper, and I only bought it yesterday.'

'What are we going to eat, then?' demanded Michael, alarmed.

'You can either have onion soup, which is safe, or you can risk a stew.'

'Not stew,' said Bartholomew quickly, knowing the monk would go a long way to avoid eating anything that contained vegetables. 'You know I think bad meat might be causing the flux.'

'Then give the students the soup, but find a couple of chickens for the Fellows,' ordered Michael, slipping her a few coins. He watched her walk away, jangling the silver in her large, competent hands. 'What did you learn from Carton's books, Matt? Were they full of heresy?'

'The witches' manual and the recipes for charms are a bit dubious, but the rest are perfectly sound. He was over-reacting, just as he over-reacted with the medical texts.'

Michael gazed down the hall, where Mildenale was advising his students on the safest route home. 'We will need to replace Carton, but I do not want *him* to take the post.'

'I doubt he would accept, anyway, not when he is on

the verge of founding his own hostel.' Bartholomew glanced at the monk. 'Is it a good idea to grant him a licence? I suspect he intends to indoctrinate any students who enrol, so they all end up thinking like him.'

Michael looked unhappy. 'Unfortunately, he has the necessary charters. The College will benefit, though. We are planning to buy three shops from Mistress Refham, and arrangements are in place for him to rent them from us at a very respectable price.'

Bartholomew frowned. 'But Mistress Refham died months ago. How can she sell us property?'

'Do you listen to *nothing* in Fellows' meetings?' demanded Michael in exasperated disgust. 'On her deathbed, she left instructions that her son and his wife were to sell us the shops cheaply. Unfortunately, they are refusing to honour her last wishes, and the matter is with the lawyers.'

Bartholomew mumbled something noncommittal – the monk's explanation rang a vague bell – and watched Mildenale finish with his students. He started to move towards the man, but William got there first, and the two friars immediately began a low-voiced discussion. Mildenale seemed to be doing most of the talking, and Bartholomew picked up the word 'Dominican' in the tirade.

'Carton was much less vocal about the Black Friars than the others,' mused Michael, who had also heard. 'I wonder what Mildenale and William thought about that.'

Bartholomew regarded him uneasily. 'You think one of them might have killed him over it?'

Michael raised his hands in a shrug. 'They are fanatics, and thus a law unto themselves. Who knows what they might do in the name of religion? I thought William knew the boundaries, but he is not intelligent and may have been persuaded that anything goes in the war against the Devil.'

Bartholomew was appalled. 'I sincerely hope you are wrong.'

'So do I,' said Michael grimly. 'But let us see what *Mildenalus Sanctus* has to say about his fallen comrade. We will tackle William afterwards; I do not feel like interviewing them together.'

As usual, Mildenale's hands were clasped before him and he was gazing heavenward. A student mimicked his pious posture, although he desisted abruptly when Michael frowned at him.

'I am not sure what I can tell you,' said Mildenale, when the monk asked whether he knew anything that might solve Carton's murder. 'His devotion to stamping out wickedness earned him enemies, but that is to be expected in a soldier of God. I wonder who will be next, William or me?'

'You think someone might be targeting zealots?' asked Michael, rather baldly.

Mildenale regarded him in surprise. 'Carton was not a zealot, Brother. What a dreadful thing to say! He was just determined to speak out against sin, as am I. And with God's help, I shall succeed.'

'If you think you might be in danger, you should stay in,' suggested Bartholomew. 'Until—'

'I will take my chances.' Mildenale's smile was beatific. 'God will stop any daggers that come *my* way, because He is keen for me to open my hostel.'

'I hear you argued with Carton over the burning of some books,' said Michael.

Mildenale nodded, rather defiantly. 'He was collecting

evil texts for a bonfire, but I thought it was dangerous to keep them indefinitely, and wanted to incinerate them at once. We quarrelled about it on several occasions, but he stubbornly refused to see that I was right.'

'Some people think Carton was the Sorcerer,' said Michael, again somewhat bluntly. He did not bother to address the fact that Carton had doubtless thought *he* was right, too.

Mildenale gaped at him. 'Of course he was not the Sorcerer! What has got into you today, making all these odd remarks? If Carton had been the Sorcerer, do you think he would have railed against him so vehemently? He was by far the most outspoken of us on that particular issue. William and I tend to denounce evil in general, rather than damning individual heathens.'

'Do you think the Sorcerer killed him, then?' asked Michael.

Mildenale thought for a moment, then shook his head. 'No, because the Sorcerer has never stooped to violence before, and we have been battling each other for weeks now. Of course, fighting would be a lot easier if we knew who he was, but the fellow eludes us at every turn.'

'He eludes me, too,' said Michael with a weary sigh. 'Where were you yesterday afternoon? No, do not look offended. It is a question I must ask everyone who knew Carton.'

'In church, praying. I am afraid no one can verify it, but I am not a man given to lies. There is no reason why you should not believe me.'

'Right,' said Michael. 'Do you know of anyone who was especially irritated by Carton's views?'

'The Dominicans,' replied Mildenale immediately and predictably. 'And the canons at Barnwell were not keen

99

on him, either, because he did something of which they did not approve.'

'What was that?'

'He told a lie about Sewale Cottage – the house they want to buy from us. He said a merchant called Spynk offered ten marks for it, whereas Spynk had actually only stipulated nine. They raised their bid to eleven marks, and were peeved when they later learned they had been misled.'

'They said nothing about this to me,' said Michael, startled and a little angry.

'I am sure they did not,' said Mildenale. 'But it is true – Carton told me himself. He liked the canons, but was prepared to do all he could to secure Michaelhouse the best possible price.'

Michael turned to Bartholomew. 'It looks as though we shall have to visit Barnwell again.'

'Mildenale did not seem overly distressed about Carton,' said Bartholomew, sitting on one of the hall benches. They still needed to talk to William. 'Carton was one of his closest companions, and they held similar views, yet he received news of the murder with remarkable aplomb.'

'That did not escape my notice, either. He is almost as difficult to read as Carton, hiding as he does behind a veil of piety. Do you think they had a fatal falling out over these "heretical" texts?'

'I cannot see Mildenale wielding a dagger, especially in a chapel.' Bartholomew rubbed his eyes, which felt sore and scratchy. 'I wish I was not so tired. We shall need our wits about us if we are to catch a man who has no compunction about killing priests.'

'I would suggest you apply for sabbatical leave, because

you do need a rest. But you were away all last year, so you have had your turn. And I would refuse to let you go, anyway. It was tiresome being without my Corpse Examiner.'

'You had a Corpse Examiner: Rougham.'

Michael grimaced. 'Who did not diagnose a single suspicious death in fifteen months. I still wonder how many murderers walk our streets, laughing at me because their crimes have gone undetected. In fact, there was one case when I was certain something untoward had happened, but Rougham was unshakeable in his conviction that both deaths were natural.'

'*Both* deaths?'

'John Hardy and his wife. Do you remember them? He was a member of Bene't College, but resigned his Fellowship when he married. Because he was an ex-scholar, I was asked to look into what had happened to him. The couple lived near Barnwell Priory.'

Bartholomew frowned. 'They owned a big yellow house. Cynric told me it had burned down.'

'There was a rumour that it was set alight by the canons. Naturally, I questioned Prior Norton, but he said the inferno had nothing to do with them. I was inclined to believe him, because there was no reason for the Augustinians to incinerate the place.'

'Were Hardy and his wife in the building when it went up?' asked Bartholomew uneasily.

'No, the fire was weeks after they died, and the house was empty. The gossip that the canons set the blaze originated with Father Thomas.'

Bartholomew regarded him askance. 'And what was Thomas's reason for starting such a tale?'

'First, he pointed out that the Hardy house was very

101

close to Barnwell Priory. And second, he claimed that Podiolo becomes a wolf once the sun goes down, and is assisted in his various acts of evil by Fencotes, the walking corpse.'

'Lord!' muttered Bartholomew, struggling not to laugh. 'Was he serious?'

'He never joked about religion. Fortunately, no one knew one small fact that might have lent his accusations more clout: the Hardys dabbled in witchcraft.'

Bartholomew thought about the pleasant couple and found that hard to believe. 'Are you sure?'

'I found all manner of satanic regalia in their home. Prudently, I removed it before anyone saw, and Beadle Meadowman burned it for me. I do not think the Hardys were great magicians like the Sorcerer but there was certainly evidence to suggest they had pretensions.'

'Then perhaps they were killed because they were Devil-worshippers.'

'It is possible. But Thomas did not know what they did in their spare time, so there is no reason to suppose anyone else did, either.'

'How did they die?'

'Rougham said of natural causes. They were in bed, side by side, and slipped away in their sleep.'

Bartholomew was incredulous. 'Both of them? That is not very likely.'

'I spent hours in their house, searching for an explanation. There was no evidence of a struggle, or that a killer had cleaned up after one. There was no sign of a forced entry, and the washed pots in the kitchen indicated they had dined alone – no visitors or guests. Their bodies were unmarked, and there was nothing that looked as if it might have contained poison. Nothing.'

'But two people do not die in their sleep at the same time.'

'Why not? Rougham said it was possible.'

'It is *possible*, but so improbable . . .'

'Rougham gave me a written statement saying his verdict was natural death, and although I spent a week asking questions, nothing surfaced to make me think he was wrong. In the end, I was forced to concede that the improbable *had* happened, and one followed the other into death. They were fond of each other, so perhaps love caused them to breathe their last at the same time.'

'In tales of romance, perhaps, but not in real life.'

Michael looked accusing. 'Then it is a pity you elected to race off to France and Spain last year instead of remaining here, doing your duty.'

Bartholomew was used to recriminatory remarks about how he had 'abandoned' Michael, and had learned to ignore them. 'I would ask Rougham about it, but he has gone to Norfolk.'

'Fled from the rumours that say he stole Danyell's hand,' said Michael, adding uncharitably, 'Or perhaps he is afraid of catching the flux. Several of his patients have died from it already, although Cynric tells me you have only lost two.'

'You may be about to lose a few more, though,' said Cynric, appearing suddenly behind them. 'You are needed at Bene't College, where three students are said to be in great distress.'

Bartholomew ensured he had enough barley and angelica in his bag, and headed for the stairs. 'You will have to talk to William on your own, Brother. Three patients may take some time.'

'I would rather wait. For all his faults, I do not want

William implicated in this nasty business, and I want you with me when I interview him. Two minds are better than one.'

Bartholomew had been right to predict that he might be at Bene't College for some time. He had been summoned early enough to help two of the ailing scholars, but the third was rapidly sliding towards death, and there was nothing he could do to prevent it. It was not the first time Bene't had waited too long before calling him, but when he remonstrated with Master Heltisle he learned that the porters had been ordered to fetch him the previous day, but had apparently forgotten.

'Their faulty memories have cost this student his life,' snapped Bartholomew. He tried to control his temper, but it was difficult when a youngster was dying in his arms.

Heltisle was a tall, haughty man with the easy confidence of someone born to power and wealth. He had been a clerk on the King's Bench before he had forsaken law for academia, and such a lofty personage did not appreciate being railed at by a physician. His expression was a little dangerous.

'I will speak to them about it,' he said tightly, warning in his voice.

Bartholomew turned back to his patient, suspecting he would do no such thing. Bene't's servants were the surliest men in Cambridge, and it was common knowledge that even the Master was nervous of them. The head porter was a lout called Younge, and when his minions retired or died in office – the latter being more common, given their propensity for violence – he possessed a knack for appointing replacements worse than the originals.

It was late afternoon when the student died, but Bartholomew lingered at Bene't, wanting to be sure the other two would not follow suit. He was used to fevers claiming lives, but losing young patients still distressed him, and he was in a dark mood by the time he had satisfied himself that the others were out of danger. He headed for the gate, and it was unfortunate that Younge happened to be lounging in the porters' lodge as he passed.

'The next time your Master issues you with an order to summon me, you would do well to follow it immediately,' he snarled, itching to punch the insolent grin from the man's face.

'And who is going to make me?' asked Younge, rising to his feet menacingly. Although he was shorter than the physician, he was considerably broader. 'You?'

'The Senior Proctor,' snapped Bartholomew, far too angry to be intimidated.

'We shall see about that,' sneered Younge. 'Master Heltisle will protect me.'

'I imagine he would rather protect his students,' retorted Bartholomew. 'They *pay* him to be here.'

Younge made no reply, so Bartholomew began to trudge back to Michaelhouse. He felt drained of energy, partly from sitting helplessly while a child died, but also because the heat remained oppressive. And, of course, there was the fact that he could not recall the last time he had had a full night's sleep. The previous one had been no exception, although he had at least managed to snatch a couple of hours before he had been called out.

When he reached the College, he found his chamber a frenzy of activity as his room-mates packed for their enforced vacation. They were all going to Waltham

Abbey, where one had a post when he was not at his studies and had decided to leave that afternoon rather than wait until morning. When their horses arrived, they bade him a hasty farewell and were gone in a flurry of hoofs. The place felt oddly empty without them, and he did not stay there long before going in search of Michael. Together they went to see William.

'William's students were the first to go,' said Michael, as they walked across the yard. 'They are relieved to be away from him, and one even asked if he might share with you when he comes back. They are all Franciscans, but they are uncomfortable with the stance he has taken towards the Dominicans.'

'He has always held those views. He has not changed.'

'But he was always a lone voice before. Now he has Mildenale – and Thomas, when he was alive – and their support has made him more extreme. He is much worse than he was.'

They knocked on William's door, and found the friar on a small prayer-stool that had been set up in one corner. When Bartholomew heard the words 'Dominican' and 'Satan' murmured in the same breath, he almost walked away, wondering what sort of god William thought was listening.

'I am sorry about Carton,' said Michael once he was comfortably seated with a cup of the friar's cheap wine. Bartholomew was not offered any – not that he would have accepted anyway; William's brews tended to give most people a headache. 'You were friends, and his death must be a shock.'

William nodded, and his heavy features creased into an expression of grief. 'I shall miss him, just as I miss Thomas, but Mildenale will recruit others to our cause.

Do you have any idea who might have killed Carton? If not, I have a theory you might like to hear.'

'Go on, then,' said Michael cautiously.

William folded his arms. 'The Dominicans hated the way Carton denounced Satan, who is their master. So they bashed out his brains with one of the sinful books he was gathering for his pyre.'

Bartholomew exchanged a glance with Michael, hoping it was significant that the friar did not appear to know how Carton had been killed.

'That is an intriguing notion, but impossible,' said Michael evenly. He did not want to antagonise William by dismissing his opinions quite so early in the interview. 'I visited the Dominican friary this afternoon, and learned that the entire convent was at a lecture in Merton Hall when Carton was murdered. Prior Morden can vouch for every one of them, and so can several other scholars, including the Chancellor. The Black Friars are innocent.'

William's jaw dropped in disappointment. 'Are you sure?'

'Quite sure,' replied Michael, although Bartholomew knew him well enough to see he was not. However, the claim might serve to muzzle William. 'And now you can tell me where you were.'

'Surely, you cannot suspect *me*?' cried William, shocked. 'I am your colleague and your friend.'

'Are you?' asked Michael coldly. 'Then why do you accuse Matt of witchcraft? You know perfectly well he would never apprentice himself to Mother Valeria *or* steal hands from corpses.'

William scowled at the physician. 'I know nothing of the kind. And I might not have voiced my concerns aloud had *he* not given Thomas the medicine that took his life.'

'It is time you stopped these vile accusations,' snapped Michael, while Bartholomew winced. 'Or does the fact that you quarrelled with Thomas the night before he died still prey on your conscience?'

William sniffed. 'I admit I wish the encounter had been less acrimonious, but he said I was stupid, and no man should accept that without voicing his objections. So I called him a Dominican.' He sat back with a satisfied expression, obviously thinking he had won the insults contest.

'Where were you yesterday afternoon?' asked Michael, while Bartholomew thought the dispute between the two friars was not as serious as he had been led to believe. Then he realised it was: to men like Thomas and William, being accused of belonging to the Order they so despised was one of the gravest slurs imaginable.

'I was out,' William replied, looking decidedly furtive. 'Investigating things.'

'What things?' demanded Michael, eyes narrowing.

William looked as though he might prevaricate, but then sighed his resignation. 'I was conducting my own enquiry, if you must know. I was trying to find out who put blood in our font, who took Bene't's goats, and who purloined Danyell's hand.'

'I see. And did you discover anything of relevance?'

'Not really. The goats have disappeared without a trace, no one has been hawking severed hands to the town's witches, and there have been no other incidents of blood left in holy places. Unfortunately, I know for a fact that the Dominicans had nothing to do with Danyell's fingers, because they were all taking part in a satanic coven at the time.'

'It was a holy vigil,' corrected Bartholomew. 'They

prayed in their chapel the whole night before Ascension Day. I went there twice, to tend Prior Morden's aching back.'

'Call it what you will,' said William unpleasantly. 'I know the truth.'

The sun pouring through the windows had transformed Bartholomew's room into a furnace, and it was far too hot for sleep. He tried, for he desperately needed rest, but tossed and turned in sweltering discomfort, even when he lay on the stone floor. He missed his room-mates, and awoke from several uneasy dozes with a start, dreaming that they had the flux and he was forced to watch them die. In the end, he decided to go for a walk, hoping exercise would calm his troubled thoughts.

It was almost dark, but the sun still bathed the western sky with shades of red and purple. A blackbird sang in a parched tree, and the town was noisier than usual, because everyone had their windows open. He could hear snatches of conversation, snoring and music as he left the College and began to walk along Milne Street. He took a deep breath, smelling scorched soil, the muddy ooze of the river, and a blocked sewer. He could detect something even more rank, too: the butchers' stalls in the market and their festering produce. Insects whined in his ears, bats swooped and a dog barked frantically at a cat that sat just out of its reach and washed itself.

He was not the only person who thought an evening stroll might help him relax; a number of people were out, many of whom he knew. His patients nodded and smiled at him; some stopped to exchange pleasantries about the weather or, more usually, to confide some aspect of their health they thought he should know. One or two colleagues told him they had enjoyed the disputation he had conducted the previous week in St Mary the Great, and Eyton, the affable vicar of St Bene't's, informed him that he should make sure he was indoors by midnight, because the town's witches intended to hold a celebration.

'A celebration of what?' asked Bartholomew suspiciously.

Eyton cocked a merry eyebrow. 'A celebration of evil. What else? So if you go to see Mother Valeria, you will find she is not in.'

Bartholomew surmised that the priest had been talking to William. 'I see.'

'Of course,' Eyton went on with a confidential wink, 'tonight's revelries will be nothing compared to what is scheduled for the witching hour next Saturday. It will be the night before Trinity Sunday, you see, which is a very holy occasion for warlocks.'

'How do you know that?'

Eyton seemed surprised he should need to ask. 'The Sorcerer's disciples have been talking about it for weeks, buying in supplies of sulphur and pitch in anticipation. I shall have to make sure I have plenty of honey to hand.'

Bartholomew regarded him blankly. It was too late in the day for obscure allusions. 'Honey?'

'To keep these witches at bay,' explained Eyton. 'We discussed this yesterday, if you recall. I do not mind a few warlocks, but I am nervous of such a *very* large gathering. You never know what they might achieve when they mass in great numbers.'

'I suppose not,' said Bartholomew weakly.

'And let us hope we have no more incidents like the one involving Margery Sewale,' added Eyton fervently.

'She was dragged from her grave for the purpose of black magic, and I do not want it to happen again. I am afraid that there will be so many Satan-lovers gathering in All Saints-next-the-Castle on Saturday that the Sorcerer may not be able to control them all.'

'I have no idea what you are talking about,' said Bartholomew tiredly. 'All Saints?'

Eyton chuckled inappropriately. 'The biggest and most influential of the Cambridge covens meets there, because it was deconsecrated after its entire congregation died of the plague. It is a perfect place for such gatherings – remote, ruinous and sinister. It is the Sorcerer's church, and he has invited all disciples of the Devil to join him there for the Trinity Eve celebrations.'

'I will tell Michael,' said Bartholomew. 'His beadles will put a stop to it.'

Eyton's smile faded to alarm. 'No, do not do that! People will not like it. The point I am trying to make is that the occasion will be the Sorcerer's début – his first appearance in front of all these different cadres. If you do not follow their ways, you would be wise to stay home in bed.'

'Then I shall do as you suggest,' said Bartholomew, purely to end the discussion. 'Thank you.'

'You are welcome,' said Eyton jovially. 'And now I had better go to guard the body of that student you failed to save today. We do not want anyone stealing his corpse.'

Eyton's babble was unsettling, and Bartholomew knew it would be a while before he was able to sleep. What he needed was something – or someone – to take his mind off his worries, and he wished Matilde was still in Cambridge. She would know how to distract him from dark thoughts, and he felt loneliness stab at him as he walked. Then he realised he was outside the grand building owned by his brother-in-law. Although Oswald Stanmore spent his leisure hours at his manor in the nearby village of Trumpington and used the Cambridge house mostly for business, he sometimes worked late. Bartholomew knocked on the door, hoping that night might be one of those times, and was pleased when it was answered by the merchant himself.

Stanmore, a handsome man with a neat grey beard, ushered him in and offered him wine, which he served in the garden. His apprentices were being entertained by a juggler he had hired, and their laughter rippled across the yard. Bartholomew's thoughts immediately returned to Matilde, because she had loved jugglers. He had planned to marry her, but, mistakenly believing he would never propose, she had left Cambridge one spring day. He had spent more than a year looking for her – his sabbatical leave had seen little time spent in foreign universities, despite what his colleagues believed – but she had disappeared like mist in sunlight. If she was not coming back, he liked to think of her happily settled with a man who would give her the kind of life she deserved. He certainly refused to contemplate what his friends thought: that a lone woman in a cart full of possessions had been too great a temptation for the murderous robbers who infested the King's highways.

'I like sitting out here in the summer,' said Stanmore, taking an appreciative sip of his wine. 'And if you look through that grille on the wall you can see right down the road, but no one can see you.'

'So you can,' said Bartholomew, thinking it was an odd thing to point out. 'Do you spend much time peering down Milne Street, then?'

'A fair amount, especially when your sister is not here. I find it takes my mind off her.'

'Trumpington is only two miles distant. If you miss her that much, go home.'

'She is not in Trumpington, she is in London,' said Stanmore rather testily. 'I told you she was going, and so did she – several times, although I had a feeling our words were not sinking in. You are always preoccupied with your own concerns these days, and ours do not seem to matter to you.'

Bartholomew was dismayed by the accusation. 'What do you mean?'

'Our son,' said Stanmore. He scowled, as if the physician had done something wrong. 'You arranged for him to meet your former student Sam Gray, who secured him a post with the Earl of Suffolk. Richard is now a valued member of the Earl's household.'

'That is good,' said Bartholomew. But Stanmore was still glaring at him. 'Is it not?'

'It would have been, had he not fallen in love with the Earl's daughter. And the Earl has rather a different match in mind than the son of a merchant. Edith has gone to talk some sense into him.'

'Into the Earl?' asked Bartholomew uneasily.

'Into Richard,' snapped Stanmore impatiently. 'We have already explained all this to you.'

'Yes,' said Bartholomew, remembering that they had done so the night after Thomas died, when he had been too full of self-recrimination to concentrate. 'You have.'

Stanmore poured him more wine. 'You are working too hard – more students than you can manage, and too many patients. Then there was that nasty business with

113

Magister Arderne. He questioned your competence, and his remarks are still having an effect.'

'My patients trust me. If they did not, I would not have so many of them.'

'They trust you to help them, but a good number think your success comes from the pact you have made with the Devil. Your controversial methods are to blame. If you were more traditional, like Paxtone and Rougham, no one would give you a second thought.'

Bartholomew sighed, thinking he was far more orthodox than he had been when he was younger, forced into conforming by relentless pressure from all sides. It was galling to be told he was unconventional, when he tried so hard to avoid controversy.

'Take your success with the flux,' Stanmore went on when he did not reply. 'You cure virtually everyone, while Paxtone and Rougham struggle to keep half from their graves. Indeed, Rougham is so appalled by his failures that he has fled the town on the pretext of visiting his family. Some folk believe Mother Valeria has helped you devise a magical remedy.'

Bartholomew was beginning to wish he had kept on walking; this was not a conversation that would put him in the right frame of mind for sleep, either. 'I give my patients boiled barley and angelica – hardly witches' fare. Although I forgot the angelica once and I cannot help but wonder whether it is the boiled water that holds the secret, not the—'

'And there is a perfect example of your odd views,' interrupted Stanmore. 'How can boiled water mend anything? Your patients do not care about your peculiarities – they just want to get better – but there are those who resent your success, and are unsettled by it. Arderne sowed the seeds of suspicion, and your enemies will be only too happy to use his claims to be rid of you.'

'My enemies?' echoed Bartholomew. He had not thought of himself as a man with enemies.

'Master Heltisle of Bene't College abhors you, because you see him for the arrogant pig he is. His porters dislike the way you decline to be intimidated by them. Mildenale disapproves of the fact that the Dominican Prior is among your patients. Spaldynge despises you for being a *medicus*. And then there are those who detest you because you are friends with the Senior Proctor.'

'Should I abandon my practice and go off to become a hermit somewhere, then?'

'It will pass, I suppose,' said Stanmore, relenting when he saw the exhaustion in his kinsman's face. 'Especially once the Sorcerer has either established himself as a viable alternative to the Church or is ousted by the clerics. His imminent coming is making people more interested in witchery than usual, and that is why you have become a topic of conversation. But it will not last.'

'Do you know his identity?'

'No one does, but he will transpire to be some lowly scholar or upstart apprentice who knows a few incantations and a cure for warts. He will not be the powerful mage rumours would have us imagine. Speaking of warlocks, there are David and Joan Refham, going to attend their coven.'

Bartholomew was beginning to be bewildered by the discussion. 'Who?'

'The pair who are going to sell your College the shops on St Michael's Lane. You should watch them, because they will cheat you. They belong to the Sorcerer's coven, which they joined to win Satan's help in making them

115

lots of money. Refham is a blacksmith, but likes to think himself an expert in all trades. He keeps trying to interfere in mine, but has no idea what he is talking about.'

Bartholomew looked through the grille, and was disconcerted to see the couple in question standing very close, perhaps near enough to hear what was being said about them. Refham was in his forties, and what hair remained had been shaved into bristle. He had hazel eyes, and a smile that revealed crooked teeth. He was sturdy and looked strong, although the softness of his hands indicated he had not been near an anvil in some time. His wife was almost as tall, and her clothes had been cut to show off her slender figure.

'If you have the misfortune to meet him,' Stanmore went on, 'take all he says with a grain of salt. I doubt Langelee will involve *you* in the delicate business of buying property, but pass my warning to your colleagues. They should know what kind of man they are dealing with.'

Bartholomew drank another cup of wine, then left to go home. When he arrived, pleasantly drowsy, the porter said Mother Valeria had sent for him, so he trudged up Bridge Street towards the northern end of the town. He saw lamps flickering in All Saints as he went by, and groups of people loitered in the graveyard. Eyton was right: folk were indeed readying themselves for some dark rite that was about to take place. As he passed the dilapidated lych-gate he was astonished to see the vicar himself standing there. Eyton was holding a tray, and people were stopping to give him money.

'What are you doing?' Bartholomew whispered, a little shocked. 'You warned me away from All Saints, but here *you* are, boldly greeting the Devil's disciples as they make their way inside.'

Eyton grinned cheerfully. 'I am selling them talismans, because you can never be sure when you might need protection at this sort of event. Would you like one? These little pouches contain secret herbs and a sprinkling of holy water. And, of course, each one is blessed by me, after it has spent a night on St Bene't's altar.'

Bartholomew tried not to gape at him. 'You hawk amulets against evil at satanic gatherings? Do the town's merchants know about this? It is an impressive piece of marketing.'

Eyton looked hurt. 'The folk who attend these events are not cloven-hoofed fiends. They are ordinary men and women looking for answers – answers they hope the Sorcerer may be able to provide. I am here to make sure they do not come to harm from any real demons that might be attracted to the occasion.'

Bartholomew struggled, unsuccessfully, to understand his logic. 'I cannot see the Bishop condoning your actions. He would want you to prevent these covens from taking place at all.'

Eyton laughed, genuinely amused. 'I doubt de Lisle gives a fig what I do! He is in Avignon, anyway, trying to persuade the Pope that he is not a criminal. Indeed, he would probably attend one of these gatherings himself, if he thought it would extricate him from his predicament.'

'The Bishop has his faults,' said Bartholomew, 'but Devil-worshipping is not among them.'

Eyton laughed again. 'De Lisle is a rogue, and does the Church no favours by staining it with his presence. But I can see you like him, so we had better talk about

117

something else. I feel a little queasy. It must be the jug of honey I drank on my way here. I do not suppose you have a remedy, do you?'

Bartholomew was about to inform him that he did *not* like de Lisle, but it did not seem appropriate to denounce high-ranking churchmen when the Sorcerer's congregation was filing past him. Instead, he looked at the massive pot that stood at the priest's feet, and was not surprised Eyton felt sick. 'Surely a spoonful will suffice?' he asked. 'It is unwise to swallow such large quantities in one go.'

Eyton grimaced. 'Perhaps, but I am unwilling to take the risk. But here come a few more customers, so you will have to excuse me. Incidentally, if you are out later, be on your guard, especially if you see anyone flying about on a black goat. It is almost certain to be a denizen of Hell.'

'Lord!' muttered Bartholomew, watching the priest move to intercept a well-dressed couple who looked pleased with themselves: the Refhams.

'I do not need protecting from Lucifer,' declared Refham, elbowing the vicar roughly out of the way. 'I gave him a gift of three chickens for the sacrifice last week, so he will feel indebted to me.'

'I will have one,' said Joan. She shrugged when her husband regarded her askance. 'Father William says demons are unpredictable, so there is no harm in being cautious.'

Refham sighed. 'Buy one for me, then. I will not be happy if Satan turns me into a toad.'

'Buy it yourself,' retorted Joan. 'I have better use for my pennies than squandering them on you.'

They moved away, still bickering, and Bartholomew watched other people make their way towards the church.

118

Despite the unpleasant stuffiness of the night, some had donned hoods or hats to hide their faces, although he recognised a few by their gait or the other clothes they wore. There was one who looked suspiciously like Podiolo, but the fellow was so heavily disguised that it was impossible to be sure. He was accompanied by a man who might have been one of the plump, balding canons of Barnwell, but equally well might have been someone else.

Bartholomew was unsettled to discover the Sorcerer's coven was quite so popular, and wondered whether the odd incidents Michael was investigating – defiled corpses, goats and bloody fonts – were indeed connected to this sudden interest in dark magic. When Eyton began a friendly chat with someone who was almost certainly the Mayor, Bartholomew slipped through the gate and entered the churchyard, thinking he would take a few moments to observe the proceedings and see whether he could learn anything to help Michael.

All Saints-next-the-Castle was a medium-sized church. Its nave roof had collapsed the previous winter, leaving only a few wooden rafters, and its glassless windows were choked with ivy. The chancel was in better condition, and the physician wondered whether the Sorcerer saw to its upkeep, so he would have somewhere dry to perform should a coven happen to fall on a rainy night. He stood on a tomb and peered through a weed-fringed window. The nave was full and very noisy. The sound was that of people meeting friends and exchanging pleasantries, and the occasional clink of a goblet indicated that refreshments were being served. It was a far cry from the deep-throated chanting he had expected, and looked perfectly innocent to him.

He left the church feeling there was nothing to see,

and was about to resume his journey to Mother Valeria when he spotted the charnel house that stood in the furthest corner of the cemetery. It had once been used to store the bones that were unearthed when new graves were dug, or to house bodies the night before they were buried. It was a sturdy building, because such places were at risk from raids by dogs or wild animals, and was in far better repair than the church itself. Its roof was intact, its door was solid, and its walls were sound. He was not sure why his attention had been drawn towards it, but as he stared, he became aware that two people were lurking in its shadows. They saw him watching, and it took considerable willpower to stand his ground when they came towards him.

'Matthew,' said Father William coolly. Mildenale was at his side. 'I almost believed you earlier, when you said you had no truck with witches. And then I find you here.'

Bartholomew stifled a sigh, and wondered whether it was worth even attempting an explanation. William seldom listened to anyone, but he was even less likely to believe anything from a man in a graveyard where a satanic ritual was about to take place. 'I was on my way to see a patient when I saw the lights. I decided to see if I could learn anything to help Michael with his enquiries.'

'He is telling the truth,' said Mildenale to William. He clasped his hands together and raised his eyes to the dark skies. 'God has given me a talent for identifying liars.'

'Has He?' asked William. Envy was etched deeply in his face. 'I wish He would do the same for me. It would be very useful for rousting out heretics.'

'Why are *you* here?' asked Bartholomew. 'This is no place for friars.'

120

'Trying to find out the Sorcerer's identity, as usual,' replied Mildenale. He sounded as weary as Bartholomew felt. 'Unfortunately, his acolytes do the honours with the public sacrifices while he sits in a darkened booth and dispenses expensive spells and curses. It is always impossible to see his face, but we shall try to gain a peek tonight. Again.'

'Personally, I think we should storm the booth and rip off his hood,' said William belligerently. 'But Mildenale believes that might put us in danger from outraged followers. However, a cautious approach is all wrong, if you ask me. I want this villain unmasked.'

'It is better to watch and listen,' argued Mildenale. 'And ascertain exactly what we are up against.'

'We had better do it before Saturday night, then,' said William to him rather threateningly. 'Because after that, it will be too late.'

He remained suspicious of Bartholomew, although Mildenale sketched a blessing and told the physician he might be safer leaving before the celebrations began – the last time the coven had met, a sudden wind had brought down a tree. Bartholomew was only too pleased to do as he suggested.

'What is the name of the patient you are going to see?' demanded William, stopping him with a hand on his sleeve. 'I may say a few prayers for him, if he is the kind of fellow who deserves the honour.'

'No one you know,' replied Bartholomew, sure it was true.

'We will petition for his recovery, anyway,' said Mildenale, prising William's fingers from the physician's arm. 'God's speed, Bartholomew, and do not be late for mass tomorrow.'

121

Relieved to be away, Bartholomew made for the gate. Behind him, he heard William berating his colleague for his timidity in confronting evil. He hoped neither of them would come to harm that night. They were zealots, but he did not want to see them dead, like Thomas and Carton.

Mother Valeria lived in a shack near the back of the castle. It had once been the centre of a thriving community, albeit a poor one, but most of the houses had fallen into ruin after the plague, and were thick with weeds and brambles. The path to Valeria's door was well trodden, though, which was a testament to the number of people who sought her out for cures, charms and advice. There was no door, and a sheet of leather covered the entrance instead. It was heavier than it looked, and had been arranged to make a stealthy approach impossible. On previous visits, Bartholomew had noticed holes in the back of the hut, and supposed they were there to facilitate a quick escape, should one ever be necessary. It was a wise precaution: folk healers often provided convenient scapegoats, to be blamed for all manner of disasters and misfortunes.

Bartholomew fought his way through the hanging and entered the dim interior. It smelled of cured meat and herbs, and dozens of jars adorned the wall-shelves. There was a hearth in the centre of the hut, with a slit in the roof above to allow smoke to escape. Valeria always had a blaze going, no matter what the weather, and there was usually something bubbling in a pot over it. That night was no exception, even though it was late, and most people – other than coven-goers – were in bed.

Valeria sat on a stool next to the fire. Bartholomew

thought she was tall, but he had never seen her standing, so it was difficult to tell. She had a long nose, matching chin and several prominent warts. As the warts moved position every so often, he suspected they were there for appearance, rather than natural blemishes. He was not sure the nose and chin were genuine, either, because there were times when he was sure they were more pronounced than others. She had once confided that she went to some trouble to look the part, claiming people were more likely to have faith in her spells if she met their requirements regarding what they thought a witch should be like.

'I was not sure you would be home,' he said, sitting next to her. Automatically, he stretched his hands towards the flames, then realised how ridiculous that was in the middle of a heatwave. He pulled them back sheepishly. 'There is a coven in All Saints tonight.'

She grimaced. 'I might go later, but only because watching the antics of amateurs is so damned amusing. They are no more witches than you are, except perhaps the one they call the Sorcerer.'

Bartholomew smiled. 'I am glad someone knows I am not a warlock.'

She spat her disgust. 'If you had been a warlock, you would have cured more people from the plague. I saved dozens, you know.'

'Did you?' asked Bartholomew, always eager to learn new ways of healing. 'How?'

'With spells and incantations. But you cannot just repeat the words by rote. You have to say them properly, using the right magic at the same time. Would you like me to teach you?'

'No, thank you.' She had offered to show him such tricks before, but he could tell from the impish gleam in

123

her eye that she was playing with him; he doubted she would share her secrets, given that they were what put bread on her table. 'Do you know the Sorcerer's real name? Michael needs to talk to him, but it is difficult to track him down when no one knows who he is.'

'He is elusive, and his acolytes keep the curious away. I have no idea who he might be, although he is growing in power and will soon become truly dangerous.'

For some reason, her words made Bartholomew shudder; he supposed it was the notion that she should be unnerved by the power of another witch. He changed the subject to one with which he was more comfortable. 'Did you call me to tend your knee again?'

She presented him with the afflicted limb, although it was so heavily swathed in leggings that a physical examination was all but impossible. He had asked her to remove them on previous occasions and had been curtly informed that it would not be decent. He did not have the energy to remonstrate with her that night, and as soon as he had palpated the swollen joint – as well as he could through the thick clothing – and provided her with a pot of ointment, he took his leave. Valeria bared her stained teeth in a smile of thanks, then sketched some heathen benediction he preferred not to acknowledge.

It was pitch black by the time he started to walk home, although lamps still burned in All Saints. The night was airless and quiet, so when there was a rattle of footsteps in an alley off to one side, he heard them quite distinctly. He stopped dead and peered into the darkness, but the lane appeared to be deserted. He supposed it was a beggar, unable to sleep for the heat.

He walked on, but then heard footsteps a second time. He whipped around and stared at the road behind him,

124

only to find it empty. When he heard the sound a third time, he ducked behind a water butt and crouched down. After a while, two figures emerged from the shadows. One was so large that Bartholomew wondered whether his eyes were playing tricks on him, while the other sported a bushy beard. Even though he could not see their faces, their silhouettes were distinctive, and he knew he would have remembered if he had seen them before – and he had not. They appeared to be reasonably well dressed, so were no common robbers, yet there was something about the stealthy way they moved that was strangely and inexplicably villainous.

They passed within an arm's length of his hiding place, and he froze in alarm when the giant stopped and sniffed the air. Whilst there was no reason to think they were looking for him, it was clear they intended to move unseen, and they struck him as the kind of men who would object to being spied on. He held his breath until he thought his lungs would burst. Eventually, they slunk on, disappearing into the alleys near the Great Bridge, but it was some time before Bartholomew felt it was safe to leave the comforting mass of the water butt and make his own way home.

Chapter 4

'I hate this weather,' grumbled Michael the next day, as he tried to make himself comfortable on the only bench that was out of the sun. He was in the conclave, a pleasant chamber that adjoined Michaelhouse's hall and that was the accepted domain of the Fellows. 'Agatha says the meat she bought this morning is already fly-blown. And you know what that means.'

'More onion soup?' Bartholomew was standing at a window, staring absently across the courtyard below. 'Spices to disguise the taste?'

'Worse,' moaned Michael. 'Reduced rations! She says some is so green she would not even give it to students. Still, the last of them left this morning, so there are fewer mouths to feed now.'

'Who is left?'

'The Fellows and Mildenale. Oh, and Deynman, who does not trust us to look after the library.'

'It feels strange,' said Bartholomew, unsettled by the silence and empty rooms. That morning, breakfast had brought back painful memories of the plague, when the scholars' ranks had thinned because of sickness. 'I do not like it.'

'It is only for a week, and now we can concentrate on finding Carton's killer – along with those responsible for digging up Margery, putting blood in our font and taking Danyell's hand. *And* the thief who stole Bene't's goats, I suppose, as Heltisle was after me about it again today.'

'I watched the Sorcerer's disciples meet in All Saints last night,' said Bartholomew, hoping Michael's crime-solving itinerary would leave him time to complete his experiments on the powder Carton had found in Thomas's room. It had not seemed important before, but now the physician felt he would be letting Carton down if he did not do as he had promised.

'Then I sincerely hope no one saw you. Your reputation already leans towards the unorthodox, and being spotted in the vicinity of satanic covens will do it no good whatsoever.'

'William and Mildenale caught me.' Bartholomew raised his hands in a shrug at Michael's horrified expression. 'They were doing the same thing – trying to see what might be learned in order to stop it. But I discovered nothing that might be of use to you, other than the fact that the Sorcerer has more followers than I realised.'

Michael regarded him with round eyes. 'Please do not do it again, Matt. It might be dangerous. Besides, my beadles were there, mingling anonymously with the crowd. They know what they are doing, and they are paid for it.'

'I was only trying to help.'

'I would rather you helped in other ways, such as telling me what you think about the theft of Danyell's hand. Did I tell you the poor man was only visiting Cambridge? He was passing through on his way from London to Norfolk, travelling with a friend called Richard Spynk.'

'Spynk.' Bartholomew had heard the name in a

different context than pertaining to the hapless Danyell. 'Carton spoke to him about buying the house Margery left us. He used Spynk to inflate the price for the canons of Barnwell.'

'So, you do listen at Fellows' meetings! Yes, Spynk is interested in the house. But recap what you told me about Danyell – your conclusions about his death.'

'I am almost certain he died of natural causes. I found his corpse when I was returning home after tending Mother Valeria, and there was no sign of foul play. Except for the missing hand.'

'You said he had probably had a seizure and the limb was removed *after* death, because there was no sign of a struggle or evidence that he was restrained. You then went on to explain that one cannot remove body parts from a live victim without the poor fellow doing all he can to stop you. It made me feel quite queasy.'

'That was the heat. Did you know there is an ancient superstition that the hand of a dead man will help someone make really good butter?'

Michael regarded him askance. 'Now you are teasing me.'

Bartholomew shrugged. 'It is an old tale, but there are some who believe it. Severed hands are also said to cure warts. I think I mentioned that before.'

Michael nodded. 'You did. Unfortunately, you said it in front of William, which led him to accuse *you* of stealing the thing. You told him people tend not to consult physicians for minor ailments like warts, at which point he decided you must have purloined it as a gift for Valeria.'

'I am surprised Spynk wants a house in Cambridge, given what happened to his friend,' said Bartholomew, declining to waste his time dwelling on William's wild fancies. 'If *your* hand were stolen in a distant town, I would be keen to leave the place as soon as possible.'

'He claims to have discovered a liking for Cambridge – says he wants to do business here in the future. His trade is importing luxury goods from the Low Countries, and he thinks we are a good commercial opportunity – linked to the sea via the river, and with a population able to afford such commodities. *Ergo*, he wants a house for his visits, and says Sewale Cottage fits the bill perfectly.'

'It is funny you should be talking about Spynk,' came a soft voice from the door that made both scholars jump in alarm. 'Because he has the flux, and wants you to visit.'

'How many times have I asked you not to slink up on me, Cynric?' demanded Michael, hand to his chest. 'If you do it again, my Junior Proctor may have to charge *you* with murder. Mine.'

When Bartholomew went to see Spynk, Michael left for Barnwell Priory. The monk wanted to ask Prior Norton why he had failed to mention Carton's attempt to manipulate a higher price for Sewale Cottage. It was an excellent motive for murder, and meant the canons should be questioned more closely. He hired a horse to take him, not just because it had been a long and unpleasant walk the day before, but because he wanted the brethren to know his visit was an official one. He was furious they had withheld information from him, and intended to intimidate them to the point where they would not dare do it again.

Bartholomew went to the High Street, where Spynk was staying in a pleasantly airy suite of rooms overlooking the road. His windows afforded magnificent views of St Mary the Great one way, and King's Hall's gatehouse the other. As these were two of the finest buildings in Cambridge, the physician wondered whether they had given Spynk a false impression of its prosperity.

'Thank God you are here,' Spynk said when he arrived. 'I have the flux. Make me well – immediately, if you would be so kind.'

He was a large man with wiry hair and thick, callused hands that suggested he was not averse to manual labour. When Bartholomew had gone with Michael to break the news of Danyell's death on Ascension Day, Spynk had spent an inordinate amount of time bragging about the fact that he had personally supervised the repair of Norwich's defensive walls. He also claimed he had paid for most of the work, and said the city had granted him lifelong exemption from certain taxes in appreciation. He gave the impression that he was a man of power and influence, although the physician had thought him vulgar, and was not sure whether to believe most of his self-aggrandising declarations.

'There is no such thing as an instant cure for the flux,' said Bartholomew. 'It takes time to—'

'I hear you have a better success rate than the other fellow – Paxtone. Meanwhile, Rougham has fled because his ineptitude was killing people. Well, that is one rumour. The other is that he stole poor Danyell's hand for anatomy and has gone into the Fens to complete his dark business.'

'Rougham would never entertain anatomy,' said Bartholomew truthfully. 'And he has gone to visit his family. It is half-term, so he is within his rights to go.'

Spynk seemed ready to argue, but was interrupted by the sudden need to dash for a bucket. While he was busy,

130

Bartholomew inspected the sample of urine that had been provided, then asked for a pot of boiled water. It was brought by Spynk's wife, a pretty woman with dark hair and a kirtle that revealed an impressive amount of frontage.

'You might have decanted it into a better jug, Cecily,' snapped Spynk, peering out through the curtain that gave him his privacy. 'That one is chipped.'

'They are all chipped,' she replied sullenly. 'Look for yourself, if you do not believe me.'

'It is fine,' said Bartholomew hastily, reluctant for them to embark on a domestic squabble in front of him. He added his powdered barley and angelica. 'It is the water that matters, not the pot.'

Cecily watched him stir the mixture. 'I hope those are powerful substances, Doctor. My husband is a strong man, and dislikes weak remedies.'

'They are what will make him well again,' replied Bartholomew, declining to admit that his cure contained two very innocuous ingredients. If Spynk believed the medicine was ineffectual he might decline to swallow it, and the flux was too serious an ailment for games.

'It tastes like starch,' objected Spynk, after a tentative sip. He thrust it back at the physician. 'I am not drinking that. Tip it out of the window, Cecily.'

'Tip it yourself,' retorted Cecily churlishly. 'I am not your servant.'

'We can add honey,' suggested Bartholomew, thinking of the priest Eyton and his penchant for the stuff. 'That might make it more palatable.'

Cecily brightened. 'That is a good idea. I bought some from Barnwell Priory on Saturday afternoon – it was an excuse for me to get inside and have a look around –

and I do not want to carry it home to Norwich. The pot might break and spoil all my new dresses.'

'Spoon some in, then,' ordered Spynk. 'As much as you like. I can afford it.'

Bartholomew stopped her from adding the whole jug to the concoction, suspecting the resulting sickliness would make the merchant feel worse then ever. Then he encouraged Spynk to swallow what he had prepared, and sent Cecily to the kitchens for more boiled water. She sighed resentfully, but did as she was asked.

'I understand you are a member of Michaelhouse,' said Spynk when she had gone. 'Is it true?'

Bartholomew nodded. 'Have you visited our College?' he asked politely.

'Yes – last week. I went to talk to Carton about the house you are selling on Bridge Street. How much do you think you will get for it?'

Bartholomew knew he would be swimming in dangerous waters if he attempted to meddle in College finances. 'I have no idea. You will have to talk to the Master or Wynewyk. They are—'

'I will give you a horse if you tell me about any other offers you have had,' interrupted Spynk. 'I am *very* interested in making this particular purchase.'

'Talk to the Master,' repeated Bartholomew. 'I do not know about the other offers.'

Spynk glared at him, then sighed irritably. 'Very well, but you have just lost yourself a decent nag. I am sorry about Carton, by the way. He tried to cheat me by starting a bidding war with Barnwell, but I do not bear him a grudge. He was only doing his duty. I understand Michaelhouse is poor, and needs all the money it can lay its grubby hands on.'

132

'We are not one of the wealthier foundations,' admitted Bartholomew cautiously.

'I sent Cecily to Barnwell on Saturday,' Spynk rambled on. 'I wanted her to get a feel for the place, work out how wealthy they are. It is always good to know your enemies. Do you not agree?'

'I do not have many—'

Spynk released a braying laugh. 'That is not what I hear! I am a stranger here, but even I know half the town thinks you are a warlock. The other half believes you are a saint, but they are mostly poor, and no one listens to them. You have enemies aplenty.'

He was going to add something else, but another bout of sickness prevented him. Afterwards, he flopped on the bed and closed his eyes, exhausted by the ordeal. Bartholomew was grateful for the silence. Eventually, Cecily arrived with another brimming pan, then stood nearer to him than was proper while he made a second batch of the mixture.

'I need more hot water,' he said, searching for an excuse to send her away until he had finished. She was so close that her breath was hot on the back of his neck, and he kept thinking that Spynk might wake up and wonder what they were up to.

'What for?' she asked. 'You have already prepared enough of this medicine to satisfy an ox. If he drinks it all, he will burst.'

'I need to wash my hands.'

'Your hands?' asked Spynk, showing he had not been asleep after all. 'God's blood, but this is a strange town! Why should you wash your hands? They look clean enough to me. Cecily and I only wash ours on Sundays, before we go to church.'

'Actually, I scrub mine on Wednesdays, too,' said Cecily with a coquettish smile. 'I like to feel fresh. Do you want a different pot, or would you mind giving them a rinse in that potion we have just brewed? We have not added the honey yet, so it will not be sticky, and Richard will not mind.'

Bartholomew regarded her askance, lost for words.

'Danyell was obsessed with cleanliness, too,' said Spynk with a grimace of disapproval. 'He took a bath every year, but look how he ended up – someone stealing his fingers for God knows what purpose. He was an odd man: careful with hygiene on one hand, but in the habit of wandering about at night on the other.'

Bartholomew's ears pricked up. 'What?'

Cecily's expression was dreamy. 'He often met me for a nocturnal stroll when everyone else was in bed. Of course, it is safe to do it in Norfolk, where we live, but Cambridge is a rough place, seething with villains. It is not wise to roam about in the dark here.'

'For him, it was probably not wise to do it anywhere,' said Spynk. 'He had a morbidly pounding heart, and should have stayed in. In fact, it was not very sensible to travel to London, either. I wish I had not asked him to come, because now his sons are going to say his death is my fault.'

'It was no one's fault,' said Bartholomew. 'He had a seizure, which could have happened any—'

'I want that in writing,' said Spynk. 'Will you oblige? I will give you the parchment.'

'What time did Danyell go out on the night he died?' asked Bartholomew. Michael had already interviewed the Spynks at length, but there was no harm in repeating the process. They might tell him something they had forgotten to mention earlier, or he might see something the monk had missed. After all, someone must know why Danyell had been relieved of his hand.

'Just after dusk,' replied Cecily. 'I was keen to go with him, but he said he wanted to be alone. He had pains in his chest and arm, and thought a walk might ease them.'

'Why did you offer him your company?' asked Bartholomew, thinking it was a peculiar thing for the wife of a wealthy merchant to do. She was right in that Cambridge could be dangerous after dark, and it was no place for a woman with only an ailing man for protection.

Cecily shot him an odd glance. 'I thought he might like it.'

Rather belatedly, it occurred to Bartholomew that Cecily and Danyell might have enjoyed more than pleasant conversation when they took their late-night strolls. When he took in her deliberately provocative clothes and the salacious way she eyed him, he was sure of it. He was not an observant man when it came to that sort of thing, and the fact that he had noticed at all meant she must be very brazen. He shot a covert glance at Spynk, and realised the merchant was even less aware of such matters than he was, for he seemed oblivious to his wife's antics.

'He said he had business to conduct,' said Spynk. 'And he was carrying something under his arm that looked like a stone sample. You know he was a mason?'

Bartholomew nodded. 'When he failed to return, were you not worried?'

He had found Danyell's body shortly after dawn, and it had been stiff around the jaws. Danyell had probably been dead most of the night, and it had struck him as odd at the time that his friends had not gone to look for him.

'I was,' said Cecily. 'But I could hardly go to look for him myself, and Richard was asleep.'

'I hate being woken up,' explained Spynk. 'And Cecily knows better than to disturb me at night.'

'I prefer him asleep anyway,' said Cecily meaningfully.

'It is de Lisle's fault,' said Spynk, bitterly and somewhat out of the blue. 'If he had not forced us to go to London, we would not have stopped here to rest on our way home. And Danyell might still be alive, despite what you say about seizures.'

Bartholomew did not understand. 'The Bishop of Ely made you travel? How? I thought he was in Avignon. And besides, you just said it was your idea to visit London, and—'

'We had to make a complaint about him, in front of the King,' explained Spynk. 'Me and Danyell, and a score of others. The Bishop is a bully, you see. He and his men stole all my cows a few years ago, and the King wanted our accusations on record.'

Bartholomew blinked. 'De Lisle is a cattle rustler? That does not sound very likely.'

'Then you do not know him very well,' said Cecily. 'I offered him a night of my company in exchange for leaving my husband alone but he said he would rather have the livestock. He is an uncouth man, and I was delighted to detail his shortcomings to the King.'

'He laid violent siege to Danyell's manor, too,' added Spynk. 'It must have been terrifying. De Lisle may be one of the most powerful prelates in the country but that has not stopped him from indulging in theft, arson, extortion, assault and even murder. He is a wicked villain.'

'Right,' said Bartholomew, declining to argue. Cambridge was in de Lisle's See, and such men had an uncanny habit of learning who had been talking about them; the physician did not want to include a prelate on his list of enemies. And while the Bishop did indeed have a reputation for being ruthless, Bartholomew was sure he was not a criminal, and thought Spynk and Cecily were exaggerating the charges that had been laid against him.

'How do you feel now, Master Spynk?' he asked, to change the subject.

'A little better,' admitted Spynk begrudgingly. 'It must have been the honey.'

At breakfast that morning, Langelee had announced that there would be a Statutory Fellows' Meeting at noon, because there was urgent business to discuss. There was not only the sad matter of Carton to debate, but the purchase and sale of various properties, too. After he had finished with Spynk, there was an hour to go before the gathering, so Bartholomew lay on his bed and fell into a restless doze. He woke when a clatter of hoofs announced Michael's return from Barnwell.

'Nothing,' said the monk in disgust, springing from his saddle with the natural grace of the born horseman, if a rather heavy one. 'It was a waste of time. Norton admitted to knowing about Carton's attempts to raise the cost of Sewale Cottage but said everyone does it these days – that he would have been surprised had we *not* tried to manipulate a better price.'

'Is it true?' asked Bartholomew, stepping forward to take the horse's bridle. It snickered at him, causing him to drop it smartly. 'Does everyone do it these days?'

'Yes, apparently. So, now I am not sure whether Norton

objected to his convent being the victim of this so-called common practice, or whether he took it in his stride.'

'You should drink some ale before the meeting,' advised Bartholomew, thinking the monk looked unnaturally flushed under his wide-brimmed hat.

'I would prefer some chicken, but even the cat would not eat what was left of the ones Agatha roasted last night. Rougham was right to leave this town. It is probably cooler in Norfolk, and meat will not spoil the moment it is ready for the table.'

Agatha was in the kitchen, sprawled in her huge wicker throne and fanning herself with what appeared to be one of the College's exemplars – anthologies of texts on a specific subject. Deynman hovered behind her, a tense expression on his face. When she glanced up to watch Michael drink, he snatched it from her hand and raced from the room. A screech of outrage followed, but the laundress was too hot to embark on a chase, and Bartholomew supposed Deynman would have to wait for the inevitable retribution. He wrinkled his nose when he smelled what lay on the table.

'You should throw that in the midden,' he said in distaste. 'I am sure bad meat is a factor in spreading the flux.'

Agatha did not reply, so he started to do it himself, thinking to save her the trouble.

'Leave it,' she barked. Bartholomew froze: only the foolish or suicidal ignored a direct order from Agatha. 'I might make Deynman eat it. How dare he deprive me of a scroll! I am a member of this College, so I am entitled to make use of the library.'

'Yes – to read,' said Bartholomew, recalling that she sometimes helped herself to the priceless tomes if there was a table that wobbled or a draught that whistled under a door.

'I do not read!' she declared contemptuously. Clearly, she considered it beneath her. 'Although Cynric found an interesting book today. It was hidden on Master Langelee's top shelf, and told us all about how the night before Trinity Sunday is a special occasion for witches.'

'Was this book wrapped in black cloth?' asked Bartholomew uneasily, not liking to think of Carton's manual of witchcraft in Cynric's tender care. Not for the first time, he wondered whether he had been wise to teach the Welshman his letters.

She nodded. 'It contained a spell for making bad meat whole again, and I shall be testing it later. You can tell me if it works – hopefully before I am obliged to eat any myself.'

'Try it on William,' suggested Michael, bundling the physician from the kitchen before he could voice his objections. He grinned maliciously once they were outside. 'We cannot lose, Matt! If William becomes ill, he will be confined to bed and will stop accusing you of being in league with the Devil. And if he remains healthy, we shall all dine on meat tonight.'

Bartholomew did not bother to point out that the flux did not strike the moment bad meat passed a person's lips. He followed the monk up the stairs, across the hall and into the conclave, where the sun was blazing through the windows. He flopped on to a bench and put his head in his hands, feeling a buzzing lethargy envelop him. When would the weather break? He did not think he could stand much more of it, and hoped it would not last until the end of summer. Michael dragged the table to a place where he would not be in direct sunlight, although it meant everyone else would have it in their eyes, and sat with a sigh.

'Here comes William,' he said, cocking his head as footsteps thumped across the hall. 'I recognise that purposeful tread anywhere. Even his feet have the air of a fanatic about them.'

The door opened and William strode in, humming one of the more militant psalms. 'I have had a profitable morning,' he announced, pleased with himself. 'I accused Sheriff Tulyet of heresy.'

Michael's jaw dropped in horror. 'You did *what*?'

'I accused Sheriff Tulyet of heresy,' repeated William more loudly. 'He owns a book on the occult, and I demanded that he hand it over, so it can be added to the ones Carton collected for burning. He refused, so I called him a heretic.'

'Lord!' murmured Bartholomew. Tulyet was a friend – to the University, as well as personally – and he did not want a valued relationship soured because of William. 'What did he say?'

'Nothing – he just walked away,' replied William. 'But he was clenching his fists at his side, so I know my words had hit home.'

'They were clenched because they were itching to punch you,' said Langelee, as he entered the conclave. 'I have just come from the castle, where I was summoned to tell him why you should not be locked up. He thinks you are a danger to the King's peace.'

'I have rattled Satan's familiars,' crowed William. 'Tulyet would not complain about me if he were innocent, would he? I shall have our town free of heretics yet. Of course, I would rather see the Dominicans leave than Tulyet. I have always liked Tulyet, to be honest.'

'Which of Carton's books do you plan to incinerate?' asked Bartholomew. 'Not the Avicenna?'

'No – I plan to destroy the ones *you* removed from his chest and took to Deynman,' replied William coolly. 'When I heard you had been given the task of deciding what was profane, I knew I would have to do it myself, given your lax attitude towards blasphemy. It was not easy to prise them from Deynman, but I managed in the end.'

'Those were theological and philosophical texts,' objected Bartholomew. 'Including some you use on a regular basis, so they cannot be blasphemous. And if you have harmed Deynman—'

'I waited until he was out, then broke his locks with a stone,' interrupted William. 'I have not inspected the tones properly yet, but I am sure there will be some that will make for a merry blaze.'

Bartholomew regarded him in distaste. 'Book-burning says you are frightened of new ideas.'

'I *am* frightened of new ideas,' said William fervently. 'If they were any good, they would be in the Bible – and the fact that they are not means they should never be entertained by right-thinking men.'

'But we are scholars,' protested Bartholomew, knowing he was wasting his time but unable to stop himself. 'We have a moral responsibility to assess novel theories, and push back the barriers of our collective knowledge.'

'Exactly,' said William. 'Men like you will be pushing these barriers back to the point where any heretical notion can be aired in the debating chamber. Well, it will not happen as long as *I* am here.'

'I usually fail to see the problem with most condemned texts,' said Langelee, rummaging in the wall-cupboard for his sceptre – the ceremonial symbol of his authority, which he used to signal the beginning and end of meetings. 'They invariably make perfect sense, but just happen to go against some doctrine cooked up by men with narrow minds. So leave Carton's collections alone, Father. We will have no book-burning at Michaelhouse.'

William's face fell, while Bartholomew and Michael exchanged pleased glances. Neither would have expected Langelee to take a positive stand on books, which he tended to hold in low regard unless they were valuable, in which case he agitated for them to be sold. There were always bills to be paid or some costly repair to be made to the College fabric, and the Master was a practical man.

'But—' began the friar.

'That is my last word,' said Langelee firmly.

As the sun rose higher in the sky, the conclave became hotter. Michael complained bitterly that the last of the Fellows – Wynewyk and Suttone – were late, while Bartholomew felt himself grow more drowsy. Langelee and William bickered over the ethics of selling, rather than incinerating, heretical texts, and the Master won the debate when he pointed out that the proceeds could be used to buy wine. Bartholomew suspected Mildenale would not be so easily swayed from his convictions, and neither would Carton or Father Thomas have been.

It was not long before Suttone waddled into the conclave to take his customary seat. He was a Carmelite friar, and when he, Langelee and Michael were in a row, Bartholomew was reminded that his College possessed some very large men. The physician was hardly diminutive himself, because he was tall and his medical practice kept him fit, but he always felt like a waif when he was with his colleagues. The bench groaned its objection, and he looked in his medical bag to ensure he had salves for the kind of injuries that might occur if it collapsed and deposited them all on the floor.

'Shall we discuss the weather while we wait for Wynewyk?' suggested Langelee. 'It is less contentious than text-burning, and we should at least start the meeting as friends.'

'I would rather talk about the plague,' said Suttone, one of those who was convinced that it was on its way back. 'Sinful men have not mended their ways, and—'

Langelee cut him off with a groan. 'I do not want to hear it. We had more than enough of that in William's Saturday Sermon. I would prefer to be regaled with your views on the weather.'

'Crops are dying in the fields because of the heat,' began Michael obligingly. 'And it is common knowledge that this harvest will be a poor one. There will be a shortage of grain for bread, and we shall all starve before the year is out.'

'Nonsense,' countered Suttone, thus proving that even the climate was a controversial subject when discussed by scholars. 'There has been rain galore in the north, and they will have plenty to sell to those whose harvest has failed.'

'But they will charge a fortune,' said Wynewyk, as he bustled in with a sheaf of parchments under his arm. 'And we are desperately short of cash at the moment, as I have been telling you.'

'Perhaps so, but we still have to eat,' said Michael, to make sure Wynewyk knew that victuals were not an optional extra.

'Do not worry, Brother; Wynewyk will keep our bellies

full,' said Langelee, shooting the lawyer a look that said there would be trouble if he did not. 'But winter is months away, and we should not worry about it now. Who knows what might happen in that time?'

'True,' said William. 'After all, look at Carton. Worrying about food for this coming winter would have been a waste of *his* time, would it not?'

Bartholomew frowned, thinking it a callous remark from a man who professed to be Carton's friend. But before he could berate him for it, Langelee banged on the table with his sceptre, and announced that the meeting was underway.

'There are two matters to consider today,' he said. 'First, the status of the houses we are buying and selling. Second, this awkward business regarding the Bishop of Ely. And finally Carton.'

'That is three matters,' said Wynewyk pedantically. 'Shall we discuss them in that order?'

'Carton first,' said Langelee. 'I know it is a painful subject, but it is also the most important. I have just read his will, and I am happy to report that he left us everything he owned – we are his sole beneficiary. Does anyone have anything else to say about him?'

'I do,' said Suttone. 'The reason I was late is because I went to visit his corpse. Margery Sewale was pulled from her grave, and I was afraid someone might defile him, too. But he was untouched.'

Bartholomew regarded him in astonishment. 'Why would anyone attack Carton's remains?'

Suttone shrugged. 'Hopefully, no one will, but Carton was a member of Michaelhouse, and Margery was *associated* with Michaelhouse. I just wanted to be sure he was safe.'

144

'Father Thomas was associated with Michaelhouse, too, because he knew me,' said William. He shot Bartholomew an unpleasant look. 'I miss him.'

'We know,' said Langelee with an exaggerated sigh, while Bartholomew stared down at the table, guilt washing over him. 'But what is done is done, and we should try to move on.'

'What shall we do about replacing Carton, then?' asked William, giving the impression that he had no intention of moving anywhere. 'I am not taking on more teaching – I have heretics to rout.'

'None of us can carry Carton's classes,' said Suttone. 'We never have a free moment to prepare future lectures as it is. I hoped to write an essay on the return of the Death this morning, to read at the meeting of the Guild of Corpus Christi next week, but it will have to wait until tomorrow.'

'You intend to wax lyrical about the Death at a Guild meeting?' asked Langelee in disbelief. 'I thought those occasions were supposed to be full of merrymaking, wine and good health.'

Suttone looked crestfallen, but then brightened. 'But the letter inviting me to give the main address stipulated no such restrictions. Besides, I would be failing in my sacred duty if I did not describe the bleak, hopeless future that lies ahead of us all.'

'I see,' said Michael, while Bartholomew thought the Guild was stupid to have chosen Suttone to orate at one of their functions, given his obsession with the plague. 'However, the Master is right – these events *are* supposed to be fun. Perhaps you should consider talking about something a little more . . . jolly.'

'Jolly?' echoed Suttone in distaste. 'I do not think I

can make the pestilence jolly. Of course, there were amusing incidents, such as when the last Prior of Barnwell was sewn into his shroud but then transpired to be alive. Do you recall how he managed to free an arm and grab a silver candlestick, as if he intended to take it with him?'

'That should have the place rocking with mirth,' said Michael. 'However, I was thinking more along the lines of a reading, which everyone might enjoy. Perhaps a ballad or a tale of chivalry.'

'Chivalry during the plague?' asked Suttone, frowning.

'No, *not* during the plague,' said Michael, becoming exasperated. 'Forget about the plague.'

'Forget about the plague?' Suttone was shocked. 'I do not think any of us should do that. It—'

'We seem to be drifting away from the agenda here,' interrupted Langelee. 'We are supposed to be talking about Carton. I have decided that he will be buried tomorrow, by the way.'

'That is too soon, Master,' objected William immediately. 'It does not give us time to arrange an occasion that is suitably stately. He was one of our own, after all.'

'I know,' said Langelee. 'But the weather is against us. Prior Pechem offered to find him a spot in the Franciscan cemetery, and I think we should accept. We shall hold a grand requiem later, when it is cooler – St Michael's can be very stuffy when it is full. Does that meet with everyone's approval? Good. Then let us move on to the second item. Wynewyk, tell us about these houses.'

Wynewyk put down his pen. 'As you know, we inherited Sewale Cottage from the generous and much-lamented Margery, and at our last meeting we agreed to sell it.'

William nodded. 'It is a pleasant place with a large

garden, but it is on Bridge Street. We decided to hawk it, and use the money to acquire the Refham shops instead, which are next door to us. It is better to expand our core site, rather than to collect houses in distant parts of the town.'

'I was cornered last week by a man interested in buying Sewale Cottage,' said Langelee. 'That is why I called this meeting, actually. If folk are going to approach individual Fellows, then we need to be sure we do not contradict each other by quoting different prices.'

'Who cornered you?' asked Michael.

'That wealthy merchant from Norwich – Spynk.'

'He came to me, too,' said Wynewyk. 'He said he plans to develop business interests in Cambridge, and a small house on Bridge Street would suit him very well.'

'He offered me a horse today,' said Bartholomew. 'In return, he wanted inside information about bids made by other potential buyers.'

'Good,' said Langelee, pleased. 'We could do with another nag. Next time you meet, you can report that Barnwell Priory is the most serious contender. Carton was negotiating with them.'

'He already knows that,' said Bartholomew. 'He sent his wife to spy there on Saturday, on the pretext of purchasing honey.'

'That is the day Carton died,' pounced Michael. 'In the afternoon.'

Bartholomew had worked that out, too. He nodded. 'She must have left before the commotion started, or she would have mentioned it.'

'Unless she was responsible,' said Michael pointedly.

'She will not have stabbed Carton,' said Langelee, with such conviction that Bartholomew glanced at him sharply, wondering why the Master felt able to make such a firm statement. 'Seduce him, very possibly. But kill? Never! I wonder why Prior Norton wants to buy Sewale Cottage. It is too small to be used as a hostel for his novice-canons, so why is he so keen to have it?'

'Barnwell will buy anything,' explained Wynewyk. 'They own more property than all the other Orders put together. And the more they buy, the richer they become, from rents.'

'It goes against the grain to sell to another Order,' said William. 'Still, better Augustinians than Dominicans. I would never sell *anything* to a Dominican.'

'Really,' muttered Langelee under his breath. 'You do surprise me.'

'However,' William boomed, fixing each of his colleagues with a beady glare. As one they braced themselves, knowing from experience that an announcement was about to be made, and that it was almost certain to be objectionable. 'I have it on good authority that the canons of Barnwell want Sewale Cottage for sinister reasons.'

'And what authority is that, pray?' asked Michael, when the friar did not elaborate, but merely sat with his lips pursed meaningfully, as if the declaration was all the explanation that was needed.

'I have my sources,' replied William haughtily. 'And they are secret. But it was Mildenale, if you must know. He says they plan to build a granary on the site.'

'That is not sinister,' said Bartholomew, puzzled. 'Sewale Cottage is close to wharves they already own, and the garden has plenty of room for such a structure. They will unload their barges, and store—'

'Actually, their purpose in building the granary is to entice rats to the town,' declared William. 'And that *is*

148

sinister. Surely, you have not forgotten how they burned the Hardy house last year?'

There was silence, as his colleagues tried to fathom the logic behind his claims. Eventually, seeing there was none and that he was just giving rumours his own unique interpretation, they resumed their discussion as though he had not spoken.

'What about the property we want to *get*?' asked Langelee. 'The Refham houses.'

Wynewyk sighed. 'As you know, Mistress Refham said on her deathbed that we should have them at a reduced cost. Unfortunately, her son and his wife are being difficult, and they have put them on the market.'

'How dare they!' exclaimed William angrily. 'She promised us first refusal.'

'But it was a spoken agreement and nothing was written,' said Wynewyk. 'Refham is determined to make himself rich from his mother's inheritance, so we are in for a battle, I am afraid.'

'Do we really want them?' asked Bartholomew.

'Yes we do, because of their location,' explained Wynewyk. 'We own the properties on either side of them, and they will allow us to expand in the future. If we do not buy them now, we might never have another chance. We will not use them in the short term – we shall rent them to Mildenale, so he can found his hostel – but their long-term importance cannot be overemphasised.'

'Why Mildenale?' asked Bartholomew.

'We discussed this last time,' said Langelee curtly. 'Take notes, if you cannot remember from one meeting to the next. However, I shall repeat myself this once: it is because we are all a bit tired of his noisy religious opinions and it is a good way to be rid of him.'

'I *like* his noisy religious opinions,' objected William. 'He is a man after my own heart and—'

'And in recognition of his service to the College,' added Suttone, more charitable than the Master. 'He was a founding Fellow, and one of our very first teachers. I know he left Cambridge shortly afterwards, and spent the next three decades as a parish priest in Norfolk, but he has often sent us gifts of money and books through the years. He has been good to us.'

'To summarise, we have two parties currently interested in buying Sewale Cottage,' said Wynewyk, bringing the discussion back on track. 'Namely Spynk and Barnwell. Meanwhile, I am trying to persuade Refham to honour his mother's dying wish, but I suspect we will end up paying more than we want.'

'Damn,' said Langelee. 'The last item is the Bishop. Have you heard from him, Brother?'

Before Michael could reply, there was a knock on the door, and Cynric came in.

'Arblaster the dung-merchant is ailing again,' said the book-bearer quietly to Bartholomew. The physician was alarmed to see the guide to witchcraft under his arm. 'He needs you immediately. And Junior Proctor Bukenham reminds you to see him on the way home, too.'

'Go,' ordered Langelee, standing abruptly and making for the door. 'It is time for a break anyway, and I am hungry. We shall finish our business when you return.'

Bartholomew was hungry, too, but the summons sounded urgent, and he did not want Arblaster to share the Bene't student's fate. He set off towards the Barnwell Causeway at a rapid clip and Michael, who had offered to accompany him part of the way, did not keep up for long. The monk disappeared into an alehouse in the Old Jewry, near where Matilde had lived, claiming it was the haunt of men who might be able to answer questions about the blood in the font.

The sun scorched the Fens so fiercely that even birds seemed oppressed by the heat, and the countryside was both still and silent as Bartholomew walked. Usually, there were some sounds, even if only the whisper of wind or a dog barking, but that day there was nothing. It felt unnatural.

He was soon drenched in sweat, and dust adhered to his wet skin and clothes. He forced himself on, wiping his face with the sleeve of his shirt. He had dispensed with his tabard the moment he had left the town – partly because it was an additional layer he did not need, but also because it was not wise for lone scholars to flaunt themselves outside the comparative safety of the town. The University was an unpopular institution, and academics made for tempting targets.

He tapped on Arblaster's door and pushed it open without waiting for an answer, desperate to be out of the sun. It took a moment for his eyes to become accustomed to the dim light, but when they did, he was astonished to see the dung-master sitting at a table with his ledgers, while Jodoca sewed by the window. He regarded them uncertainly, wondering whether someone had made him the butt of a practical joke. Arblaster did not look as though he had taken a turn for the worse. On the contrary, there was colour in his cheeks, and the fact that he was out of bed showed he had made a good recovery. Furthermore, Jodoca's presence suggested he was no longer afraid of dying and having Mother Valeria come to snatch his soul.

'I am sorry,' said Bartholomew, beginning to back out in embarrassment. 'There has been a misunderstanding. Cynric said you needed me urgently.'

'I do need you urgently,' replied Arblaster. 'Although it has nothing to do with my health. At least, not yet. If things do not work out, I may suffer an imbalance of humours from the annoyance of it all. But the medicine you gave me worked admirably, and I am much better.'

'I am glad to hear it,' said Bartholomew, nonplussed. 'So what do you want with me?'

Arblaster gestured to the bench. 'Sit down, and I shall explain. Would you like some ale? Jodoca brewed it herself, and it is excellent – cool, fresh and sweet.'

Bartholomew did want some ale, but sensed he was about to be told something he would not like, and was reluctant to accept overtures of friendship until he knew what. He waited where he was, ignoring both the seat Arblaster patted enticingly and the goblet Jodoca held out to him.

'There are two matters I want to discuss,' said Arblaster, coming to close the door. Bartholomew was not sure whether it was to keep out the heat, to stop the conversation from being overheard, or to prevent his reluctant visitor from escaping. 'First, and most important, dung.'

'Dung?' echoed Bartholomew in disbelief. The dash along the sweltering Causeway had left him slightly light-headed, and he was not sure he was up for another of Arblaster's expositions.

'I hear Michaelhouse is digging new latrines. That means the contents of the old ones are available, and I would like to make you an offer for them. There is nothing like well-aged manure for spring beans, and I am very keen to get my hands on yours.'

'Christ!' muttered Bartholomew, gazing at him in disbelief.

'Isnard the bargeman will be after you for the same reason,' Arblaster went on. 'But he will ship it outside the town on one of his boats, and will sell it to the abbey in Ely, whereas *I* will make sure it benefits the citizens of Cambridge. Ask your Master not to agree to Isnard's terms until he has spoken to me.'

'All right,' said Bartholomew, trying not to be angry about the fact that he had exhausted himself for such a peculiar matter. 'What is your second concern?'

'Sewale Cottage. I would like to buy it, and I want you and your colleagues to look favourably on my application. Tell them I will pay eleven marks, which is one mark more than the price offered by the Prior of Barnwell, and two more than Spynk.'

Bartholomew was not inclined to look favourably on anything connected with Arblaster at that precise moment. 'You made me run all the way here to discuss manure and houses?'

Arblaster nodded earnestly. 'We are willing to pay handsomely for your help. *Very* handsomely.'

'I do not want your money,' said Bartholomew stiffly, turning towards the door. He could not see how it opened, so failed to make the dignified exit he had intended. He sighed his resignation when it became clear that he would not escape without help, and turned back to them. 'Talk to Langelee. He will make the final choice.'

'Not so. Michaelhouse is a democracy, where Master and Fellows make decisions together. However, I understand how these things work, and one eloquent man can sway his colleagues. I know *you* are eloquent because I heard your public lecture last term. Do as I say and—'

'No,' said Bartholomew, struggling to keep his irritation in check. 'Speak to Langelee. And do not summon me again unless you need urgent medical attention. I have other patients, and coming all the way out here for no reason might have put them in danger. Please do not do it again.'

Jodoca came over to rest a hand on his arm. 'Do not be angry, Doctor. We did not mean to upset you, but we were not sure how else to proceed. We spoke to Carton about Sewale Cottage, but he must have forgotten to do as we asked, because Langelee is not including us in his negotiations.'

Bartholomew regarded her thoughtfully. 'When did you speak to Carton?'

'Last week. We knew he was conferring with Barnwell, so we collared him one night. He stayed here for ages, talking and drinking my ale. He was a pleasant, friendly man and I am sorry he died.'

Bartholomew could not imagine Carton spending a sociable evening with anyone who did not share his dogmatic religious convictions. He was also surprised to hear Carton described as pleasant and friendly. 'What did you talk about?'

'Dung,' replied Arblaster. 'Dominicans. Sorcery. Poison. You know the sort of thing.'

It seemed an odd collection of topics to Bartholomew. 'What about them, exactly?'

Jodoca clearly wanted to be helpful, and to give an accurate account of the occasion. She screwed up her face, and thought hard. 'First, he agreed that fresh manure produces poor parsnips. Second, he said the Dominicans are thinking of raising a new chapel, but thought the Sorcerer might object to more houses of

God, who is his rival. And third, he asked if dung could be poisonous.'

Despite her efforts, Bartholomew was not much enlightened. As a Franciscan, Carton was unlikely to be privy to the Black Friars' building plans, and nor should he have known what the Sorcerer might make of them. And why should he ask about poisons? Bartholomew thought about the packet Carton had found in Thomas's room. Had Carton developed an interest in toxic substances because he believed he had lost a colleague to one?

'There is a rumour that Carton was the Sorcerer,' said Jodoca to her husband, when Bartholomew said nothing. 'But I do not think it can be true.'

'Of course it is not true,' replied Arblaster. 'The Sorcerer presided over his coven last night. But Carton is dead, so clearly he and the Sorcerer are two different people.'

'Unless he rose from the grave,' suggested Jodoca. 'Warlocks are good at that sort of thing.'

Bartholomew retraced his steps along the Barnwell Causeway, deeply resenting the fact that the Arblasters had chosen the hottest time of day to summon him. Why could they not have waited until evening, when there might have been a breeze? He was staggered by their audacity, and tried to imagine Carton relaxing enough to be sociable with them. Had the Franciscan been fishing for information, perhaps pertaining to Thomas's death, because he had been conducting his own investigation? Or had he merely taken the opportunity to enjoy the company of people who did not know him, and who did not expect him to hold forth about lofty academic matters? Bartholomew certainly appreciated the mundane conversation of men like Isnard on occasion, when his colleagues were in overly argumentative frames of mind.

His throat was dry and sore, and he wished he had not stalked out of the Arblasters' house quite so frostily – that he tasted Jodoca's ale first. After all, he deserved some recompense for his frantic dash along the baking Causeway. Then he saw the red roofs of Barnwell Priory, and smiled. The canons would give him something to drink.

He knocked on the gate, and was admitted by Fencotes, who laid a corpse-cold hand on the physician's head in blessing. Norton was passing, and beckoned Bartholomew towards the infirmary, which he said was the second-coolest place in the convent; the first was the chapel, but he was wary of inviting scholars from Michaelhouse into that, given what had happened the last time he had done it. As they walked, Norton and Fencotes chatted knowledgeably about the buildings that were for sale in the town and the prices they were likely to fetch. They even knew about the Refham shops, and how Michaelhouse should have been allowed to purchase them for a pittance, but was likely to end up paying a lot more.

'Everyone is interested in property these days,' Norton explained, when Bartholomew asked why the canons were so well informed. 'Ever since the plague. First, house prices dropped, because there was no one to live in the houses. Now the cost of desirable properties is rising, because *they* are in good repair, while the uninhabited ones have fallen into ruin. It is all very exciting.'

'Even for men sworn to poverty?' asked Bartholomew, failing to see why such a subject should seize anyone's interest, but particularly those who had vowed to eschew worldly vices.

'I have no wish to own houses myself,' said Fencotes, a little reproachfully. 'However, I have always been interested in homes, and bought and sold more than my share before I took the cowl.'

'He was a secular most of his life,' explained Norton, adding mysteriously, 'In Norfolk.'

'I see,' said Bartholomew, not sure how else to respond.

Fencotes drew his cloak more closely around his skeletal shoulders and shivered. 'Is it my imagination, or has the temperature dropped? It feels as cold as the grave out here.'

'It is your imagination.' Norton's eyes bulged as an idea occurred to him. 'But you can have a hot tisane, while we enjoy some of the ale you keep in your crypt.'

'His *crypt*?' asked Bartholomew, regarding Fencotes askance.

'The one under the infirmary,' explained Fencotes, gesturing with one of his corpse-pale hands. 'It was stuffed full of coffins when I first arrived, which did not seem appropriate, given all the old men living out their last days in the chamber above it, so Podiolo helped me clear it out. It is a horribly frigid place, which is why we store ale there.'

'Michael came to see us earlier today,' said Norton unhappily, as they walked across the courtyard. 'He wanted to know why we failed to mention Carton deceiving us about the price of Sewale Cottage. I hope he believed our explanation – that it is common practice, and we were expecting fibs. I would hate him to think we were being obstructive, when we want Carton's killer caught more than anyone.'

'We did not tell Michael one thing, though,' added Fencotes. 'That Carton was not very skilled at manipulating a price war; we knew he was lying when he said Spynk had offered nine marks.'

'He was too wrapped up in religious matters to pay the proper attention, you see,' elaborated Norton. 'It takes effort and care to drive such bargains, and he was always distracted.'

'We have an offer of eleven marks now,' said Bartholomew, resisting the urge to point out that friars were supposed to be wrapped up in religious matters, and that the comment said more about Barnwell than Carton. 'From Arblaster.'

Norton stopped dead in his tracks and regarded the physician intently. 'I cannot tell if you are bluffing or not,' he said eventually. 'You *are* good.'

'I think he is bluffing,' said Fencotes. 'But even if he is telling the truth, we should offer twelve. It will be worth it. That property is perfectly situated for a granary.'

'Actually, it is not, because the ground slopes,' argued Norton. 'And the house is very small.'

'The building can be extended if necessary,' countered Fencotes. 'Sewale Cottage will be a good, solid investment.'

They were still debating when they entered the infirmary, where Podiolo abandoned doing something odoriferous with pipes, flames and metal dishes, and came to greet them.

'I am experimenting with sulphur today,' he said, in response to Bartholomew's questioning glance. 'If I succeed in making gold from lead, it will be the culmination of my life's work.'

'Do your patients not object to the smell?' asked

Bartholomew, thinking an infirmary was not a good place to conduct tests that involved rank substances.

'They are used to it. Look at Norton and Fencotes bickering over Sewale Cottage! I shall be glad when the place is sold, because I am tired of hearing about it. Will you share your cure for the flux with me? I have three men sick of it at the moment, and I lost the last two who succumbed.'

Bartholomew not only gave him the remedy, but examined the patients. Podiolo remarked that the cure was mild for such a virulent sickness, but was uninterested in hearing Bartholomew's theory about the beneficial properties of boiled water. He silenced the physician with an impatient wave of his hand, and turned the discussion back to sulphur.

'People keep talking about the Sorcerer,' said Bartholomew, thinking about the similarity between witchcraft and alchemy – both relied on powders, potions and a liberal sprinkling of incantations. 'Do you have any idea who he might be?'

'There are those who say it was Carton, because he was strange,' replied Podiolo, grinning wolfishly. 'There are others who claim it is I, because of my interest in making gold. I have even heard men say it is you, because you cure the flux where others have failed.'

Bartholomew was uneasy. 'I hope you tell them it is not.'

'I say you would not know how to cast a spell to save your life,' said Podiolo, amusement in his yellow eyes. 'And that if *I* were this great Sorcerer, I would have manufactured gold years ago.'

Bartholomew was then treated to a lengthy monologue about the advances Podiolo had made in his quest, but did not mind. It was cool in the infirmary, and Podiolo was generous with the ale. The Florentine was more interested in talking than listening, so all the physician had to do was nod occasionally. He began to relax for the first time in days. Eventually, Norton came to join them.

'Will you pass this to Brother Michael? I meant to give it to him earlier, but his remarks about us not mentioning the bidding business were rather accusatory, and it slipped my mind.'

He held out his hand to reveal a stone with a hole in it, through which had been threaded a leather thong. Bartholomew had seen pebbles with natural cavities before, and knew they were highly prized as charms. This one was adorned with symbols that were unfamiliar. They were not Greek, Hebrew or Arabic, and he supposed they belonged to a language he had never seen written.

'What is it?' he asked, taking it and examining it with interest.

'A holy-stone talisman,' replied Norton, rather more knowledgeably than Bartholomew thought was appropriate for a man who should have known nothing of sorcery. 'Used by folk who want to protect themselves against wolves. Obviously, it does not belong to any of us, so it must have been either Carton's or his killer's. Either way, it is a clue.'

'How can you be sure it does not belong to any of you?' asked Bartholomew, bemused.

Norton raised his eyebrows. 'Because we are not afraid of wolves. Witches are another matter, but you do not wear a holy-stone to ward off witches. Any fool knows that.'

'Of course,' said Bartholomew, who had known no

such thing. He thought about Podiolo, and the rumours of his lupine ancestry. 'Why are you not afraid of wolves, exactly?'

Norton's eyes bulged so much that Bartholomew found himself braced to catch them when they popped out. 'Because wolves would never invade us,' he said, as though the answer were self-evident and Bartholomew was lacking in wits because he had been obliged to ask.

'Where did you find it?' Bartholomew asked.

'Fencotes must take the credit for its discovery. He went to kneel on the spot where Carton died, to pray and cleanse the chapel after the violence that sullied it. While he was there, he saw this in a crack between the flagstones. It was near where Carton's right hand would have been.'

Bartholomew frowned. 'Are you saying Carton was holding it when he died?'

Norton shrugged. 'It is possible. It is equally possible that the killer dropped it, perhaps when he was arranging the poor man's limbs.'

'And you are sure it was not there *before* Carton died? Perhaps one of your servants—'

'They are not allowed in that chapel, which is the domain of canons alone. And, as I said, *we* have no need for this kind of talisman. The only explanation is that Carton or his killer must have brought it. *Ergo*, if you identify its owner, you may catch your murderer.'

Chapter 5

The sun beat down relentlessly as Bartholomew trudged along the Barnwell Causeway towards the town, and the air seemed more sultry and oppressive than ever. It was so hot he felt he could not catch his breath, and he was exhausted by the time he reached the King's Ditch and passed back into civilisation. Junior Proctor Bukenham lived in a hostel near the Small Bridges, in the south of the town. To get there, the physician took a shortcut past some marshy land that was dominated by one of the town's mills. The great waterwheel was still that day, because the river was too low to drive it, and the miller lounged outside his house with a stem of grass gripped between his teeth.

'I need a spell to ward off the flux,' he said, as Bartholomew walked past him.

'Avoid bad meat,' suggested Bartholomew helpfully. 'It will serve you better than spells.'

'You do not know any,' said the miller, rather accusingly. 'Magister Arderne the healer told me you were bereft of them, but I thought he was just being spiteful.'

'No, he was right,' said Bartholomew, the heat making

162

him respond more tartly than was his wont. 'I do not deal in magic.'

'I had better consult a witch, then. Cynric will be able to tell me which one is best value.'

Bartholomew had not gone much further when he heard a rustle in the bulrushes at the side of the path. At first, he thought it was a cat or a bird, but the sound grew louder, and he realised it was something considerably larger. He glanced around uneasily, aware that he was alone in a fairly isolated part of the town. The nearest house was Bukenham's, but that was still some distance away.

'Physician! It is me.'

Bartholomew peered into the reeds, but could see no one there. 'Who?'

'*Me*,' came the whisper, a little impatiently. 'Who do you think?'

Bartholomew had no idea, but then he spotted a vague shape deep among the grasses. 'Mother Valeria?' he asked, recognising the crumpled hat, although there was not much more about her that was identifiable; he could not see her face. 'What are you doing there? I thought you never left your house – that people came to see you.'

'Of course I leave my house!' She sounded disgusted with him. 'How could I collect the plants I need for my charms if I was at home all day? I have been less mobile of late, because of my knee, but you helped with that and it is much better.'

'It will not stay that way if you make a habit of sitting around in bogs.'

'I have been collecting marsh-mallow, and this is the best place for miles, although I prefer to keep myself hidden. But I saw you coming and wanted to tell you something. It is about Carton, whose murder you are investigating. I hear things when I am about my business, and today I learned he was not the man you thought you knew. Prior Pechem is looking into his background.'

Bartholomew frowned. 'What do you mean?'

'I overheard Pechem telling Mildenale that he could not find a record of Carton's ordination. And, as I am here and you seem to be in the mood for listening, I shall tell you something else, too. The man they call the Sorcerer is growing in power, and you would be a fool to try to stop him.'

'Last time I asked, you said you did not know him. Have you learned his name, then?'

'No one knows his name, but he is stronger now than he was a week ago, and has twice as many followers. He frightens me. And he would frighten you, too, if you had any sense.'

There was a sharp rustle and the shape was gone, almost as if Valeria had vanished into thin air. Bartholomew shook himself, and dismissed such fanciful notions from his mind. It had been a long day and he was tired. He considered hunting for her, to demand a clearer explanation of her so-called intelligence, but someone was coming, and he did not want to be caught doing anything that might be deemed odd. He pretended to be buckling his shoe, then resumed his journey to the Junior Proctor.

'You own a holy-stone, I see,' said Bukenham conversationally, when the physician rummaged in his bag for camomile syrup and the talisman dropped to the floor. The Junior Proctor was a soft-faced, shy man, who had stuck at his post longer than most of Michael's deputies; Bartholomew suspected it was only because he was too frightened to resign. He was patently terrified of the monk, and his current illness – an inexplicable aching of the head – was almost certainly a case of malingering. 'I used to have one of those.'

'Did you?' asked Bartholomew in surprise. 'Why?'

'Arderne sold it to me. He said it would protect me from wolves, although wolves tend not to be much of a problem in the streets of Cambridge. But it was a pretty thing, and I grew used to it hanging around my neck. Then the cord broke and I lost it. Did you buy yours from Arderne?'

There was no reason not to tell him the truth – Bukenham was Michael's deputy, after all. 'Fencotes found it in the chapel after Carton was killed, but I never saw Carton wearing an amulet of any description, so I am inclined to think it belonged to his killer.'

'You are probably right. Carton was a friar, and they usually renounce objects of superstition.'

'*Was* Carton a friar? I have been told the record of his ordination cannot be found.'

Bukenham shrugged. 'That does not mean anything, especially with the Franciscans. They gather recruits by the cartload, and their registers are often unreliable. Did you know there is a rumour that Carton was the Sorcerer? I do not believe it, personally.'

'Neither do I,' said Bartholomew. 'But what are your reasons?'

'No scholar would dabble in such dark matters, so my feeling is that it will be a townsman.'

'Scholars have dabbled before,' said Bartholomew, unconvinced by this logic. 'And they are, on the whole, clever men who like pitting their wits against the great mysteries of the universe. It would not be the first time one went down the wrong path.'

Bukenham sighed. 'I was hoping to keep this to myself, but I see I shall have to confide. The Sorcerer's Latin is poor, and *that* is why I think he is unlikely to be an academic.'

Bartholomew narrowed his eyes. 'That suggests you have heard him speak. How?'

Bukenham sighed again, deeply unhappy. 'About a week ago, I was on patrol when I stumbled across one of his meetings. I know I should have used my authority to stop it, but I was alone and I am no Brother Michael. So I watched instead, hoping to learn something that would allow our beadles to arrest him the following day.'

'I did the same at All Saints last night,' admitted Bartholomew. 'So did William and Mildenale.'

Bukenham looked at him in surprise, then grimaced. 'But the ceremonies in All Saints are always well attended, so it would be unreasonable for you and two friars to take action. However, the one I witnessed was in the charnel house, with only two disciples present.'

'What did you see?' asked Bartholomew.

'Hooded men touting the hand of a corpse, the head of a goat, and a bowl of something I am sure was blood. The Sorcerer was chanting in a horrible voice, like claws on glass.'

'Did you notice anything that might allow us to identify him?'

'Nothing. He was swathed from head to toe in a thick black cloak. The only outstanding thing about him was his terrible Latin.'

'Who was with him? You said there were two others.'

'I did not see their faces, either. All I can tell you is that their ritual struck a deep fear into my heart, and I am glad my head-pains keep me in bed. I am sorry to leave Brother Michael to fight alone, but there are limits to what any man should be asked to do in the line of duty, and tackling the Sorcerer is well past them. And if you had any sense, you would see I am right.'

When Bartholomew arrived back at Michaelhouse, the shadows were lengthening. The sun was transforming the College's pale stone into burnished gold, darkening the thatch on the outhouses, and turning the tiles on the hall into a deep russet red. He stopped for a moment to admire it, thinking how lucky he was to live in a place that was so lovely.

'Arblaster tried to bribe me,' he said to Langelee as they walked towards the hall together, to resume the Fellows' meeting. 'He wants the contents of our latrines, and said he would offer eleven marks for Sewale Cottage. Then the canons of Barnwell offered twelve.'

'Excellent!' declared Langelee, rubbing his hands. 'I cannot imagine why Arblaster should want Sewale Cottage, though. It is nice, but very small. What was the bribe?'

'I have no idea,' said Bartholomew, slightly offended that the Master should think he might have accepted it. 'I did not let the discussion go that far.'

'You mean you agreed to be his advocate for nothing?' Langelee shot the physician a look of abject disgust. 'Please do not do it again. It will make folk think we are an easy mark.'

Bartholomew removed the talisman from his bag as a means of changing the subject. Discussions with Langelee could often be wearing. 'Did you ever see Carton wearing this?'

Langelee took it from him, and turned it over in his

thick fingers. 'A holy-stone! I have not seen one of these in years. The Archbishop of York gave me one once, to protect me from wolves, but I lost it. It was Carton's, you say? That surprises me – I thought he disapproved of pagan regalia.'

'Unlike the Archbishop of York, apparently,' muttered Bartholomew. He spoke a little louder as the Master handed the trinket back. 'It might belong to Carton's killer.'

'Folk tend to wear such items under their clothes, given that they are deeply personal, so I doubt you will have much luck asking if anyone recognises it. Still, it is worth a try, I suppose.'

'I have been told there is no record of Carton's ordination. Do you know where he is supposed to have taken his vows?'

Langelee frowned. 'The certificate he showed me said it was Greyfriars in London – one of the largest Franciscan houses in the country. I suppose it might have been forged, but I think it unlikely. The Franciscans accept anyone, so there is no need to pretend to be a Grey Friar when they would recruit you in an instant anyway. They are always after me to join them.'

'They are always after me, too.'

Langelee gripped his arm in a soldierly fashion. 'Then we must unite against them. If you feel yourself weakening, come to me and I shall slap some sense into you. You can do the same for me. Major holy orders would be a massive encumbrance; I do not want to spend half the night doing penance every time I have a whore.'

'It would be inconvenient,' said Bartholomew, wondering how many other Fellows were subject to such confidences by their Master. 'Did you make any further checks on Carton's credentials?'

Langelee shook his head. 'I did not feel there was any need, since his application was supported by Clippesby. I suspect the record of his ordination has just been misplaced. Carton was a friar to his core – you only had to hear his sermons on sin to know that.'

'Clippesby,' mused Bartholomew. 'He is a Dominican, yet he sponsored a Franciscan.'

'You have spent too much time with William,' said Langelee with a grimace. 'Not all friars detest other Orders, and Clippesby has always been gracious in that respect – he has had to be, given the rubbish William hurls at him. Of course, Clippesby is insane, which probably helps. He is too mad to know he should be offended. However, that said, I do not think he would have asked us to elect Carton, had there been anything shady about him.'

Bartholomew smiled. He liked Clippesby, and knew the man was not as deranged as everyone liked to think. Clippesby was also a better judge of character than some of his colleagues, and Bartholomew agreed with the Master that he was unlikely to have supported the application of anyone who might harm the College. 'Perhaps my source was mistaken about what was heard.'

'There is William,' said Langelee. He raised his voice as if addressing half of Cambridge. 'Hey, Father! Do you think Carton's ordination was genuine?'

William's expression was pained. 'Have you been talking to Prior Pechem? He asked me the same question, and said Thomas had been agitating about it. Carton took his vows in London, but Thomas said the river was flooded that day, so the ceremony was cancelled.

He virtually called Carton a liar, and Carton was deeply offended. It was one of the things Thomas and I quarrelled about the night before he died: I told him he should apologise, but he refused.'

'Trouble in the ranks,' mused Bartholomew, regarding him thoughtfully.

'It was because he was not a *Michaelhouse* Franciscan,' explained William. 'I never quarrel with Mildenale and Carton, and any dissent was always of Thomas's making. I do not like to speak ill of the dead, but he was dreadfully argumentative.'

'How is Arblaster?' asked Michael, catching them up as they crossed the hall. Their footsteps echoed hollowly, reminding them again that their College was deserted.

'Perfectly well,' replied Bartholomew shortly. 'Other than an unnatural desire to be at the contents of our latrines.'

'Arblaster meddles in the dark arts,' claimed William, opening the conclave door and nodding a greeting to Suttone and Wynewyk, who were already there.

'Is that so?' said Michael without much interest. William thought most people meddled in the dark arts, and so could not be taken seriously when he made such assertions.

'It is, actually,' replied Langelee. 'I heard he sent to Mother Valeria for a cure for his flux, but she declined to provide him with one.'

'I heard that, too,' said Suttone. 'Apparently, he had refused to pay for a spell she had cast for him earlier, and she said she would not make him a remedy until he made good on the debt. He objected, so she threatened to snatch his soul instead. So, you saved him, did you, Matt?'

'Personally, I suspect Arblaster is the Sorcerer,' said

Wynewyk, watching the others take their places at the table. 'He is the right height and size, and I know he is a coven member.'

'How?' demanded Michael. 'I hope *you* have not attended any of these unsavoury gatherings.'

Wynewyk pursed his lips. 'Of course not, Brother! I have a friend in the castle – a soldier – and he was escorting me home one night when we saw lights in All Saints. He insisted on investigating, but we both thought better of ousting the trespassers once it became clear the Sorcerer was in charge.'

'You did not try to obstruct their wicked ceremonies?' asked William accusingly.

'Did the two of us storm the church and attempt to tackle fifty cloaked satanists? No, Father, we did not. They were not doing anything terrible, anyway – just chanting spells they hoped would cure Margery Sewale. It was all rather sad, actually; most were in tears. She was a popular lady.'

'But you saw the Sorcerer?' asked Michael eagerly. 'Can you describe him?'

'Not really.' Wynewyk looked apologetic. 'He kept his face hidden. He was taller than average, and looked bulky, although that could have been because of his cloak. And his Latin was dismal.'

'I am going to bring him down,' vowed William. His eyes were fierce, and his jaw set in a determined line that said he meant it. 'Mildenale and I will see this heretic—'

'Item three on the agenda,' interrupted Langelee briskly. 'We have already dealt with Carton and the houses. All that remains is the Bishop. Have you heard from him, Brother?'

Michael looked pained. 'He has not written to me since he left England last year.'

'*I* can tell you about the evil de Lisle,' said William viciously. The Bishop was a Dominican, so naturally William did not like him. 'He has been indicted for sixteen separate crimes, which include murder, extortion, abduction, assault and theft. But he fled overseas before the King could find him guilty and seize all his assets.'

'You should learn the facts before you make that sort of statement,' said Michael coldly. 'My Bishop did *not* commit those crimes – they were perpetrated by men in his retinue, and he cannot be held responsible for what stewards, reeves and bailiffs do.'

'Actually, he can,' countered Langelee. 'When I committed crimes for the Archbishop of York, he would have been held accountable, had I been caught. Fortunately, I never was. De Lisle, however, hires inferior men to do his work, and now he must bear the consequences.'

His Fellows regarded him uneasily. None were comfortable when their Master confided details of his colourful former life.

'Well, I am glad you did not break the law for de Lisle, Brother,' said Suttone after a brief but awkward silence. 'Or you might be languishing in prison, like his other spies.'

'I am not his *spy*,' objected Michael. 'I am his agent. And all I do is furnish him with news about the University. It is part of his See, so of course he should be kept informed of what is happening.'

'Well, whatever the truth, we do not need to worry about him any more,' said Langelee. 'I have it on good authority that he will never come home. The King is too angry with him, and his fellow bishops do not want him as their friend. He is an outcast.'

Suttone was shocked. 'But what will happen to his See?'

'He has able deputies for that,' said Wynewyk. 'Priests – not the reeves and bailiffs who race around setting houses alight and stealing cattle. There is nothing wrong with the way he manages the episcopal side of things – he is just a bit of a brute when it comes to secular business.'

Michael sighed wearily. 'De Lisle is *not* a criminal—'

'You should keep that opinion to yourself,' advised Langelee. 'It is unwise to side with a man who is ostracised by the King. Futile, too, because de Lisle will never be in a position to reciprocate.'

'The Master is right,' said Wynewyk. 'Remember how the Bishop was accused of murdering one of Lady Blanche de Wake's servants some years back? Well, Blanche is the King's cousin, and His Majesty still holds the incident against him.'

'Lord!' exclaimed Bartholomew, regarding the monk in alarm. 'I had forgotten all about that. You asked him openly about his involvement in the killing, but he never did give you a straight answer.'

'That does not mean he is guilty,' persisted Michael stubbornly.

'Dozens of people have presented the King with evidence of de Lisle's misdeeds,' said Wynewyk. 'And while I appreciate that some may have done it out of spite, they cannot all be lying. Incidentally, did you know that Spynk is one of them? So was Danyell.'

Langelee shook his head in disgust. 'Prelates are always short of money, and it is common practice to raise

173

revenues by theft, extortion, blackmail and abduction. But the real crime here is that de Lisle let himself be caught. The man is a damned fool! I only hope it does not result in other high-ranking churchmen being forced to answer for their actions.'

'The things you say, Master,' said Suttone, regarding Langelee with round eyes. Bartholomew suspected he expressed what all the Fellows were thinking, even William. Everyone was relieved when a knock on the door brought a merciful end to the discussion. It was Cynric, with Beadle Meadowman at his heels; Meadowman was one of the army of men Michael employed to help him keep order among the scholars. The beadle pushed past Cynric, and made directly for Michael, bending to whisper in his ear. Bartholomew's heart sank. He could tell from the man's pale face and agitated manner that he had something unpleasant to report.

'There has been another one,' said Michael in a low voice, looking sombrely at his colleagues. 'I am summoned by Master Heltisle and Eyton the vicar. A second corpse has been removed from its grave, this time in St Bene't's churchyard.'

Bartholomew knew he was dragging his heels as he followed Michael and Cynric along the High Street towards St Bene't's Church, but he could not help it. Images of Margery Sewale's body kept flashing in his mind, and he did not want to see another like it. As the University's Corpse Examiner, he had seen more than his share of the dead, and had grown inured to such sights over the years. But there was something about exhumations that bothered him profoundly.

'Superstition,' said Michael dismissively, when the physician tried to explain his misgivings – his sense that he was being watched by the disapproving dead. 'I am surprised at you, Matt. You are a man of learning, and your scientific mind should reject such notions for the rubbish they are. Of course the souls of these poor cadavers will not be paying attention to you; they will be in Heaven, Hell or Purgatory, depending on how they fared when they were weighed.'

'I know,' said Bartholomew tiredly, realising he should not have expected the monk to understand. 'But that does not stop me feeling uneasy about it. And seeing Margery like that . . .'

'Margery was your patient, and you had known her for years,' said Michael, his voice a little kinder. 'Of course you disliked seeing her out of her grave. But none of your patients are buried in St Bene't's churchyard, so you are unlikely to know the victim this time.'

'That cemetery is used by the scholars of Bene't College, members of the Guild of Corpus Christi, *and* the people who live nearby. I have a lot of patients buried there.'

'Lower your voice,' advised Michael dryly. 'That is not a good thing for a physician to be yelling – it may make your surviving clients nervous.'

'It is not a joke, Michael,' snapped Bartholomew, beginning to wishing he had not started the discussion.

'It is, if you start thinking these ravaged corpses might take umbrage at you for doing your job. You sound like Cynric, man. Pull yourself together!'

Bartholomew glanced behind him, to where his book-bearer was walking with Meadowman. There was no real need for Cynric to have accompanied them, but the

Welshman enjoyed being out at night and had insisted on coming. Bartholomew was glad he had, and found comfort in the knowledge that Cynric's sword was to hand, should there be trouble. He tried to ignore his sense of foreboding, and think about the monk's investigations instead.

'I did not have time to give you this earlier,' he said, removing the talisman from his bag. 'It was found in Barnwell's chapel. Norton says it belongs either to Carton or his killer.'

Michael took it from him. 'What is it?'

'A holy-stone that is supposed to defend its wearer against wolves, apparently. Arderne sold them in the spring, regardless of the fact that wolves tend not to frequent Cambridge these days.'

'Perhaps one of the canons bought it to protect himself from Podiolo,' said Michael. 'There is definitely something lupine about that man.'

'Now who is being irrational? *That* sounds like something Cynric might say.'

Michael grimaced. 'Yes, but in this case Cynric would have a point. Have you never noticed Podiolo's yellow eyes and pointed teeth? Of course, everyone at Barnwell is strange, as far as I am concerned. All those fat, balding canons who look identical, Norton's bulging eyes, Fencotes the walking corpse . . .'

'They probably say the same about Michaelhouse: William's fanaticism, Langelee's criminal past, Wynewyk's penchant for Agatha's clothes, Clippesby's lunacy, Suttone's obsession with plague . . .'

Michael sniggered. 'Did you hear about the shambles surrounding Suttone's address to the Guild of Corpus Christi? The invitation was meant for *Roger* Suttone of

176

Peterhouse, who is famous for amusing speeches. As head of the Guild, Heltisle wrote the letter but his porters did not listen to his instructions and took it to the wrong Suttone.'

Bartholomew smiled. 'There will be nothing amusing about any homily our Suttone will deliver. Will they admit their mistake, and un-invite him?'

'It is too late – our Suttone has accepted.'

Bartholomew watched Michael swinging the holy-stone around on its thong. 'Your Junior Proctor seemed certain that was not Carton's.'

'Can we conclude the killer dropped it, then? Who is on our list of suspects?'

'Norton claimed his brethren would never own such a thing, on the grounds that none of them are afraid of wolves. He did not explain why.'

'Perhaps he trusts Podiolo to keep them all at bay,' suggested Michael. 'However, I do not accept Norton's reasoning, so the canons can remain on the list. Not all of them – just Podiolo, Fencotes and Norton himself, who are the three without alibis.'

'Then there is Spaldynge, said Bartholomew, thinking of the man who bore him such unjust animosity. 'He was friends with Arderne, and might have bought one of his amulets. And being reminded of that ancient murder – James Kirbee – is a reason for him wanting Carton dead.'

'They are the obvious culprits,' said Michael. He sighed heavily. 'But then we have all the folk who objected to Carton's uncompromising sermons, and about sixty insulted Dominicans.'

'Arblaster said something odd today. He told me Carton asked whether dung was poisonous. Carton seemed preoccupied with poison – he found that powder among Thomas's possessions and insisted I test it for him.'

Michael's agitation showed in the way he whipped the talisman around on its string. 'Will you ask Mother Valeria whether she knows who owns this amulet? I had better not do it; the Senior Proctor cannot be seen fraternising with witches, especially a frightening and unpopular one.'

Bartholomew nodded. 'But I doubt she will be able to help. Arderne alone sold dozens of the things, and—' He ducked quickly when the thong broke and the holy-stone flew past his ear.

'Damn!' cried Michael, diving after it. 'The wretched thing has a will of its own!'

'You should watch yourself at St Bene't's, boy,' whispered Cynric, taking the opportunity to speak to the physician alone, while Michael scrabbled about in the grass at the side of the road. 'The Sorcerer will be behind this excavated corpse, just as he was behind what happened to Margery.'

'How can he be? You told me Carton was the Sorcerer.'

'The Sorcerer would not have let himself be murdered, so Carton is innocent.' Cynric was never shy about abandoning one theory and adopting another. 'But these bodies are being hauled from hallowed ground on the orders of the Devil. You had better take this.'

Bartholomew accepted the proffered bundle cautiously. 'What is it?'

'Bat-eyes,' replied the book-bearer, as if it was the most natural thing in the world. 'In a pouch. If you hang it around your neck it will render you invisible to Satan.'

'Hang it round your neck, then,' said Bartholomew, trying to pass it back to him. If William caught him wearing such an object there would be trouble for certain.

'I already have one. Shove it in your purse if you do not want it at your throat, but do not refuse it. It cost me a groat.'

So as not to hurt Cynric's feelings – and not to prolong the debate – Bartholomew slipped the pouch in his bag, intending to toss it in the midden when he went home.

'I learned recently that June is a great month for witchery,' Cynric went on conversationally. 'The stars and moon are right, see. It explains why the Sorcerer is suddenly so powerful.'

'I do not suppose you gleaned this from the witches' manual in Langelee's office, did you?' asked Bartholomew coolly. 'One of the tomes that Carton had collected for burning?'

Cynric looked furtive. 'It fell into my hands when I was dusting, and it seemed a pity not to hone my reading skills on it. You are always saying I need to practise.'

'Put it back,' ordered Bartholomew. 'William will have you dismissed if he catches you enjoying something like that. I am serious, Cynric. Put it back and promise you will not touch it again.'

Cynric pulled a disagreeable face, but nodded assent. He bent down and retrieved something from the ground. It was the amulet, and Bartholomew wondered whether he had known it was there all along – that he had delayed telling the monk because he wanted to give his master the bat-eyes.

Michael took it from him. 'Good. And now we had better hurry, or Heltisle and Eyton will think we are never coming.'

'Who has been laid to rest in St Bene't's recently?' asked Meadowman as they walked. The beadle looked nervous, steeling himself for what was to come.

'Sir John Goldynham was buried on Ascension Day,' said Michael. 'He was Rougham's patient, one of his wealthiest. Then there were two Bene't scholars and Mistress Refham the month before.'

Bartholomew had known both Goldynham and Mistress Refham, and did not want to see them excavated. He faltered. 'Are you sure you need me, Brother? The culprit left no clues when he exhumed Margery, so why should this be any different?'

The monk grabbed his arm and pulled him on. 'I am hoping he has been more careless tonight.'

St Bene't's was an ancient church with a sturdy tower that was said to pre-date the coming of the Normans. Bartholomew liked it, because its thick walls muffled the clamour of the streets, so it was always peaceful. Its churchyard was overgrown and leafy, a tiny haven of stillness next to a road that was full of taverns, shops and the houses of tradesmen. It was not quiet that evening, however, for a crowd had gathered. Bartholomew recognised scholars from Bene't College, the taverner from the Eagle, and members of the Guild of Corpus Christi; some carried pitch torches, which threw an unsteady light through the trees. The Guild had helped found Bene't College some five years earlier and was a rare example of University–town co-operation.

At the centre of the spectators was Eyton. The priest had a pot of honey under his arm and seemed to be anointing people with it, because a number of folk had sticky foreheads. Others wore charms, and Bartholomew recognised them as the ones Eyton had been selling outside All Saints. He could only suppose there had been a run on amulets after the discovery of a second exhumed corpse, so the priest was obliged to improvise in order to meet the demand for mystical protection. Watching him, not altogether approvingly, was Master Heltisle.

Not everyone had clustered around Eyton. Isnard was clinging to a nearby tree, clearly having come straight from the Eagle. Bartholomew smiled when he saw him, knowing perfectly well that the bargeman was hanging back because he did not want Michael to see him drunk, lest it damaged his chances of being readmitted to the choir. Behind Isnard, deep in the undergrowth, were the pair Bartholomew had seen lurking near the Great Bridge the previous night. One was identifiable by his enormous size, and the other by his bushy beard. He started to point them out to Michael, but the monk's attention was elsewhere.

'Damn!' Michael muttered. 'We could have done without an audience. And we could do without Eyton smearing everyone with honey on the pretext of repelling witches, too. The fact that a vicar believes there is a danger will send the rumour-mongers into a frenzy.'

'Brother Michael, you are here at last,' said Heltisle, striding forward imperiously. 'We were beginning to think you might not come. And who can blame you? I do not appreciate being summoned to witness this sort of thing, either.'

'Once men are in their graves, they should stay there,' agreed Eyton with a cheerful grin, as if he were talking about the weather. 'They should not be walking around the town.'

'Walking around the town?' echoed Michael uneasily. 'Meadowman told me the body had been excavated by some evildoer, as happened to Margery Sewale. He said nothing about walking—'

'Then he did not tell you the whole story,' said Eyton. 'Goldynham clawed his way out of his tomb, and was heading for his favourite tavern when I stopped him with a splash of holy water.'

Michael gaped at him. 'But that is—'

'Impossible?' interrupted Eyton. 'I would have said so, too, had I not seen it with my own eyes. The Devil imbued Goldynham's corpse with sinister strength, and who knows where it might have wandered, had I not stopped it.'

'Right,' said Michael warily. 'What did you see, exactly?'

Eyton was enjoying the attention. He stood a little straighter, and beamed at his listeners. 'I had just finished saying compline, and was about to go home when I heard odd sounds coming from the graveyard. I grabbed a phial of holy water and set off to investigate.'

'Why holy water?' asked Bartholomew, thinking a cudgel might have been a more appropriate choice. It was not unknown for the graves of wealthy citizens to be plundered by robbers, and such degenerates were unlikely to be deterred by religious regalia.

'Because it is an effective weapon against the denizens of Hell,' replied Eyton matter-of-factly. He turned back to Michael. 'I moved towards the source of the noise, and saw a shadow. It was Goldynham, rising from his grave. So I raced at him and sprinkled the water on his unholy form, shouting *in nomine Patris, et filii et Spiritus Sancti* as I did so.'

There was an awed gasp from the crowd. Amulets were clutched, and fingers touched honey-drizzled foreheads. One or two traditionalists even crossed themselves.

'Then there was a great puff of smoke and he fell backwards,' Eyton went on, brandishing his spoon for effect. 'When the mist cleared, he was dead again – good had triumphed over the Devil.'

Michael raised his eyebrows. 'Why would the Devil attack Goldynham? He was an upright man.'

'The Sorcerer arranged it, I expect,' replied Eyton with a shrug. A number of his parishioners nodded their agreement. 'I cannot think of any other explanation. Can you?'

'I can think of several,' replied Michael coolly. 'And I detect a human hand in this outrage, not a supernatural one. What happened next?'

'I fetched Master Heltisle,' said Eyton. 'And we thought *you* should investigate the matter.'

'Oh, I shall,' said Michael. It sounded like a threat.

'I wanted the Sheriff to come, too,' said Heltisle. 'The churchyard is University property, but Goldynham was a townsman – I am not quite sure where jurisdiction lies. But he is out chasing robbers on the Huntingdon Way, and so is unavailable.'

'We will liaise,' said Michael. He and Tulyet worked well together, and there were none of the usual territorial tussles that took place between powerful institutions.

Meanwhile, Bartholomew became aware that people were looking expectantly at him, and realised it was time to do his duty. He moved cautiously towards the body, forcing his feet to move, because although he did not believe Eyton's tale it had done little to dispel the sense of unease that had been dogging him ever since he had left Michaelhouse.

'Has anyone touched anything?' he asked.

'Certainly not,' said Heltisle, shooting him an unpleasant

glance. 'I am no Corpse Examiner, thank you very much. And my porters have kept everyone else back.'

Bartholomew saw Younge by the grave, shoving the more ghoulish of the onlookers away with unnecessary force. He was assisted by three cronies, all rough, sullen men with missing teeth and scarred knuckles. Their Bene't uniforms were filthy, and all four looked disreputable and unkempt.

As he approached the tomb, Bartholomew was painfully reminded of what had happened to Margery – loose soil scattered carelessly around a gaping hole, and a body flung across it like a piece of rubbish. One of Goldynham's arms dangled into the pit, as if he was trying to crawl back in. A wooden cross, which had marked the tomb until a more permanent monument could be erected, had been hurled to one side. So had a shovel.

'Goldynham was excavated with that,' said Bartholomew, indicating it with a nod. It was old but in good repair, with a sharp edge for cutting through sun-hardened soil. Damp clay still adhered to it, indicating that the silversmith's grave, like Margery's, had been deep.

'No, Goldynham exhumed himself,' argued Eyton. 'He used his bare hands.'

'His hands are clean,' said Bartholomew, kneeling to pick one up and show him. He resisted the urge to shudder at the feel of the cold, earth-moist skin. 'Had he been scrabbling his way clear of a grave, there would be dirt on his fingers. He did not do this himself.'

Heltisle regarded him with a good deal of contempt. 'You seem very sure of yourself. Why are you so familiar with what happens when a grave is despoiled?'

'It is a matter of simple logic,' said Bartholomew evenly,

declining to let the man's hostile manner rile him. 'Clawing through soil results in dirty hands. And the spade is there, for all to see.'

'He is right,' said the Eagle's taverner, stepping forward to look for himself. 'The earth is damp at the bottom of the grave, and it matches the damp soil on the spade. That means it *was* used to—'

'But I know what I saw,' cried Eyton, dismayed. 'There was no one digging but Goldynham himself. Perhaps he had the spade with him when he was buried.'

'He did not,' said Bartholomew, astonished that the priest should make such a claim – and alarmed that some of his congregation seemed ready to believe it. They were nodding and nudging each other, and there was more amulet-gripping. 'Someone would have noticed. Besides, he was a wealthy man, and if he had wanted a spade in his coffin, he would have chosen a better one than that.'

'He died suddenly, so perhaps he did not have the luxury of being selective,' suggested Eyton, unwilling to give up. 'Or perhaps that was a favourite implement, one he had owned a long time. Your colleagues – William and Mildenale – would understand what is happening here.'

'And what is that?' asked Bartholomew. The question was out before he could stop himself, and too late he realised he had provided the priest with the perfect opening for a rant. Eyton took a deep breath and began, advising his audience not to forget about the Sorcerer and his recent increase in power. Then he took the opportunity to let the crowd know that another batch of his holy amulets would be available for sale the following morning, and that God-fearing folk who did not want to fall prey to witches should consider investing in one.

185

'What about warts?' called one parishioner. 'The Sorcerer is better at curing them than any of the other witches, but if he is growing powerful and dangerous, does that mean we cannot approach him for help with warts?'

'Of course you may approach him,' replied Eyton amiably. 'Just make sure you are wearing one of my amulets when you do so.'

Michael shook his head. 'Eyton is a strange fellow,' he murmured. 'On the one hand, he claims to have hurled holy water over a demon-possessed corpse, while on the other he advocates visits to the Sorcerer for cures. But never mind him. What can you tell me about Goldynham?'

Reluctantly, Bartholomew turned his attention to the body. The silversmith had not fared well from his time in the ground. His skin was dark and mottled, and his stomach distended. The physician conducted the most perfunctory of examinations, unwilling to perform a more detailed one in front of spectators, so it was not surprising when he found there was little to say.

'Rougham said he died of a quinsy,' he replied in a low voice, so as not to be overheard. 'And he seems to be intact – no missing fingers, toes, hands, ears or hair. He has been excavated in exactly the same way as Margery: the culprit took a spade and dug down to the body, throwing soil in all directions. He did not pile it neatly to one side, suggesting he had no intention of reburying his victim. He does not care who sees his handi-work.'

Michael was thoughtful. 'Goldynham and Margery were decent folk, and I cannot believe either had serious enemies. They knew each other, but were not friends or kin. *Ergo*, I doubt this act of desecration is personal, so there must be another reason why they were picked. What could it be?'

Bartholomew shrugged. 'They were both buried on Ascension Day. Perhaps that date has some dark significance for one of the town's covens.'

'It is possible,' acknowledged Michael. 'However, it is equally possible that someone wants the witches blamed, to bring them trouble. What else can you tell me?'

Bartholomew tried to review the situation objectively, closing his mind to the fact that he was in a churchyard at night, kneeling next to a corpse that had been unlawfully exhumed. 'Perhaps we are reading too much into the situation. Margery and Goldynham were wealthy, so their graves are tempting targets for thieves. Hence Eyton saw not Goldynham moving about, but a robber, who fled because he was about to be caught, not because he was doused with holy water.'

Michael nodded. 'You are almost certainly right. Has the villain left anything that might allow us to identify him this time?'

Bartholomew took a torch, and spent a long time inspecting the ground around the tomb, but despite the fact that the thief had almost been caught red-handed, he had left no clues behind.

Michael was disappointed by the physician's findings – or lack thereof – although he was careful not to let his frustration show. He did not want it said that the incident had him confounded. Calmly, he asked Heltisle whether everyone might adjourn to Bene't College. Heltisle was not keen on having laymen in his domain, but was not so rash as to refuse a direct request from the Senior Proctor. He nodded acquiescence, and led

187

scholars, parishioners and Guild members through the back gate and into his hall. Younge was on hand to make sure no one misbehaved, and exerted his authority by forcing everyone to remove their shoes before stepping on the beautifully polished floors.

'What shall we do about Goldynham?' asked Heltisle, while they waited for the horde to assemble. He stood on the dais with Michael and Eyton, while Bartholomew hovered to one side. 'We do not want him escaping a second time, so I am not sure reburial is a good idea.'

'It *is* a good idea,' countered Bartholomew immediately. 'He represents a danger to health as long as he remains above ground. He should be re-interred tonight.'

'I do not choose to toss him back in the earth like so much rubbish,' declared Heltisle haughtily. 'I know Michaelhouse did it to Margery Sewale, but Bene't treats *its* dead with more respect. My porters will take him to the church, and I shall rebury him when I see fit.'

Bartholomew shrugged, knowing from the arrogant jut of Heltisle's chin that there was no point in trying to persuade him otherwise. 'It is your decision, and I suppose the chapel is cool . . .'

'I had better splash a bit more holy water on him when we have finished here, then,' said Eyton with a merry wink. 'That and a prayer or two should stop him from wandering off again tonight.'

'And that goes to show how fine is the line between religion and sorcery,' murmured Michael to the physician. 'Eyton's incantations and charms are not so different from those used by warlocks to ward off undesirable forces.'

Bartholomew watched two porters leave to do their Master's bidding, wondering whether he *had* acted with indecent haste when he had reburied Margery. He supposed he would find out if Eyton – who, as St Bene't's priest, would spend the most time in Goldynham's noxious company – became ill.

Once everyone was in the hall, standing in shuffling, jostling rows, Michael began to speak.

'Goldynham was a wealthy man, and his grave was robbed because a thief was after jewellery,' he declared. 'The same is true for Margery Sewale – she was buried without ornaments, but the culprit was not to know that. Eyton saw the thief – *not* Goldynham – who immediately took to his heels and fled when he realised he was about to be caught. This unsavoury incident has nothing to do with witchery.'

Sensible men, like the landlord of the Eagle, nodded acceptance of this version of events, but it was a dull explanation, and others were less inclined to believe it. Unfortunately, one was Heltisle.

'You are letting Bartholomew's opinions cloud your judgement,' he said coldly. 'Father William told me he dabbles in the dark arts, and is learning secrets from Mother Valeria. And he killed Father Thomas, too, when the poor man spoke out against heretics.'

'Doctor Bartholomew is no heretic,' shouted a familiar voice. It was Isnard the bargeman. He had lost his crutches, which was not an unusual occurrence when he was drunk, and was being held up by members of the Guild of Corpus Christi. 'Nor does he kill his patients. Not deliberately, at least.'

'Your testimony is tainted, Isnard,' said Heltisle scornfully. 'You are so desperate to be allowed back in the Michaelhouse Choir that you will say anything to curry favour.'

189

'Well, yes, I would,' admitted Isnard blithely. 'But in this case, it happens to be the truth. And before you say it, he is not the Sorcerer, either. He has no time for that sort of caper, what with all this flux about.'

'Who is the Sorcerer, then?' demanded Heltisle, as if he imagined the bargeman might know. 'The fellow holds half the town in his sway, but none of us know his name.'

'I have a few ideas,' said Eyton genially. There were calls for him to share his suspicions, so he began to oblige. His list was extensive, and included the Sheriff, Mother Valeria, Chancellor Tynkell, Podiolo, Arblaster and the University's stationer. Bartholomew was relieved when no one from Michaelhouse featured in his analysis.

'Can you not stop him?' Michael asked of Heltisle, as people began to call out reasons why one suspect was more likely to be the Sorcerer than the others. 'He is a member of your College, and you must have some control over the fellow. These accusations are likely to cause trouble.'

'I have no wish to stop him,' said Heltisle coldly. 'He is right to warn folk of the dangers they face. The town has been plagued by some very odd happenings of late, and we should ignore them at our peril. Take our goats, for example. Seven were stolen – and seven is a mystical number.'

'Is it?' asked Bartholomew tiredly. 'I did not know that.'

'I am sure you did,' countered Heltisle nastily. 'It is the kind of thing all wicked—'

Michael interrupted by elbowing him and Eyton off the dais and repeating his speech about grave-robbers. By the time he had dismissed the crowd, half seemed ready to believe him, although the rest remained sceptical. He was disappointed not to have convinced more, although Bartholomew thought he had done well enough, given the town's current preference for supernatural explanations over rational ones.

'I suppose it could have been worse,' said Heltisle, watching Younge oust the lingerers, so that only he, Eyton, Michael and the physician remained. 'We buried a student today – the one you failed to save, Bartholomew. My lads would have been distressed had it been him rising from his grave.'

'He would have been a prettier sight than Goldynham,' quipped Eyton rather inappropriately. 'However, we should be grateful it was not Mistress Refham. She is important to both our Colleges, because not only did she order those three shops sold to Michaelhouse at a very reduced rate, but she was generous to Bene't, too. I would not have wanted to throw holy water at her.'

'I thought it *was* her at first,' said Heltisle. 'I never have been very good at remembering who went where in cemeteries. Unlike the Corpse Examiner, I imagine.'

'What do you mean by that?' demanded Bartholomew, becoming tired of the man's sly insinuations. There had always been a degree of antagonism between him and Heltisle, but they usually managed a veneer of civility. He wondered what he had done to upset the balance.

Heltisle regarded him with dislike. 'I mean you have been implicated in some very dubious happenings of late. It was *you* who found Danyell's mutilated corpse, and there was the blood in *your* College's baptismal font. Moreover, you have never hidden your belief that anatomy is a viable branch of medicine. Perhaps the blood was Danyell's, spilled as you lopped off his hand.'

'You do not "lop off" limbs in anatomy,' snapped

Bartholomew, thinking the remarks highlighted the man's ignorance. 'It is a precise art, in which lopping plays no part.'

Heltisle took a step away, startled by his vehemence. Michael laid a warning finger on the physician's arm, to prevent him from sharing any other details about a technique that was not only illegal in England but that was generally considered abhorrent. Fortunately, the discussion was cut short by Younge, who approached with two people trailing at his heels. He was scowling.

'Here are David and Joan Refham, Master Heltisle. It is late for visitors, and I would have sent them packing, but you said I should be nice to them because you think they might give our College some of their mother's money.'

Heltisle winced at his porter's bold remarks, then turned to the couple with an ingratiating smile, although the indignant expression on Refham's face suggested any effort to make amends for Younge's words would be a waste of time. With oily charm, Heltisle ushered them to a bench and plied them with wine. Refham snatched the proffered goblet, downed its contents in a gulp, and tossed the goblet on the floor. Joan sniffed hers, then set it aside with a moue of distaste that was offensive.

'Is that my mother's grave, all dug up?' demanded Refham. 'Your lout Younge refused to tell me. Why you continue to employ him is a mystery to me. I would have hanged him years ago.'

'It was Goldynham,' replied Heltisle soothingly. 'Your mother has not been touched.'

'Good,' said Refham coldly. 'I would not have been happy if she had.'

'Nor would I,' added Joan. 'And when we are not happy, it is not good for anyone.'

'No?' asked Michael mildly. 'And why is that?'

'Because I say so,' replied Refham. 'And woe betide anyone who steps in my way. Believe me, you want to keep me happy.'

'And me,' added Joan.

'Well, there is no cause for unhappiness here,' said Heltisle hastily. 'Not yours, anyway.'

'Good,' said Refham again. 'Better someone else suffers than me, I always say. Are you Michael? The University's henchman?'

'I am its Senior Proctor,' replied Michael coolly. 'I understand we may be seeing more of each other, if Michaelhouse decides to buy the three shops you have just inherited.'

'Oh, you will decide to buy them,' said Refham smugly. 'I know what they are worth to you, being lodged between two plots you already own. The real question is whether you will get them. There are others who are interested, and we shall favour whoever offers us the most money.'

'Your mother's dying wish was that Michaelhouse should have them,' said Michael, displaying admirable calm in the face of such unpleasantness. 'You were in a tavern as she breathed her last, but I was at her side. She also stipulated a very reasonable price that we were to pay.'

'My lawyer says I need not be bound by her deathbed babbles. And what can she do about it now, anyway? She is dead, and all her property is mine.'

'And mine,' added Joan. 'And we intend to make as much money as we can from it. Then we shall leave this godforsaken town and go somewhere nice, like Luton.'

'So prepare to loosen your purse strings, henchman,' jeered Refham. He turned to Heltisle. 'We might favour Bene't with a donation. It depends on how we are treated, to be honest. I like good wine and decent horses.'

'Are you sure Michaelhouse should do business with a man like him?' asked Bartholomew in distaste, as Heltisle ushered the couple away, fawning over them in a manner that made even Younge cringe. 'My brother-in-law says he cannot be trusted, and he may do us harm.'

'Not as much harm as I will do to him, if he attempts anything shady,' retorted Michael.

Because spectators had prevented Bartholomew from performing a thorough examination of Goldynham, Michael suggested he should do it before returning to Michaelhouse. It was late, he said, so St Bene't's Church would be empty and he could do what was necessary without fear of being seen. Reluctantly, the physician followed him inside the dark building; Meadowman and Cynric stationed themselves by the door, ready to cough a warning should anyone try to come in. When they reached the body, Bartholomew faltered, feeling he had already done more than should have been expected of him.

'We need answers as a matter of urgency,' said the monk tiredly, seeing his hesitation. 'I have no idea where to begin looking for this fiend, and you are my only hope for clues.'

With a sigh, the physician did as he was asked. It was distasteful work and, as usual, he was assailed by the uncomfortable feeling that he was being watched by disapproving spirits. Manfully, he pushed his unease from his mind and tried to concentrate on the task in hand.

Goldynham had been tall, even in old age, and had sported an unusually full head of white hair, like a puff-ball. The hair was still there, although it was lank and dirty from its time in the ground. He was also wearing a gold-coloured cloak he had always liked – it had been a kind of trademark with him, and he was seldom without it, even in the heat of summer. Bartholomew supposed his colleagues at the Guild of Corpus Christi had ensured it had accompanied him to his grave.

'He died two weeks ago,' said Michael, standing well back with a pomander pressed tightly against his nose. 'Natural causes, you said. A quinsy.'

'That is what Rougham told me. Goldynham was not my patient, so I cannot confirm it, but there is no reason to doubt the diagnosis. Quinsy is often fatal in the elderly.'

'I cannot say I took to Refham and his wife,' burbled the monk, hoping to take his mind off what was happening in the parish coffin. It did not work. 'Lord, Matt! Is that really necessary? Perhaps Heltisle has a point when he claims you are overly interested in anatomy.'

Bartholomew glanced up at him. 'Of course I am interested in anatomy – so is any physician with a desire to understand the human body. And yes, it is necessary to look down Goldynham's throat if you want me to see whether he died of a quinsy. How else am I to do it?'

Michael did not rise to the challenge, and resumed his analysis of the Refhams instead. 'I will not let my dislike interfere with us buying their property, but I shall not enjoy dealing with them.'

'Really? I would have thought you would relish the opportunity to pit your wits against theirs – to find loop-holes in the law that will see them the poorer.'

Michael's eyes gleamed. 'That is true – it will be fun to wipe those smug smiles from their faces with a bit of cunning. Have you finished now? Thank God! So what can you tell me? Is Goldynham mutilated? You said not earlier, but that was before you had a chance to assess him properly.'

'There are marks to suggest he was handled roughly, but I imagine that was because the culprit was hurrying, not wanting to be caught.'

Michael pointed. 'His rings are still on his fingers, so the thief did not benefit from his crime before Eyton arrived. All his hard work was for nothing.'

Bartholomew was not so sure. 'The body was pulled right out of the ground, and it was buried deep, so that cannot have been an easy task to accomplish. It was the same with Margery. Why, when it would have been quicker to remove any jewellery *in situ*?'

Michael narrowed his eyes. 'What are you saying? That the purpose of this atrocity was *not* theft?'

Bartholomew looked away. 'We know corpses sometimes play a role in satanic rituals, so perhaps the Sorcerer *is* to blame. I know you just announced publicly that he is not, but you may be wrong.'

'I cannot be wrong,' argued Michael. 'You have just told me nothing is missing. And do not say the culprit was disturbed before he could make off with anything, because no one disturbed him when he was with Margery, and nothing was missing from her, either.'

'When she was defiled, you proposed that it might be the act of pulling a corpse into the open that is significant. Or perhaps the culprit needed soil from beneath a body for some specific ritual. I am afraid you will have to ask someone who knows about this sort of thing,

196

because contrary to popular opinion, I do not. However, I shall be surprised if the culprit's motive was not witch-craft.'

'Damn!' breathed Michael. 'And your suggestion makes sense, of course, given the other odd things that have been happening. All anyone talks about is this wretched Sorcerer, so it probably is unreasonable to hope there is no connection between despoiled graves and a powerful warlock. We *must* discover his identity before he or his minions dig up anyone else.'

'I would rather concentrate on catching Carton's killer.'

'I am beginning to think that once we have the Sorcerer, we may have the killer, too. After all, Carton spoke out against him, and now he is dead. Can we go home now? I do not like it here.'

Bartholomew rinsed his hands in a bucket of water that had been left in the porch, and followed the monk outside. He felt soiled all over, and could not shake the conviction that Goldynham would have deplored what he had just done. When Cynric slammed the door closed behind them, he almost jumped out of his skin. They began to walk through the churchyard, but stopped when they saw Eyton kneeling by the open grave. The priest grinned in a friendly manner.

'I am just performing an exorcism,' he said, sounding as though he was thoroughly enjoying himself. 'But do not worry about me – I am quite safe. I am wearing three amulets around my neck.'

'We are not worried,' replied Michael ambiguously. He turned to Bartholomew. 'His antics can do no harm, given that there is no one here to see him. Let him stay, if dark graveyards at the witching hour are the kinds of places he likes. We are going home.'

'Good,' said Bartholomew, not sure Michael was right about the priest being alone. He was sure someone was lurking in the trees at the back of the cemetery. While Michael briefed Beadle Meadowman about keeping ghoulish spectators away, he went to look, but there was no one there. However, the leaves rustled gently, even though there was no breeze.

He shivered, and went to rejoin the monk.

Chapter 6

There were two new cases of the flux that night, and Bartholomew trudged wearily from the castle as the night-watch called three o'clock, grateful it was half-term and there would be no teaching the following day. He could not quite bring himself to be grateful for the fact that there were no students to hound him with questions, though, because he missed their lively curiosity. In fact, he missed it enough to find he was in no hurry to return home, and decided to visit Mother Valeria instead. He was due to inspect her knee that day anyway, and to see her now would save him a walk later.

'It will leave more time for finding out who stabbed Carton,' he explained to Cynric, who had accompanied him on the grounds that he might need protection from restless corpses.

'But Mother Valeria is a witch,' the book-bearer pointed out uneasily. 'A real one, not some sham pedlar of ineffective spells. You should not associate with her.'

'You do – you bought one of her bat-eye charms,' remarked Bartholomew, remembering it was in his bag. He still had the one to guard against wolves, too, and

199

reminded himself again to throw them away later, when Cynric was not looking. It would not do for anyone to find them.

'That is different,' said the book-bearer in a tone of voice that told the physician disagreement was futile. 'I went for a purpose, I paid my money, and I left when she gave me what I went for. You, on the other hand, talk to her and ask her questions. You *fraternise*.'

'I ask after her health. I cannot help her unless I know how she feels.'

Cynric shot him the kind of glance that said he was not believed. 'I had better get you another charm, then – one against witches.'

'That might be difficult. Witches are unlikely to sell something that works against themselves.'

Cynric regarded him scornfully. 'You get that kind from priests, boy, not witches. I will buy one from Eyton if he has any left – the rise of the Sorcerer means there has been a bit of a run on them lately. His are better than the rest, because he is generous with the holy water.'

'Have you returned that witchcraft guide yet?' asked Bartholomew, not liking to think of Cynric adding yet more to his already extensive body of knowledge on the subject.

'I will do it this morning. I have finished with it anyway. It was interesting, but did not tell me much I did not know – except that June is an auspicious time for warlocks. As I said, it is why the Sorcerer is making his stand now.'

'Yes,' said Bartholomew tiredly. 'Here is Valeria's lane.'

'I am not going down there,' said Cynric firmly. 'I will do a good deal for you, as you know, but hobnobbing with powerful and dangerous witches is not one of them. I will see you later.'

200

He disappeared into the semi-darkness, as light-footed as a cat. Bartholomew watched him go, then took a deep breath of air that smelled of hot grass. It was a scent he associated with the dry, arid climates of the Mediterranean, and was not one he ever expected to encounter in England. It was thick and rich, and familiar and unfamiliar at the same time. Then a waft of something less pleasant assailed his nostrils, causing him to gag. Idyllic images of olive groves and herb-coated hills promptly disappeared, and one of blocked drains took their place.

He made his way along the nettle-lined path to Valeria's hut, marvelling at how well it was trodden. People claimed to be frightened of her, but that clearly did not stop them from seeking out her expertise. He thought the relationship between witch and customer was an odd one: folk like Cynric were desperate to buy her charms and amulets, yet were ready to condemn her dark powers without hesitation. Bartholomew felt sorry for her; she was in an acutely vulnerable position.

He reached the clearing, and saw smoke issuing from her hut, even though the hour was horribly early. She claimed she never slept, but he was not sure whether to believe her. When he tapped on the door frame and pushed aside the leather hanging, he saw her filling two cups from something that bubbled on the hearth.

'I have been expecting you,' she said. 'I saw you go up the hill earlier and knew you would visit on the way home. You always come at a time when you think no one will see you.'

'Unfortunately, it has done me scant good,' he said ruefully, sitting on a stool. 'People still think I am your apprentice, and that I come to learn dark secrets.'

201

'I know I have teased you about it, but I would never really teach you my skills.' The old woman made it sound as though he was the last man on Earth she would consider for the honour. 'You would spend the whole time telling me why they would not work, and that would be tiresome.'

'I wish William could hear you say that. I do not suppose you have a cure for fanaticism, do you? He is very sick with it.'

'There are measures you can take to silence a barbed tongue. It involves acquiring a certain kind of stone, and burying it under the hearth of a—'

'No!' Bartholomew held up his hand in alarm. 'I was not serious.'

'Never jest about magic, lad. It is nothing to be frivolous about, as men have learned to their cost.' Her voice had become low and sibilant, and for the first time during their association, Bartholomew felt uneasy in her company. He studied her in the flickering light of the fire, but her hat shadowed her features and all he could see was the sharp glitter of eyes. She seemed to be scowling, and he saw he had offended her. Perhaps this was the face she presented to petitioners like Cynric, and suddenly he understood exactly why they were inclined to treat her with caution.

'I am sorry,' he said, contrite. 'It has been a long night, and I am tired.'

'I can see that,' she said, relenting. 'And I know what it is like to be at the wrong end of a Franciscan's zeal. I have suffered it many times during my long lifetime, and it is never pleasant.'

'How old are you?' asked Bartholomew, although most of his patients struggled to answer that question. He could tell by her hunched posture and wrinkles that she was ancient, and he wondered what remarkable events she had witnessed during her life.

'I have seen more than a hundred summers, but only seven in Cambridge. I came just after the plague. This house and all the others around it were empty because every living soul had been snatched by the Death. But that does not worry me. I like a place with a few ghosts.'

Bartholomew had vague recollections of her arrival, although his memories of those bleak times tended to be blurred and uncertain. He hoped the doom-sayers like Suttone were wrong, and that the disease would not return, because he did not think he could bear watching helplessly again while his patients died. He realised his mind was wandering, and forced his attention back to the present.

'A hundred summers,' he mused, not really believing it. She was too spry for that sort of age, although he was not about to annoy her by saying so. 'It is a long time.'

'Not among my kind. I am actually rather youthful for a witch.' She presented a leg that was clad in some of the thickest leggings Bartholomew had ever seen. 'Now, inspect my knee, like a good lad, and give me more of that paste to ease the swelling.'

'It would be easier – and more effective – if you let me see it without these coverings,' he said, as he always did. He lived in hope that she would eventually trust him enough to comply.

She fixed him with beady eyes. 'The pain is in the bone, so how will removing clothes help? There are already layers of skin, muscle and fat in the way, so I do not see how a veil of wool will make a difference. Besides,

I do not let men see my naked limbs. It would be unseemly.'

Bartholomew knew there was no point in pursuing the issue. He knelt and probed the joint as best he could, pleased to feel the swelling had reduced considerably. He handed her another jar of the ointment, and repeated the instructions on how to use it.

'Yes, yes,' she said impatiently. 'I remember from last time. I cannot pay you in coins, so how about a bundle of mugwort instead? Mugwort protects books from the worm, so scholars are always pleased to have it. I picked and dried it myself, so I can guarantee its efficacy.'

Bartholomew accepted, because the herb was also useful for women's ailments, and his own supply was depleted. He put the bundle in his medicine bag and stood to leave, but Valeria reached out and grabbed his sleeve. She wore gloves, but her fingernails poked through the ends, long and curving, like talons.

'Stay and drink some breakfast ale. Everyone else comes to talk about themselves, and it makes a change to have a guest who is interested in me. I know you are tired, but my ale will revive you.'

Bartholomew did not want to stay longer than was necessary, but it was cool inside the hut, and he was thirsty. 'Just for a while, then.'

Mother Valeria's idea of good conversation was a mono-logue on the pleasures of growing roses, and although Bartholomew was not very interested in why different types of manure should produce such varying results, he found himself relaxing. Valeria had a pleasant voice that was almost as low as a man's, and there was something about her sharp humour and wry manner of speaking that reminded him of Matilde.

'You should have this discussion with Arblaster,' he suggested. 'He is keen on dung.'

'Have you seen his compost heaps? I put a spell on every one of them last year, and he claims my incantations are the secret of his success. He belongs to the cadre that meets in All Saints, but I cannot say I like the man. He is too greedy, always haggling over the cost of the charms I provide.'

'He is a witch?' asked Bartholomew. Then he recalled William, Langelee and Suttone telling him at the Fellows' meeting that the dung-master meddled in the dark arts, and realised he already had the answer to his question.

'He is a coven member,' she corrected pedantically. 'Their numbers have risen since the Sorcerer made himself known, which is good and bad. On the one hand, it means more people will support traditional healers, like me, when zealots like your William rail against us. On the other, it means witchery is attracting folk who only want to use it to their advantage.'

'I do not understand.'

'I mean it is encouraging false converts. As soon as something else comes along, they will be off worshipping that instead. Refham and his wife are good examples: they have no real interest in or liking for dark magic and just want it to make them rich. It makes them an unsavoury pair.'

'I see,' said Bartholomew, hiding his amusement that treating witchcraft shabbily should result in someone being considered disagreeable. 'You talked about the Sorcerer when we met in the marshes yesterday. Have you had any success in working out who he is?'

'None at all, and I was serious in my warning to you: do not confront him. Let the priests and the monks do it. They have taken sacred orders to combat his kind of evil. You have not, so you should stand aside and let them take the risks.'

Bartholomew was unsettled to see that a confident, allegedly powerful witch like Valeria was intimidated by the Sorcerer. And the fact that she described him as evil had not escaped his attention, either. It sounded sinister coming from someone who was not exactly heavenly herself. Her notion that friars should confront the Sorcerer reminded Bartholomew of Carton. He took the talisman from his bag and showed it to her.

'Have you seen this before?'

She did no more than glance at it. 'It is a holy-stone. Magister Arderne was selling them earlier this year. Now *there* was a disreputable fellow, full of lies and false cures.'

'Do you know who owned it?'

She shook her head. 'He hawked dozens of them and that one is not distinctive. Why?'

'It might have belonged to Carton's killer.'

She took it from him and studied it carefully. Eventually, she handed it back. 'All I can tell you is that the cord is greasy, which means it hung around a neck for a considerable length of time. From this, I deduce that its owner will not be a person like Refham, whose conversion to dark magic is recent, but a fellow whose convictions have been held for a good deal longer.'

It was not an especially helpful observation, because people tended to keep such beliefs to themselves – or had until the Sorcerer came along. And asking how long someone had put his trust in witchery was hardly the sort of question that would meet with an honest answer.

206

'I suppose it eliminates the canons of Barnwell,' he said, more to himself than to Valeria. 'One of them could not have worn an amulet for an extended period, because they live communally and a colleague would have taken issue with it eventually. They may be an odd crowd, but they are still monks, and therefore supposed to eschew such things.'

Valeria laughed. 'Podiolo would worship the Devil himself if he thought it would help him make gold, while Fencotes came late to his vows, and lived a wild life before. Norton is hardly saintly, either, with his love of property. Do not eliminate anyone just because he wears a habit.'

'The town has an unsettled feel at the moment,' said Bartholomew, changing the subject because he found her observations disconcertingly astute. 'The false converts you mentioned are sending those who support the Church into a frenzy of condemnation. Perhaps you should leave until the mood has quietened. It would not be the first time someone instigated a witch-hunt, and you are vulnerable here.'

'I have nowhere else to go. But you should heed your own warning, because I know what folk say about your unorthodoxy. They may blame *you* for missing hands, defiled corpses and bloody fonts. And there is the fact that you like anatomy. You are just as much at risk as I am.'

Bartholomew had an uncomfortable feeling that she was right.

Dawn was not far off when the physician stood to take his leave, swallowing the last of the ale as he did so. It was spicy and made him dizzy, but the sensation passed, and he found himself feeling quite energetic as he walked down Bridge Street. He wondered what she had put in it, and belatedly it occurred to him that he probably should not have had it. Witches were known for producing powerful beverages, and he could not afford to be drunk quite so early in the day.

His route took him past Margery Sewale's house, and he experienced a momentary flash of sadness. She had been his patient for years, and he was sorry he had not been able to save her. He paused outside her cottage, recalling how she had made him cakes while she told him about her symptoms. Not everyone was so hospitable, and he would miss her. He glanced across the street to the patch of scrub opposite, where he had found Danyell's body. He had been returning from visiting Mother Valeria, then, too. He frowned as he thought about the Norfolk mason. Who had taken his hand, and why? Was it the Sorcerer?

No answers were forthcoming, and he was about to walk on when he became aware of a glimmer of light under Margery's window. The house had been empty since her death because the Master had not wanted the trouble of renting it for the short time before it was sold. It had been locked up and left, so should have been in darkness. Curious and concerned, Bartholomew walked towards it. Anticipating a set-to with burglars, he took a pair of heavy childbirth forceps from his bag – a gift from Matilde, he remembered with a pang – placed his hand on the door, and pushed. It swung open with a creak.

There were two men inside, and they stopped what they were doing with a start. It was too dark to see faces, but the pair had silhouettes that Bartholomew recognised immediately. It was the giant and his bearded friend. For a moment, no one did anything, then the intruders whipped their swords from their scabbards. Bartholomew had been in the company of soldiers long enough to recognise the confident way they handled their weapons, and for the first time it occurred to him that bursting into a house that was obviously in the course of being ransacked was a reckless thing to have done. He stepped back, intending to turn and make a run for it, but the men anticipated him. The giant feinted with his blade, forcing the physician to dodge to one side, while Beard ducked behind him and slammed closed the door. Bartholomew was trapped.

Short of other options, he attempted to bluster his way out of his predicament. 'This is Michaelhouse property, and you are trespassing. What do you—'

The giant moved with a speed that took him by surprise, and he only just managed to jerk away from the blow intended to deprive him of his head. It was almost impossible to defend himself against such determined tactics, and he knew it was only a matter of time before he was skewered. Without giving himself time to think, he issued the bloodcurdling battle cry he had learned from Cynric during the French wars, and launched an attack of his own, forceps held high. The giant fell back, startled, but Beard stood firm. His sword flashed towards Bartholomew, who stumbled away so the blow went wide. The man muttered a curse under his breath, and prepared to strike again.

Suddenly, the door flew open with a tremendous crash, and a shadow tore inside. Even in the dark, Bartholomew recognised Cynric's short Welsh killing sword. While the book-bearer engaged Beard in a furious, stabbing skirmish,

Bartholomew swung around to face the giant. The man was already moving towards him. Bartholomew flailed wildly with the forceps, and heard a grunt of pain as they connected with flesh. Then the giant let fly with a punch that missed, and while the physician was still off balance, he shoulder-charged him *en route* to the door. It was like colliding with a bull, and Bartholomew was knocked clean off his feet. The crash he made as he fell distracted Cynric, giving Beard the opportunity to dart after his accomplice. Bartholomew tried to stand, but his legs were like rubber. Cynric raced to his side; the physician pushed him away.

'Follow them, see where they go,' he gasped. 'Do not let them escape.'

But the intruders had moved fast, and Cynric had wasted valuable seconds making sure his master had not suffered serious harm. It was not long before he returned.

'There are too many alleys and yards around here,' he muttered, disgusted. 'I have no idea where they went, and the streets are still deserted, so there is no one to ask.'

'You cannot track them?' Bartholomew had great respect for Cynric's skill in such matters.

'Not in a town, boy. Broken blades of grass, footprints and bruised leaves mean nothing in a place inhabited by so many people. And I listened as hard as I could, but they are too experienced to let the rattle of footsteps give them away.'

'Experienced?'

'They were fighters, men who have done battle before. It was rash to tackle them with nothing but forceps.' Cynric's tone was deeply disapproving.

'They were going to steal something.'

'Like what? The place is empty, because we removed

all the furniture after Margery died. In fact, a burglary was why we emptied it, if you recall. Someone broke in the night after she passed away, and ransacked the house. So we took everything out while we still had it.'

The incident had slipped Bartholomew's mind. 'Did we catch the culprit? I cannot remember.'

The book-bearer shook his head. 'But the news of her death was all over the town, and it is not unknown for the homes of the recently deceased to be targeted by unprincipled thieves.' He frowned in puzzlement. 'They do not usually bother once a place has been stripped, though. I wonder what that pair thought they were doing.'

Bartholomew struggled into a sitting position. The intruders' lamp had been knocked over during the skirmish, but he recalled how bare Margery's home had looked after the servants had taken benches, pots and shelves. They had even unpeeled the ancient rugs from the floor, revealing uneven tiles that would need to be replaced before the cottage could be sold. He supposed thieves could still take door hinges or wall brackets, but Beard and the giant were relatively well dressed, and he could not see such men being interested in second-hand ironmongery.

'What are you doing here?' he asked the book-bearer, when answers continued to evade him, no matter how hard he thought. 'You went home ages ago.'

'I saw the light, and was watching from across the street,' explained Cynric. 'I was going to follow them when they came out, to see where they went. But you were in before I could stop you.'

His voice held a note of admonition, and Bartholomew realised his recklessness had spoiled a perfectly sensible plan. Cynric would have stalked the two men to their lodgings and reported the incident to Michael, who would then have gone to question them. The monk might even have locked them in his gaol until he was sure of their story. Bartholomew's intervention meant he had risked his life for nothing – and created yet another mystery for the Senior Proctor to unravel.

'I am sorry, Cynric,' he mumbled. 'I did not think.'

'It is all right.' Cynric held out his hand, and hauled the physician to his feet, shooting him a grin at the same time. 'Your battle cry was impressive, though. Was it one you heard at Poitiers? Now there was a time to gladden the heart of a warrior!'

Bartholomew swallowed hard. It had not gladdened *his* heart, and the horror of the close fighting still haunted his dreams. Working among the injured afterwards had been worse still, even for a man familiar with such sights, and he failed to understand why Cynric seemed to gain so much delight from reminiscing about it. He forced the rush of bad memories away and smiled back at Cynric, supposing his Welsh had been unintelligible.

'You arrived just in time. Thank you.'

Cynric began to prowl, looking for clues to what the two men could have wanted, while Bartholomew leaned against the wall. He was unsteady on his feet, and wondered whether it was the aftermath of the skirmish or the lingering effects of Valeria's ale. He tottered to the door and inspected it. Indentations along one side showed where someone had taken an implement to the wood and carefully pried his way inside. It looked like a determined effort, and Bartholomew wondered – again – why Beard and the giant should think it worthwhile.

212

'We should go and inform the Master,' said Cynric, peering at the damage.

'We can tell him someone broke in, but we cannot tell him why. Do you have any theories?'

'Margery had no kin, so that pair cannot be disinherited nephews or distant cousins coming to see what they can salvage. They are not local men, because the size of one and the beard of the other make them distinctive, and I would know them. So they must be visitors.'

'I have seen them around. Their clothes suggest they are men of some standing.'

Cynric nodded. 'I thought the same. Do you think one might be the Sorcerer?'

It was the sort of leap in logic Bartholomew had come to expect from Cynric, so the question did not surprise him as much as it might another man. 'You said they were not local, but the Sorcerer *is* local. Or, at least, he has been here a while, amassing his power. *Ergo*, neither of the two burglars can be him, because an observant man like you would have noticed either one of them weeks ago.'

'True,' said Cynric, preening slightly at the compliment. 'Pity. They were imposing fellows, and I shall be disappointed if the Sorcerer transpires to be someone puny.'

Bartholomew left him to watch the house while he returned to Michaelhouse, promising to dispatch the porter with tools to mend the door. He crossed the Great Bridge, passed the grand houses that belonged to the Sheriff and other town worthies, and had just reached the shadowy churchyard of All Saints-in-the-Jewry when his attention was caught by a rustle.

'Heathen!' came a fierce whisper from the bushes. 'Your days are numbered.'

It was still not fully light, and Bartholomew could not see very well. 'Who is there?' he demanded, wondering whether Beard or his gigantic companion were having some fun with him in retaliation for interrupting whatever it was they had been doing.

'Your heart is steeped in wickedness,' the voice went on. 'And it will bring about your death.'

Bartholomew reached into his bag and withdrew the forceps again, wondering what Matilde would say if she knew the use to which he was putting them. 'If you have something to say, then come out and say it. Do not hiss in the dark like a demented kettle.'

'I know how you spend your nights,' breathed the voice. 'You consort with witches.'

Bartholomew was beginning to be annoyed. He dived into the vegetation, aiming to grab the fellow and demand an explanation. He heard a twig snap ahead of him, so fought his way towards it, swearing under his breath when brambles ripped his shirt. Suddenly, he was through the undergrowth and out into the road on the other side. He looked up and down the street rather wildly, but there was no one in sight. Except one man, who regarded him in startled concern.

'Matt?' asked Michael. 'What in God's name is the matter? Who were you shouting at? And what have these poor shrubs done to warrant such a vicious attack?'

'And you saw nothing at all?' asked Bartholomew, following the monk across Michaelhouse's yard for breakfast. They had just buried Carton in the Franciscan cemetery – the hour after dawn was the coolest time of day, and all funerals were currently taking place then – and he desperately wanted to think about something

214

else. William and Mildenale had complained that their colleague was being shoved in the ground with indecent haste, while not all the Grey Friars were pleased that their priory should be chosen as the final resting place for a dead fanatic. The occasion had been both dismal and uncomfortable, and Bartholomew was glad it was over.

'Only you. I heard you leave in the middle of the night, and was worried when you did not come home. I was on my way to find you when I saw you fighting the trees. Thankfully, no one else did, because I would not like it said that Michaelhouse is full of lunatics – it would be hard to refute, as we are already the proud owners of Clippesby, Mildenale and William.'

'Is Cynric back?'

Michael nodded. 'He tells me you attacked two swordsmen with your forceps. What is wrong with you today? You have never shown a fondness for violence before, and none for suicide, either. Cynric thinks Mother Valeria put a spell on you.'

'She gave me some ale.'

Michael regarded him in horror. 'And you drank it? Lord, Matt! Valeria's ale is known to make hardened drinkers totter like children, while Sheriff Tulyet uses it for scouring his drains. She occasionally challenges folk to swallow more of it than she can, and no one has ever bested her.'

'Why would she do that?' Bartholomew was not sure whether to believe him.

'For easy money. Men pay handsomely for the chance to defeat her in a drinking bout, and there is always some fool who thinks he can win. As you seem to be her friend, you should advise her to rein back for a while. There is a lot of ill-feeling towards witches at the moment, and she should make herself less visible.'

They reached the hall and headed for their seats at the high table. William and Mildenale were standing together, the commoner muttering in the friar's ear. William was nodding vigorously, and Bartholomew wished he would listen as avidly to the more moderate members of his College.

Michael followed his gaze. 'Mildenale told me yesterday that he will do anything to save the Church from the Sorcerer "when the times comes", whatever that means.'

'Probably the night before Trinity Sunday. That is when the Sorcerer is expected to make his bid for power. Apparently, it is an important day for dark magic.'

Michael continued to stare at the Franciscans. 'William is like a nocked arrow in a bow, ready to be sent hurtling towards a target, and Mildenale is clever enough to use him so. *Mildenalus Sanctus* will not baulk at using force if he thinks it will further his righteous cause. I have a feeling he is readying himself to do serious harm to the Sorcerer and his disciples.'

'But most of the people who attend these covens are not great warlocks – they are folk like the Mayor, Podiolo and others we have known for years. And if it does come down to a battle between them and the likes of William and Mildenale, I am not sure which side I will choose.'

'Hopefully, you will be with me, trying to stop any such battle from taking place,' said Michael tartly. 'Damn Mildenale and his fierce ideas! And damn Refham's greed, too!'

'Refham?' echoed Bartholomew. 'What does he have to do with anything?'

'If he had sold us these shops at the price his mother

216

stipulated, Mildenale would be established in his own hostel by now. And then he would be too busy to ferment religious wars.'

The remaining Fellows entered the hall with the Master; Deynman trailed at their heels. Suttone was saying he had decided against a reading for the Guild of Corpus Christi, because a lecture on the plague would make for better entertainment. Wynewyk was holding forth at the same time about how Barnwell Priory had offered thirteen marks for Sewale Cottage, thus outbidding Arblaster. Langelee was giving a detailed account of a game of camp-ball he had played the previous evening, which seemed to revolve around how many townsmen he had punched while pretending to grab the ball. And Deynman was muttering a venomous diatribe about the fact that someone had marked his place in Aristotle's *Rhetoric* with a piece of cheese. No one was listening to anyone else, and their braying chatter made the hall feel a little less empty.

The Fellows took their places at the high table, while Deynman and Mildenale sat in the body of the hall, although not together. Mildenale found the librarian's slow wits tiresome, while Deynman was furious with the commoner for tearing pages from a book he had deemed heretical. Langelee intoned a grace, and Bartholomew let the words wash over him, thinking about Carton.

'—*ut non declinet cor meum in verba malitiae ad excsandas excusationes in peccatis.*'

When Bartholomew looked up with a start – the Latin was uncharacteristically grammatical, and asking for help against deeds of wickedness was not the usual subject for prayers at meals – he saw the Master reading from a scrap of parchment. William was regarding the physician

217

rather defiantly, while Mildenale's expression was unreadable above his piously clasped hands.

'Sorry, Matt,' murmured Langelee, when he had finished and they were seated. 'William asked me to do that, and it was easier to agree than to fight him over it. He thinks you are a necromancer.'

'A necromancer?' echoed Bartholomew, bemused.

'Necromancy is predicting the future by communicating with the dead, apparently, although I had never heard of it. Have you?'

'I know what it is,' replied Bartholomew cautiously. 'But that does not mean I—'

'Well, he says he fears for your immortal soul,' said Langelee, not really interested in the answer. 'Although I suspect the fear comes from Mildenale, and William has no more idea of what necromancy is about than I did. Your interest in anatomy must have set them off.'

Most meals at College were eaten while listening to the Bible Scholar – Michaelhouse men were supposed to hone their minds even when dining – but the Bible Scholar was among those who had been sent away, so they ate in silence, the only sounds being the occasional tap of a knife on a plate, or William gulping his ale. Bartholomew did not object to the rule against conversation that morning, because it gave him time to consider the various mysteries that confronted him.

Who were the two men in Sewale Cottage, and what did they want? Cynric had not seen them before, which meant they had probably not been in the town for very long. Their clothes indicated they were not paupers, yet they had been burgling an empty house. Bartholomew's interruption had driven them out, which suggested they had not found whatever it was they were looking for.

Should he go back, to see if he had better luck? Of course, not knowing what he was hunting would make any search difficult, but at least he would have daylight on his side. And Cynric. The book-bearer was good at scouring other people's houses.

Then there was the voice in All Saints' churchyard. Who hated him enough to whisper such poisonous remarks? Master Heltisle? Spaldynge? Younge the surly porter? The kinsman of some patient he had failed to save? One of the many enemies Stanmore thought he had acquired? It was not pleasant to think he had engendered such dislike, and he did not dwell on the matter for long.

Finally, there was the death of Carton and the incidents Michael thought were connected to it. Had the Sorcerer killed Carton because he had spoken out against him? Had he pulled Margery and Goldynham from their graves as part of a spell to accrue power? Would such atrocities become commonplace in the future, and no corpse could rest easy in its tomb for fear of being disturbed?

'I cannot eat this,' the Master declared suddenly, taking a piece of smoked pork between thumb and forefinger and holding it aloft. 'It is rotten.'

'So is the fish-giblet soup,' said William, nodding at his own untouched bowl. He was a glutton for fish-giblet soup, a flavoursome dish that no one else liked. Neither he nor Langelee were fussy eaters, and the fact that they deemed the meal inedible said a good deal about the state of its decomposition. 'The heat must be spoiling seafood, as well as meat.'

'Can bad victuals bring plague, Matthew?' asked Suttone conversationally. He had concentrated on the bread and honey, although the bread was oddly shaped from having the mould cut off it.

'Do not ask him such a question unless you have an hour to spend listening to the reply,' advised Michael. 'But you cannot have an hour, because there is a murder to solve, and I need his help.'

'You have tales of walking corpses to quell, too,' said Langelee, cutting across Bartholomew's indignant retort. 'Eyton's claim that Goldynham dug himself up is circulating like wildfire and I am sure you want to provide an explanation that does not credit the Sorcerer with organising it.'

'I do,' agreed Michael. 'But unfortunately, Eyton is a priest, so people are inclined to believe—'

'Eyton is not a liar,' said William fiercely, hastening to defend his friend. 'He is a Franciscan.'

'I am not saying he is a liar,' snapped Michael. 'I am saying he is mistaken. The churchyard was dark, and it was very late. Shadows can play strange tricks on agitated minds.'

'Speaking of agitated minds, yours must have been deranged last night,' said Langelee, rounding on Mildenale with sudden belligerence. 'I saw you talking to Refham. How could you demean yourself by conversing with such a man? Do you not know he is trying to cheat us?'

'Of course I do,' said Mildenale, startled. 'And if he sells those three shops to someone else, I shall not be able to establish my hostel, so I stand to lose a great deal from his cussedness. So, when our paths happened to cross yesterday, I politely informed him that deathbed wishes were God's will and that he would be breaking holy laws by going against what his mother wanted.'

'And what did he say to that?' asked Langelee. 'I cannot imagine he was moved.'

Mildenale raised his eyes heavenwards. 'He was not. But then the Almighty spoke to me, and suggested I try a different tactic. So I offered Refham a commission – said he could have the job of decorating the buildings once they are in our possession.'

Langelee grinned, pleasantly surprised. 'God is a clever fellow! We have said from the start that the shops will need a lick of paint before they can be rented out. Refham likes to think he can turn his hand to any trade, so that will be an extremely attractive proposition to him.'

'So it might, but it will cost him his immortal soul,' said William grimly. 'He will be cursed by God if he does not do what his mother ordered with a willing heart – accepting bribes before complying with her wishes is essentially the same as disobeying her. And that is breaking one of the Ten Commandments.'

'God does not curse people for defying their mothers,' said Langelee disdainfully. 'Ten Commandments or no.'

'He does,' argued William vehemently. 'And He might curse you, too, if you take that sort of attitude with me. In fact, He will curse anyone who does not follow the straight and narrow, and they will find themselves condemned to the deepest pits of Hell. I know these things, because I am a friar, and one of those chosen to preach His message. Is that not so, Mildenale?'

'Indeed it is,' agreed Mildenale piously. 'God only selects the truly righteous to do His work.'

'We should talk to William about the blood in the font,' said Michael to Bartholomew, when the meal had ended and the Master had intoned a final grace. 'No matter how righteous *Mildenalus Sanctus* believes him to be.'

221

'Why?' asked Bartholomew, who wanted nothing to do with the Franciscan while he was in his current state of bigoted intolerance.

'Because he was the one who discovered it, and he might have noticed something he later forgot to mention. Then we shall visit Spynk and ask more questions about Danyell. And finally, we shall go to Bene't College and make enquiries about Goldynham. We can chat about the goats when we are there, too, so Heltisle will know I have not forgotten them.'

'But we have done all this before,' objected Bartholomew, suspecting none of the interviews would be likely to provide them with the answers they so desperately needed, and that they would be wasting precious time. 'Or you have.'

Michael shot him a weary glance. 'Do you have any better ideas? No? Then let us go and corner our rabid friar – preferably when he is alone and not being prompted by *Mildenalus Sanctus*.'

Bartholomew did not feel equal to an encounter with William. His sleepless night was taking its toll in the form of muddy wits, and the mouldy bread he had eaten for breakfast sat heavily in his stomach. But Michael was right: he did not have any better ideas as how to proceed, and he saw there was no choice but to follow the monk's suggestions.

'Let me do the talking,' ordered Michael, as they walked to the north accommodation wing, where William lived. 'Just listen to his answers, and see if you think he is holding out on us.'

'You think he might try to mislead you?' Bartholomew doubted William would do any such thing. The friar might be a zealot, but he was not normally obstructive of the monk's investigations.

'He is so obsessed by his war against heterodoxy at the moment that he has lost any grasp of reason he may once have had. He has always been suspicious of the way you practise medicine, but friendship – or comradeship, at least – has curbed his tongue in the past. Now he tells Langelee you are a necromancer.'

'It is because of Thomas,' said Bartholomew unhappily. 'My mistake led to the death of a fellow Franciscan – a friend.'

Michael waved a dismissive hand. 'He and Thomas were never close. Indeed, I was under the impression that Thomas did not like him – he accepted William's companionship only because they held similar views about sin. William's so-called grief derives from the fact that he said some very unpleasant things the day before Thomas died, and now he feels guilty about it.'

William's voice could be heard booming through the open window as they approached, although Bartholomew suspected the friar imagined he was whispering. He was not surprised to learn the subject was heresy. Deynman was sitting on the bed, looking trapped, while William paced in front of him, finger wagging furiously. Bartholomew was seized by the urge to grab it; he had long been of the opinion that people who felt the need to wag fingers invariably did not know what they were talking about. The friar looked sheepish when Michael strode in with the physician at his heels.

'I am not saying there is actual *evil* in you,' he said to Bartholomew with a pained smile. 'Just that you are incapable of telling the difference between the sacred and the profane.'

'How odd,' said Michael, watching the librarian escape. 'I was just saying the same about you.'

William was indignant. 'Me? *I* have been preaching on the subject for years, and know it better than anyone alive. Of course, my ideas have become a lot clearer since I joined forces with Mildenale, Carton and Thomas. It is a pity two of them are dead.' He glared at the physician, who was unable to meet his eye.

'Never mind that,' said Michael curtly. 'Today, we are here to discuss the blood you found in our baptismal font.'

'Good,' said William, pleased. 'It is time someone took these matters seriously. Have you come to procure my help? I was your Junior Proctor once, and excelled at weeding out heretics.'

'How could I forget?' murmured Michael. 'Tell me what happened that day.'

William frowned. 'But you were there, Brother. You both were. Why do you need me to recount the incident?'

'Humour me,' instructed Michael tersely.

William looked bemused, but did as he was told. 'I went to church early, to pray for Thomas. As I was collecting some candles to light, I realised there were a lot of flies about, and that most were congregating by the font. Curiously, I pulled off the cover, to reveal it filled with blood.'

'Not *filled*,' corrected Michael pedantically. 'There was a dribble.'

'It was certainly human, though,' said William, determined, as always, to have the last word. 'I could tell by its particular shade of red.'

Michael stared at him for a long time. 'Matt cannot

224

tell the difference between human and animal blood,' he said eventually. 'And he is a physician, trained to detect subtle variations in the colour of bodily fluids. Your skill is a worrying one, Father, and not something to be admired in a God-fearing man. You should keep it quiet, or you will have half the witches in the county flocking to hire your expertise. They know a kindred spirit when they see one.'

William's jaw dropped. 'How dare you say such things! I am a friar, and I—'

'You admit to special skills with blood,' snapped Michael. 'Friar or not, *that* is suspicious.'

'This is outrageous!' cried William. 'You know I have no truck with witchery. I have always spoken out against wickedness, and—'

'Sometimes men protest over-loudly, to distract folk from their real beliefs.' Michael pressed his point relentlessly, cutting across the friar's shocked protestations. 'But I shall consider your claims of innocence later. Now, I want to talk about the blood. Did you notice anything odd or unusual that day? Think carefully before you reply, Father. You might know something that will allow me to solve this case, which *may* prove you are not in league with these demons you are so interested in.'

William opened his mouth to argue, but saw the expression on the monk's face and thought better of it. Even he knew it was wise to capitulate sometimes. 'There was nothing odd or unusual,' he said. Then he frowned. 'Except . . . but no, that cannot be relevant.'

'Let me be the judge of that,' ordered Michael curtly.

'There was a glove near the font. It is too hot for anyone to wear gloves, so I assume someone used it as

225

a cloth, perhaps to wipe up some spillage. I threw it in the ditch on my way home.'

'Was it stained crimson, then?' demanded Michael.

William shrugged. 'I think so. I did not look very closely.'

'Was it human blood?' pressed Michael mercilessly. 'I am sure you noticed the colour.'

'Well, I did not,' snapped William, becoming agitated. 'The glove is almost certainly irrelevant, as I told you. You forced me to mention it, even though I am sure it means nothing, so do not try to batter me with it. It could have been in the church for weeks.'

'Actually, it could not,' said Bartholomew. 'I swept the nave myself the day before all this happened. There were no gloves lying around then, because I would have noticed.'

And he knew he had done a thorough job, because he had gone to the church for some peace. His students had been engaged in a lively debate in his room, the conclave had contained William and his accusing stares, and the streets were full of patients who wanted to tell him about their ailments. He had sought refuge in St Michael's, and had spent an hour with a broom, enjoying the solitude and the act of doing something that did not require him to think.

William rounded on him. 'You were alone there? Here is something you have kept to yourself! You might have used the opportunity to despoil the font, leaving it for me to find the next day.'

'You are the one with the sinister knowledge of blood, not him,' retorted Michael. 'Incidentally, was it Mildenale who told you to give Langelee that particular grace to read just now?'

'What if it was?' demanded William. 'He is right.

Matthew *does* fraternise with unsuitable people, such as Mother Valeria. I do not want it said that my College houses warlocks.'

'Has it occurred to you that no one would say anything, if you did not give these rumours credence?' asked Michael archly. 'If you were to tell everyone they are untrue, rather than race to condemn him as a necromancer?'

'I did not start these tales,' objected William. 'Magister Arderne did. He was the first to say—'

'His lies would have been forgotten by now, had you not kept them alive,' snarled Michael. 'If people do take against Michaelhouse it will be *your* fault, not Matt's.'

'No!' cried William. 'Can you not see what is happening? Satan is putting evil thoughts in your head. Mildenale is right: the Sorcerer is becoming more powerful by the day, and we must do all we can to fight him. People are leaving the Church in droves, and—'

'Yes, they are,' flashed Michael. 'However, they would be less inclined to go if the Church's chief proponents were not so frighteningly dogmatic. Your zeal is doing more harm than the Sorcerer, Mother Valeria and all the other witches put together.'

'Was William right about the blood, Matt?' asked the monk, as they walked across the yard, heading for the gate. It was time to speak to Spynk about Danyell again. 'Was it human? You told me it was impossible to tell, and it did not occur to me to question your opinion.'

'I cannot tell the difference, and there was not much of it, anyway – no more than a splash, as you said. Rougham and Paxtone take ten times that amount when they bleed their patients.'

Michael shuddered. 'What do you think about this glove?'

Bartholomew looked away, so the monk would not see the unease he was experiencing. 'William threw it away, so I do not see how it can be of any use as a clue.'

But Michael was not so easily deceived. 'Prevaricating with me will not work for three reasons. I know you too well. You are by far the worst liar in Cambridge. And I happen to be aware, as do you, that one person *always* wears gloves, no matter how hot the weather.'

'Mother Valeria,' said Bartholomew heavily. 'I was not sure you had made the connection.'

'And you were not going to enlighten me,' said Michael tartly, 'which would have been wrong. She is a witch, and leaving blood in churches may well be part of some ritual she performs.'

'Others wear gloves, too,' said Bartholomew, alarmed that the old woman might be implicated in the strange events. 'Or perhaps the culprit wore them to keep his hands clean. This glove does not necessarily imply that Valeria is responsible.'

'No, but it implies that we should ask her about it – a treat I shall leave to you, since you seem to be the best of friends these days.'

'She will not be responsible, Brother. She has been in the town for years and has never engaged in this sort of behaviour before. It will be the Sorcerer. After all, these odd events have coincided with his sudden rise to fame. And Valeria told me his magic is more dangerous than hers, which suggests he engages in activities other witches do not condone. Like putting blood in fonts.'

Michael did not answer, but his frown showed he was considering the physician's points. They began to walk up St Michael's Lane towards the High Street. Three beige dogs lay panting in the shade at the side of the alley. Bartholomew felt sorry for them, and fetched a bowl of water from the porters' lodge. Nearby, sparrows twittered as they took dust baths, and the monk gagged as they passed the back of Gonville Hall; the runnel that carried the College's waste to the river had been dry for so long that there was a blockage, and the resulting stench was eye-watering. Michael was still hacking when they reached the High Street, and his tears meant he could not see where he was going. He bumped heavily into someone walking in the opposite direction.

'Have a care, Brother,' cried Sheriff Tulyet, grabbing Bartholomew in an attempt to keep his balance. 'A man of your girth cannot thunder around the town with no thought to other pedestrians.'

'I am not fat,' said Michael immediately. He had barely noticed the collision, but the Sheriff was less than half his weight and was lucky to be standing. 'I just have big bones. Tell him, Matt.'

'The biggest in Cambridge,' said Bartholomew obligingly. The monk was always ordering him to invent anatomical excuses for his lard, and he had given up trying to explain that the size of his bones had nothing to do with his impressive girth.

In deference to the heat, Tulyet had dispensed with his robes of office, and wore a plain shirt and loose leggings. He looked a good deal more comfortable than the scholars in their obligatory habits and tabards. His light brown hair, elfin face and insubstantial beard led some men to underestimate him, a mistake no one made twice. He possessed a sharp mind and a keen sense of

229

justice, and townsmen and scholars alike knew they were lucky in his appointment.

'Lord, but it is hot,' he said, wiping his face with a piece of linen. 'Will you come to the Brazen George and allow me to buy you some ale?'

'If you insist,' said Michael, immediately heading for the tavern that was one of his favourite places. It should have been out of bounds to him, but he had never let the University's ban on scholars entering alehouses interfere with his creature comforts. He opened the door and made a beeline for a small room at the back, which was private and secluded.

'I suppose you want to talk about Goldynham,' said Bartholomew, when they were settled on a bench with a jug of ale. It was not as cool as it should have been, and the pot-boy apologised for the cloudiness, which he blamed on the weather. 'But we have no idea who hauled him from his grave.'

'Is that why you were walking towards Michaelhouse?' asked Michael. 'To mull over the case with us?'

'Actually, I was on my way to discuss Sewale Cottage with your Master,' said Tulyet. 'But yes, I do want to know your theories about Goldynham. The sooner we have the culprit under lock and key, the sooner our town will become peaceful again.'

'You expect trouble?' asked Bartholomew uneasily. 'More riots?'

'Not in the sense of the ones we had earlier this year, where University and town pitted themselves against each other. But I do not like this sudden interest in witchery – or in this almost universal belief that the Sorcerer is about to offer our citizens a viable alternative to the Church. The Church is its own worst enemy in that respect – letting the likes of William and Mildenale plead its case. And, I am afraid to say, the Bishop does not help, either.'

'You mean because he is a criminal?' asked Bartholomew baldly.

Tulyet nodded. 'Had he been a layman, he would have been hanged by now. But I am more interested in Cambridge than in de Lisle. We need to learn who is unearthing these corpses before there is trouble between those who adhere to orthodox religion, and those who think there is something better to be had.'

Michael sighed. 'This town! When one rift heals, it does not take long for another to develop. And you have not been here much of late, Dick. I hear you have been chasing highwaymen.'

Tulyet nodded a second time. 'A particularly violent band of robbers has been operating on the Huntingdon Way. I would just as soon stay here and quell this trouble with the Sorcerer, but the King dislikes villains terrorising his highways, so I am duty bound to concentrate on them.'

Michael's eyes narrowed. 'You have never let the King dictate your priorities before. And Goldynham was a burgess, so the fate of his corpse comes under your jurisdiction, not mine. *Ergo*, you have another reason for preferring to chase thieves.'

Tulyet laughed. 'I should have known better than try to deceive you. The truth is that Goldynham and I had a long-standing disagreement. People know I disliked him, so it would be better if you were to investigate his desecration.'

'What was the argument about?' asked Bartholomew.

'I own a tome called the *Book of Consecrations*, and

231

Goldynham wanted to buy it. However, it belonged to my father, and it is not for sale. He was furious when I refused him, and used all manner of sly tactics to make me change my mind. He even attempted to steal it.'

Michael was puzzled; townsfolk did not usually go to such lengths over books. 'Why did he want it so badly?'

Tulyet shrugged. 'I really cannot imagine – I have never read the thing. But it was one of my father's most prized possessions, and I want to pass it to my son in time. I will never sell it.'

Bartholomew raised his eyebrows, suspecting they still did not have the whole truth. 'And is there yet another side to the quarrel? Perhaps one that involves Dickon?'

Eight-year old Dickon was the Sheriff's only child, and the apple of his father's eye. He was large for his age, and a bully. The servants were terrified of him, while other parents had banned him from their homes. For an intelligent man, Tulyet was strangely blind when it came to Dickon, and refused to believe anything bad about him. There was a rumour, started by Cynric, that Dickon was not Tulyet's offspring at all, but the Devil's, and Dickon's aggression, cunning and total lack of charm meant most of the town was ready to believe it.

'Goldynham accused Dickon of throwing mud and calling him names,' admitted Tulyet tightly. 'It was all lies, of course.'

'Perhaps Dickon is the Sorcerer,' murmured Michael to Bartholomew. 'And spends his nights excavating the corpses of his enemies. God knows, he has enough of them. Including me – I cannot abide the brat.'

'Incidentally, it is not just excavated corpses that are adding fuel to the rumours about witches,' said Tulyet, straining to hear what the monk was saying. 'There are other incidents, too.'

'Such as the blood in our font?' asked Michael.

'Actually, I was thinking about the magic circle that was drawn outside Sewale Cottage,' replied the Sheriff.

'What magic circle?' asked Bartholomew.

'Someone chalked a peculiar design on Margery's doorstep the day she died,' explained Michael. 'I scuffed it out, because I did not want folk chatting about it. But we do not know it was a *magic* circle, Dick. It was just a sphere with some meaningless symbols scrawled inside it.'

'That is what magic circles are,' said Bartholomew, surprised Michael had not mentioned it before. 'Covens often develop their own alphabets, which are meaningless to outsiders.'

'Like the religious Guilds, you mean?' asked Tulyet. 'My own Guild of Corpus Christi has secret signs that only we know. We sometimes have them carved on pendants or other jewellery. Look.' He pulled a gold disc on a cord from under his shirt to show them.

It reminded Bartholomew of the talisman Fencotes had found, and he removed it from his bag. 'Have you seen this before? It might belong to Carton's killer, who we think may be the Sorcerer.'

'We have a couple just like it at home,' said Tulyet, giving it a cursory glance. 'Magister Arderne sold them to my wife, although I was not very pleased with her for squandering good money. I use them as parchment-weights. I do not recognise this one, though. Pity. The sooner we have this upstart in the castle gaol, the happier I will be. But I must go. Langelee told me to meet him at ten o'clock, and it must be nearing that time now.'

'You said you were going to discuss Sewale Cottage with him,' said Michael. 'Why? Surely you cannot want to buy it?'

'Actually, I do. It stands near my own house, and will make a pleasant home for Dickon when he comes of age and wants a place of his own. It will be a good investment.'

'It will,' agreed Michael, watching him leave. 'It means he can be rid of the brat as soon as he is old enough to look after himself. And who can blame him?'

Chapter 7

The High Street seemed hotter than ever after the cool of the tavern, and Bartholomew was reminded of a desert he had once crossed. The air was so dry that it had interfered with the experiment he had been running on the packet Carton had found among Thomas's belongings, and given him results that were questionable. He had been obliged to start it a second time.

'So,' summarised Michael as they walked towards the house where Spynk and Cecily were staying, 'I think I understand what is happening now.'

'Do you?' asked Bartholomew tiredly. 'I do not.'

Michael cleared his throat and began to explain, using the pompous tone he often adopted in his lectures. 'A few weeks ago, one of Cambridge's witches decided he could do rather better for himself. He called himself the Sorcerer, and began to dig up corpses, purloin dead men's hands, fill fonts with blood, draw circles and steal goats. As his activities were discussed, people decided to join his coven.'

'Why would they do that?' asked Bartholomew uncertainly.

'It is obvious. First, many folk lost their faith in the Church when the Death took their loved ones. And second, men like William, Thomas, Carton and Mildenale are braying about the return of the plague and how it will claim all the sinners it missed the first time. When priests talk like that, it frightens people – in this case, it has frightened them into the arms of the Sorcerer.'

'All right,' acknowledged Bartholomew cautiously. 'And so the Sorcerer killed Carton because Carton was one of those who spoke out against him?'

'Precisely. All these incidents are connected – even Thomas's death. After all, someone lobbed the stone that put him in need of a physician. I know your initial thought was that it dropped from a roof, but you are almost certainly wrong. After all, Thomas's sudden demise has been a serious blow to those who are doing battle on the Church's side.'

Bartholomew rubbed his eyes. 'So not only did I kill a patient, but I helped a witch grow in power?'

Michael nodded blithely. 'I wonder why the Sorcerer chose to defile Margery and Goldynham in particular – there are plenty of other recent burials to pick from.'

'I have a theory about Goldynham,' said Bartholomew, pushing uncomfortable thoughts of Thomas from his mind. 'Dick clearly has no idea what the *Book of Consecrations* is about, but I do. It is a handbook of necromancy, containing spells for raising demons. You look surprised, Brother, but you should not be – we both know Dick's father experimented with the dark arts after the plague. I assumed he returned to the Church when we exposed him, but perhaps he did not.'

Michael stared at him. 'I am not surprised to learn Tulyet the Elder owned a sinister text, given his penchant for witchery. My amazement stems from the fact that *you* should be familiar with one.'

'I skimmed through it at the University in Padua last year, although it seemed like a lot of nonsense to me. However, it is a famous treatise, and its incantations are alleged to work. Perhaps Goldynham believed in its efficacy, because it sounds as though he was very keen to lay his hands on the thing.'

'Goldynham was a necromancer?' Michael was shocked. 'Is that why he was dug from his grave?'

'I do not know. All I am saying is that if Goldynham was involved in witchcraft, then it means his exhumation may not be as random as we first assumed.'

'And Margery? Was she a witch, too?' demanded Michael. 'A dear, gentle lady who never missed church and who left all her worldly goods to Michaelhouse in exchange for prayers for her soul?'

'Of course not,' replied Bartholomew tiredly. 'Perhaps she *was* random.'

Michael shot him a dubious glance. 'So, your theory is that Goldynham was excavated because he might have been a satanist, but Margery was excavated by chance? I am not sure that explanation is entirely logical. Either witchery is a factor in these desecrations or it is not – you cannot have it both ways. Incidentally, did you know Tulyet the Elder died last year, when you were in France?'

'Yes – you told me when I came home.'

'Dick wanted a Corpse Examiner to inspect the body, on the grounds that his father had been in excellent health and the death was completely unexpected. Rougham obliged, and decided Tulyet had died of a natural seizure.'

237

'Did you believe him?'

'I did at the time, although I confess that now I am not so sure. Perhaps Goldynham did away with him in order to acquire that book.'

'Then he would have taken it immediately, not offered to buy it from Dick later.'

'Just like the Hardys,' said Michael, lost in his thoughts. 'Rougham said they died of natural causes, too. Lord! I hope he did not make a series of terrible mistakes. I have been assuming that the Sorcerer began to gather his power a few weeks ago, but supposing he started to do it last year?'

'You said the Hardys were diabolists themselves, so they and the Sorcerer were on the same side.'

'Or were rivals,' said Michael grimly.

'There is no evidence to support that. And people do die of natural causes, even in Cambridge.'

'But that is the problem, Matt! *Everyone* who perished in Cambridge last year died of "natural causes". Your absence and Rougham's presence may have precipitated something dangerous and foul. And now we are about to reap the consequences.'

Spynk and his wife were in the garden of the High Street house in which they were lodging, sitting under a tree. They were drinking ale, which they offered to share with their visitors, but it had been left in the sun, so was unpalatably hot. Neither scholar took more than a token sip. Spynk waved away Bartholomew's solicitous enquiries about his recent brush with the flux, and said he was weak, but essentially recovered.

'Fourteen marks,' he said, as Michael sat on the bench and attempted to find a position where flecks of sunlight did not touch him. Bartholomew leaned against a nearby wall, in the shade.

'What?' snapped Michael irritably, squinting up at the sky and moving slightly to his left.

'For Sewale Cottage,' said Spynk. 'Fourteen marks. That is higher than the last bid made by Barnwell. And if you ensure my offer is favourably received, I will give you a bale of silk.'

'I shall bear it in mind,' said Michael, flapping furiously at a wasp that hovered around his face. 'But we are not here to discuss property. We want to talk about Danyell.'

'You caught the villain who stole his hand?' asked Spynk eagerly. 'At last! Who is it? Scholar or townsman? I cannot see why either should have taken against us, given that we are strangers here, but this is an odd sort of place.'

'Our enquiries are continuing, so we have no culprit yet,' replied Michael coolly. 'And why are you so keen to buy Sewale Cottage, if you find Cambridge an "odd sort of place"?'

'Oddness does not bother my husband,' said Cecily with a smirk. 'And he is prepared to overlook a great deal if folk buy his goods. He plans to spend a lot of time here in the future, selling to the Colleges and wealthy townsmen, and says I am to come with him. Will that please you, Doctor?'

Heat and a lack of sleep had combined to make Bartholomew drowsy, and he had not given the discussion his full attention. Thus he was not sure how to reply.

'Yes,' he said, hoping it was the right answer. He saw a frown cross Spynk's face. 'Probably.'

Cecily lowered her eyelashes and smiled. 'I thought it

might. I suspect you are a man who likes having friends to visit of an evening. To walk with them in quiet places.'

Bartholomew blinked, not sure where the conversation was going, and was relieved when Spynk stepped in and changed its direction. 'I learned something disturbing yesterday, Brother. A clothier named Stanmore told me you were the eyes and ears of the Bishop of Ely. That you are his spy.'

Bartholomew seriously doubted his brother-in-law had said any such thing. Stanmore was far too sensible to risk the Senior Proctor's ire by gossiping about him to strangers. He said so.

'Well, perhaps he did not use the term *spy*,' admitted Spynk. 'But that is what you are, regardless.'

Michael's expression was glacial, and the hapless wasp met a sudden end between the table and his fist. 'I keep de Lisle apprised of University affairs. Why? Is there a problem?'

'Not with you,' said Spynk. 'But there is a huge one with your Bishop. His men have bullied me for years, and I detest the man.'

'Ah, yes,' said Michael flatly. 'You are one of the people who complained about him to the King. That is why you and Danyell went to London. I had forgotten.'

'Well, someone needed to take a stand,' said Spynk stiffly. 'De Lisle cannot be allowed to terrorise anyone he pleases. And do not tell me he is innocent, because there were sixteen charges in all, including arson, murder, abduction, extortion and blackmail. Why do you think he has fled to Avignon? Because he knows there is not a court in the country that will find in his favour.'

'I do not think this is the best way to secure Michaelhouse's good graces, dearest,' said Cecily with a

240

good deal of sarcasm. 'And I am sure Brother Michael knows all about the Bishop's intrigues.'

'He has nothing to do with them,' said Bartholomew sharply, unwilling for people to think the monk complicit in anything de Lisle might have done.

Cecily came to stand closer to him than was decent, and he recalled thinking she had probably behaved improperly with Danyell, too. He supposed she could not help herself, and tried to ignore it.

'Are you sure about that, Doctor?' she asked, adjusting the neckline on her kirtle. It slipped, revealing more frontage than was civilised. 'Every man has his secrets. And so does every woman.'

Bartholomew shot her husband an uneasy glance, but Spynk's attention was on Michael, whom he was regarding minutely, as if he thought he might see something there if he looked hard enough. The physician was tempted to tell him not to waste his time – he had known Michael for years, and the monk was not that easily read. Indeed, there were still occasions when Michael said or did things that made Bartholomew think he barely knew him at all.

'I am a good judge of people, Brother,' said the merchant eventually. 'And I sense you are an honest, straightforward fellow. You will have had nothing to do with the Bishop's reign of terror.'

Bartholomew stifled a laugh, thinking Spynk was not as good a judge as he imagined; Michael was the last man who could be considered straightforward. Or honest, for that matter. Then he was obliged to jump away smartly, when Cecily edged even closer to him.

'You examined Danyell's body,' she said, reaching out to rest her hand on his chest when his sideways jig trapped him between the wall and a tree. 'Are you sure he was not murdered?'

'No one can ever be sure about such matters,' replied Bartholomew. When she frowned, considering the implications of his remark, he seized the opportunity to slither past her. His new position put him in the full glare of the sun, but that seemed a small price to pay.

'What do you mean?' demanded Spynk. His eyes narrowed as he became aware of the curious dance that was taking place between his wife and her intended victim.

'What I say,' replied Bartholomew, balancing on the balls of his feet, ready to initiate evasive manoeuvres if Cecily advanced again. 'Determining causes of death is not an exact art. However, your descriptions of the pain Danyell had been experiencing in his chest and arm strongly indicate a natural seizure. Why do you ask whether he was murdered?'

'Because the case against the Bishop is weakened without his testimony,' replied Spynk, going to take Cecily's hand and pushing her rather unceremoniously on to the bench next to Michael. She glowered sulkily at him. 'And we are suspicious of it. Perhaps de Lisle ordered Danyell's death.'

'De Lisle is not stupid,' said Michael, standing hastily and going to lean against the wall. 'He would not kill in any circumstances, but he is not such a fool as to attack someone who has challenged him in a court of law. How will he prove his innocence, if the complainant is dead?'

Spynk shot him a look that said it was impossible de Lisle could be innocent. 'What about Danyell's clothes?' he demanded. 'Have you found them yet?'

'His body had been stripped when Doctor Bartholomew found it,' explained Cecily, when Michael looked blank. 'He said Danyell had been dead for hours, so there was plenty of time for thieves to act.'

'Damned vultures!' snapped Spynk, resting a heavy hand on her shoulder as she attempted to rise. 'They even stole the sample stone he carried. I saw it under his arm when he left the house that night.'

'More importantly, what about his missing hand?' asked Cecily, trying to squirm away. Spynk's grip intensified, and she winced. 'The Bishop—'

'The missing hand had nothing to do with de Lisle,' said Michael quickly. He did not want her to start the rumour that the Bishop had a penchant for dead men's limbs, because that was a tale that *would* be popular. The prelate's haughty manners had not earned him many friends in Cambridge.

Spynk did not look convinced. 'Perhaps his henchmen took it, to prove Danyell was dead.'

'What henchmen?' asked Bartholomew, puzzled. 'You mean his vicars?'

'I mean the louts who run his estates. There are about fifteen of them, all surly villains who would slit anyone's throat for a piece of silver. The two worst are Osbern le Hawker and John Brownsley. Osbern persecuted me while Brownsley led the attack on Danyell's house.'

Bartholomew was not sure what he was saying. 'Are you telling us these men are in Cambridge?'

Spynk looked shifty. 'Well, I have not seen them personally, but Danyell's death has their mark upon it. They are the kind of villains who would hack a limb from a man while he still lives.'

'The physical evidence suggests the hand was taken *after* Danyell died,' said Bartholomew. 'I know this because the blood vessels of a corpse are—'

'The Bishop and his people played no role in Danyell's death,' interrupted Michael, before the Spynks could be told something they would probably rather not know. 'Your friend died of natural causes, and someone later stole his fingers because witches are rather active here at the moment. However, the outrage will not go unpunished, and I will catch the man who desecrated him. But I need your help.'

'We know about Cambridge's warlocks,' said Cecily, finally managing to escape her husband's restraining grip. Bartholomew aimed for the table, putting it between her and him. 'There was a tale only this morning that a silversmith dug his way clear of his grave in order to visit his favourite tavern. Perhaps you are right in claiming that this has nothing to do with de Lisle, Brother. It will not be the first time my husband has been proven wrong.'

Spynk glared at her, but then a crafty expression infused his face. 'If we help you prove the Bishop is innocent of harming Danyell, will you back my bid to buy Sewale Cottage?'

'No,' replied Michael curtly. 'You will help me because obstructing my investigation might see you in prison. The house business is a completely separate matter.'

Spynk was unperturbed by the threat, and treated Michael to a conspiratorial wink. 'I understand. You say this because you still want the silk I offered earlier.'

'I will help you, Brother,' said Cecily, cutting across the indignant denial. She stalked provocatively towards the table; Bartholomew tensed, waiting to see which way he would need to dodge to avoid her.

'She knows nothing,' said Spynk contemptuously. He turned to the monk. 'However, I can repeat what I told you when we first learned Danyell was dead. He was a

244

regular visitor to our Norwich home – I cannot recall all the times I found Cecily entertaining him. When I heard de Lisle's other victims were going to formalise their complaints in London, I asked him to travel with us, and do likewise.'

'He was the best company in Norfolk,' added Cecily, shooting her husband a look that showed the remark was intended to wound. 'He made me laugh. I imagine you like a joke, too, Doctor?'

'He never laughs with women,' said Michael, moving to interpose his bulk between predator and prey. 'He prefers men.'

'The best ones always do,' sighed Cecily, with a grimace of resignation.

'We are supposed to be talking about Danyell,' said Michael irritably, trying to bring the discussion back on track. 'You told me the last time we spoke that he went for a walk alone, even though he was not in the best of health. Why did he do that?'

'Perhaps he wanted to consult a *medicus*,' replied Spynk, shrugging in a way that said he thought the question was an irrelevancy.

'He did not see Paxtone, Rougham or me,' said Bartholomew. 'And we are the only physicians in Cambridge. Or are you saying he went to consult a different kind of healer?'

'He might have done,' admitted Spynk. His tone was distinctly cagey. 'He thought witches' cures are more efficacious than those of book-trained men.'

'I see,' said Michael. 'What else did he think? That sorcery offers more answers than the Church?'

Cecily smiled at him, and ran her fingers down his sleeve. 'We all think that, Brother. I used to be a devout

245

Christian, but then the plague came and showed me that priests are no better than the rest of us. However, I am ready to be persuaded otherwise.' She winked at him.

'My wife makes a good point,' said Spynk, stepping forward to grab her hand and pull her back. 'Who can respect an organisation that has de Lisle as one of its leaders?'

'De Lisle worked untiringly during the Death,' said Michael quietly. 'Some prelates deserted their posts, but he went out among the sick and the dying, giving what aid he could.'

'Perhaps that was why so many of his parishioners died,' suggested Spynk. 'God declined to answer the petitions of such a sinner. Do not try to make him a saint, Brother. He is a villain, and men like him are the reason why so many of us have lost our faith – not in God, but in the Church.'

'The Church is run by *men*,' added Cecily, her eyes fixed on the monk. They seemed to glisten. 'And we all know how fallible *men* can be.'

'Danyell,' prompted Michael, ignoring her. 'You suggested he went out that night because he wanted a cure for his illness. Which healer did he intend to consult?'

'He heard Mother Valeria was good,' replied Cecily.

'No,' said Bartholomew, his mind working fast. 'You claimed a few moments ago that a sample stone was stolen from his body, but why should he carry such a thing to Valeria? It sounds to me as though he was going to see a potential client. You have developed business interests here, so perhaps he did, too. He was a mason, and there is always a demand for good craftsmen.'

Spynk inclined his head. 'You may be right. He specialised in tile floors, and never lacked for clients. I hear

Sewale Cottage is in need of a new floor and that Michaelhouse will lay one as part of the terms of its sale. You should ask whether any of your colleagues secured his services, Brother. After all, he did die opposite that very house. And then he died before he could buy his cure.'

'No Michaelhouse Fellow would have opened such negotiations without telling the rest of us,' said the monk. 'It is not how we operate.'

'Really?' asked Spynk slyly. 'Your Franciscans are a law unto themselves, and neither you nor the Master seem able to silence their vicious tongues. Maybe one of *them* decided to see if he could get a good price for a new floor.'

'And then chopped off Danyell's hand to make it look as though witches killed him,' added Cecily.

'Cecily has taken a fancy to you, Matt,' said Michael, as they left Spynk's house. 'Perhaps she hopes her amorous attentions will improve their chances of getting Sewale Cottage.'

'Her interest faded the moment you made that remark about me preferring men. Now she will concentrate her efforts on you instead.'

Michael did not seem as discomfited as the physician felt he should have been. He smiled. 'I will be a better proposition, anyway. You pay little attention to what transpires at Fellows' meetings, so she was wasting her time if she expected you to put in a useful word on her husband's behalf.'

'I doubt that was her intention – there is scant affection in her marriage, and I suspect she is more likely to hinder Spynk than help him. Shall we go to see Mother Valeria, to ask if Danyell visited her the night he died?'

'You can do that later, after dark, when hopefully no one will see you. We need to know whether she gave him a "cure" that may – deliberately or otherwise – have hastened his end.'

Bartholomew did not like the implications of that remark. 'She is a healer, Brother. She does not kill her clients. Besides, I thought you had accepted my diagnosis that Danyell died of natural causes.'

'I am inclined to keep an open mind, because nothing is as it should be at the moment. Perhaps the Sorcerer has an ability to bring about seizures, and saw Danyell – who seems to have been a fellow heathen – as competition. Or perhaps Valeria killed him because she wanted a dead man's hand. You told me yourself that such items are believed to hold dark power.'

Despite the warmth of the sun, Bartholomew shuddered. 'I will talk to her tonight.'

The monk sighed. 'I dislike this kind of case – where we are obliged to tackle people's religious convictions. I can tell Eyton that Goldynham did not scratch his own way out of his grave until I am blue in the face, but there is nothing I can do to *make* him believe me.'

'It cannot last. Something will happen to show that all these events have perfectly logical explanations.'

'Unfortunately, I suspect folk will be looking for supernatural ones for everything from now on, and that sort of thing is virtually impossible to combat. For example, William used a piece of cheese to mark his place in a library book last week, and it left a greasy stain. Deynman scattered the book with mugwort – a witch's remedy – and this morning the blemish was gone. He says the Sorcerer is responsible, because the book was about astrology.'

Bartholomew looked sheepish. 'That was me. I rubbed out the mark with chalk powder, because I could not sleep after the business with Goldynham, and it seemed a good way to pass the time.'

Michael grimaced. 'But no one will believe you. It is much more exciting to think the Sorcerer mended the book, than a physician with chalk and time on his hands.'

They walked in silence for a while. It was a market day, and wares were being ferried to and from the stalls behind St Mary the Great. The heat was causing tempers to run high, and there was a fierce confrontation between Isnard and a butcher. The butcher was incensed by the accusation that he was selling bad produce, and hurled a kidney at the bargeman. It missed and struck a dog, which sniffed the missile, then trotted away with a whine and its tail between its legs.

'Agatha says she will not buy any more meat until the Sorcerer has mended the weather,' said Michael unhappily, watching the Sheriff's men step in when punches began to fly. 'According to her, he intends to chant a few spells that will bring the heatwave to an end.'

'And when the weather breaks of its own accord, he will say it was his doing. He cannot lose.'

Suddenly, Michael narrowed his eyes. 'Refham is over there with Blaston the carpenter. What is a decent man like Blaston doing in such low company?'

'I barely know Refham – his forge is out on the Huntingdon Way, so he does not spend much time in the town – but he does not seem overly pleasant.'

'He is sly and greedy,' declared Michael uncompromisingly. 'Is money changing hands between him and

Blaston? Yes, it is! And look at the furtive cant of Refham's eyes. Joan is there, too, shielding what is happening from passers-by. It is clear they are up to no good.'

Blaston was one of Bartholomew's patients, along with his wife Yolande and their twelve children. He was an amiable, trusting soul, and the physician did not like the notion that Refham might be in the process of cheating him. He started to walk towards them. Joan saw him coming and grabbed her husband's arm, trying to steer him down an alley, but Refham was not so easily shifted. He freed his hand impatiently, his attention fixed on the carpenter.

'Doctor!' exclaimed Blaston pleasantly, when he turned to see what was causing Joan to act so strangely. 'Do you know David Refham? He is a blacksmith by trade, and—'

'I have not bothered with that work for some time now,' interrupted Refham. 'Manual labour is not for me. I prefer making money in other ways, such as by the sale of the properties I inherited. My aim is to buy a cottage in Luton and do nothing but lie in the sun and drink ale.'

'What do you want with us?' asked Joan, regarding the two scholars with barely concealed dislike. 'If you think you can persuade us to lower the price on those houses, you can think again. We mean to get as much as we can, and they will be sold to the highest bidder.'

'Everyone hates the University, so you will not find many townsmen sympathetic to your plight,' added Refham nastily. 'You will have to pay what we decide we should have.'

'On the contrary,' said Michael with quiet dignity. 'Your mother's decency and kindness made her a popular lady, and lots of folk deplore the way you are flouting her last wishes.'

Refham's expression hardened. 'It is none of their damned business, and I shall do what I like with my inheritance. And now you can leave us alone, because Blaston and I have business to discuss.'

'What kind of business?' asked Bartholomew.

'None that is your affair,' said Joan indignantly. 'Go away, or I shall summon the Sheriff and tell him you are harassing innocent citizens.'

'There is no need for quarrelling,' said Blaston, dismayed by the hostile remarks that were being bandied back and forth. 'And no need for secrecy, either. I am delighted to be doing business with you, Refham, and do not see why we should keep it secret.' He turned to Bartholomew and smiled, genuinely pleased. 'He has asked me to do some work for him, on those three shops.'

'You mean the ones we are thinking of buying?' asked Michael uneasily. He exchanged a brief glance with Bartholomew. What was Refham up to?

Blaston grinned happily. 'He wants them in the best possible condition for when he makes his sale, and has asked me to replace the old rafters in the roof. It is a big job, and I could do with extra money at the moment, because Yolande is expecting again. This time, I think it might be twins, she is so big.'

'I chose Blaston because I knew he needed the work,' said Refham. His expression was unreadable and Bartholomew immediately suspected trickery.

'Are you being paid in advance?' the physician asked the carpenter, suspecting he could guess exactly what Refham planned to do.

'I am to buy the timber myself and start work

251

tomorrow,' replied Blaston airily. 'I will be paid half when the work is finished, and the rest when the buildings are sold.'

'That is not a good—' began Bartholomew, appalled.

Refham spat on his hand and thrust it towards the carpenter, an indication that he wanted the transaction agreed without further delay. Before Bartholomew could stop him, Blaston had seized it. Refham sneered at the physician. 'The deal is made, and no one can undo it now.'

'I will not renege,' said Blaston, misunderstanding him. 'You can trust me to be honourable.'

'I know,' said Refham. 'Come, Joan. Let us celebrate our good fortune with a cup of wine.'

'Note they are going to celebrate *their* good fortune,' said Michael to Blaston when the pair had gone. 'And did not invite you to join them. I doubt you will benefit from this arrangement.'

But Blaston was too gleeful to listen to doom-merchants, and Bartholomew recalled he had always been that way. It explained why he was poor, while his fellow craftsmen earned a decent living.

'Yolande will be delighted,' he crowed. 'We are desperately short of money, and have nothing put by for the winter. And as she is with child, she cannot work.'

Yolande supplemented the family income by prostitution, and Bartholomew had long been fascinated by how many of her brood bore likenesses to prominent burgesses and scholars. However, she could not ply her trade when she was pregnant, and the family would find the winter hard.

'There is not much work for skilled carpenters these days,' Blaston went on. 'There are too many itinerants who offer to do the job for half the price. Of course, their work is no good, but by the time the customer sees it, it is too late – his money has gone.'

'Tell Refham to buy the materials you need,' said Bartholomew, wishing the carpenter had let his wife negotiate the deal. Yolande would not have been so gullible.

'His money is stored at Barnwell Priory for safekeeping, and he asked me to pay for the wood so as to move matters along.' Blaston nodded his hands together, delighted with the bargain he thought he had secured. 'The sooner I finish, the sooner I will be reimbursed.'

'His family will starve,' said Michael, watching the carpenter saunter away. 'While Refham and Joan grow fat on the fruits of their dishonesty. Lord, how I loathe that man!'

It was mid-afternoon, and Bartholomew thought the day was slipping away far too fast. They reached Bene't College, where their knock was answered by Younge. The porter lounged against the door with a stem of grass between his teeth, regarding the Senior Proctor and his Corpse Examiner with disdain.

'What do you want?' he demanded.

'Nothing I am prepared to discuss with you,' retorted Michael coolly.

'Then you cannot come in.' Three of Younge's cronies came to stand behind him. 'I am head porter here, and no one is admitted without my say-so. Bene't is different from other Colleges because of its ties with the town Guild of Corpus Christi. You do not have the same sway here as you do in the likes of Peterhouse or Clare.'

Calmly, Michael reached out, placed a hand in the middle of Younge's chest and pushed. The porter tried to resist the monk's forward momentum, but Michael put his full weight behind the manoeuvre and it was not many moments before he was through the door. Bartholomew followed uneasily.

'Now,' said the monk pleasantly. 'Go and tell Master Heltisle we are waiting.'

Younge drew his dagger, but there was uncertainty in his eyes, and the move was more to prevent a loss of face in front of his colleagues than a serious attempt to intimidate the Senior Proctor.

'Send him back to his Chancellor in pieces,' suggested one, outraged by the monk's audacity. 'He has no right to throw his weight around here.'

'Especially when there is so much of it,' quipped another.

It was the wrong thing to say to a man who was sensitive about his appearance. Michael put his hands on his hips and fixed the joker with a stare that made the laughter die in his throat. 'Tell Heltisle I am here,' he ordered. His tight voice indicated he was only just controlling his anger.

'Bugger off, monk!' blustered Younge. 'You cannot tell me what to—'

Michael moved faster than Bartholomew would have thought possible for so large a man, and suddenly Younge was pinned against a wall with the monk's fingers around his throat. The porter promptly dropped his dagger and began scrabbling at his neck. Bartholomew saw that his feet had almost been lifted clean off the ground and he was balanced on the very tips of his toes.

'I could teach you some manners,' said the monk in a voice, that was low and dangerous. 'But I am a man of God, so I try to avoid violence if possible. So, you will conduct me to Master Heltisle, and if I have occasion to visit Bene't again, you will not question my orders. Do I make myself clear?'

Younge nodded hastily, and the monk released him so abruptly that he slumped to the ground. He rubbed his throat, fixing Michael with a look of such loathing that Bartholomew was alarmed.

'I do not think Younge will give me any more trouble now,' said Michael to Bartholomew, after the head porter had picked himself up and was leading the way across the courtyard. 'Especially after I send Meadowman to collect a fine of three groats, which is the going rate for annoying the Senior Proctor.'

'Brother Michael,' said Heltisle in surprise, standing as the monk strode into Bene't's fine hall. 'What are you doing here?' He glared at Younge. 'And why did you not announce him, as I have trained you to do?'

The scholars of Bene't had gathered to hear a sermon, which was being delivered by Eyton. Bartholomew had heard Goldynham's name being bellowed from the yard, and knew exactly what subject the vicar had chosen for his discourse.

'Younge is not very good at his job,' said Michael to the Master, shooting the porter a disparaging glance. 'Furthermore, he and his friends are surly, aggressive and stupid.'

'That may be so, but they repel unwanted tradesmen and protect us during riots,' countered Heltisle. 'They are also loyal, and would not hesitate to risk their lives on our behalf – unlike the staff at Michaelhouse, who would slink away at the first sign of trouble.'

'Cynric would not,' said Bartholomew, offended that the likes of Younge should be considered better than his devoted book-bearer.

The look Heltisle gave him was full of dislike. 'No, but he would arm himself with all manner of pagan charms before he joined in any battle. He is the most superstitious man in the town.'

'Actually, I suspect that honour goes to the Sorcerer,' said Eyton cheerfully, coming to join them. 'He is superstitious – and powerful, too. Indeed, it was he who gave Goldynham the strength to dig his way out of his own grave. Is that not true, Heltisle?'

'Yes,' replied Heltisle coolly, although Bartholomew could not tell whether he really agreed with the vicar. He had never been very good at reading the Master of Bene't.

Michael sighed irritably. 'How many more times must we go through this? I cannot imagine why you, an ordained priest, must persist in spreading these ridiculous tales.'

'They are not tales, Brother,' said Eyton, his expression earnest. 'I know what I saw. The Sorcerer is gaining in power, and only a fool refuses to see it. The Church must stand firm against him.'

'Bene't will stand firm,' said Heltisle. He smiled rather slyly. 'However, just in case matters do not go according to plan, I have commissioned a special charm, which is guaranteed to keep the Sorcerer away from our portals when he assumes his mantle of power on Saturday night.'

Eyton beamed at him, then turned to the monk. 'He commissioned it from me, and I prepared it last night with a piece of the Host, a drop of goat's blood, a dab of honey and a clove of garlic. This time-honoured combination is highly effective in keeping demons at bay. Oh, and I soaked it in a bucket of holy water, too.' His expression clouded. 'Although I left the holy water in the church porch last night, and this morning I discovered someone had washed his hands in it. Can you credit such sacrilege?'

'I will absolve you later, Matt,' whispered Michael, seeing the physician's stricken expression.

'Perhaps you will continue with your lecture, vicar,' said Heltisle to the priest. 'I can see our students are itching to hear what else you have to say about sin and the Devil.'

The students' rolled eyes suggested they would rather listen to what the Senior Proctor had to say to their Master, but Eyton skipped merrily back to the dais and resumed his tirade.

'I am surprised you let him loose on your scholars,' said Michael, after listening for a few moments. 'His theology seems more firmly based in folklore than in religion, while his logic is seriously flawed. Why have you given him free rein to rant?'

'Because it is an excuse to keep the students indoors,' replied Heltisle. 'I do not want them out when trouble is brewing. Besides, they are supposed to be keeping track of the number of doctrinal errors he makes, and there is a prize for the lad with the highest score.'

Bartholomew tried to stop himself from gaping as Eyton informed his audience that a dash of bat dung rendered holy water ten times more powerful than the normal stuff. 'I cannot imagine a Michaelhouse priest making that sort of claim.'

Heltisle treated him to an unpleasant look. 'William might. His logic is just as dismal as Eyton's, which probably explains why they are friends. Unfortunately, the Sorcerer's rise has led them both to be more outspoken – Eyton insulted Refham last night, and I am trying to

257

stay on the right side of him, in the hope that he will give Bene't some of his mother's money. But enough of my problems. What brings you to our humble abode, Brother?'

Bene't was not humble. It comprised some of the most sumptuous dwellings in Cambridge, and was often patronised by wealthy barons. Its splendid hall boasted a beautifully polished floor, and there was a wooden gallery at one end, which allowed a choir to sing during the foundation's many feasts. The long oaken table was generally acknowledged to be one of the finest pieces of furniture in the town, which delighted Robert de Blaston, who had made it.

'Goldynham,' said Michael. 'We understand he had an interest in the dark arts.'

Heltisle raised his eyebrows in surprise. 'I seriously doubt it – he always struck me as a deeply religious man. In fact, I was thinking only this morning that his death was a blessing in disguise, because I do not think he would have liked living through this business with the Sorcerer.'

'Tell me about your missing goats,' said Michael, changing the subject abruptly. Heltisle blinked at him. 'How many did you lose again?'

'Seven, although not all at once; they went one by one. Eyton tells me the Sorcerer has been stealing them, and thinks I should just let him have them, so as not to annoy him. But goats are expensive, and we are not made of money.'

'Where do you keep these animals?' asked Michael.

Heltisle went to a window and pointed. Outside was a walled garden, containing an orchard of mature fruit trees. The goats roamed freely among them. The walls were well maintained, and the only access was through

258

a gate that stood opposite the porters' lodge. It would not be easy to enter without being seen by Younge and his men – and even more difficult to escape with a goat.

'The gate is always locked at night,' Heltisle went on. 'And my servants are vigilant. I would have thought this was one of the safest compounds in town, and I am amazed that someone has been able to break in. Eyton thinks they might have been removed magically.'

'Perhaps Eyton is partial to goat stew,' murmured Michael to Bartholomew, as they took their leave. 'Because I detect a human hand at work here.'

'So do I,' said Bartholomew. 'Although I suspect the hand is directed by a very clever mind. Heltisle is right: it will not be easy to slip past Younge, grab a goat and leave with no one noticing.'

Michael looked thoughtful, then abruptly headed for the porters' lodge. Bartholomew held his breath as the monk marched inside. Younge was massaging his neck, but his hand dropped to the hilt of his dagger when Michael appeared.

'I am about to look very closely into your missing goats,' said the monk without preamble. 'Is there anything you would like to tell me before I begin? I will not be pleased if I later learn that information has been with-held from me – and when I am not pleased, I fine people.'

'We would never steal from Bene't,' said Younge, understanding perfectly what was being asked. He seemed genuinely shocked by the notion. 'We have no idea who is taking them, but if I catch the villain, he will not live to explain himself. I will run him through.'

The sun was setting in a blaze of red gold as Bartholomew and Michael left Bene't. The monk went to his office in

St Mary the Great, to brief his beadles on the night to come. He ordered them not only to watch for students sneaking illicit cups of ale in the town's taverns, but to be alert for any covens that might convene, too. They nodded obediently, but he suspected they would not do much about the witches; they were superstitious men and would sooner leave such matters well alone. Not for the first time, he felt he was fighting alone, and that the only ally he could trust was Bartholomew.

Meanwhile, several patients had sent summonses for the physician while he had been out, including three new cases of the flux and a crushed finger. The latter was normally the domain of the town's surgeon, but Robin of Grantchester had also been hurt by Magister Arderne's accusations earlier in the year. Now he confined himself to cutting hair and drawing teeth, and could not be persuaded to do anything more complicated. Bartholomew was not sure whether the situation was good or bad: on the one hand, Robin was not a skilled practitioner and lost a large number of clients, but on the other, he was better than having no surgeon at all.

He decided to deal with the finger first, because the victim was a child – one of Stanmore's apprentices, whose hand had been squashed in a door. To reach him, Bartholomew had to walk past Clare College, and he was unfortunate in his timing, because Spaldynge happened to be coming out.

'How many people have you killed today, physician?' the Clare man asked unpleasantly.

'None yet,' said Bartholomew, hot and weary enough to be goaded into responding. 'But that might be about to change. I am getting a bit tired of you and your accusations.'

'Are you threatening me?' demanded Spaldynge, clenching his fists and looking as though he would very much like to use them.

'Yes, I suppose I am,' replied Bartholomew. He thought about the last time he had met Spaldynge, when Carton had been with him. 'My colleague told me about the man you killed – James Kirbee. How can you condemn me, when you are guilty of taking a life yourself?'

Spaldynge's expression became dark and angry. 'You will be sorry you mentioned that.'

'And you will be sorry if you provoke me again,' snapped Bartholomew. 'I was not your family's physician during the plague, and neither were Paxtone and Rougham. Leave us alone.'

There must have been something in his voice that told the Clare man he was treading on dangerous ground, because he growled something unintelligible and slunk away. Bartholomew watched him go and wondered whether he should have applied a little aggression months ago, when Spaldynge had first started issuing his nasty challenges. But confrontation did not come readily to the physician, especially with men who might not be in command of all their faculties, and once Spaldynge was out of sight, Bartholomew felt vaguely ashamed of himself.

He treated the apprentice's injury with a poultice of comfrey, and left him to rest, watched over by solicitous friends. He wished Edith was there, because cronies, no matter how well meaning, were no substitute for her motherly care. Stanmore escorted him to the door.

'You seem to be in town all the time these days,' said Bartholomew. 'When were you last home?'

'Not since Edith left,' replied the merchant. 'Trumpington

is not the same without her, so I engross myself in work – which has paid off, because I have just signed an agreement with Spynk, who can find me a cheaper source of dye for my cloth. And it is advisable to be here when the town is on the verge of one of its episodes, anyway. It means I can protect my property myself, rather than leaving it to my steward.'

'You refer to the unrest brought about by the Sorcerer? He is due to make his appearance on Trinity Eve, apparently.'

'At midnight,' agreed Stanmore. 'He has people seriously rattled, because they are joining his coven in droves – no one wants to be on the losing side. Arblaster and Jodoca must be delighted – the little cadre they established in All Saints has gone from having a dozen members to being the largest in the shire, all in the space of a few weeks.'

'Do you think Arblaster is the Sorcerer, then?' asked Bartholomew, a little surprised. The dung-master had not seemed the type. Of course, he reflected wryly, Arblaster had not seemed the type to be in a Devil-worshipping cult at all, so clearly Bartholomew's notions of what constituted a diabolist were sadly off course. 'Michael has been struggling to learn his identity, but no one is talking.'

'If it is Arblaster, folk will be disappointed,' grinned Stanmore. 'They will not like paying homage to a man who has made his fortune in muck.'

'Hiding his identity until he has accrued a decent amount of power is clever,' said Bartholomew. 'It is difficult to fight someone you do not know and cannot see. He is proving to be a formidable adversary.'

Stanmore nodded. 'The Church has a lot to answer for.'

'What do you mean?'

'I mean that its most vocal proponents are William and Mildenale, who are not nice men – the Sorcerer is a lot more appealing. *He* does not tell us it is our own fault the plague took our loved ones, or that it is sinful to buy good-luck charms from witches. And he cures warts into the bargain.'

'What about Eyton? He is a member of the Church, but his beliefs seem rather more flexible.'

'If all Franciscans were like Eyton, the Church would be a lot more popular. But enough of religion. I hear Michaelhouse is forcing Barnwell, Arblaster, Spynk and Dick Tulyet to bid against each other for Sewale Cottage, and that you are almost certain to sell it for more than it is worth. Is it true?'

'If Arblaster is the Sorcerer, then perhaps we should let him have it,' said Bartholomew. 'We do not want an enraged magician after our blood.'

He had been joking, but Stanmore nodded quite seriously. 'It is certainly something to bear in mind, although I would rather see it go to Dick, personally. He is a friend – you should show him that means something.'

Bartholomew left him, and began to walk to his next patient. He was passing the unkempt jungle of churchyard around St John Zachary when he glimpsed movement. A figure was in the shadows, but the sun was in his eyes and he could not see clearly. It looked to be wearing a long pale cloak and to have a head of thick white hair. He blinked, for his first thought was that it looked like Goldynham. But the silversmith was dead, and lay in St Bene't's Church. Bartholomew squinted against the light and took a step forward, but the figure had gone, and he realised his eyes must have been playing tricks. With a sigh, he went on his way.

The next day, Bartholomew was overwhelmed with demands from patients, and it was late afternoon by the time he had finished with them. His stomach was rumbling, and he realised he had not eaten since breakfast. He went to the Michaelhouse kitchens, where Agatha slouched in her great wicker throne, pulled from its usual place next to the hearth and put near the door, in the hope of catching a breeze. She was fanning herself with the lid of a pot, legs splayed in front of her. She was not alone; Cynric, Mildenale and Langelee sat at the table, a jug of ale in front of them. It was an unusual combination, because Cynric did not usually deign to socialise with scholars, and Mildenale was abstemious in his habits. Langelee, on the other hand, was willing to drink with anyone.

'I noticed the damn thing was missing this afternoon,' Langelee was saying. 'Sometimes, I hate being Master, because as soon as you solve one problem there is another to take its place.'

'There will be a problem if you do not give me some of that ale,' growled Agatha. 'I am parched.'

Mildenale took it to her. She drank noisily, then handed it back. The friar filled it from the barrel that stood at the top of the cellar steps and handed it to Cynric, who thanked him with a nod before passing it to Langelee. Bartholomew looked around for food, but there was none that he could see, and he was not so foolish as to hunt for some while Agatha and the Master were watching. Fellows were expected to buy their own snacks – called 'commons' – and were not supposed to raid the kitchens every time they were peckish. Michael declined to let

264

these rules interfere with his gastronomic requirements, but Bartholomew was not Michael, and he was too hot to engage in the kind of skulduggery it would take to acquire a meal while laundress and Master were nearby. He settled for ale, and was pleasantly surprised to find it sweet and cool.

'What is missing?' he asked of Langelee, as he sat on the bench next to Cynric.

'That guide to witchery you found in Carton's room,' replied the Master. 'He had been planning to burn it, along with other heretical texts – the ones you put in the College library after his death.'

'Those were all religious or philosophical books that have been on the curriculum for decades,' explained Bartholomew, seeing Mildenale's eyes begin to widen in horror. 'Such as Guibert of Nogent's *De Sanctis*.'

'I would never use Guibert in *my* lectures,' said Mildenale in distaste. 'He was a Benedictine, for a start. *And* he hailed from Nogent.' He pursed his lips disapprovingly.

Bartholomew had never understood why a scholar's ideas should be dismissed because of the Order to which he belonged, or because he came from a different country. 'Even if you disapprove of his theology, you must admire the precision of his grammar,' he told the friar reproachfully.

Mildenale thought about it. 'He does use longer sentences than anyone else,' he conceded eventually. 'However, I am disappointed to learn Carton included him among his collection of heretical texts. I was under the impression he had gathered some *really* devilish works – such as this manual for witches.'

'He considered anything written by non-Franciscans

anathema,' said Langelee. 'Except, for some unaccountable reason, books by Greeks on law. Still, I suppose we all have our foibles.'

Mildenale was crestfallen. 'This is a blow! I was hoping he had gathered a chest full of heresy, so we could have a decent pyre in the Market Square – and Guibert, for all his flaws, does not deserve the flames. Unfortunately, now this manual on sorcery has disappeared, I cannot even set fire to that.' He clasped his hands together, and his eyes drifted heavenwards as his lips began to move in prayer, presumably asking to be supplied with something suitably flammable.

'I do not have it,' objected Cynric, when the physician looked at him. 'I handed it back this morning, just as you ordered, although that was a mistake. It would not be missing, if I still had it.'

'He is telling the truth,' said Langelee, seeing Bartholomew's sceptical expression. 'He gave it to me in person.'

'It is no great loss,' said Cynric, refilling the jug and prudently offering Agatha the first mouthful. Her mouth was evidently larger than he imagined, because when she handed it back he was obliged to make another trip to the barrel. 'It contained new snippets but most of it was basic general knowledge.'

Langelee took the jug from him. 'It is a pity it has gone missing now, because it might have been a useful source of information for those of us who are not intimately acquainted with witches and their habits. For example, telling us what the Sorcerer might do on Trinity Eve. Mother Valeria was going on about his predicted début when I went to purchase a charm the other day.'

'You did *what?*' cried Mildenale in horror, while even Bartholomew was taken aback.

Langelee shrugged, clearly thinking the friar was overreacting. 'I wanted a spell that would make Refham relent over selling us his mother's shops. But it transpired to be rather pricey, and required me to break into his house at night and bury a dead rat under his hearth. I decided not to bother.'

'I would have dealt with the dead rat,' said Cynric helpfully.

'Actually, it was the cost that put me off,' confided Langelee. 'I could have managed the rat with no trouble myself, although I appreciate your offer.'

Bartholomew found himself exchanging a shocked look with Mildenale, although the Franciscan's disquiet derived from the fact that Langelee was willing to resort to magic; the physician was uneasy with the fact that the Master had just confessed to being a competent burglar.

'Are you sure this guide has not found its way back to you, Cynric?' asked Langelee, after a short interval during which he and the book-bearer speculated on the best way to gain access to Refham's hearth. Agatha joined in, adding that she had already purchased such a charm on the College's behalf, although hers was from Eyton, who was considerably cheaper, and the rat under the hearth was replaced by chanting three *Pater Nosters* beneath the nearest churchyard elm.

'I wish it had,' said Cynric. 'Now it might be in the hands of someone dangerous.'

Mildenale gaped at him. 'I would say that *anyone* who takes an interest in such tomes is dangerous.'

'That is not true, because *I* am interested in them,' said Cynric guilelessly. 'And I cannot imagine who else in

College might want the guide, especially now the students have gone. They are curious about forbidden texts, but the Fellows are not – or they have read them all already.'

'The porters are less vigilant now the place is virtually empty,' said Langelee. 'So someone must have come in from outside and taken it.'

'How would a stranger know where to look?' asked Bartholomew. 'You kept it on the top shelf in your chambers, which is not the most obvious place to search for valuables.'

Langelee looked sheepish. 'Actually, it was in the garden. Cynric handed it to me when I was supervising the digging of the new latrines. I set it down and forgot to bring it in when I came back.'

'So the labourers have it,' said Mildenale, looking as though he was ready to go and demand it back there and then. His expression became angry. 'Have you interrogated them?'

'I *questioned* them,' replied Langelee. 'But none can read, and I doubt they are the—'

'Books are valuable,' snapped Mildenale. 'They do not need to be able to read in order to sell one.'

Langelee regarded him coolly, not liking his tone. 'I told them it was a dangerous text on witchery, and that anyone hawking it was likely to be cursed. I know how to intimidate labourers, and I am certain none of them is the thief, so please do not accuse them. It is not easy to get men to work in this heat, and I shall be furious if they walk out on us.'

Mildenale sniffed disapprovingly, and turned to another topic. 'The Church does not sanction the use of charms and curses, and for you to visit a witch in order to procure one—'

'I did not procure one,' argued Langelee pedantically. 'I told you – it was too expensive.'

'And do not rail at *me*, either,' growled Agatha, when the Franciscan inadvertently glanced in her direction. She seemed hotter and crosser than ever, and the ale had done nothing to cool her temper. Bartholomew thought she looked dangerous, and began to edge towards the door. 'My beliefs are my own business, and I do not allow mere priests to tamper with them.'

'But it is my duty to tamper,' declared Mildenale indignantly. 'I am supposed to save people from the burning fires of Hell.'

Agatha glared at the sun, then at the friar. 'So, it is your fault we are all roasting alive down here, is it? Your duty is to save us from the fires of Hell, but the fires of Hell are *here*, spoiling meat and ale.'

'That is not what I—' began Mildenale.

'This vile weather has gone on quite long enough,' she growled, rising to her feet. 'I should have known the Church was responsible. You lot preach and pray, but none of you know what you are talking about. Well, let me tell *you*, something, *Mildenalus Sanctus*. If I ever have reason to—'

Bartholomew reached the door and shot through it. Cynric and Langelee were close behind him, neither willing to linger when Agatha was on the warpath. Mildenale was left alone with her.

'You know, boy,' whispered Cynric, 'there are times when I wonder whether *she* is the Sorcerer.'

Once Bartholomew had escaped from the kitchens, he went to look at the experiment he had been running in his storeroom. He was pleasantly surprised to find it had worked, and he was left with two piles of powder.

He had managed to separate the compounds, and now all he had to do was identify them. Ignoring Deynman's advice, which entailed mixing them with fish-giblet soup and feeding it to William, he performed a number of tests. Eventually, he sat back, knowing he had his answer.

'What Carton found in Thomas's room was not poison,' he told Deynman. The librarian was not particularly interested in what Bartholomew was doing, but he was lonely and bored without the students, and craved company. With Michael still at St Mary the Great, and the other Fellows in the conclave, where mere librarians were not permitted to tread, the physician was the only choice left.

'So your sedative was responsible for Thomas's death, after all,' said Deynman, rather baldly. 'Carton was hoping this powder would be the culprit, so you would be exonerated. He told me he disliked the way Father William keeps taunting you about it.'

'Did I hear my name?' came a booming voice from the doorway. Bartholomew sighed. He did not have the energy for a verbal spat with William.

'Doctor Bartholomew has just learned that it was definitely him who killed Thomas,' said Deynman, ever helpful. It was not the way the physician would have summarised his findings, but he supposed it was accurate enough.

'The powder Carton found was a remedy against quinsy,' Bartholomew elaborated. 'I thought as much when he handed it to me.'

'Thomas did worry about quinsy,' said William. 'He told me so himself, after Goldynham died of it. Well, you had better make your peace with God, Matthew. It cannot be easy, having a man's death on your conscience. And Thomas was a fellow prepared to fight against the Sorcerer, too, unlike most of the town. Either they are actively supporting him, or they are standing well back to see what will happen when he makes his play for power. There are not many true Soldiers of God left.'

'There are plenty,' objected Deynman. 'Isnard, Eyton and even Yolande de Blaston have pledged to side with the Church. And there are lots of scholars, too. In fact, the only College that has *not* condemned the Sorcerer is Bene't – and that is only because its Fellows are afraid of their porters.'

'Younge and his friends are members of the All Saints coven,' said William, nodding. 'But they will learn they have chosen the wrong side when Satan devours them all on Saturday night.'

'I wonder if he will devour those who use bits of cheese as bookmarks, too,' mused Deynman pointedly. 'I imagine so, because I cannot think of a worse crime for a scholar to commit.'

They began to bicker, and Bartholomew was grateful when Cynric came with a summons from a patient, although his relief evaporated when he learned it was Dickon Tulyet who needed his services. Few encounters with the Sheriff's hellion son were pleasant.

Dickon – large enough to verge on the fat and with eyes that were remarkably calculating for a boy his age – had cut himself while attempting to relieve another child of a toy. When Bartholomew arrived, he was screaming at the top of his lungs, but the physician was sure frustration at the failed theft was the cause of the racket, not pain from the relatively minor wound. Dickon's parents fussed and cooed, showering him with sweetmeats and other rich treats that were likely to make him sick. With a resigned sigh, Bartholomew took salve and bandages, and prepared to do battle.

'I am sorry he bit you, Matt,' said Tulyet, for at least the fourth time, as the physician took his leave. 'But the kick was not his fault. I should have held him more tightly, but I was afraid of hurting him.'

Bartholomew rubbed his eyes, not liking the way he was always tempted to be rougher than usual when he was obliged to deal with Dickon. It was unworthy of him as a physician, and as a man. However, it was hard to feel too sorry when his hand burned from its encounter with Dickon's sharp teeth, and when his ribs ached from the flailing boots. The next time, he decided, he would ask Michael to sit on the brat. That would keep him under control.

'You are right to buy Sewale Cottage,' he said, flexing his fingers carefully. The wound hurt. 'It will not be many more years before living with him becomes too perilous for you.'

'What do you mean?' cried Tulyet, stung. 'He is a good boy. You cannot blame him for taking exception to painful cures. Of course he will fight – I have trained him to look after himself.'

Bartholomew nodded a goodnight, refusing the offer of wine. Dickon had a habit of joining his father in his office, and the physician did not want a resumption of hostilities that night. He was eager to go home and sleep, but Cynric was waiting outside, to say Mother Valeria wanted to see him.

'Can it not wait until morning?' he asked weakly. The skirmish with Dickon had drained him, and all he wanted was to lie down.

'She said not,' replied Cynric disapprovingly. 'However, if you decide not to go, please do not ask me to tell her you are not coming. I do not want to be turned into a toad.'

Wearily, Bartholomew trudged up the hill. Cynric accompanied him part of the way, then disappeared into the Lilypot tavern. Bartholomew had not been alone for more than a moment when he saw a shadow – one that was exceptionally large and that loitered near Sewale Cottage. When a second shadow joined it, Bartholomew was sure they were the giant and Beard. Keeping to the darker side of the street, he crept towards them, intending to do what Cynric had done, and watch to see what they were doing.

But when he reached the spot, they had gone. He pressed his ear to the door, but there was no sound from within and he was sure they had not broken in a second time. He looked down one or two alleys, but the two men had disappeared into the darkness of the sultry summer night, almost as though they had never been there at all.

Chapter 8

It was late by the time Bartholomew reached Mother Valeria's little house, but tallow candles burned in gourds outside, lighting the path through the nettles. As he trudged along the well-worn track, he met two people walking in the opposite direction. He could not see their faces, but both greeted him by name as they passed. One held an amulet, and he supposed the witch was still open for business. He tapped on the door frame and battled his way through the leather hanging.

'There you are,' said the old woman sourly. 'You took your time.'

'Dickon Tulyet,' explained Bartholomew, sitting on the stool she prodded towards him with her foot. 'He screeched like a hellion, and I am surprised you did not hear him. I imagine the Bishop could, and he is in Avignon.'

'I heard he was trying to steal a toy from a lad twice his size,' said Valeria. 'He will be a fierce warrior one day.'

'He is a fierce warrior now,' said Bartholomew. It occurred to him that he should refuse to answer the next summons. But Dickon was a child, when all was said and done, and Tulyet was a friend.

'Bite him back,' recommended Valeria, looking at the livid mark on the physician's hand. 'That will teach him not to do it again.'

Bartholomew was not so sure. 'It might teach him to do it harder, to incapacitate me.'

'Then wear gloves. They will protect you from sly fangs.'

Her mention of gloves reminded him of the one William had found in St Michael's Church when the blood had been left in the font. He told her about it, then waited to see if she would admit to it being hers. Unfortunately, the hut was far too dim for identifying subtle variations in facial expressions, so he had no idea whether she was surprised by the tale or not.

'If Father William can distinguish human blood from animal, then he is a better witch than me,' was all she said as she stoked up her fire. Several pots were bubbling over it.

'The glove was not yours?' he asked, deciding to be blunt.

She raised her eyebrows. 'You think I am the kind of woman who leaves blood in holy places?'

'What can I do for you?' he asked, not sure how to answer such a question and reverting to medical matters before he said anything that might offend her. Whilst he did not believe he could be turned into a toad, the late hour and the shadows that danced around the fire were playing havoc with his imagination nonetheless. 'Is your knee paining you? It will not get better if you do not rest it.'

'I am obliged to be out more now the Sorcerer is preparing to make his stand. I cannot stay here, skulking

275

while he accrues power. He is a great magician, and I must find ways to protect myself.'

'You think he might try to harm you?' said Bartholomew uneasily.

She regarded him in disdain. 'I am competition. Of course he will try to harm me.'

'Then you should leave. Come back on Sunday, to see whether his début is all it is anticipated to be.'

'Oh, it will be,' she said softly.

The conviction in her voice sent a shiver of unease down his spine, and he hastily turned his attention to the heavily clad leg, seeking comfort in the familiarity of his trade. A hotness under the coverings indicated she had been using the joint more than was wise, and it was inflamed again.

'Shall I recite a spell to take the poison from Dickon's bite?' she asked while he worked. 'Or would you prefer some of my salve? I imagine it contains the same ingredients as the one you would prescribe yourself, except that mine is prepared while I recite incantations, so it will be more effective.'

'If you do not rest your knee tomorrow, it will become more swollen than it is now,' he said, preferring to change the subject than explain why he would not accept her offer. Her prediction of the success of the Sorcerer's investiture had troubled him, and he wanted nothing to do with magic in any guise, but especially in the dark and in the home of a witch.

'Give me more of your poultice, so I can rest tonight. I cannot sit, stand or lie down, it hurts so much.' She grinned suddenly, revealing black teeth. It was rather an evil expression. 'You have never asked why I do not remedy myself. I am a healer, and a good one, too. Powerful.'

Bartholomew shrugged, feigning a nonchalance he did not feel. 'We all need help sometimes.'

She smiled again, less diabolically this time. 'Yes, we do, although you always refuse mine. Still, you can take the advice of an old wise-woman instead, which is to stay in your College on Saturday night. I do not intend to be out when the Sorcerer makes his appearance, and neither should you. You have been kind to me – keeping secret my failure to heal myself – and I want to return the favour. But you look tired, and I should not keep you any longer.'

Bartholomew stood, but then sat again when he remembered what else he had agreed to do for Michael. 'A man called Danyell died the night before Ascension Day. It was probably a seizure, but his hand was removed from his corpse. I do not suppose you have any idea why that should happen?'

'Is that an accusation? Do you think I am responsible?'

'It is a question,' said Bartholomew hastily, visions of toads flooding unbidden into his mind. He took a deep breath. He was not usually impressionable, and wished he was not so unutterably weary. 'I need to know why someone could want such a thing.'

'I use corpse hands to improve my customers' butter-making spells. Other witches use them to prepare amulets for burglars – carrying one will render a thief invisible, you see.'

'Your fellows help criminals?' asked Bartholomew uncomfortably.

'We help anyone who pays, although I am rather more selective. Spaldynge came last week, wanting to buy a hand, but I declined to oblige, even after he offered to double the price. I heard he acquired one from the three crones in the Market Square in the end.'

Bartholomew's thoughts tumbled. 'Did he say why he wanted it?'

'Well, I doubt it was for making butter. But corpse hands are very useful, and I usually have a few in stock.' She sighed impatiently when she saw him glance around. 'I do not keep them out on display, not with customers streaming in all day long. Do you think me a fool?'

'Who might have taken Danyell's?'

'The Sorcerer, I imagine. But there has not been much demand for body parts of late, other than Spaldynge. It is too hot for butter-making *or* burglary.'

Bartholomew supposed she was telling the truth. 'Danyell was unwell the night he died, and his friends say he intended to come to you for a cure. Did he?'

'Not if he died on Ascension Day Eve. That is an important time for witches, and I was out, gathering. You came to see me before dawn the following morning, because the exertion had hurt my knee.'

'Gathering what?' he asked, recalling that he had been walking home after tending her swollen joint when he had stumbled across Danyell's body.

'Materials for my spells,' she replied. She grinned when she saw her reply was vague enough to tell him nothing at all, and he found himself beginning to grow exasperated with her.

'Be careful,' he warned, as he rose to leave. 'The Church may be losing popularity but it is still a powerful force, and its members may turn on innocents if they cannot catch their real enemy. It would not be the first time.'

'Then heed your own words, physician. I am not the only one said to dabble in the dark arts.'

Bartholomew retraced his steps along the path, and

crossed the Great Bridge. The guards waved him through, knowing *medici* often needed to be out after the curfew was in place. The streets were quiet and empty, although Cynric's voice emanated from the Lilypot. Bartholomew caught several military-sounding words and supposed the Welshman was recounting one of his battle stories.

He had just reached the Church of All Saints-in-the-Jewry when there was a sharp rustle of leaves. Remembering the poisonous remarks that had been hissed at him the last time he had passed a graveyard in the dark, he crossed to the opposite side of the street. If the whisperer was there, he did not want to hear what the fellow had to say. Then there was a slightly louder crackle, and he turned to see a figure, faintly illuminated by the light of the waning moon.

It was a tall man in a yellow cloak, who had a head of pale curls and a book under his arm; the book had a circle on its cover, as though it was a tome about magic. Unlike the incident in St John Zachary, when the sun had dazzled him, Bartholomew could see quite clearly this time. He sighed tiredly. Goldynham had been famous for his bushy white hair and gold cloak, and it was clear some prankster intended to give credence to Eyton's tale about the silversmith's post-mortem wanderings. He grimaced in disgust as the figure glided theatrically into the churchyard and disappeared among the shadows.

For the first time in weeks, Bartholomew was not required to visit a patient during the night. It was not a very long night, given that the summer solstice was not far off, but sleeping through it was a pleasant change regardless. He did not wake when the bell rang to summon the College's few remaining scholars to their dawn devotions, and

Michael, mistakenly assuming he had only recently returned home after tending the most recent victims of the flux, told Langelee to let him be; the monk wanted his friend alert to continue their investigations. William objected, maintaining Bartholomew needed to do penance for what had happened to Thomas, but the physician was a heavy sleeper, and did not stir when the Fellows began a bitter, sniping argument right outside his window.

Michael prevailed, and Langelee led a reduced procession to St Michael's – just four Fellows, with Mildenale and Deynman bringing up the rear. Bartholomew was still asleep when they returned, and not properly awake at breakfast, when Deynman took it upon himself to act as Bible Scholar. His Latin, delivered in something of a bellow, was all but incomprehensible, and everyone was relieved when Langelee surged to his feet and recited a concluding grace.

'The dung-master needs you,' said Cynric to Bartholomew when the scholars trooped out into the yard. 'He sent word at dawn, but I thought he could wait this time. It did not sound urgent, anyway.'

'You are right to make him wait, Cynric,' said Deynman, nodding approval. 'He made Doctor Bartholomew run all the way to his house on Monday, when all he wanted was to chat about Sewale Cottage and latrines.'

'If he mentions either matter again,' said Suttone, 'tell him that we have an offer of fifteen marks from Spynk, and that we have promised the manure to Isnard.'

'But neither arrangement is sealed in stone,' added Wynewyk hastily. 'We are open to offers, and Michael is not very keen on Isnard at the moment.'

'No, I am not,' agreed the monk. 'But do not worry

about remembering all this, Matt, because I am coming with you. I want to speak to the canons of Barnwell about Carton. Again.'

'The canons have asked you to visit them, too,' said Cynric to the physician. 'Fencotes took a tumble in the night, and Podiolo needs you to tell him whether to use elder or figwort for the bruises.'

Either would work, and Bartholomew was reminded yet again that the infirmarian was not a very proficient practitioner.

'What will another trek to Barnwell tell you, Brother?' asked Langelee curiously. 'Surely, there are only so many times you can demand to know what the canons saw, and be told they saw nothing?'

Michael shrugged, unwilling to let anyone know he was not sure how else to proceed. 'Perhaps one will be so exasperated by repeating himself that he will let something slip.'

'Do you think one of them is the killer?' asked Suttone unhappily. 'I hope you are wrong. I do not like the notion of murder between Orders. It will cause trouble.'

'If an Augustinian has killed an innocent Franciscan, there *will* be trouble,' vowed William hotly.

'Have you written your speech for the Guild of Corpus Christi yet, Suttone?' asked Langelee, before William could start a tirade. 'Heltisle says he is sure it will be memorable.'

Suttone preened himself. 'No one knows the plague like me. However, I intend to stay away from your notion that it came because everyone is sinful, William. It might put folk off their wine.'

'But it *did* come because folk are sinful,' said William immediately. 'It is your sacred duty to—'

'What wine?' interrupted Deynman curiously. 'It is a

meeting, not a feast. It is to be held in All Saints-next-the-Castle on Saturday night.'

'Is it?' asked Michael, his eyes round. 'I thought that was the time and place set for the Sorcerer's grand appearance. Are you saying the Sorcerer is supported by the Guild of Corpus Christi?'

'You are mistaken, Deynman,' said Suttone, startled. 'I have not been told to orate in All Saints.'

'I am quite sure,' said Deynman. 'I heard about it from Peterhouse's Master Suttone, who is disappointed that he was not the one invited to give the speech. He says he would relish the opportunity to pontificate in a half-derelict church at the witching hour.'

'Well, I shall not go if it is true. I do not lecture in ruins, especially in the dark and when they are full of witches.'

'You said you would have Carton's killer, once you discovered the Sorcerer's identity, Brother,' said Langelee, more interested in his dead Fellow than in Suttone's preferences for speech-giving venues. 'The man is everywhere you turn these days, so surely it cannot not be too hard to find out who he is?'

Michael sighed wearily. 'I wish that were true, but he is more elusive than mist.' He looked at each Fellow in turn. 'Do you have any idea who he might be? Or a suspicion to share?'

'I certainly do not,' replied William indignantly. 'I do not consort with that sort of person.'

'How do you expect to defeat him, then?' demanded Langelee. 'You say you are ready to pit yourself against him when he appears on Saturday, but only a fool engages an enemy he knows nothing about.'

'We will know him when he shows himself,' said

Mildenale in a way that sounded vaguely threatening. He looked hard at Bartholomew. 'No matter who he turns out to be.'

'He will not be one of us,' said Wynewyk, angry on the physician's behalf. 'How dare you!'

'He will be someone with an interest in necromancy,' hissed Mildenale, clasping his hands. He glanced at William, silently demanding his support. 'And *God* will help us to defeat him.'

'We believe the villain will be a man who loves anatomy,' added William, although he would not meet the physician's eyes. 'Someone who procures body parts to practise on.'

'What is wrong with your hand, Bartholomew?' asked Mildenale suddenly. He crossed himself. 'It looks like a bite. Is it the Devil's mark?'

'In a manner of speaking,' said Bartholomew, looking at the clear imprint of teeth along the side of his hand. 'Dickon did it.'

'Definitely Satan's sign, then,' said Langelee, laughing.

They all turned when the gate opened and a visitor was ushered in. Bartholomew was surprised to see it was Eyton, although Mildenale and William seemed to be expecting him. The vicar trotted across the yard towards them, eyes twinkling merrily. He nodded a genial greeting and immediately launched into an account of how he had spent the previous night in his churchyard, making sure no corpse tried to follow Goldynham's example. He had just finished his vigil, he claimed, and had come to say a few prayers with his fellow Franciscans. He carried a pot.

'Honey,' he explained cheerfully. 'To protect us from whatever might come our way over the next few days. And this afternoon we shall scatter holy water across the whole cemetery. I have several pails of it, back at the church.'

'You should not create holy water by the bucketload,' admonished Suttone. 'It is not seemly, and will make the general populace think it is cheap.'

'Oh, it is not cheap,' grinned Eyton. 'These days I can charge three times the amount I would have got before Ascension Day. Supply and demand, you see. And market forces.'

'Those sound like dark arts to me,' said William uncertainly.

Eyton punched him playfully on the arm. 'But they are making me rich. They paid for that fine meal you and I enjoyed together yesterday, so do not complain too vehemently.'

'Has Goldynham been reburied yet?' asked Bartholomew, recalling what he had seen the previous night. Everyone had been asleep when he had returned, so there had been no opportunity to tell them about the prankster. He wondered whether the culprit had used the original cloak or a similar one.

Eyton shook his head. 'I was going to commit him to the ground yesterday, but the Guild of Corpus Christi asked me to wait a while so they can launder his graveclothes. Why? Do you want to examine him again, to see how he managed to dig his way free?'

'It was the Devil's work,' declared William, speaking fervently now he was on more familiar ground. 'But I said some prayers that should keep him dead. Only a very evil person will be able to override them and encourage him to wander about again. Someone like the Sorcerer.'

Bartholomew decided it was not the time to inform his colleagues that someone was pretending to be

Goldynham. William and Mildenale might assume he had seen the real silversmith, and claim it as proof that he was a necromancer.

'Give me the amulet that Fencotes found at Barnwell, Matt,' ordered Michael. 'I need to go to the Franciscan Priory later, to ask Pechem about Carton's ordination. I shall see whether any of them recognise that holy-stone at the same time.'

'I have already told you about Carton's ordination,' objected William, not liking the notion that he had not been believed. 'He took his vows in London. Thomas agitated about floods and cancellations, but he was just being stupid.'

'Thomas was suspicious of everyone,' said Mildenale. 'Carton was the better man, God rest his soul.'

'Actually, I preferred Thomas,' countered William, always argumentative, even with allies. 'Carton could be a bit slow to denounce Dominicans, and I once heard him say that he thought they had interesting points to make about Blood Relics.'

'Shocking,' said Michael flatly. 'How could he?'

Bartholomew had been trying to find the talisman while his colleagues bickered, but Dickon had been in his bag the previous evening and its contents were in a muddle. Items began to drop out.

'What is this?' demanded Mildenale, darting forward to lay hold of the bat-eye charm that had been a gift from Cynric. He answered his own question before the physician could reply. 'It is an amulet, designed to ward off evil! You should know only God can do that.'

'I own a few of those,' said Langelee casually. 'I do not carry them around me with, of course, but I have a fair collection in my rooms. They are foolish things, but it is safer to buy them than have the seller curse you for refusing. We ought to burn them all one day.'

Eyton looked at the bat-eye pouch and shuddered. 'It is not one of mine, so it probably came from a witch, and if you set those alight, the resulting stench might summon Satan. Of course, he will not come if you allow me to bless your firewood first. I know the right prayers.'

Mildenale's attention was still on Bartholomew's bag. 'Here is an amulet against wolves *and* some mugwort – a herb favoured by warlocks. Mother Valeria *has* been teaching you dark secrets!'

'I am disappointed, Matthew,' said William reproachfully, while the physician silently cursed his absent-mindedness; he should have remembered to throw Cynric's gifts away. 'I believed you when you said you were no necromancer. Now we find magical herbs and amulets in your bag.'

'And do not forget his love of anatomy,' added *Mildenalus Sanctus*, fixing the physician with a fanatical glare. 'No man who truly worships God can condone such a wicked practice.'

Michael gave a hearty sigh. 'Mugwort is a common cure – Paxtone and Rougham use it all the time. Ask them, if you do not believe me.'

'Rougham is away, and Paxtone has the flux,' said William. 'We cannot ask them. How convenient!'

Bartholomew was relieved to be away from Michaelhouse. Normally, he would have ignored the Franciscans' ridiculous assertions and dismissed them for the nonsense they were, but he had not liked being accused of witchery in the current climate of unease, and their claims had unsettled him deeply.

286

'Do not worry,' said Michael, as they headed for the Brazen George. He had no intention of walking all the way to Barnwell, and Cynric had arranged for horses to be waiting at the tavern. 'They will come to their senses when this Sorcerer business fades away, and William in particular will be sorry for what he has said.'

'But by then it may be too late,' said Bartholomew unhappily. 'A lot of damage can be done in a short period of time, as we saw with Magister Arderne in the spring. He was not here long, but the harm he did with his tongue still haunts me – and haunts Paxtone, Rougham and Robin the surgeon, too.'

'Then we must ensure we bring the Sorcerer down as soon as we can.' Michael rubbed his stomach. 'There was no meat for breakfast this morning, so I had better eat some while we wait for the horses to be saddled. You should do the same. You are pale, and it will put colour in your cheeks.'

But Bartholomew had no appetite. 'Wait for me – I will be back in a few moments.'

Before the monk could question him, he turned along the High Street, aiming for St Bene't's Church. If Eyton was at Michaelhouse with his fellow Franciscans, then it was a good opportunity to inspect Goldynham's corpse, to see whether the prankster had done more than just imitate the dead silversmith. Goldynham might have been intact when Eyton had found him, but he had been lying unattended for the best part of three days, and who knew what might have happened in that time? He walked fast, oblivious to the sweat that began to trickle down his back. When he arrived, he made straight for the chancel, putting his sleeve over his nose as he approached the body.

Goldynham looked much as he had the night he had been disinterred, although someone had combed the dirt from his hair and washed his face. The gold cloak was missing, and the physician recalled Eyton saying the grave-clothes were being cleaned on the orders of the Guild of Corpus Christi. Was it true? And if so, was the prankster a Guild member? Or was it the same man who had whispered at him from the churchyard on Sunday night – perhaps Spaldynge or Heltisle, because they hated him, and wanted to give him a fright? Or was it the Sorcerer, because that was the sort of thing that was expected of him?

He walked back along the High Street still thinking about it, and was near the Brazen George when he heard a scuffle taking place in one of the dark, sewage-laden alleys that ran between the main road and Milne Street.

'You are hurting me!'

Bartholomew peered down the narrow opening; it was choked with weeds and a dead pig lay near its entrance. The corpse was full of maggots, and the stench in the confined space was overpowering. Further in, where it was much darker, he could see two people engaged in a curious, struggling dance. One was enormous, and Bartholomew recognised him as the giant. The other was Refham. The giant had his hands around the blacksmith's throat and was holding him so his feet were off the ground. When Refham started to make choking sounds, Bartholomew drew his dagger and went to the rescue.

'Leave him alone,' he yelled, holding his knife in a way that told the giant he was ready to use it. It would not be much use against a sword, but he could hardly go home to fetch a bigger weapon before tackling the bully. He recalled how well the man had fought the last time

288

they had met, and hoped he was not about to be skewered for the likes of Refham.

The giant jumped at the sound of a voice coming towards him, but when Bartholomew edged closer he sensed another figure lurking in the deep shadows beyond. It was Beard. It was too late for second thoughts, so Bartholomew continued his advance, clutching the dagger and hoping he looked more menacing than he felt. Fortunately, the sun was behind him, which meant that all his opponents could see was a silhouette. They would not know he was the man they had fought in Margery Sewale's cottage – at least, Bartholomew hoped not, or they would know for certain that they could best him.

The giant ducked suddenly, and Beard lobbed something over his friend's head. It was a rock, which Bartholomew prevented from braining him by raising his hand. He staggered when it bounced off his forearm, and by the time he had regained his balance, the pair were running away. Instinctively, he started to give chase, but skidded to a halt after a few steps. What would he do if he caught them? Once they were out of the shadowy alley, they would see he was armed only with a dagger and would make short work of him with their swords.

He returned to Refham and knelt next to him. The blacksmith was gasping and retching, clutching his throat as if serious harm had been done. Bartholomew prised his hands away and inspected the damage. There were red marks where the giant's fingers had been, and there would be bruising the following day, but he knew Refham would survive without long-term problems. He helped the smith to his feet and escorted him out of the lane and into the High Street, away from the stench of the dead pig. People glanced in their direction as they emerged, and Bartholomew saw several smirk when they saw Refham stained, dishevelled and unsteady on his feet. Evidently, he was not a popular man.

'Satan tried to grab you, did he, Refham?' asked Isnard conversationally, as he hobbled past on his crutches. 'And then realised you are too wicked, even for him?'

'Bugger off!' hissed Refham, taking a step towards him. The threat was hollow, though, because he could barely stand. 'Do not pretend you are better than me. Even the Michaelhouse singers do not want you in their ranks, and they have a reputation for accepting anyone, regardless of musical talent.'

An insult to the choir was far too grave a matter for Isnard to ignore. His face turned black with fury. 'I will kill you for that,' he said, looking as though he meant it.

'Go home, Isnard,' said Bartholomew, interposing himself between the two men. 'Michael will not reinstate you if you brawl in the street.'

'He will not reinstate me anyway,' said Isnard. A dangerous light gleamed in his eyes. 'Cynric tells me he does not even want me to have the College latrines. I have nothing to lose now.'

'I will talk to him again,' promised Bartholomew. 'But only if you go home.'

Isnard wavered, but a chance at rejoining the choir was far more important than trouncing Refham. He treated the blacksmith to an unpleasant sneer and went on his way.

'And you can mind your own business, too,' snapped Refham, pushing Bartholomew away from him, albeit weakly. 'Leave me alone.'

'Willingly,' said Bartholomew, thinking he should not

have bothered to save the man. 'Can you walk, or do you want me to send for your wife?'

'I do not need help – yours or anyone else's. And do not expect me to thank you for pushing your nose into my affairs. I would have bested that pair, had you not come along.'

Bartholomew was tempted to grab him by the throat himself. 'Who were they?'

'Business associates. And I am not telling you any more, because it is nothing to do with you.'

Bartholomew regarded him thoughtfully. 'I could spend the rest of the day following you around, seeing whom you meet and asking them questions. That would give me the answers I want, although I imagine it would be tiresome for you.'

Refham flexed his fingers, and for a moment the physician thought he might swing a punch. He braced himself to duck, but Refham was not a total fool, and knew he was in no condition for a spat. 'If you must know, they have been renting my forge while I am in Cambridge selling my mother's property. They have not told me their names – it is not that sort of agreement.'

Bartholomew was bemused. 'They do not look like smiths to me. Why would they want a forge?'

'They needed a place to lay their heads of an evening, and I wanted their money, although our contract is no longer in force. I have no idea what else they did there, and, frankly, I do not care.'

'But they might mean the town harm,' said Bartholomew, thinking it was a curious arrangement, and one that reeked of illegality. He wondered whether Cynric was right, and one of the pair was the Sorcerer – and that the man had succeeded in concealing his identity for so long because he was not in Cambridge for much of the time.

Refham shrugged. 'So what? I cannot wait to leave this place and buy myself a pretty house in Luton. It does not matter to me whether this town thrives or burns to the ground.'

Bartholomew thought about what he had seen. 'Your "business associates" do not like dealing with you. Most respectable men do not negotiate by grabbing each other by the throat.'

'That was because I told them the rent is going up, and they did not like it – they just ended our little pact. But you get what you pay for in this world, as Michaelhouse is about to find out. If you want my mother's shops, they are going to cost you.'

His expression softened slightly when he saw his wife coming towards him. She took in his dishevelled clothes and the marks on his neck, and turned to Bartholomew with a furious expression.

'It was not him,' said Refham, seeing what she was thinking. 'He is no warrior. Indeed, I heard Dickon Tulyet gave him a pasting only last night. It was the men from the forge.'

'They did not agree to our new terms?' asked Joan. 'Well, it was worth a try. Anything for money.'

Bartholomew returned to the Brazen George in a thoughtful frame of mind. He considered going to Refham's forge on the Huntingdon Way, to see if he could learn more about the two men who had burgled Michaelhouse's property, but decided there was no point if Refham's demand for a higher rent had already driven them away. He told Michael what had happened – about the prankster and Refham's near-throttling – as he battled to mount the pony the monk had hired for him. It was a docile, steady beast, but Bartholomew was no horseman. He rode with all the elegance of a sack of grain, and Michael, who was one of the best riders in the county, was invariably ashamed to be seen with him.

'The prankster is an annoying irrelevancy,' said the monk dismissively. 'It is some student's idea of fun – although he will find himself in the proctors' gaol if he plays his nasty tricks on me. But Beard and the giant are rather more intriguing. Do you really think one of them could be the Sorcerer? It makes sense that the culprit is a stranger – it seems unlikely that a long-term resident would suddenly decide to make his mark in the world of witchery.'

'But why would a stranger kill Carton?' asked Bartholomew.

Michael performed some fancy wheels on his fine stallion while he waited for the physician to mount up. 'Because Carton spoke out against sin – not as uncompromisingly as William and Mildenale, but a lot more rationally. Perhaps the Sorcerer thought that made him the most dangerous of the three. And there is always the possibility that Carton had worked out the Sorcerer's identity.'

'Carton remains a mystery to me,' said Bartholomew, flinging himself across the saddle and clinging on gamely while the pony bucked at the unexpected manoeuvre. 'He wanted me to test the powder he found in Thomas's room because he did not believe my medicine had killed his friend.'

'I know – although his hopes were unfounded, because the substance was a remedy for quinsy. So what is your point?'

Bartholomew struggled into the correct position at last; both he and the pony heaved a sigh of relief. 'That *he* may have thrown the stone that hit Thomas. He was certainly there when it happened.'

Michael gaped at him. 'How in God's name did you reach that conclusion?'

'At the time, I assumed part of a tile had fallen from a roof, because I could not imagine anyone hurling rocks at friars. But perhaps I was wrong. Later, Carton was very insistent that I should not blame myself – he even told Deynman that he disliked me feeling guilty.'

Michael frowned. 'But your explanation makes no sense: Carton lobs a stone at Thomas – although he had no reason to do so, because they preached the same message about witchcraft and sin – and then tells you that Thomas died of poison. It is tantamount to announcing that a murder has been committed, and needs to be investigated, and no sane killer does that. Besides, I am not sure Carton *did* care whether you were distressed over Thomas. He was not a kindly man, not once he became a Fellow.'

Bartholomew supposed he was right, but there were so many questions about Carton that he was not ready to dismiss his theory just yet. It would sit at the back of his mind until there was more evidence to consider. He followed Michael out of the yard and on to the High Street, not quite at ease with the pony's rhythmic walk. The animal smelled of manure and dry hay, which was a lot more pleasant than the waft from the meat stalls as they rode through the Market Square. As they passed the booths that sold spices, they met Heltisle of Bene't College. Younge hovered behind him with a basket over his arm, scowling furiously.

'It is his punishment for being rude to you yesterday,'

explained Heltisle, when Michael raised questioning eyebrows. 'He hates shopping.'

'I am sure it will teach him not to be offensive again,' said Michael, his tone of voice suggesting that he would have imposed something rather more radical. 'But it is not his rudeness that concerns me – it is the fact that he wanted to chop me into little pieces with his dagger.'

Heltisle's expression was cold. 'You provoked him. He is paid to protect the College, and it is unfair to penalise him for doing his job. Incidentally, my Fellows have voted unanimously to pay the fine you levied against him. Three groats, was it?'

Michael gave him a smile that was all teeth and no humour. 'And it will be six if I have occasion to deal with him again.'

Because he was impotent against the Senior Proctor, Heltisle rounded on Bartholomew. 'I met Refham just now, and he told me you attacked him. We hope to benefit from his generosity, so I would be grateful if you did not antagonise him with loutish behaviour. It took me a long time to pacify him.'

Bartholomew almost laughed. 'I doubt Bene't will see anything from Refham. He does not seem the kind of man to make benefactions.'

'Perhaps, but we are unwilling to take that chance. Food will be expensive this winter, with the crops on the verge of failure, and that will drain our resources. We need all the money we can get. Refham asked me to make Michaelhouse's Franciscans desist in their denunciations of the Sorcerer, too.'

'Did he indeed?' asked Michael, exchanging a glance with the physician. Did that mean Refham was the

Sorcerer?' Bartholomew knew the blacksmith belonged to the All Saints coven, and he was certainly unpleasant enough to be a demon-master. 'How interesting. Pray tell us more.'

But Heltisle was not of a mind to be helpful. He turned his attention to the spices on sale, mumbling something about using them to disguise the taste of some mutton he had bought. 'This heat will not last much longer,' he muttered, more to himself than the Michaelhouse men. 'It will break soon. The Sorcerer said so.'

'How do you know what the Sorcerer thinks about the weather?' demanded Michael immediately. 'Are you acquainted with him? Does he look anything like Refham?'

Heltisle's eyebrows shot up. 'No, he does not. And if you must know, I heard the Sorcerer speak at All Saints. But he was swathed in a dark cloak and I did not see his face, so I cannot tell you his name.'

'You heard him speak?' Michael sounded shocked. 'Surely *you* do not attend covens?'

'I went with Refham once, because he invited me and I did not wish to offend him by refusing. The Sorcerer swept in, threw some powder, bones and various other oddments in bowls, and created a lot of smelly fumes. Then he left, and his disciples took requests.'

'Requests?' echoed Michael warily.

'For cures, curses and so on. He was not there long, but his presence was imposing nonetheless.'

'Was Refham with you when the Sorcerer made his appearance?' asked Bartholomew.

Heltisle regarded him coldly. 'He may have wandered away to talk to friends – I do not recall. However, I advise you to stay away from the Sorcerer, because he will make for a formidable enemy.'

'Did Refham tell you to pass us that particular message, too?' asked Michael archly.

Heltisle's expression was distinctly furtive. 'He may have done.'

'Do you think Refham is the Sorcerer?' asked Michael, as he and Bartholomew continued their journey towards Barnwell. 'There is proof, of sorts.'

'Or Heltisle,' suggested Bartholomew. 'He is clever enough to deceive you about it by feeding you information that makes Refham look suspect.'

'You are just saying that because you do not like him.'

'No, I am saying it because there is evidence,' objected Bartholomew. 'First, he was defiant about attending a coven – blaming Refham for his presence there, but careless of the fact that it is hardly an activity for the head of a powerful College. Second, if he is the Sorcerer, then Younge and his cronies will make for excellent helpmeets – and they are definitely members of the All Saints cadre, because we have been told so by several people.'

'That is not evidence, that is conjecture. However, we shall bear your suspicions in mind.'

They passed the Franciscan convent just as Prior Pechem was emerging. The leader of Cambridge's Grey Friars was a dour, unsmiling man, who was nevertheless embarrassed by the excesses of some of his brethren. He did his best to curb their diatribes, but was better at scholarship than at imposing discipline and was not the most effective of rulers. William, Mildenale, Thomas and Carton had ignored his pleas for moderation, and he had proved himself powerless to restrain them.

'Ah,' said Michael blandly, reining in. 'Just the man I have been looking for.'

Pechem blanched. 'I have asked Mildenale and William to stop preaching until the Sorcerer crisis is resolved, but they ignore everything short of a bolt of divine lightning. And sometimes I wonder whether even that would work. However, they are members of Michaelhouse, so I should not bear all the responsibility for their unfettered tongues.'

'No,' admitted Michael. 'We are both to blame for that. But that is not what I wanted to speak to you about. I am more interested in the fact that you have been looking into Carton's ordination.'

'Yes, I have. Thomas said Carton lied about the date. Apparently, Greyfriars in London was flooded when he claimed to have taken his vows.'

'Did you believe him?' asked Bartholomew, fighting to keep his pony from stealing hay from a passing wagon. The horse won handily, and emerged with a sizeable snack. 'Thomas, I mean.'

Pechem thought about it. 'I believe there *was* a flood on the day in question – Thomas was a fussy, pedantic sort of man, and would not have made a mistake over something like that. But do I accept his claim that Carton was not one of us? No, I do not.'

'Why?' asked Bartholomew.

Pechem regarded him in surprise. 'You ask me this question, when he was a member of your own College? You only had to spend a few moments in his company to appreciate his deeply held convictions – and his detailed knowledge of a friar's duties.'

'Do you think he was defrocked at some stage in his career, then?' asked Michael. 'And he invented a new date for his ordination, so no one would discover that his name had been scrubbed out? Perhaps he was banished for giving overzealous sermons.'

Pechem almost cracked a smile. 'We Franciscans do not expel members for preaching radical messages. William would have been gone years ago if that were the case. On the contrary, our Minister-General likes a bit of fanaticism. He says it grabs the laity's attention.'

'Well, there is that, I suppose,' acknowledged Michael. 'William and Mildenale have certainly done well with the attention-grabbing side of things.'

'But only since the Sorcerer became popular,' said Bartholomew. 'Before that, everyone ignored William for the fool he is. And Mildenale was preoccupied with organising his new hostel.'

Michael was thoughtful. 'Thomas was not a particularly remarkable preacher until a few weeks ago, either. Oh, he railed about sin immediately after the plague, and was quite eloquent at first. But when people began to forget its horrors, some of the fire went out of him. After that, he just paid lip service to his message. That only changed when the Sorcerer arrived and he joined forces with Mildenale.'

'Thomas was a good man,' argued Pechem. 'He often reminded us of how he went among the sick during the Death, and he put his survival down to the fact that he was godly.'

'You went among the sick, too,' said Bartholomew, recalling how hard Pechem had worked in those bleak days, with no heed for his own safety. 'Does that make you godly, as well?'

Pechem looked flustered; he was a modest man. 'I would not presume to say.'

'Unlike Thomas,' muttered Michael. He pulled the holy-stone from his purse. 'Did you ever see Carton wearing this?'

Pechem made no move to take it from him. 'I most certainly did not! Those sorts of things are not permitted in my Order, and anyone caught wearing one can expect to be reprimanded most severely. Incidentally, Thomas insisted I write a letter to London, asking for confirmation of Carton's ordination. I am expecting a reply any day now.'

'So you do suspect Carton of misleading you,' pounced Michael. 'Or you would not have done as Thomas demanded.'

'Actually, I did it because it was the only way to stop him from pestering me. Personally, I suspect the flood meant the ceremony was held elsewhere, and Thomas's suspicions were groundless.'

'I thought Carton and Thomas liked each other,' said Bartholomew. 'They spent a lot of time together.'

'Yes, they did, but I think it was a case of fanatics laying aside their differences to fight for a common cause. I doubt there was much real affection between them.' Pechem shuddered. 'I do deplore zealots! Look at the trouble they bring, even after they are dead.'

The ride to Barnwell was no more pleasant on horseback than it had been on foot, because the sun still beat down relentlessly and there was the additional nuisance that ponies attracted flies. Michael flapped furiously at the dark cloud that buzzed around his head, while Bartholomew ignored them, in an experiment to see which tactic worked best. Michael's frenzied arm-waving attracted more insects, but he was considerably less bitten. When they finally reached the priory, both were out of sorts.

'I had better come with you to see the dung-merchant,' said Michael, red-faced from his exertions. 'I do not want you accepting a bribe that makes us look cheap.'

'I said I would plead Isnard's case to you again,' said Bartholomew as he dismounted, the mention of manure reminding him of his promise to the bargeman. 'Let him rejoin the choir, Brother. He heard it was you who argued against him having our latrines, and he is very upset about it – especially as he planned to sell the dung to Ely Abbey, no doubt because it is *your* Mother house.'

'I am *glad* he is dismayed,' said Michael venomously. 'However, I would sooner he had it than Arblaster. Arblaster collects the lion's share of muck these days, and I disapprove of monopolies. Are those goats?'

Bartholomew looked into the field he had seen on previous visits, where a number of the animals were tethered under the shade of a tree. 'Yes. I understand they can often be found in the countryside.'

Michael glowered, his temper raw from heat and flying insects. 'Well, there are seven of these, which is the same number that were stolen from Bene't College. And they are black – Satan's favourite colour, according to William, although Deynman says he prefers red.'

'So, Arblaster is the Sorcerer now? And he is keeping seven goats for a demonic special occasion?'

'Why not? He has made a fortune from dung, which you would not think was a lucrative trade.'

Bartholomew shrugged. 'He bought spells to increase his profits. Perhaps they worked.'

He knocked on Arblaster's door and waited to be admitted, recalling that the last time he had burst in unannounced, anticipating a medical emergency, and had taken the occupants by surprise. The door was opened by Jodoca, who was wearing a kirtle of pale yellow that made her look cool and fresh. She ushered them in and provided them with ale, which was cold, sweet and clear. Michael's eyes gleamed when she produced a plate of Lombard slices, his favourite cakes.

'I would offer you chicken,' she said, smothering a smile at the rate at which the monk devoured the refreshments, 'but I am not sure it is still good, even though it was only cooked this morning.'

'You are wise to be cautious,' said Bartholomew approvingly. 'I have noticed flies alighting on meat – cooked and raw – which I believe accelerates the rate at which it spoils. It is—'

'Ignore him, madam,' said Michael. She had won his heart with her hospitality. 'He does not usually regale people with accounts of insects and rotting food. Sometimes he can be quite erudite.'

'I am sure he can,' said Jodoca, eyes twinkling with amusement. 'My husband is out with his muck heaps at the moment, but I have sent the servant to fetch him. He should not be long.'

'I thought he was ill,' said Bartholomew, although not with much rancour. It was simply too hot to be annoyed. 'Or has he summoned me a second time for no good reason?'

'Oh, I have good reason,' said Arblaster, bustling in on a waft of fertiliser. He was thinner than he had been, and there was a gauntness in his face that had not been there a few days ago, but he was clearly recovered from his flux. 'It is just not a medical one. I see you have brought a colleague to hear my offer this time. That is good.'

Bartholomew rubbed his eyes. 'I asked you not to send for me unless you needed a physician.'

'You said we should not send for you *urgently*,' corrected Arblaster. 'And we made sure your book-bearer understood that it was not. I want to offer fifteen marks for Sewale Cottage, and there will be a goat in it for you if you persuade Master Langelee to accept. I know you said you were not interested in personal inducements, but these are special circumstances.'

'If you give him a goat, you will be left with only six,' said Michael pointedly. 'Not seven.'

Arblaster shot him a puzzled smile. 'There are plenty of goats in the world, Brother. Well, what do you say? Fifteen marks for the house and an opportunity to put in a bid on your latrines.'

'We will inform the Master,' said Michael. 'Although, I have never been fond of goat . . .'

'A sheep, then,' said Arblaster immediately. 'Or would you prefer a pig?'

'I am not in the habit of bartering for livestock,' said Michael haughtily. 'However, we might be interested in a year's supply of fertiliser for our manor in Ickleton.'

'Livestock is beneath you, but manure is not?' asked Jodoca with a mischievous grin. 'You are a man after my husband's own heart, Brother.'

Bartholomew laughed when the monk looked discomfited. He reached out to take the last of the Lombard slices, but Michael did not like being the butt of jokes. He staged a lightning strike on the remaining pastry, then shot his friend a smug little smirk of victory as he raised the prize to his lips.

'We already have an offer of fifteen marks,' he said, barely comprehensible through a cake-filled mouth. 'I doubt the Master will be interested in a second.'

'Sixteen, then,' said Arblaster, without hesitation. 'It is a good price for such a small property, especially if you count a helping of the finest dung, too. I shall make sure it contains plenty of horse, which you will know is the best. In fact, it is such a good bid that I doubt anyone will best it.'

'The canons are still interested,' said Michael, wiping his sticky hands on a piece of linen. 'And Tulyet wants it for his son, while Spynk is also keen. Who knows whether the negotiations are over?'

Jodoca raised her goblet in a salute to both scholars. 'Then we shall just have to enjoy the pleasure of your company again, so we can discuss the matter further.'

Michael was reluctant to leave the pleasant cool of the Arblaster home, despite the proximity of the dung heaps and their distinctive aroma, and made excuses to linger. Arblaster started to hold forth about silage, but Jodoca sensed such a topic was unlikely to interest scholars, and tactfully changed the subject to music. She listened to the monk confide his plans for the Michaelhouse Choir, then sang a ballad she had composed; both men sat captivated by her sweet voice, although Bartholomew thought her French left something to be desired. It put him in mind of Matilde, whose grasp of the language was perfect, and some of the pleasure went out of the situation when a pang reminded him of how much he missed her. He stood to take his leave, making the excuse that he had medical duties at Barnwell.

When he and Michael arrived at the priory, Fencotes was resting in the infirmary. Prior Norton's eyes bulged dangerously as he led the way across the yard.

'What happened to him?' asked Bartholomew.

'He had a fall, although I am not sure how. He refuses to talk about it, but I suspect it may have been in the chapel. The paving stones are dreadfully uneven, but no canon wants to admit to taking a tumble in a church – it looks as though he is not holy enough to warrant the protection of the saints.'

'Have you learned any more about the talisman you found?' asked Michael taking the holy-stone pendant from his scrip and swinging it about on its thong. 'We believe Carton might have been killed by the Sorcerer, which means this nasty little bauble belongs to him.'

'To the Sorcerer?' Norton was aghast, and his eyes opened so wide that Bartholomew was sure he was going to lose them for good. 'You mean he was here? In our convent?'

'It seems likely,' replied Michael, with what Bartholomew thought was unfounded confidence. 'After all, you have virtually no security, so anyone can come and go as he pleases. Even powerful warlocks.'

'Do you have any ideas about the Sorcerer's identity?' asked Bartholomew, feeling sorry for Norton.

The Prior swallowed hard, still shocked by Michael's revelations. He glanced around uneasily, as if he imagined the dark magician might suddenly appear. 'We discuss little else at the moment. We may be removed from the town physically, but that does not mean we are unaffected by what happens in it. We are all worried about the Sorcerer.'

'So tell me what these discussions have concluded,' ordered Michael.

Norton looked unhappy. 'We have suspicions, but no real evidence. Arblaster founded the All Saints coven, and remains one of its most influential members. Then there is Refham the blacksmith, who started to dabble in the occult at about the time folk began to talk about the Sorcerer. Spaldynge is another – he is nasty and vicious. Then Sheriff Tulyet owns books that deal with witchery, and there are some very unpalatable priests – Eyton, for example. And Pechem.'

Bartholomew stopped listening when it became clear Norton was reciting a list of men he did not like. He wondered how many more people were doing the same across the town, and hoped they would have the good sense to demand proof of guilt before accusing anyone openly. It occurred to him that anonymity was a cunning ploy on the Sorcerer's part, because it added to his air of mystery – which would further impress those who admired him, and serve to unsettle those who did not.

'What is wrong with Pechem?' he asked, not seeing what there was to dislike about the head of the Cambridge Franciscans. The Prior was not a bundle of fun, but he was decent and honourable.

Norton grimaced. 'Some of his friars accused us of setting the Hardy house alight.'

Bartholomew struggled to understand what he was talking about. 'You mean the couple who died in their sleep together last year? Their empty home was incinerated a few weeks later?'

'The place was said to be inhabited by their restless spirits,' recalled Michael. 'And Thomas said it was your canons who burned it down.'

'And did you?' asked Bartholomew. He shrugged when Norton regarded him indignantly. 'If it was haunted, then perhaps you thought it was better destroyed. It stood close to your grounds, and—'

'We are not arsonists,' objected Norton. 'But the building *was* haunted – there is no doubt about it.'

'Why do you think that?' asked Bartholomew curiously.

'Because two people do not die in their sleep at the

same time, and the house always had an eerie feel after they had gone. I know you investigated vigorously, Brother, and your Corpse Examiner of the time did his best, but I remain convinced that the Hardy deaths were unnatural.'

'So you said at the time,' said Michael. 'But you were unable to say why.'

'It was just a sense I had that something untoward had happened. The Hardys practised witchery, but you dismissed that as irrelevant. Perhaps you will reconsider now you understand that dark magic is actually a rather potent force.'

Michael gave him a sharp look, not liking the notion that fellow clerics should acknowledge the power of witchcraft. 'And did you fire their house after they died?'

Norton shook his head, but there was an uneasiness in his eyes; he was not a good liar.

'But you know who did,' said Bartholomew. 'Who was it? It will not be Podiolo, because he would never tear himself away from his alchemy for long enough. Was it Fencotes? He is not the kind of man to tolerate a haunted house on his doorstep.'

Norton mumbled something that sounded like a denial, but Bartholomew glanced at Michael and thought they had their answer. Norton saw the look and became testy. 'I said it held an evil aura, Brother, but you declined to come out at midnight and experience it for yourself. So, yes, perhaps we did take matters into our own hands. And why not? We have had no trouble from it since.'

Michael regarded him tiredly. 'So you admit to arson. What about the Hardys, then? Did any of your canons take matters into his own hands there, too? Because they played with dark magic?'

Norton shook his head again, this time vehemently. 'When they were alive, we thought nothing of their religious preferences. It was only when they were dead that their house took on an . . . atmosphere.'

There was no more to be said, so Bartholomew left Michael to show the talisman to the canons, while he went to tend Fencotes in the infirmary. Norton went with him, apparently afraid that he might accuse the old man of something that would upset him.

The infirmary was blissfully cool, and Podiolo was in his office, dozing while something bubbled over a brazier. It smelled rank, and it occurred to Bartholomew that an ability to produce noxious odours was something that might benefit the Sorcerer. He shook himself, aware that he was beginning to suspect everyone for the most innocuous of reasons. Fencotes was reading in the infirmary's chapel, but did not seem to be suffering unduly from his tumble. There were three large splinters in the palm of one hand that Podiolo had felt unequal to removing, and a bruise on the point of his shoulder.

'How did you say this happened?' asked Bartholomew.

'I fell,' replied Fencotes shiftily. 'It happens when you reach my age.'

'Falls usually involve grazed knees or hands,' said Bartholomew. 'But yours—'

'Do not question the veracity of an old man,' chided Fencotes mildly. 'It is not seemly. I told you I fell, and that should be enough for you.'

Bartholomew frowned. The chapel floor was stone, so Fencotes should not have acquired splinters from it, while it was strange to suffer a bruise on the shoulder but nowhere else. It was more likely that the old man had fallen out of bed, but did not want to admit to such an embarrassing episode to his colleagues. Obligingly, the physician dropped the subject.

'Your Prior tells me you dislike witches,' he said instead. He saw Norton roll his eyes; he had not expected Bartholomew to launch into the subject with no warning.

Fencotes nodded, unabashed. 'I dislike anything that challenges God. I did more than my share of it when I was a secular, so now I must make amends. And yes, I did burn the Hardy house to the ground, if that is what you are really asking. Their deaths were suspicious, and I am sure the building was plagued by their restless spirits. I said prayers as the house went up in flames, and I feel they are at peace now.'

'How can they be at peace if they were witches?' asked Bartholomew curiously. 'Surely, they will be in Hell?'

Fencotes smiled wanly. 'These are weighty theological questions, beyond my meagre wits. Suffice to say that I detect nothing sinister about the location now.'

'How do you think they died? You clearly did not accept Rougham's verdict.'

'I think they were slain by the Devil, because they summoned him and he found them lacking. They were not truly evil folk, just misguided. Their daughters died of the plague, and that is enough to send any man into the arms of Satan.' Fencotes's expression was immeasurably sad, leading Bartholomew to wonder whether he had lost children to the Death, too. 'I did what was necessary.'

The physician supposed no real harm had been done, given that the property had been unoccupied and there were no heirs to suffer from a loss of revenue. And the incident seemed unimportant compared to the other

309

investigations he and Michael were pursuing. He turned his attention back to medicine, and was silent as he smeared a goose-grease salve on the old man's shoulder.

'Will you tell Langelee we are ready to offer sixteen marks for Sewale Cottage?' asked Norton, watching him work.

'We already have an offer of sixteen,' said Bartholomew absently, most of his attention on his patient. 'Sixteen and a consignment of dung, to be precise.'

'Seventeen, then,' said Fencotes immediately. Bartholomew glanced up to see Norton regarding the older man in surprise. Fencotes shrugged, wincing as he did so. 'Why not? It will be worth twice that in a few years, the way prices are rising, and we are in the market for the long haul. Besides, it really will make an excellent site for a granary. It will be worth every penny.'

'What about the bribe, then?' asked Norton. 'We do not have much manure, so what about a few goats instead? I think we have about seven that you could choose from. They are black, though. Do you have a problem with black? Some folk do not like it.'

'Lord!' muttered Bartholomew, his thoughts reeling.

'Or if livestock is not to your taste, you can have this,' said Fencotes, rummaging in his scrip and producing a small pouch. 'It is an amulet against evil, and contains one of St James's teeth.'

Bartholomew was astonished that Fencotes should be willing to part with such a thing – and that he had converted a holy relic into what was essentially a magical charm. 'You must want this house very badly,' was all he could think of to say.

'I would not mind living in Sewale Cottage when I am too old to carry out my duties here. It will allow me to sit in the window and watch the world go by. I cannot do it at Barnwell, because the world does not come this way.'

Bartholomew packed away his salve. 'I did not know you owned an amulet.'

'Nor did I,' said Norton uneasily. 'It is not right to tout the teeth of saints around, Fencotes. Men have been struck dead for less.'

'And this one *is* sacred,' said Fencotes, regarding it fondly. 'It came from Rome. Do not confuse it with the kind of "holy-stone" hawked about by Arderne, or the charms dispensed by Mother Valeria.'

'She is losing her power,' said Norton, ranging off on another subject. 'People are talking about it in the town. Her cures are less effective now, and her curses do not work as well as they did.'

'She does not curse people,' objected Bartholomew loyally.

'Of course she does,' said Fencotes, while Norton nodded his agreement. 'She is a witch. Ask her if you do not believe me – I am told you and she are on very good terms. Her waning power must be worrisome to her, though. Her reputation is based on the fact that she frightens people, but if they realise she cannot harm them, she may find herself reviled. People do not like witches.'

'What people are these?' asked Bartholomew, supposing Valeria's sudden lurch from favour was why she had felt compelled to wander about on a knee that should have been rested. 'Most folk I meet seem to be very much in favour of them.'

'Then you are mixing with the wrong crowd,' said Norton. 'Because ones *we* meet – and there are a lot of them, because they come here for our honey – are violently opposed to the rise of evil.'

311

'These folk do not think witchcraft is evil,' said Bartholomew. 'They are only—'

'Witchery *is* evil,' interrupted Fencotes firmly. 'And if you disagree with me, it shows you favour Satan. It is obvious you consort with him, because I can see his teeth-marks on your hand.'

'Dickon Tulyet,' explained Bartholomew.

'Something worse than the Devil, then,' said Norton wryly. He brought the discussion back on track. 'So seventeen marks, a goat and St James's incisor it is, then.'

'Tell Langelee,' said Fencotes. He looked sly. 'If you decline, I may inform folk that you healed my bruises by invoking the Devil.'

Bartholomew raised his eyebrows. 'People will believe that, will they? That I can bring a demon into the sacred confines of your convent?'

Fencotes winked. 'Convey our latest offer to Langelee, and you will not have to find out.'

Bartholomew was relieved to escape from the infirmary and declined to answer Podiolo's half-hearted questions about salves. Normally, he was happy to teach the Florentine about the medicines he was supposed to dispense, but Fencotes had unsettled him, and he wanted to leave. He walked into the yard and looked for Michael. Norton followed him.

'I think poor Fencotes might be losing his wits,' said the Prior uncomfortably. 'It must be this dreadful weather. It is responsible for luring decent folk to the Sorcerer's side, and now it has led Fencotes to offer you talismans and threats.'

'So much for your claim that the canons do not own such things.'

'They do not,' declared Norton. 'You heard Fencotes.

312

There is a world of difference between an amulet containing a saint's tooth and the profane thing he found at the spot where Carton died.'

Michael was not long finishing his enquiries, and returned to report that none of the canons or the servants admitted to recognising the holy-stone Fencotes had found in their chapel.

'What do you think?' he asked, as they rode home. 'Is Carton's killer – the Sorcerer – at Barnwell? Norton is a well-built man, and would make an imposing figure in a hooded cloak. Meanwhile Podiolo will be excellent at creating fumes and smoke.'

'Your Junior Proctor told me the Sorcerer's Latin is not very good,' said Bartholomew. 'Does that mean we should eliminate the canons from our lists at suspects?'

Michael shook his head. 'Podiolo and Norton have excellent Latin, but they are both clever enough to disguise that fact. Fencotes's Latin is genuinely poor, though, because he has not been a canon for very long.'

Bartholomew was thoughtful. 'His injuries were curious, and I know he did not get them from a fall in the chapel. Then there is his amulet. The fact that he is ready to relinquish such a valuable thing means he must want Sewale Cottage very badly. I wonder why.'

Michael frowned. 'Arblaster wants it badly, too, as do Spynk and Dick Tulyet. Also, it was burgled the night Margery died, and you have seen Beard and the giant loitering nearby twice since.'

'What are you saying?' asked Bartholomew, uneasy with the notion that Tulyet was being mentioned in company with men he did not much like.

'I was thinking about the chalk circle on Margery's doorstep. I rubbed it out and forgot about it, but perhaps

313

my action was precipitous. I wonder whether it had anything to do with the fact that at least four parties are very eager to own that house.'

Bartholomew regarded him doubtfully. 'I am not sure that makes sense . . .'

'No, it does not, but neither does anything else about this case. However, I suggest we visit Sewale Cottage later, and go through it carefully to ensure we do not sell something we later wish we had kept. Something the Sorcerer may want, for example. Or something his enemies are keen to keep from him.'

'But there is nothing in it. It is empty.'

'That did not stop the giant and Beard from searching, did it? We shall take Cynric with us and do a bit of investigating ourselves, but I would rather no one saw us. We shall do it at midnight.'

Bartholomew groaned. 'That will set the gossip alight, Brother. Two Michaelhouse Fellows grubbing about in an abandoned house at the witching hour. *We* will be accused of being the Sorcerer.'

'Good,' said Michael grimly. 'Perhaps it will force the real one to show his hand.'

Chapter 9

There was a commotion in the Market Square as Bartholomew and Michael rode back into the town. One of the three crones who sold wizened vegetables was screeching at the top of her voice. She was surrounded by people, and more were hurrying to join the mob with each passing moment. Bartholomew's brother-in-law was among them, standing with Arblaster and Jodoca. Meanwhile, Mildenale and William formed a tight cluster with the scholars of Bene't College, who included Master Heltisle and Eyton. Spaldynge lurked near his Clare colleagues, but was separate enough to suggest they spurned his company. Bartholomew was shocked at the change in him: his normally neat clothes were dirty and dishevelled, and his beard was matted. He looked like a man on the verge of insanity. Refham and Joan were not far away, exchanging cordial remarks with Spynk and looking as though they were thoroughly enjoying the commotion. Cecily merely looked bored.

There were other folk, too, including a gaggle of black-clad preachers who had come to warn Cambridge about the imminent return of the plague. Suttone was talking animatedly to them, and Bartholomew hoped they would not inspire him to preach too grim a sermon to the Guild of Corpus Christi in two days' time. Next to the preachers was a well-dressed man who wore a red rose in the hat that shaded his eyes from the sun. He moved with a self-assured grace that suggested he was used to being in control of things, although his clean-shaven face was youthful.

'Who is he?' Bartholomew asked of Cecily, who had come to leer at Michael. The question was partly for information, but mostly to distract her from her prey. 'I have not seen him before.'

'Nor have I,' replied Cecily. 'But you are right to ogle him, because he is a pretty fellow. He rejected *my* company in no uncertain terms, but he is smiling at you. Make a play for him.'

Bartholomew was not quite sure how to reply to that advice, and the man's 'smile' was actually a squint from the brightness of the sun, anyway. He was about to say so, but Spynk noticed what Cecily was up to, and came to haul her away, scowling as he did so. Michael ignored them both.

'I sense real menace in this crowd,' said the monk, as he dismounted. 'They have aligned themselves according to faction: those who support the Church, and those who prefer the Sorcerer.'

Bartholomew slid off his pony with a sigh of relief. 'Actually, I suspect most do not know what to think, and will make their decision on Sunday, after they have seen what the Sorcerer is capable of.'

'What are they doing with that old woman?' Michael winced when a particularly loud screech tore through the air, and other voices rose to make themselves heard above it.

316

'Of course she is a witch,' Heltisle was saying. He held the crone's skinny arm in a grip that was the cause of her noisy distress. 'And she loiters too close to my College for comfort. I want her gone.'

'Let her be,' said Eyton quietly, trying to prise the Master's fingers open. 'She is an elderly lady and is doing no harm. I will give her a bit of honey, which will—'

'She is a denizen of Hell,' countered William. 'She spat at me yesterday.'

'One does not necessarily imply the other, Father,' said Stanmore. 'Lots of people spit at you.'

'Yes,' agreed William, glowering around. 'And it means there are lots of heretics about.'

'What is going on here?' demanded Michael. The crowd parted to let him through.

'Heltisle and William say this person is a hell-hag,' explained Mildenale helpfully. 'Arblaster and Jodoca say she is not. And Stanmore and Eyton say that even if she is, we should leave her alone. I say we let God decide by—'

'She is *not* a witch,' said Jodoca, regarding Heltisle and William with reproachful eyes. 'She has been selling her wares here for decades, so why take against her now?'

'That is a good question,' said Michael, looking at the two scholars. 'Do you have an answer?'

'The answer is that the Sorcerer is gathering his minions,' replied William. 'And the best way to attack him is to strike at his servants. That will weaken him and strengthen the Church.'

'We had better eliminate Bartholomew then,' muttered Spaldynge. 'He is stronger and more dangerous than any crone.'

317

'You are doubtless right,' said Mildenale, eyeing the physician uneasily. 'He keeps charms and mugwort in his medical bag, and probably stole Danyell's hand for anatomy. Necromancy—'

'You can leave him alone, too,' interrupted Jodoca. 'He saved my husband from the flux – rescued not only his physical form, but his soul, as well. Mother Valeria was going to have it if he died.'

There was a gasp from the crowd. Some folk crossed themselves, but more hands went to amulets that were worn around necks. Eyton had been busy. Bartholomew regarded Jodoca in surprise – he had not expected support from such a quarter.

'Bartholomew might be the Sorcerer himself,' said Spaldynge, fixing the physician with eyes that did not seem quite sane. 'He can cure warts, which is the Sorcerer's speciality.'

'Actually, he is hopeless with warts,' argued Stanmore. 'I had one for months, and none of his remedies worked. But the spell I bought from the Sorcerer banished the thing in a few days. Look.'

Spaldynge barely glanced at the proffered hand. 'Mother Valeria used to be good with warts, but she is losing her power now the Sorcerer is on the rise. Perhaps that is why Bartholomew has taken to lurking in grave-yards of late – he has stolen her remedy and is collecting the mystical ingredients to use himself. There is a rumour that Goldynham still wanders at night, so perhaps they do it together.'

'Do not talk nonsense,' said Eyton, while Bartholomew regarded Spaldynge in horror, appalled by the accus-ation. 'Goldynham has not been discussing warts with anyone, because I have kept him in the church.'

The attack on Bartholomew meant attention had strayed from the crone, and she seized the opportunity to escape. She was not fast on her feet, and anyone could have laid hold of her, but no one did. She hobbled into the trees at the back of St Mary the Great and disappeared from sight.

'You should be ashamed of yourselves,' said Michael, glaring around at the crowd in distaste. Some had the grace to look sheepish. 'Picking on old women! What is wrong with you?'

'True,' agreed William. 'We should set our sights on more powerful magicians. Like Valeria.'

'No,' said Bartholomew. 'She is an old woman, too, and—'

'See how he races to defend his familiar?' pounced Spaldynge. 'He *is* a warlock!'

'He raced to defend an elderly lady,' corrected Stanmore with quiet reason. 'Lord knows, I have no love for witches, but it is not right to lynch them without a proper trial.'

'Besides, Valeria might be one of the Sorcerer's servants,' said Mildenale thoughtfully. 'And we should not antagonise him unnecessarily, not until we know what we are up against. God tells me—'

'I have been thinking about this Sorcerer,' interrupted Heltisle. 'And I do not believe he has amassed all this power everyone keeps talking about. I think it is just rumour and speculation, with no hard fact to back it up. So, I have decided to side with the Church. Who will stand with me?'

'Me,' said William, immediately striding forward with Mildenale at his heels. Other scholars joined them, although it was clear they were uncomfortable siding with

319

the Franciscan fanatics and the arrogant Master of Bene't College.

'The Church will crush all sinners,' declared Mildenale, glaring at the people who held back. 'Their souls will be condemned to everlasting torment.'

'Perhaps they will, but I shall wait until Trinity Sunday before stating a preference,' said Eyton. His normally cheerful face was unhappy. 'We should not make up our minds without having all the facts.'

'I am with you, Eyton,' said Stanmore, while William gaped at the priest. 'We should wait and see.'

A good part of the crowd mumbled their agreement; the cautious by far outweighed the zealots.

'Well, *I* think the Sorcerer will not approve of folk who only support him once they have seen his strength,' said Refham. 'So who is with him – the man who will make us wealthy with his magic?'

Arblaster, Cecily and Joan rushed to stand next to him, along with a number of folk from the Guild of Corpus Christi. Suttone watched them in horror, and Bartholomew suspected that his Saturday night speech might contain a section about the perils of witchery, too. Jodoca hesitated for a moment, but then went to join her husband.

'So,' murmured Michael. 'The battle lines are drawn.'

The altercation in the Market Square fizzled out when it became clear that most people did not know what to think about the confrontation between conventional religion and magic. Mildenale began a haranguing sermon about the Church's disapproval of heretics, which served to drive many onlookers away; more still joined the exodus when William added his thoughts on the matter. It was not long before the mob had dissipated, and folk had gone about their business.

Bartholomew and Michael returned the horses to the Brazen George, where the landlord said he was pleased to have them back, because the Sheriff wanted them. Tulyet's own mounts were worn out or lame from chasing robbers on the Huntingdon Way, and he needed more if he was to stand any chance of catching the villains. He looked hot and weary when he came to collect the nags, and there was dust in his beard. For the first time, Bartholomew saw the toll the felons' activities were taking on him.

'Dickon is healing well,' Tulyet said, a smile lighting his exhausted face as he thought about his son. 'Thank you for coming to tend him. How is your hand?'

'It has seen me accused of fraternising with the Devil,' replied Bartholomew. 'First by *Mildenalus Sanctus*, and then by Canon Fencotes.'

'You have been to Barnwell?' asked Tulyet keenly. 'Did they make a new bid on Sewale Cottage?'

'Seventeen marks and some dung,' replied Bartholomew. 'And an amulet with teeth in it.'

'I will offer eighteen marks,' said Tulyet. 'And we had better discuss bribes when I am more alert. Corruption is not something that comes readily to His Majesty's officials – well, not to me, at least – and I should not attempt it when I am tired.'

'Eighteen?' echoed Michael. 'Why in God's name would you pay that much? It is not worth it.'

'It is to me. It is close enough to allow me to keep a fatherly eye on Dickon, but not so near that he will complain about me looking over his shoulder. It will be a perfect place for a young man.'

Michael regarded him doubtfully. 'But eighteen marks, Dick! I am astonished.'

'Why? Michaelhouse will be paying a good deal over the odds to acquire the Refham properties. You are not happy about it, but you will raise the required amount, because the location is important to you and it is a once in a lifetime opportunity. It is the same for me and Sewale Cottage.'

Michael nodded, but Bartholomew could see his suspicions were not allayed. The monk might have accepted Tulyet's logic, but why were the others so keen to purchase the place? Did they really want an occasional residence for when they happened to visit Cambridge, like Spynk, or because it would make a good place for a granary, like Barnwell, or because its garden was suitable for compost, like Arblaster? And why were the giant and Beard interested in it?

'Dickon is doing well with his reading,' said Tulyet with considerable pride, changing the subject to one he considered more pleasant. 'He sits for hours with one particular tome, and I cannot help but wonder whether he might become a scholar.'

'Lord!' breathed Michael in horror. 'I sincerely hope not!'

Bartholomew did not want to talk about Dickon, either, so he told Tulyet about the giant and Beard, and the various encounters he had had with them. 'Refham has been renting them his forge,' he concluded. 'It lies on the Huntingdon Way – the road your felons have been haunting.'

'You believe they might be two of my robbers?' asked Tulyet. 'There must be fifteen or twenty villains in this gang, so it is certainly possible that a couple slink into the town on occasion. They are not known to the people who live on the highway, which is unusual, because most criminals are local.'

'Outsiders, then?' asked Michael.

'I believe so. The resident felons object to this invasion of their territory, so they are actually trying to help me. My men tell me the Sorcerer is responsible – not by taking part in the raids himself, but by providing the robbers with charms that render them invisible to my men. I am beginning to think they might be right, because no thieves are *that* good. I do not understand how they continue to elude me.'

'I heard they have killed people,' said Bartholomew. 'Is it true?'

Tulyet nodded. 'Several times, so as to leave no witnesses. They are careful and ruthless.'

'And they are keeping you occupied, so you cannot help me with the Sorcerer,' mused Michael. 'Perhaps they are just one more strand in the mystery we are trying to unravel.'

'How so?' asked Tulyet. He leaned against a wall and took the jug of ale that the landlord brought him, gulping it thirstily. But his eyes never left Michael's face. 'Explain.'

'We believe Carton was murdered by the Sorcerer,' began Michael. 'We also think the Sorcerer is responsible for leaving blood in the baptismal font, for stealing Danyell's hand, for making off with Bene't College's goats, and for exhuming Margery and Goldynham.'

'He is also setting the town at each other's throats, as people begin to align themselves with him or the Church,' added Bartholomew. 'Older, established witches, like Mother Valeria, are said to be losing their power, and charms and amulets appear wherever we look.'

'Everything is connected to the Sorcerer,' concluded Michael. 'And now it seems that even your robbers may have a link with him.'

Tulyet finished his ale and headed for the horses. 'Then we must work together to ensure his nefarious plans do not succeed.'

Watching Tulyet drink reminded Michael that he was thirsty, too, and he suggested going inside the Brazen George for refreshment. Bartholomew agreed, because tavern ale was likely to be better than anything on offer at Michaelhouse, and it was time they analysed some of what they had discovered.

'The Sorcerer. The murder of Carton. Sewale Cottage,' said Michael, counting points off on his fingers once they were settled. 'If we can determine the identity of this wretched warlock, we will know Carton's killer *and* why everyone is so determined to have Margery's house.'

'I am not so sure about the last bit,' said Bartholomew. 'Just because some of our would-be buyers are diabolists does not mean the house is connected to the Sorcerer.'

'Actually, I am inclined to think *all* our would-be buyers are diabolists.'

'Not Dick. I know his father was one, but Dick is not.' Bartholomew turned his thoughts to the other buyers. 'Arblaster belongs to the All Saints coven, while Spynk hates the Church because of his quarrel with the Bishop. And we should not forget that Spynk arrived in Cambridge just before Ascension Day, which is when all these odd events began.'

Michael nodded thoughtfully. 'Meanwhile, the canons of Barnwell are unusual fellows. Podiolo is an alchemist,

324

and Norton and Fencotes have both revealed superstitious beliefs.'

'But there is nothing to say any of them is the Sorcerer. However, it might be someone like Refham, who is a ruthless, grasping sort. Or Spaldynge, who seems to be losing his sanity.' Bartholomew was thoughtful. 'Yet while I am uncertain whether Sewale Cottage is central to our investigation, I am not sure the same can be said for Danyell.'

'I have no idea what you are talking about,' said Michael wearily.

Bartholomew took a moment to rally his thoughts. 'He died of natural causes, but someone mutilated his body. He was returning from London, where he was complaining to the King about your Bishop. He was travelling with Spynk, who is desperate to buy Sewale Cottage, and he was probably enjoying romantic relations with Cecily.'

'Along with anyone else who has the time,' muttered Michael.

'He believed in witchery, and Spynk thought he might have been going to see Mother Valeria for a remedy the night he died. She told me he did not arrive. She also said she did not take his hand, and thought the Sorcerer might have had it . . .' He fell silent.

'Is this analysis going somewhere?' asked Michael. 'Or am I supposed to guess what it all means?'

'I am afraid you are going to have to guess,' said Bartholomew apologetically. 'I thought I saw the beginnings of a solution, but I was wrong. All I see are more questions. However, there is something about Danyell that makes me think he is important.'

They were quiet for a while, each racking his brains for answers, but none were forthcoming, so they left the tavern and braved the outside again, squinting in the sun's brightness after the gloom within. They met Isnard, who said Cynric was looking for Bartholomew because he was needed by a patient who lived near St Giles's Church. Bartholomew began to walk that way, and Michael accompanied him, vainly hoping that the physician might have a flash of insight regarding Danyell.

'Look,' said the monk suddenly, pointing. 'There is *Mildenalus Sanctus*, loaded down with books. I hope he has not taken them from the library, or Deynman's displeasure will be felt from here to Ely.'

'I hope he is not going to burn them,' said Bartholomew, alarmed. 'He sees heresy in the most innocent of texts, and books are too valuable to be tossed on a bigot's pyre.'

'I noticed you two did not leap to the Church's defence earlier,' said the Franciscan accusingly as he approached. He was red-faced and panting; the books were heavy and he was carrying a lot of them. 'I expected more of you.'

'And I expected more of you,' flashed Michael. 'You encouraged Spaldynge's belief that Matt dabbles in witchery. How could you accuse a colleague of necromancy in public?'

'I do what God tells me,' replied Mildenale coolly. 'And amulets, mugwort and a love of anatomy are things that should not be swept under the carpet. It is my duty to expose heretics.'

There was no point in arguing once God was involved, and Michael did not try. 'Where are you going with those?' he asked, gesturing to the tomes.

'They are for my hostel – gifts from friends. I firmly

believe Michaelhouse *will* succeed in purchasing the Refham houses, and I plan to open my doors to students by the end of the term. I shall call it St Catherine's.'

'I am astonished by your confidence,' said Michael, a little suspiciously. 'Because *I* think Refham will force the price too high for us. I have seen you with him on several occasions of late. Were you discussing the sale? Or perhaps negotiating a price for the painting job you offered him?'

'Neither – he has been building me some bookshelves. Unfortunately, they are not up to standard, and I have been obliged to tell him they will have to be reassembled.'

'That should not surprise you,' said Bartholomew. 'He is a blacksmith, not a carpenter.'

Mildenale grimaced. 'Yes, but he agreed to make the shelves for a very reasonable price, and told me he is talented with wood. But he lied: his craftsmanship is terrible.'

'What did he say when you challenged him?' asked Michael curiously. 'I cannot imagine he was pleased, because no man likes to be told his work is shoddy.'

'He said I have no eye for quality, and threatened to raise the price of his mother's shops if I complained about him to anyone else. So you had better not let on I told you, Brother.'

Bartholomew had been looking at the titles of the volumes in Mildenale's arms. He pointed to one called *The Book of Secrets*, which brazenly sported a black pentagram. It was similar to the tome that was missing from Michaelhouse, but was smaller, newer and far less worn. 'Which friend gave you that?'

'William found it in the servants' quarters, and I intend

to burn it. A bonfire of heretical texts will be the climax of my hostel's inauguration ceremony, so I shall be collecting them avidly from now on. Carton was struck down before he could complete his work, so I have taken up where he left off.'

'I am sure he would be very proud of you,' said Michael flatly.

Mildenale did not seem to notice his colleagues' distaste for what he was proposing. 'You might want to give me some of your texts, Bartholomew. I know you own scrolls by the woman healer called Trotula, because I have seen them.'

'Trotula's works are not heresy,' objected Bartholomew. 'They tell how to cure common—'

'I know what they contain,' said Mildenale shortly. 'Just because I consider them anathema does not mean I am unfamiliar with their content. That would make me an ignoramus, would it not?'

Michael watched him go. 'God save us from zealots,' he breathed, crossing himself vigorously.

They walked up Bridge Street, and Bartholomew looked at Sewale Cottage as they passed. The door had been repaired, and bright new wood showed where part of the door frame had been replaced. He went to inspect it more closely, and was unimpressed with the work. Blaston had been careless.

'Actually, Refham did it,' said Michael. 'He charged half what Blaston wanted, and Langelee is always eager to save money. Unfortunately, the price kept going up as the work went on, and we ended up paying twice as much. And now you say he has done an inferior job into the bargain?'

'By the time he migrates to Luton, there will not be

a soul in Cambridge he has not cheated,' said Bartholomew in disgust.

Michael pointed to the cottage's single front window, where the shutter had been prised open, and then pushed closed to disguise the damage. 'That was not broken when I last looked. Someone has been inside *again*, searching for God knows what. I suppose it was Beard and his giant friend. Still, we shall conduct our own hunt tonight, and we *will* find whatever it is they have been looking for.'

It was late afternoon by the time Bartholomew arrived home. He was obliged to leave again almost immediately, because there were several more patients who wanted him. Michael went to his office at St Mary the Great, but before he left he reminded the physician to meet him at Sewale Cottage at midnight.

Bartholomew visited Isnard first, but the bargeman had grown tired of waiting for him and had gone for a drink. Next, he went to the Chancellor, who had the flux, and then to a student in Clare, who had a dried pea lodged in his nose. The lad had partaken enthusiastically of the lunchtime wine, and his friends had played a prank as he lay insensible. Unfortunately, they had been none too sober themselves, and had rammed the pulse home with considerable force. Its removal was an unpleasant experience for everyone concerned, but particularly for Bartholomew, who had the misfortune to meet Spaldynge on his way out.

'How dare you enter my College!' The scent of wine was on Spaldynge's breath, and his eyes had a glazed look that suggested the students were not the only ones who had had too much of it. 'Get out!'

'Willingly,' said Bartholomew, trying to step past him.

But Spaldynge blocked his way. 'I am going to tell the Sorcerer to put a curse on you. He will do it if I ask him nicely.'

'You know him well, then, do you? Who is he?'

Spaldynge sneered. 'That is for you to wonder.'

Bartholomew pushed past him and headed for the gate, sure Spaldynge was just as much in the dark about the Sorcerer's identity as everyone else. Or was he underestimating the man? Spaldynge's increasingly erratic behaviour might be an act designed to make people think he was losing his wits, while all the time he was amassing power. He sighed, disliking the way the case was making him question everyone. He tried to put Spaldynge from his mind as he walked to Bukenham's house. When he arrived there, he found the Junior Proctor lying on his bed with a wet cloth draped across his forehead.

'It is the weather,' said Bartholomew, after an examination told him there was nothing amiss.

'But I feel terrible,' groaned Bukenham pitifully. 'My head pounds.'

Bartholomew suspected he was not drinking as much as he should, and helped him sip some of his remedy for the flux. He was rapidly coming to the conclusion that boiled barley water was one of the most powerful medicines in his arsenal, although he knew he could never share his theory with anyone else. No one would believe him, and there was no point in deliberately courting controversy.

'You can return to work tomorrow,' he said, when Bukenham had finished the bowl and reluctantly conceded that he felt a little better. 'That will please Michael. He needs your help.'

Bukenham looked alarmed, then clapped his hand to his temple. 'I am having a relapse! No, do not remedy me. I would sooner be indisposed, because I do not fancy tackling the Sorcerer.'

'Yes, the Sorcerer *is* dangerous, so it is unfair to lie here while Michael battles him alone.'

'He has you. Besides, I do intend to assist, but in my own way. Michael came to see me earlier, and I have been mulling over what he told me, along with what I know myself – considering all the evidence in a logical manner. Perhaps that is why my head hurts: these are perplexing problems.'

'And?' asked Bartholomew. 'Did all this contemplation result in any useful answers?'

'Not really,' said Bukenham sheepishly. 'But I shall continue my work. Unfortunately, logic tells me the Sorcerer could be just about anyone. However, I have recalled one thing I forgot to mention the last time we talked. Do you remember me saying I witnessed a gathering of the Sorcerer's elite in All Saints' charnel house?'

Bartholomew nodded. 'You said he spoke dismal Latin.'

'Well, I happened across a second, larger gathering a few days later, and I recognised one of the participants. It was Margery Sewale.'

Bartholomew gaped at him. 'I do not believe you! She was a deeply religious woman.'

'Yes, but she was also a witch. Did Michael not mention the magic circle that was drawn outside her house on the night she died? Witches do that as a warding spell, to protect each other's souls when they die. One of her cronies put it there, as a final act of friendship.'

Bartholomew tried to see the gentle Margery crouched

over a cauldron in a dingy hut, like Mother Valeria, and the image would not come. Respectable widows of the mercantile class simply did not do such things, and Bukenham's suggestion was so ludicrous, it was amusing. 'Next you will be telling me this is the reason so many people want to buy her house – they are keen to own a witch's lair.'

Bukenham's gaze was steady. 'Spynk and Arblaster are diabolists, and so was Tulyet's father.'

'The canons of Barnwell are not.'

'Are you sure? Podiolo chants spells in an attempt to make gold from lead. Fencotes owns charms, and even Prior Norton is superstitious. Cynric has always seen them for what they are.'

'Cynric would accuse the Pope himself, were he ever to visit Avignon.'

'And perhaps he would be right – the current Pope is a friend of Bishop de Lisle, who is hardly salubrious company. But we are digressing. Margery *was* a witch, although that did not make her evil. However, I am not sure the same can be said about the Sorcerer. I think he started innocuously enough, but he is not innocent now. He has sold himself to Satan, and is full of dark magic.'

'Magic?' echoed Bartholomew warily. 'Do you really believe in that sort of thing?'

'Why not? I am not a member of a coven, if that is what you are asking, but I am not so stupid as to believe the Church has all the answers.'

Bartholomew left feeling uncomfortable. It was growing dark, and the town seemed to be full of whispers. He passed St Bene't's Church, then stopped dead in his tracks when he saw a tall, white-haired figure dressed in a gold cloak.

'You let me die, physician. And I am here to make things even.'

Bartholomew sighed, aware that 'Goldynham' had chosen to make his appearance at a time when that part of the High Street was momentarily empty, so as to ensure there were no witnesses. He wondered why he had been singled out for such treatment – or did the prankster perform for others, too? He might have suspected his students, were it not for the fact that they had all been sent home.

'You are likely to get yourself killed doing this,' he said warningly. 'Someone might believe you really *are* Goldynham, and take steps to ensure your "corpse" wanders no more.'

'You will die, physician,' said the figure in a low, sinister hiss. 'You will join me in the ground.'

Bartholomew felt his patience evaporate. It was one thing to appear in the guise of a dead man, but another altogether to make threats. It was nasty, and he was tired, hot and in no mood for shoddy japes. He stepped forward, intending to lay hold of the fellow and demand an explanation, but someone collided with him before he could do so. The force of the impact almost knocked him from his feet.

'Sorry,' gasped Isnard, staggering in an attempt to keep his balance. For a man with one leg, Isnard could move at an astonishing clip. 'I was not expecting anyone to have stopped in the middle of the road.'

'Did you see him?' asked Bartholomew, turning back to the cemetery. But the prankster had gone.

'See who?' asked Isnard. 'Eyton? He will be inside, praying next to the corpse that escaped from its grave the other night. The Sorcerer mentioned at a coven meeting that sunset is a favourite time for the dead to walk, so poor Eyton is trapped in his church at this time every night now. He will have to do it until Goldynham is back in his grave, with a few charms to keep him there.'

Bartholomew was reluctant to tell Isnard what the prankster had done: the bargeman had been drinking, and could not be relied on to accept that the 'apparition' was not the dead silversmith but some sorry individual with a spiteful sense of humour. He did, however, want to search the cemetery to see if the culprit was still lurking there, but was loath to do it alone lest the villain had an accomplice. So he grabbed Isnard's arm, mumbling something about a missing student, and dragged him through the vegetation, childbirth forceps at the ready. But the place was deserted.

'We can try the church,' suggested Isnard helpfully, picking dead leaves from his tunic. 'Perhaps your lad is hiding there.'

It was a distinct possibility, so Bartholomew strode inside St Bene't's, the bargeman hobbling at his heels, but it was empty except for Eyton who was on his knees in the chancel. The priest was reciting an exorcism over Goldynham's coffin, and Isnard shuddered – even though the words were Latin, and he could not understand them, Eyton still managed to give them a distinctly sinister inflection.

'May I help you?' asked Eyton, glancing up as he flicked holy water across the casket. Then he reached down and drew a pentagram on the floor with what appeared to be a black candle.

Bartholomew looked at him hard, wondering whether *he* had disguised himself as Goldynham, perhaps to frighten people into buying more of his charms. He would not have to appear to many folk – just one or two would be enough to start the rumours flying. But, Bartholomew thought grimly, Eyton would be disappointed if he thought *he* was going to blab about what he had seen.

'We came to see how you were,' said Isnard, feeling some sort of response was needed and seeing the physician was not going to supply one. 'I imagine it is unnerving in here, all on your own.'

'I do not mind,' said Eyton with a grin. 'And I like to be of service to the town. Did you know my incantations are the only thing preventing Goldynham from visiting the Eagle and ordering himself a jug of ale?'

'Just as long as he does not expect *me* to treat him,' murmured Isnard. 'I am not in the habit of buying drinks for corpses: you cannot rely on them to be around to return the favour later.'

'Where is his cloak?' asked Bartholomew. His voice echoed around the church, and he realised he had spoken far louder than he had intended. Priest and bargeman looked at him in surprise.

'Sent to Trumpington for cleaning,' replied Eyton. 'The Guild refuses to bury him until he is decently dressed, although as far as I am concerned, the sooner he is back in the ground, the better.'

Isnard and Eyton immediately embarked on a discussion about the importance of clean grave-clothes, while Bartholomew prowled the shadowy church. Did the prankster know some little-used path that had allowed him to escape from the cemetery? Or had Eyton divested himself of his disguise and dropped to his knees the moment the door had opened? Bartholomew liked Eyton, and sincerely hoped he was not the kind of man to jump out on passers-by while pretending to be a corpse. Eventually, he took his leave, and was relieved when Isnard offered to accompany him as far as the Great Bridge – the physician had been summoned to see Mother Valeria again. He was not in the mood for more japes, and suspected the prankster would think twice about pestering him if the bargeman was there.

'You seem to have made a remarkable recovery,' he said as they walked. 'The message Cynric received earlier said you had the flux and were at death's door.'

Isnard looked sheepish. 'I was hoping Brother Michael would come to give me last rites. Then I was going to stage a miraculous revival, so he would think I am blessed by the saints and will let me back in the choir. But I grew tired of waiting, and the King's Head beckoned. Perhaps I will try it tomorrow. What do you think?'

'That he is unlikely to be deceived, and you will make him more hostile towards you than ever. You may have better luck with the latrines, though. He does not want Arblaster to have them.'

Isnard beamed. 'Thank God! Will you tell him I escorted you around the town at great personal risk to myself? It is not safe being out here, not with the Sorcerer on the loose. Here is your brother-in-law.'

Bartholomew glanced sharply at him, wondering whether the two statements had been put together for a reason. Stanmore was walking home after a business meeting, several apprentices at his heels.

'You should not be out, Matt,' Stanmore said. 'No sane man should, not with the Sorcerer at large.'

'See?' whispered Isnard in the physician's ear.

'Did you offer to clean Goldynham's cloak?' asked Bartholomew, wondering whether the prankster had

336

appropriated the real one, or whether he had just happened to have a similar one in his wardrobe.

Stanmore was startled by the abrupt question, but answered it anyway. 'Yes. I took it to Trumpington because I thought it best to wash it well away from superstitious eyes.'

'You mean Cynric's?' asked Isnard wryly.

Stanmore nodded. 'And I did not want witches trying to cut bits off for their sinister rites, either.'

Bartholomew continued his journey towards the castle, grateful that Isnard's presence meant he was not obliged to walk very fast. The evening was stifling, and he was drained of energy.

Isnard peered at him in concern. 'You should go home. Or are you seeing Mother Valeria for a cure? She is good, but not the woman she was a month ago. The Sorcerer has seen to that – her powers have waned as his have risen. Everyone is talking about it.'

'Who is the Sorcerer? Do you know?'

Isnard shook his head vehemently. 'And nor do I want to! I have seen him in his cloak, and that is more than enough for me. Between the two of us, I do not like all this jiggery-pokery. I would rather go to church.' He looked a little anxious. 'You will not tell anyone, will you?'

Bartholomew shook his head, thinking it was a sad state of affairs when a man felt sheepish about admitting that he preferred church to covens.

'Good. There is a rumour that enemies of the Sorcerer will burst into flames on Sunday – the day after his début. I think I shall lie low for a while, until he has invoked so many demonic powers that the Devil will come for him. But here is the Great Bridge, and this is as far as I go.' He shuddered and crossed himself.

337

'If Mother Valeria is losing her power, then why are you afraid to come with me?'

'She may be losing it, but she is not helpless yet. And she does not like me, because I can drink almost as much of her ale as she can. Anyway, good luck and be careful. And if she offers *you* her ale, politely refuse it. You will not stand a chance in that sort of competition.'

It seemed a long way from the bridge to Mother Valeria's hut, partly because Bartholomew was tired, but mostly because the night seemed unusually dark, and for once he did not like being alone. He was alert to the smallest of sounds, expecting to see the prankster or the poisonous whisperer emerge out of the gloom at any moment. And if not them, then there were always the giant and Beard to accost him. He glanced at Sewale Cottage as he passed, but it seemed deserted. Eventually, he reached Valeria's copse, where he tramped along the path and tapped on the door frame to her house.

She called out for him to enter, and he battled through the leather hanging only to find himself surrounded by washing that hung from the rafters. It had evidently been laundry day, and a number of garments were strung up, including a large number of gloves. Bartholomew counted them absently. The hut was tidier than usual, and everything was in neat piles. He wondered why. When at last he reached Valeria, the old woman was crouched on her customary stool with a book. He was surprised, not only that she should own such a thing, but that she should be able to read it. Literacy was not a skill commonly found in wise-women. He recognised the cover, though.

'Michaelhouse is missing a witches' manual,' he said. 'It was stolen yesterday.'

338

'I know – it belonged to Carton. Cynric asked me to use my Seeing Eye to locate it. He is afraid you did not believe him when he said he did not have it, and your good opinion is important to him. This is not Carton's copy, however.'

Bartholomew saw that was true: hers was a different colour and in better condition than the one in Michaelhouse, and he wondered how many of the things were circulating in Cambridge: he had seen Mildenale with one too, destined for his Market Square pyre. 'It is yours?'

She raised an eyebrow, and her expression turned cool. 'It is a guide for witches, and I am a witch, so you should not find that so startling. Or are you questioning my ability to read?'

Bartholomew did not want to reply, so went to look at the page she was perusing. It was in a peculiar combination of Latin and the vernacular. 'You are learning a spell for predicting the future?'

She nodded, and her lips were a thin, pale line between her hooked nose and long chin. 'Necromancers do it by consulting the dead, but I dislike the dead – they have a tendency to be awkward. I prefer potions.' She gestured to the fire. 'I have been brewing that one for days now. It contains powerful herbs, like mandrake and henbane, and a few items that are sacred among my kind. Do not look alarmed, I know what I am doing.'

'Do you?' he asked, forcing himself not to back away. She seemed especially witchlike that night.

She made a low croaking sound that might have been a laugh. 'I have never performed this particular ritual before, but the situation with the Sorcerer has turned deadly and I need to know what I am up against. The rite is not for novices, though, and even skilled warlocks have lost their lives executing it. But I should be able to manage. Would you like to watch?'

'No, thank you!'

She grinned at his alarm. 'Not even to see what your future holds? Whether Matilde will return to you one day? Folk have begged me to cast this spell for them in the past – men like the Sheriff's father, Refham the blacksmith, Spaldynge, John Hardy, the Mayor and the Chancellor – but I have always refused because of the danger. Now I offer you the opportunity – for free – and you decline?'

For a moment, Bartholomew wavered. He would like to know about Matilde, perhaps more than anything in the world, but then the rational part of his mind took over. It was not possible to divine the future, and he would never believe anything Valeria claimed to see anyway. He smiled, and gestured to the mixture, changing the subject slightly, so as not to offend her with a second refusal.

'I hope you do not intend to drink that. Henbane and mandrake are poisonous in the wrong doses.'

'I am aware of that, physician.' Valeria patted the stool next to her. 'Come and sit with me, while we watch it boil. Is there anyone you would like me to curse for you? I can do it, you know.'

He regarded her uneasily. 'I thought you used your knowledge to heal the sick, not to harm folk.'

'I do both. No successful witch puts all her eggs in one basket, and it is sensible to develop a range of skills. I can do something about Father William, if you like. Would you like me to—'

'No! Please leave him alone.'

Valeria's expression was suddenly malevolent, and Bartholomew had an unsettling insight into to why so many people were afraid of her. 'I do not approve of hypocrisy, and I dislike that man, so perhaps I will leave him alone, but perhaps I will not. Still, he is not as bad as that vile Refham.'

Bartholomew was assailed with a sudden sense of misgiving. 'What have you done to him?'

'Done to him?' she asked innocently, although malice burned bright in her eyes. 'Nothing – except bury a stone in a churchyard with his name carved on it. He will be dead before the week is out.'

Bartholomew was vaguely relieved. 'I see.'

Valeria laughed, although it was not a pleasant sound. 'You do not believe it will have any effect. That is good. It means that when he dies, you will not blame me.'

'What has Refham done to warrant your disapproval?'

'He came for a charm that will allow him success in financial matters, but the silver he gave me was base metal. He cheated me, and no one cheats a witch and lives to tell the tale. I reversed my spell, so Michaelhouse can expect to benefit now. That should please you.'

Bartholomew decided he had better bring the discussion around to matters he understood, for he was well out of his depth with the current one. 'How is your knee?'

'Better, thank you. But I asked you to come because I have something to tell you. Last time you were here, you showed me a holy-stone and asked if I recognised it. I told you I did not – it looked like one of the dozens Arderne sold. But then I remembered that all Arderne's were plain, whereas yours had letters on it. I consulted my sisters, and we think it is *not* one of his, but a real one.'

341

'A real what?' asked Bartholomew, puzzled.

'A real charm to protect against wolves and the Devil. And several of my sisters say they saw Carton wearing it. So it did not belong to his killer, but to Carton himself. Such amulets are very, very expensive, so he must have thought he was in serious danger.'

Bartholomew was not sure whether to believe her. 'He was a friar. He would not have—'

'Do not tell me priests spurn charms. Look at Eyton and the canons of Barnwell. Besides, Carton was extremely interested in sorcery. He owned a number of books on the subject and often came to ask me questions. This talisman belonged to Carton, I am sure of it.'

'Then he wasted his money,' said Bartholomew, declining to argue. 'It did not save him.'

'Because he was not *wearing* it,' explained Valeria patiently. 'These amulets are only effective when they are on the person – and Carton's was found near his body, but not on it. Perhaps it fell off during a struggle, perhaps he removed it himself for some reason. You will probably never know.'

Bartholomew considered her claims. Carton *had* owned books on witchcraft, but told everyone they were for a bonfire. Yet who was to say that was true? Perhaps he had collected them with the sole intention of expanding his knowledge on the subject. After all, they had been in a chest, carefully locked, not hurled into a corner like rubbish. Then there was Cynric's testimony. The book-bearer and Carton had watched covens together for months before Carton had suddenly decided to stop.

Mind reeling, Bartholomew stood to leave. 'One of the crones who sells cabbages in the Market Square was almost lynched today. You should consider going away for a few weeks. The Church has some dangerous fanatics, and no witch will be safe until they have burned themselves out.'

Valeria's expression was sad. 'Unfortunately, I suspect it will be a long time before Father William cools down. But perhaps I will do as you suggest. Either way, we shall not meet again.'

Bartholomew stared uneasily at her, hoping it was a revelation of travel plans and not a prediction that one of them was going to die. Then he glanced around the hut and berated himself for his stupidity. The answer was right in front of him. All her belongings were in piles, ready to be packed, and she had washed her clothes. 'You *are* going to leave.'

Valeria smiled. 'I decided you were right. It is no longer safe here, much as it grieves me to say so.'

When he reached the door, he paused and looked back. 'When I first arrived, I noticed a certain asymmetry in your laundry.' He raised his hands at her startled expression. 'I am interested in physics, and these things stand out to me. The oddness comes from the fact that you have only washed seven gloves. I suspect the eighth was dropped in St Michael's Church. Why did you despoil our font?'

She seemed about to deny it, but then shrugged. 'Because of William. I was tired of him preaching against me and my sisters. We have always been here, and we always will be, so why does he rail against us? We do not rail against the Church, tempting though it is to point out its contradictions.'

'Was this blood part of some spell you cast on him?'

Valeria grimaced. 'Yes, but it did not work. I put

chicken blood in the font and sent him the carcass. He ate it – I watched him myself – but it did not give him the flux.'

Bartholomew was appalled. 'That is a terrible thing to have done! People die of the flux.'

'To lose a man like that would be no great tragedy.'

Now he knew what she was capable of, Bartholomew began to wonder what else she had done. 'Last time I asked, you denied taking Danyell's hand. Were you telling the truth?'

'Do you want it back?' she asked, reaching behind her for a small bag. 'As it transpires, the hand is worthless, because Danyell was a warlock himself – only the appendages of good men make decent butter. But I did not know Danyell's nature when I happened across his corpse.'

'Christ,' muttered Bartholomew, declining to take it. 'You had better not tell anyone else, or you will hang for certain. Did you draw the circle outside Margery's house, too?'

Valeria inclined her head. 'She had asked me to do it, because she did not want the Devil to take her soul. I agreed because I liked her, although she was a different kind of witch to me. People were not frightened of her, dear gentle creature that she was. They are afraid of *me*, though.'

Bartholomew was beginning to be afraid of her, too, and hoped it did not show. 'Just one more question,' he said, now very keen to leave. 'Did you unearth Goldynham?'

'That would mean I unearthed Margery, too, and I would never do that. She was a sister.'

Bartholomew believed her, but he could not have said

why. 'Goldynham was a necromancer, though. He desperately wanted Tulyet's *Book of Consecrations*.'

She gave an amused cackle. 'Goldynham was no necromancer! He hated dark magic, and if he was after Tulyet's texts then it would have been to destroy them. But you should go. Goodbye, physician.'

Bartholomew walked briskly down Castle Hill, wishing the night had brought relief from the heat, but it seemed more airless than ever. As he passed All Saints, he saw lights flickering in the chancel again. Knowing he would probably regret the detour, he crept towards them, intending to climb on a tomb and look through a window to see who he could identify. He was astonished to find that such antics were not required, because the churchyard was full of people, all talking and laughing. Some wore hoods, but most were bare-headed, as if they did not care who saw them. Indeed, the way they had gathered in small knots suggested it was a time to meet friends and to exchange news and gossip.

He made a mental note of several familiar faces, and was about to go to meet Michael in Sewale Cottage when it occurred to him that All Saints was the Sorcerer's coven, and that this might be a good opportunity to try to learn the man's identity. He hid behind some trees, intending to devise some sort of plan. As he did so, he saw lights were burning in the charnel house, too, and shadows moved within. Someone was busy, but there were too many people loitering nearby to let him get closer. He glanced at the church itself, and his eye lit on the door that gave access to the tower. He knew from past visits that the bell chamber had a window that overlooked the

345

nave. Would he be able to spy on the gathering from there? He supposed it was worth a try.

Stealthily, he crept across the grass and managed to reach the foot of the tower undetected. He was surprised to find the door was new, and that someone had furnished it with a sturdy lock. He could only assume the Sorcerer had done it, to keep trespassers out. Fortunately it was open, so he began to climb, feeling his way up the spiral stairs in complete darkness.

The bell chamber was further up than he remembered, but he made it eventually, and pushed open a second door to enter. It was illuminated by the lamps in the body of the church, which was lucky, because the floor was rotten and it was necessary to watch where he put his feet. Carefully, he picked his way across the joists to the window, now devoid of the elegant tracery that had once adorned it, and looked directly into the nave below.

He could not have hoped for a better view, and the fact that the bell chamber was relatively clean of debris and bird droppings made him wonder whether the Sorcerer used it to watch his congregations himself. By the window was an eccentric tangle of ropes and scaffolding, which had presumably been left after an attempt to shore something up. Several bowls were stacked to one side, along with a variety of powders in jars. One was sulphur; Bartholomew recognised its colour and foul stench. Another smelled even worse, and he could only suppose it was some kind of dung, which he knew could be used to produce smoke, rank odours and even small explosions.

Most of the nave roof had collapsed the previous winter, although the one in the chancel was still intact.

Thus if it rained during a ceremony, the Sorcerer would have a dry place to stand – and a dry place to create pyrotechnic displays, too, Bartholomew thought wryly. A few rafters formed a skeletal ceiling above the nave, but they were entwined in ivy. Unfortunately, the drought had killed even that tough plant, and what had been a mass of greenery was now a mat of dead leaves, dry, brittle and dusty.

As he watched, people began to pour into the church from outside, indicating the ceremonies were about to commence, and someone at the front started to warble. He had assumed it would be a chant designed to appeal to demons, but it was actually a popular song about the end of summer. It was often sung after harvest, and was an acknowledgement of sunshine, rain, ripe fruits and plentiful corn. The line about the rain was delivered in a bellow, while the one about the sun was whispered. It was repeated several times to accompanying laughter. The coven members were enjoying themselves.

Joan Refham led the music from the front of the church. Among the more enthusiastic choristers were her husband, Spaldynge, Arblaster – Jodoca was with him, but looked uncertain and uneasy – and Bene't College's porters. There was a figure in a cloak who looked suspiciously like Podiolo, while Eyton had made no attempt to disguise himself. The physician stopped scanning faces when he thought he recognised his brother-in-law. There were some things it was just better not to know.

When the song was over, Arblaster began to chat to Spynk and Cecily in a way that showed he was being sociable and welcoming, and Bartholomew was under the impression he was pleased to have them there. Meanwhile, Spaldynge went to pour ale into goblets, and

Refham lifted cloths from baskets of bread. As they did so, Joan took a crust and burned it over a candle, then spilled a few drops of ale on the floor. There was a smattering of applause.

'And that will make it rain next week?' asked Spaldynge, pulling uncomfortably at his shirt. 'Only I do not think I can stand much more of this heat.'

'I shall say a prayer tomorrow in my church,' said Eyton. 'Something will work.'

There was a murmur of approval, and stories began to be told about withered cabbages, plagues of wasps and rotting food. An upside-down cross and a chalk circle in the chancel indicated it was no holy gathering, but it did not seem innately evil to Bartholomew. Then he saw Refham slip a goblet up his sleeve, and a moment later Joan did the same. He suspected the more respectable members of the gathering would be appalled if they knew there were thieves in their midst.

Bartholomew decided he had seen enough, so he descended the stairs and headed for the lych-gate. He had not gone far when someone emerged from the church and began to run towards him. He dodged behind a tree in alarm, wondering how he would explain himself. He was even more alarmed when he saw that the person was Refham, and braced himself to be dragged from his hiding place and presented to the coven as a spy. But the blacksmith stopped short of where Bartholomew held his breath in anxious anticipation, and removed the goblet from his sleeve. He looked around furtively before placing it in a sack that had been concealed behind a tomb. The bag bulged, and it looked as though he had been busy.

'So, you steal from your friends, do you?' came a soft voice from the trees. Bartholomew ducked away a second time, and his heart began to hammer in his chest. He had not known anyone else was there. 'You are a dishonest man, Refham.'

Refham raised his hands in the air, and smiled nervously. 'Steady, Blaston. We can discuss our misunderstanding like civilised men. I will not be happy if you hit me.'

'Prepare for a bit of misery, then,' snarled Blaston, swinging a punch. His fist made an unpleasant smacking sound as it connected with the blacksmith's jaw.

Refham reeled back, clutching his face. 'It was a mistake! I will pay you back, I promise. I will have money from Michaelhouse soon, because they are going to pay well above the odds for my mother's shops. There will be plenty for everyone.'

'You mean everyone you have cheated?' asked Blaston, wincing as he rubbed his knuckles. 'Heltisle, Mildenale, Eyton, Paxtone, the Chancellor? You will repay all of us for making promises you had no intention of keeping? For doing shoddy work and charging top prices?'

Refham was alarmed. 'Well, perhaps not everyone. However, you are a special case—'

'Well, I will take my payment now, if you please,' said Blaston. 'And I do not want the goblets and jewellery you have just stolen from your fellow witches, either. I want coins.'

Refham rummaged in his purse. 'Here is a token of my good intentions. You can have the rest—'

'I do not want your good intentions,' growled Blaston menacingly. 'I want your good money.'

Scowling, Refham handed over what the carpenter apparently deemed was an appropriate sum, because he nodded his satisfaction. Refham glowered. 'I am not happy—'

Blaston's fist shot out a second time. Refham staggered, then fell flat on his back. He coughed and gasped, while Blaston walked away whistling to himself.

'I would not mind doing that myself,' said Bartholomew, catching up with the carpenter.

Blaston jumped in surprise, then chuckled when he recognised the physician. 'I was a fool to have trusted him, but his offer sounded so good. That is what happens when you are poor – you do not have the sense to distrust gift horses.'

When Bartholomew arrived at Sewale Cottage, it was in total darkness, and he thought Michael and Cynric had decided to forget the plan to search it, and stay in their beds instead. But then a shadow materialised, and the physician recognised Cynric's compact form. The Welshman took his arm and ushered him inside, looking up and down the street outside first, to ensure he had not been followed.

'You are late,' he said, when the door had been closed.

'Am I?' Bartholomew took a few steps forward, then stumbled on the uneven floor. 'Damn it! Did you not think to bring a lamp?'

'I told you the floor needed re-laying,' came Michael's voice as Cynric fiddled with the lantern he had doused when he had let the physician in. Bartholomew could not see him, but then the monk emerged rump first from under the stairs. He looked ridiculous in such an inelegant position, and the physician suppressed the urge to laugh.

'We should finish here as soon possible,' said Cynric. 'The All Saints coven is meeting tonight, and we do not want to be walking home when they break up. They will wonder what we have been doing.'

'It is a sad indictment when innocent men are obliged to race home lest a coven member thinks he is acting suspiciously,' remarked Michael, holding out a hand for Bartholomew to help him up. The physician was unprepared for the weight, and almost ended up on the floor with him. 'But you are right: we should hurry. There are limits to what senior members of the University should do, and ransacking houses in the middle of the night are well past them.'

'It was your idea,' said Bartholomew. 'And we have every right to be here. It is our property.'

'It has been searched again since we were last here,' said Cynric. He pointed to some splinters. 'The door was forced a second time, although the culprits took care to mend it this time. A casual glance would reveal nothing amiss, but *I* noticed. It was the same method used to break in last time, so I suspect Beard and the giant are responsible.'

'Perhaps they intended to conceal it then, too,' suggested Bartholomew. 'But were disturbed before they could do it. Have you found anything yet?'

'Holes in the garden,' replied Cynric. 'Someone has been digging it up.'

Michael was disgusted. 'Perhaps they found what they were looking for, and we are wasting our time. They seem to have been very thorough.'

'They mended the door but left holes in the garden?' asked Bartholomew. 'Are they trying to hide what they are doing or not?'

'Cynric said the craters are more recent than the damage to the door, which suggests they are becoming desperate.'

Cynric scratched his head thoughtfully as he considered

the task that lay ahead of them. 'I suspect randomly tapping floorboards and jabbing at ceiling beams will tell us nothing. We need to be methodical.'

'You do it, then,' said Michael, sitting on the stairs and waving a flabby hand. 'You are used to this sort of thing, and I have had a difficult evening. You search while I tell Matt what happened when he was off drinking fine wine with his rich patients.'

'I have been investigating,' objected Bartholomew. 'And I have solved some of your mysteries. For example, it was Mother Valeria who put the blood in the font.'

Michael regarded him uneasily. 'Was it human?'

'She claims chicken. She also stole Danyell's hand, but says we can have it back. I think she plans to leave the town tonight, and I cannot imagine she will take it with her. You can collect it tomorrow.'

'I will send a beadle,' said Michael with a shudder. 'So, we were right about that, at least: we said the blood and the missing hand were connected to witchcraft, and they are.'

'But not to the Sorcerer. Further, I have learned that the talisman was Carton's, not his killer's, and that Margery was a witch. Your Junior Proctor says that may be why so many people are determined to buy her house, and why Beard and the giant have searched it so often.'

'There must be a powerful charm hidden here, or a book containing satanic secrets,' said Cynric, making his way carefully along a gap between two floorboards. 'After all, Spynk, Arblaster and the canons of Barnwell are Devil-worshippers.'

'Spynk and Arblaster are attending a coven as we speak,' acknowledged Bartholomew. 'And I think I saw Podiolo, too. Dick Tulyet is not there, though – I imagine he is chasing robbers on the Huntingdon Way. Not that he would entertain attending a Devil-worshipping coven, of course.'

Cynric's eyes were gleaming. 'It will be something that will either allow the Sorcerer to become the most powerful man in Cambridge, or that will see him defeated.'

'It is more likely to be treasure,' said Michael. 'People do not go to this sort of trouble for magic. Margery must have hidden riches in her house.'

'I doubt it,' said Cynric, dismissive of the notion. 'She was too generous to the poor to have left a lot of gold lying around.'

'Perhaps it is not charms or wealth,' suggested Bartholomew. 'Perhaps the people who want the house are telling the truth – it *would* make a good home for Dickon; it *is* a nice place to stay if you have business here; it *will* make a good site for a granary; and its grounds *are* big enough to store dung.'

Michael gave a derisive snort. 'And I am the Pope. Of course this is about money!' He sighed heavily before Cynric or Bartholomew could take issue with him, and changed the subject. 'Do you want to know how I spent my evening? Trying to convince *Mildenalus Sanctus* and William that you are not the Sorcerer. It was not easy – they have heard a rumour that you talk to yourself in churchyards.'

'Actually, I talk to the scoundrel who keeps pretending to be Goldynham,' said Bartholomew tiredly. 'Unfortunately, he manifests himself only when there are no independent witnesses – and then he must spread tales about my reactions to his tricks.'

'You have seen Goldynham?' breathed Cynric, eyes bright with awe. 'The Sorcerer must have resurrected him again, and chose you to bear witness. You are honoured.'

'It is *not* Goldynham,' said Bartholomew firmly. 'It is someone who finds it amusing to dress like him.'

'Could it be the Sorcerer?' mused Michael. 'I imagine that is the sort of jape he might enjoy.'

'Of course it is not the Sorcerer,' said Cynric scornfully. 'Imitating corpses will be beneath his dignity, so it must be a minion. Unless it really is Goldynham—'

'Do not tell Mildenale and William any of this, Cynric,' warned Michael. 'I could not convince them of Matt's innocence earlier, and they may use this prankster's antics as a way to incriminate him. Damned fanatics! They think he stole that witchery guide, and said I should abandon my other investigations and find it before he puts it to use.'

'Do you want to know the *real* reason they want you to find it?' asked Cynric. 'It is nothing to do with Doctor Bartholomew being the Sorcerer – it is because it contains a spell for seeing into the future. William caught me reading it the other day, and was about to screech himself hoarse when he saw what it was about. He was very interested, and asked me if I thought it would work.'

Bartholomew did not believe him. 'You misunderstood. William would never contemplate learning about such things.'

'Well, you are wrong,' said Cynric firmly. 'He said he would be able to foil the Devil more easily if he could see into the future.' He held up his hand suddenly. 'What was that?'

He doused the lamp, then opened the shutter at the back of the house to let the moonlight in. As Bartholomew gazed into the garden, he saw a shadow. He pointed it out to the book-bearer, who drew his dagger and gestured that they should trap the intruder in a pincer movement.

'You stay here,' Cynric whispered to Michael. 'It may be a diversion, to lure us out. Guard the house.'

'Thank you very much,' grumbled the monk. 'You have given me the dangerous bit.'

Bartholomew was not very happy about the plan, either, but did as he was told and began to creep down the left side of the long toft. He could smell the river at the end of it, and hot soil. A compost heap smouldered gently.

Suddenly, there was a sharp crack and a violent rustle as vegetation was flung aside. Cynric yelled a warning, and Bartholomew braced himself as someone hurtled towards him. He had drawn his dagger, but turned it aside at the last moment. The intruder would have run straight on to it, and Bartholomew was no killer. He grabbed the man's clothing, and the fellow spun around, lashing out with his fist as he did so. Bartholomew ducked and the blow went wide. He could hear Cynric battling off to his right, but knew the Welshman could look after himself.

He turned to his own attacker, who had drawn a knife. As the intruder hurled it at him he dodged to one side so it sailed harmlessly over his shoulder. When he had righted himself, he heard footsteps thumping away. He started to give chase, but tripped over something that lay in the dry grass and went sprawling. By the time he had staggered to his feet, his attacker was gone. Cynric was next to him, limping and swearing furiously because his own assailant had also escaped.

'Damned villains,' he muttered venomously. 'Chopped at my ankles to slow me down.'

355

'Let me see,' said Bartholomew, concerned.

The book-bearer shook his head. 'Good boots, boy; I am all right. But it looks as if you were less easily defeated. You have killed one of our attackers. Well done!'

Bartholomew whipped around, and saw that Cynric was pointing at the object he had tripped over. His stomach lurched when he saw it was Richard Spynk.

Chapter 10

It was still quite dark when Bartholomew woke the next day, and he was surprised to find Cynric in the room with him, lying on one of the students' straw mattresses and staring at the ceiling with his fingers laced behind his head. Then the events of the previous night came rushing back to him. He and Michael had taken Spynk's body to St Mary the Great, while Cynric had led the beadles in a search for the intruders. The monk had decided it was too late to tell Cecily what had happened, saying there was no point in waking her at such an hour just to dispense bad news. Recalling the way the couple had behaved towards each other, Bartholomew suspected the news might not be perceived as 'bad' at all.

'Carton was stabbed in the back,' said Cynric softly. 'By someone tall, you said.'

Bartholomew supposed the book-bearer was reviewing events in his mind. He rolled over to face him. 'You think Spynk was killed by the same man? By the Sorcerer?'

Cynric nodded slowly. 'It is possible. Spynk joined a coven the moment he arrived in the town. Perhaps the

Sorcerer thought that was a bit keen, and saw him as a potential rival.'

'Was it the Sorcerer we fought last night, then?' asked Bartholomew doubtfully. 'Did you see his face? There were at least two of them, but I could not tell much else. Everything happened so fast.'

'You did battle with Beard, and I had the giant. However, I saw a third person, too, dashing for freedom while we fought. Perhaps *that* was the Sorcerer, and Beard and the giant are his henchmen.'

'So, one of these three must have killed Spynk. He cannot have been dead for long, because I had just seen him at the coven in All Saints.'

'Their first priority was escape,' mused Cynric. 'Beard and the giant are decent swordsmen, and you were armed only with a dagger. They could easily have bested us, but they preferred to run rather than risk capture by skir-mishing.'

Bartholomew sat up, knowing he should examine Spynk's body as soon as possible. He washed in the bowl of water Cynric left for him each night, which was tepid, smelled brackish and did not leave him feeling as refreshed as it should have done. He donned a clean shirt, his black tabard, and supposed he was ready to face the world. Uneasily, he realised it was already Friday, which meant there were only two days and a night left before the Sorcerer made his move on Trinity Eve. Time was running out fast.

He was glad when Cynric offered to go with him to St Mary the Great, suspecting the prankster was unlikely to bother with his nasty tricks if his victim had company. They left the College just as the sky was beginning to lighten, and walked along St Michael's Lane. Their foot-steps echoed hollowly, and Bartholomew could hear someone coughing in nearby Gonville Hall. When they passed St Michael's Church, Cynric stopped suddenly and peered into the gloom of its graveyard.

'Is someone lying on the ground over there?' he asked.

Bartholomew followed the direction of his pointing finger and saw a pale figure next to what looked like a hole. Piles of earth were scattered around. He swallowed hard as his stomach lurched in horror. 'Oh no!' he whispered. 'It is another exhumation.'

'It is,' agreed Cynric unsteadily. 'And this time I think the victim is Father Thomas.'

'Christ!' Bartholomew felt sick. 'Are you sure?'

Cynric crossed himself, then drew his sword and walked towards the shape. Reluctantly, Bartholomew followed, closing his eyes in despair when he recognised the wiry hair and grey habit of the man whose death he had brought about. By rights, Thomas should have gone in the Franciscans' cemetery, but St Michael's had happened to have a ready-dug grave, and Langelee had persuaded Prior Pechem to accept it – the Master hoped the arrangement would encourage the town to think that the Grey Friars harboured no ill-feelings about Thomas meeting his death while under the care of Michaelhouse's physician.

'What shall we do?' asked Cynric uneasily. 'Will you stay here while I fetch Brother Michael?'

'We cannot let anyone else see this,' said Bartholomew, trying to pull himself together. He found his hands were shaking. 'The last thing we need is another rumour that the Sorcerer has been at work. Help me carry him to the Stanton Chapel. Then I will stay with him while you prepare his grave, and we will rebury him as soon as you are ready.'

Cynric obliged, then took a shovel and went outside

again, leaving Bartholomew alone with the body. The physician had just dropped to his knees, supposing he had better say some prayers, when a shadow materialised behind him. He yelled in alarm, which made the shadow howl its own fright.

'God's teeth, Brother!' he exclaimed, feeling his heart hammer furiously as he scrambled to his feet. 'Was it really necessary to creep up on me like that? What are you doing here, anyway?'

'I came to recite an early mass.' Michael leaned heavily against the wall, hand to his chest. 'You scared the life out of me, shrieking like that – the Sorcerer has us as skittish as a pair of virgins in a brothel. Cynric told me what happened, by the way. You did the right thing by bringing Thomas in here. Will you inspect him while we wait for the grave to be readied?'

Bartholomew gazed at the friar's face, which was beginning to be unrecognisable after its time in the ground, and was assailed by a wave of guilt. 'It should not be me,' he said, trying to control the tremor in his voice. He was unwilling to let even Michael see how much the situation bothered him. 'Not with him.'

'You have no choice. Paxtone refuses to touch corpses, and Rougham is still away – not that I would trust him anyway, with his penchant for verdicts of natural causes. I am still haunted by the Hardys.'

'The Hardys,' repeated Bartholomew, knowing he was using them as a tactic to delay dealing with Thomas, but unable to help himself. 'I know what happened to them. I worked it out from comments made by the canons at Barnwell, Cynric and Mother Valeria.'

Michael looked worried. 'Was I right to think there was something amiss?'

Bartholomew nodded. 'Cynric told me the witches' handbook contains a spell for predicting the future. Mother Valeria was going to use it last night. It involves a potion that contains powerful herbs, and she said even skilled warlocks have died performing the ritual. She also said people have asked her for it in the past, but she always refused because of the risks involved.'

'Lord!' muttered Michael. 'The fact that she feels the need to resort to it now bodes ill. The Sorcerer has even Cambridge's most-feared witches uneasy.'

'One person who asked her to perform was John Hardy; another was Tulyet the Elder. I have a feeling that when she refused, they took matters into their own hands. Henbane and mandrake are potent plants, and they miscalculated how much they could drink. The Hardys died side by side in bed – probably later, after they had tidied away the evidence, since your subsequent search found no sign of it – while Tulyet's death was so sudden that Dick wanted the services of a Corpse Examiner.'

Michael's face was white. 'Not natural causes, then.'

'No, but these substances are hard to detect, so you cannot blame Rougham for missing them.'

'An accident?'

'Yes, they learned the hard way that witchcraft is not a game. It was the plague that drove them away from the Church, though. That disease has a lot to answer for.'

'It has,' agreed Michael. 'Look at Spaldynge – the man is still half-deranged with grief. So, you have solved two cases that have been nagging at me for more than a year, Matt. Thank you.'

Bartholomew tried to think of a way to prolong the

discussion, but Michael was having none of it. He gestured that the physician was to begin his examination, and held the lamp to help him. As he did so, it illuminated a dark spot on the friar's forehead, where the stone had struck him. Even now, it did not look serious, and Bartholomew wondered why the man had died.

'I know how you feel about Thomas,' said the monk, seeing him hesitate. 'But here is a chance to make amends. When we catch the fiend who defiled his rest, you may find your conscience eases.'

Bartholomew doubted it, but did as he was asked. His hands shook, and it was one of the least pleasant tasks he had ever performed. He fought the urge to bolt for the door as he assessed the grave-clothes to see if anything was missing, and then did the same for fingers, ears and toes. Suddenly Thomas's head rolled awkwardly to one side. Puzzled, he adjusted the lamp to look more closely. It took him a few moments to be certain, and he turned to Michael in confusion.

'His neck is broken.'

'Damaged as he was pulled from the ground?' asked the monk. 'Or perhaps when he was in it?'

'I do not think so, because there are marks – bruises – on his throat, and a sticky residue on the collar of his habit. It looks as though the garment was glued into place.'

'What are you saying?' demanded Michael, shocked. 'He was strangled and his clothes arranged to disguise it? He was *murdered*?'

Bartholomew nodded. 'But strangulation will not break a neck – at least, not usually. I imagine this was rather more savage, perhaps involving a violent tussle. And the presence of glue suggests someone was covering his tracks. Did Rougham examine Thomas's throat?'

Michael's expression was grim. 'No, he only looked at the head – at the initial injury.'

'Carton was suspicious of Thomas's death,' said Bartholomew, trying to piece the facts together. 'He wanted me to test that powder he found, because he thought there was something odd . . .'

'Do you think this is the reason Thomas was excavated? Someone wants justice done?'

But Bartholomew shook his head. 'I think our discovery is incidental. There were several other burials on the day we put Thomas in the ground—'

Michael clapped a hand to his forehead as the answer became clear. 'Margery and Goldynham! Like Thomas, they were interred on Ascension Day because they believed that could mean less time in Purgatory. But what are we to deduce from this? That witches like to exhume corpses entombed on that particular occasion?'

'Danyell was buried on Ascension Day, too,' Bartholomew reminded him. 'Perhaps he will be next.'

'I will set a watch on his grave. But let us think about Thomas. Who killed him?'

'Our suspects must be the same as the ones we have for Carton. They were both Franciscans, both believed the plague was a punishment for past sins, and both made enemies of heretics.'

'And let us not forget that William argued bitterly with Thomas the day before his death,' said Michael soberly. 'Perhaps he was still angry when Thomas was carried to Michaelhouse to recover from being hit by the stone – that he came to the sick-room and throttled Thomas in a fit of pique.'

'No, Brother. William would still be on his knees doing penance, if that were the case. We would know he was guilty by his behaviour.'

Michael disagreed. 'He is a fanatic, and such people are quite capable of putting their own unique interpretation on such incidents – that God asked them to do it, or some such nonsense.'

Bartholomew did not like the notion of his colleague being a killer. 'Perhaps Mildenale put him up to it. He is the one who encourages William's zeal.'

'*Mildenalus Sanctus* would never stain his soul with murder. He is no hothead, not like William. However, I suspect we should be looking to the Sorcerer for our culprit. After all, Thomas and Carton did speak out very vehemently against him.'

The Michaelhouse Fellows arrived for mass shortly afterwards, all talking at once about what had transpired at All Saints the previous night. Apparently, the revelry had grown very wild towards dawn, and the people who lived nearby had complained about the noise. More worrying, however, was the fact that dung had been thrown at the houses of folk known to support the Church.

'Where are William and Mildenale?' asked Suttone, looking around him suddenly. 'They were here with us a moment ago.'

Langelee scowled when a quick search revealed they must have slipped away. 'Damn them! I issued orders this morning that everyone was to stay in College until this Sorcerer business is resolved. I should have guessed they would be unable to resist the temptation to do battle with him.'

'Yes, you should,' Suttone admonished him. 'You know

how strongly they feel about witchery. Of course they will not skulk inside Michaelhouse while a popular diabolist assumes his mantle of power. They were incensed by last night's dung-lobbing, and will be eager to avenge it.'

'Lord!' groaned Michael, heading for the door. 'I had better tell my beadles to be on the lookout for them. I would rather Michaelhouse men were not on the streets when there is trouble brewing. And I must tell Cecily her husband is dead, too.'

When the monk had gone, Bartholomew pulled Langelee aside and gave him a brief account of what had happened at Sewale Cottage the previous night. He told him about Thomas, too, and the Master agreed that the body should be replaced in the ground as soon as possible.

'We had better do it now,' he said grimly, immediately making his way outside. 'And then you must go and examine Spynk for Michael. He will need a report as a matter of urgency, and you *must* catch this Sorcerer before he steps on his pedestal and proves difficult to push off.'

'I do not suppose you have heard any rumours regarding his identity, have you?'

'Lots – and you feature in more than is comfortable. So do Heltisle, Spaldynge, Refham, Younge the porter, Arblaster, Podiolo, Norton, Prior Pechem, Sheriff Tulyet, the Chancellor, Eyton, the Mayor, the Market Square crones, Michael, Wynewyk and Spynk. I think that is everyone. Oh, and there is also one that names Doctor Rougham, on he grounds that he is conveniently absent at the moment.'

When Bartholomew and Cynric arrived at St Mary the Great, the physician feeling soiled and uneasy after laying Thomas to rest a second time, Cecily was in the Lady Chapel. She smiled when he offered her his condolences, and rubbed her hands together gleefully.

'He cannot tell me what to do now,' she crowed. 'I am free of him. I ran all the way here when Brother Michael brought me the good news, just to be sure it was true.'

'What will you do?' asked Bartholomew. He had met wives who were relieved by their husband's demise before, but none had been as openly delighted as Cecily. 'Go home to Norwich?'

'I think I shall stay here a while. Not in that High Street house, though. I would rather have Sewale Cottage.'

'I see,' said Bartholomew, aware of Cynric shooting him meaningful glances from the shadows. Was it significant that Cecily – a coven member – should still want Sewale Cottage?

Cecily gave a sultry smile. 'Perhaps you would take a message to your Master for me. Tell him I am willing to pay nineteen marks for the house, and might even make a handsome benefaction to your College, too – in return for prayers for my husband's soul, of course. Richard would have *hated* that!'

'How handsome?' asked Bartholomew, surprising himself with the question. He rubbed his eyes and supposed he was more tired than he realised, because he was not usually in the habit of making such bald enquiries of recent widows, not even ones who so obviously revelled in their new status.

Cecily laughed. 'Not handsome enough, probably, so you had better offer him a couple of ells of cloth as well. Tell him to invite me to dinner. I know for a fact that *he* prefers female company.'

There was a distinct bounce in her step as she flounced out of the Lady Chapel, and she was humming. Bartholomew hoped she would stop before she reached the street. It would not be considered seemly behaviour, and might lead folk to wonder whether she had killed Spynk herself.

Cynric watched the physician begin his examination. 'Spynk was not much of a husband, but Cecily was not much of a wife, either. I cannot say I like either of them.'

Bartholomew did not reply, because his attention was focused on the corpse in front of him. There was a single stab wound in Spynk's back, although it was lower than the one that had killed Carton. Cynric showed him a knife he had found near the body, and the physician saw it was another of the ones that could be bought for a pittance in the Market Square.

'A cheap weapon that the killer did not bother to retrieve,' he mused, more to himself than to the book-bearer. 'It looks as though we have the same killer here.'

'Why should Cecily kill Carton?' asked Cynric, showing where *his* suspicions lay. 'She has a good motive for killing Spynk, but she cannot have known Carton.'

'Are you sure about that? Carton certainly met Spynk, because he told Langelee about a bid Spynk made on Sewale Cottage. I imagine Cecily was there when they bartered, so she probably did know him. However, a brief encounter cannot have been enough to warrant Carton's murder.'

'Maybe she made advances, and was piqued when he rejected her. Or she lost kin to the plague, and he told her it was her own fault. However, she did not kill Thomas, because *he* died of a snapped neck, while Carton and Spynk were stabbed. You probably have two murderers at large now.'

Bartholomew did not need reminding.

Michael was in the proctors' office, signing deeds and letters with Chancellor Tynkell. Tynkell, a thin, unhealthy looking man, was setting his seal to whatever the monk ordered, and when Bartholomew arrived, he asked if he might be excused. The relationship between the Chancellor and his most powerful official had changed over the years, and there was no longer any question that Michael was in charge.

'Well?' Michael asked, when Tynkell had gone. 'What can you tell me about Spynk?'

Bartholomew sat heavily on a bench. 'Just that he was killed with the same type of knife as Carton. Both were stabbed in the back, which suggests some degree of stealth.'

'Who would slaughter a Franciscan friar and a merchant? Cecily?'

'Cynric thinks so. I have no idea.'

'The Sorcerer is still *my* favourite suspect. If only we knew his name.'

'Langelee gave me his list of potential candidates. It included virtually every prominent scholar and townsman in Cambridge.' Bartholomew jumped when there was a sudden clamour outside, followed by the sound of smashing. They ran out of the office to find that one of the Lady Chapel's fine stained-glass windows was now a mass of coloured shards on the floor.

Michael groaned. 'Not again! We have only just repaired that after the last riot.'

He stalked outside, and was alarmed to see that a

sizeable crowd had gathered. For a brief moment, Bartholomew thought he glimpsed the giant and Beard on the fringes, but when he moved to get a better view, they were not there. He found himself near the man who wore a rose in his hat, whom he had noticed during the near-lynching of the Market Square crone. The fellow made a moue of disgust when people began to yell at each other, and moved away, clearly having better things to do with his time. Bartholomew climbed on a tombstone so he could see what was going on over the heads of those in front. Michael stood next to him, hands on hips.

'Tell me what is happening, Matt,' he ordered wearily.

'There is a squabble in progress. It seems William broke the window, to register his objection that the corpse of a self-confessed diabolist lies within. And Arblaster is berating him for destroying an attractive piece of artistry.'

'From the vicious tone of the screeching, I would say Arblaster is doing more than "berating", while William sounds deranged.'

Bartholomew stood on tiptoe. William was on one side of the ruined window, backed by a number of Franciscans from the friary; Mildenale lurked behind him, whispering in his ear. William's eyes flashed with zeal, although his other colleagues seemed ill at ease. Heltisle was with them, his porters and Eyton at his back. The St Bene't's priest looked distressed, and was trying to pull Mildenale away from William, but Mildenale kept freeing himself, determined to continue his muttered diatribe.

On the other side of the window was Arblaster; his hands were stained, as though he had been busy with dung before breaking off to quarrel with William. Jodoca was next to him. She held a piece of the broken glass and her face was crumpled with dismay. Coven member

369

she might be, but it was clear she deplored the destruction William had wrought. Refham and Joan were behind her, and so was Cecily. Joan was glowering, because Cecily was clinging to Refham's arm, and Refham was grinning at the unsolicited female attention in a foolish, leering kind of way. Not far away was Spaldynge, slovenly and wild-eyed. Dark hollows in his cheeks suggested that his mental health continued to deteriorate.

'Where are the Sheriff's men?' grumbled Michael. 'I broke up the last Church *versus* Sorcerer spat, and Dick promised to tackle the next one. It is bad for University–town relations if I keep doing it. And bad for our windows, too.'

'You may have no choice, Brother,' said Bartholomew. 'There is not a soldier in sight.'

'Who is hollering now?' demanded Michael, cocking his head. 'Someone else has just joined in.'

'Heltisle. He is accusing Isnard of being a necromancer, because of his penchant for sleeping in graveyards. Eyton is pointing out that these naps are drunken stupors and have nothing to do with witchery. Isnard is furious at the slur on his character, and people are taking sides about that now.'

Bartholomew saw Mildenale abandon William and go to stand behind Heltisle, lending him his support. He did not whisper at him, but the Master of St Bene't College seemed to draw strength from his presence even so.

'We shall cleanse the town of witches once and for all,' Heltisle bellowed. He regarded Isnard in disdain. 'Beginning with *this* vile specimen.'

'A wicked heretic,' Mildenale agreed, clasping his hands and gazing skywards. 'God overlooked him during the plague, so He sent a cart to crush his leg instead, as a punishment for his sins. The Church despises such men, and they will all be damned to the fires of Hell.'

There was a murmur of consternation, mostly because Isnard was no worse a sinner than anyone else, and if he was damned, then so were a lot of people.

'Now just a moment,' said Arblaster, shocked. 'There is no need for that sort of talk.'

There was a rumble of agreement, from folk on both sides of the debate.

'Why should you care?' snarled Heltisle. 'As a coven member, you should be happy to go to Hell.'

'Arblaster is a witch?' cried Mildenale, staring at the dung-master with an appalled kind of disgust. 'Then we should excommunicate him. William? Get me a Bible, a candle and a bottle of holy water.'

There was a stunned silence. Excommunication was a serious matter, and while priests often used it as a threat, it was rarely carried through. Even William looked uneasy at the notion that he might have to participate in one.

'Hey!' shouted Arblaster, outraged. 'I still go to church on Sundays! And do I ever complain about the fact that the vicar is usually too drunk to officiate, and will pardon any sin for a glass of claret?'

'You moan about it every week,' muttered Refham. 'But who is counting?'

'So what if I organise the occasional gathering of like-minded people at All Saints?' Arblaster went on, getting into his stride. 'It does not make me material for excommunication, and I object to this . . . this *discrimination*!'

'Perhaps *you* are the warlock,' said Spaldynge, pointing a dirty forefinger at Heltisle. 'You are the one with the mysteriously missing goats, and Goldynham was trying to escape from your churchyard.'

371

'How dare you!' cried Heltisle. He turned to Younge. 'Punch him! He insulted me *and* Bene't!'

Younge leapt forward with a grin of delight. Michael was about to intervene when Sheriff Tulyet arrived, accompanied by mounted soldiers. Heltisle was among the first to slink away from the mêlée, and Bartholomew saw several clods of dirt follow him; his tirade had earned him enemies.

'Did anyone hit him?' asked Michael, jigging this way and that to see what was happening.

'No, but not from want of trying.'

Bartholomew returned to the College, leaving Michael to discuss peace-keeping tactics with Tulyet. He was tired after his disturbed night, and for the first time was glad of the silence that came with the absence of students. He fell asleep almost immediately, to dream of Goldynham, Thomas and Carton. He started awake several times, sure one of them was in the room with him.

Eventually, real voices impinged on his consciousness. He recognised Michael's and Langelee's, but the others were unfamiliar. They were in the monk's chamber on the floor above, and it sounded as though some sort of party was in progress. Men were laughing, and he could hear the clank of goblets as toasts were made. Sun tilted through the window at an angle that told him it was already mid-afternoon. Why had Michael let him rest so long, when there were killers to be caught and the Sorcerer was planning some grand ceremony the following night?

He sat up to find he was not alone. Cynric was sitting at the desk in the window, working on a grammar exercise.

He was not usually so assiduous with his studies, and Bartholomew could only suppose the treasures found in the witches' handbook had encouraged him to hone his skills. Still, his shuffling presence explained Bartholomew's dreams about having company in his chamber.

'You were asleep so long that I was beginning to think Mother Valeria had put a spell on you,' said Cynric, rather disapprovingly. 'She has disappeared, you know.'

'Disappeared as in gone up in a puff of smoke? Or disappeared as in no one can find her?'

'The latter, because all her belongings are gone, too.' Then Cynric reconsidered, never one to pass up the opportunity to speculate on something supernatural. 'Although the former is still a possibility. Just because no one actually *saw* her explode does not mean she did not do it.'

'She told me she was leaving. I do not blame her. She is no longer safe here, what with William, Mildenale and Heltisle persecuting witches, and the Sorcerer about to challenge rivals.'

There was a gale of manly laughter from the room upstairs, but Michael's infectious chuckle did not form part of it. Langelee's guffaw did, though, and Bartholomew supposed the Master had just related some tale from his past that was more suitable for secular ears than monastic ones. The monk was no prude, but he only indulged in ribald jokes with people he knew really well.

'You might want to rescue him,' suggested Cynric, seeing what the physician was thinking. 'Tell him he is needed on important business. He is with visitors from the Bishop, and feels obliged to entertain them, although he cannot afford the time. And I do not like the look of them, personally.'

'Why not?'

Cynric pursed his lips. 'You will know why when you see them.'

Bartholomew headed for the stairs, reaching Michael's door just as another explosion of mirth issued forth. There was a strong smell of wine, as if some had been spilled.

'That,' said Michael coldly, 'is *not* amusing.'

'It is,' countered Langelee. His voice was inappropriately loud. 'I laughed until my sides hurt.'

'I am sure you did,' said Michael venomously. 'But that does not make it funny.'

'Relax, Brother,' came another voice. 'You worry too much. The Bishop is not concerned, and that is good enough for me.'

Bartholomew pushed open the door and entered. He was startled and disconcerted to see that Michael's guests were the giant and his bearded friend. For a moment, he was too astonished to speak, but the room's occupants were not very interested in his arrival anyway. The giant glanced once in his direction, then immediately turned his attention to the wine jug, sloshing some claret into his goblet and some on Michael's beautifully polished floorboards. Langelee held out his cup, then toasted the man; a red stain appeared down his chin and on his tabard. The Master was drunk. It did not happen often these days, but when it did, it was best to avoid him, because his lively bonhomie had a habit of turning dangerous very fast.

'Matt,' said Michael, standing with obvious relief. 'I expect you have come to tell me I am needed elsewhere.' He was halfway through the door before he remembered his manners and gave a pained smile. 'Have you met John Brownsley, bailiff to the Bishop, and his companion Osbern le Hawker?'

'Yes,' said Bartholomew, regarding the pair coolly. 'On several occasions.'

'I do not believe so,' said Beard. He seemed genuinely surprised that the physician should think otherwise. 'I would have remembered, because the Bishop often talks about the University's Corpse Examiner and I have been keen to make your acquaintance. My name is Brownsley, by the way.'

The giant – Osbern – nodded a greeting, but not one that showed any recognition. He tried to scuff the spilled wine from the floorboards with his boot, grinning conspiratorially at Langelee as he did so. Bartholomew was confused. It was clear Osbern and Brownsley did not connect him with the encounters in Sewale Cottage or the rescue of Refham, yet he was sure they were the same men.

'We arrived this morning,' Brownsley went on smoothly. 'And neither of us has been here before. Perhaps you visited the Bishop in Ely at some point? It is possible you may have seen us there.'

'Have some wine,' said Langelee, before the physician could take issue with him. 'The Bishop sent it, and it is excellent stuff. He is never a man to stint on such things.'

'He is generous to his supporters,' agreed Osbern. 'Less generous to those who oppose him.'

'I hear he persecutes those,' slurred Langelee. 'Abducts their women and demands ransoms for their return. Or he sends ruffians to burn their homes and steal their cattle. Spynk and Danyell told me.'

'Did they now?' said Brownsley flatly. He was not

375

amused, and Bartholomew wished the Master would shut up before he said something that might induce the Bishop's ruffians to harm him.

'They are both dead now,' Langelee blustered on. He grinned, rather evilly. 'I do not suppose the Bishop decided to still their tongues, did he? I imagine their demise is very convenient for him.'

Bartholomew glanced at him sharply. Is that why Beard and the giant had been in Margery's garden the previous night? Killing one of the men who had complained about their master to the King and forced him into exile? But why had Spynk been there in the first place?

'De Lisle had nothing to do with those unfortunate incidents,' said Brownsley. It was impossible to read his expression. 'If you do not believe me, then ask him.'

Langelee roared with laughter. 'But I cannot find it in my heart to judge de Lisle too harshly. After all, he is only doing what other barons do, and it is not easy to make ends meet when you have a large retinue to fund. It would not be right to let loyal servants perish from want, would it?'

'It would not,' agreed Osbern jovially. 'This cask is empty, Brother. Do you have another?'

'No,' said Michael shortly. 'You will have to have ale instead.'

'Why *are* you here, Brownsley?' asked Langelee conversationally. 'You have not told us yet.'

'We have been in London, trying to protect the Bishop's good name against liars,' replied Brownsley. 'Men like Spynk and Danyell, in fact. Afterwards, we were supposed to travel to Avignon, but there was a change of plan, and we were obliged to come north again first.'

'What change of plan?' asked Langelee, intrigued.

376

Brownsley's smile was enigmatic. 'He asked us to bring him some money when we visit him at the papal court. We collected all we could, but life with the Pope is probably expensive, and we decided he might need a bit more than we had with us. So we are on our way to Ely, to beg some from the abbey.'

'You will have no success there,' predicted Langelee. 'They have that big cathedral to maintain, and have only just finished setting a fancy wooden octagon on top of it. I doubt they have money to spare.'

'No?' asked Brownsley, and Bartholomew was under the impression that the conversation had been skilfully manoeuvred to this point. 'Then what about the University? It is in his See, and even a casual glance around shows there is money here.'

'Michaelhouse is as poor as a church mouse,' declared Langelee immediately. 'A bit of cash will come our way when we sell Sewale Cottage, but we shall have to spend it all again when we buy the Refham shops.'

Brownsley and Osbern exchanged a glance. 'We heard Sewale Cottage was up for sale,' said Brownsley pleasantly.

'How?' asked Bartholomew. He smiled, to make his question sound more friendly – there was no point in deliberately antagonising powerful men. 'You said you have only just arrived in Cambridge.'

Brownsley grinned back, although there was no warmth in the expression. 'We must have heard it as we rode here. But Sewale Cottage is a nice house in a good location. I would not sell it, if I were you.'

'Unfortunately, it is too small to be of any use to us,' said Langelee. 'And the Refham property will be much more valuable in the long run. We have no choice but to hawk the place.'

'De Lisle would rather you kept it,' said Brownsley softly. 'He will make it worth your while.'

Langelee's wine-reddened face creased into a puzzled frown. 'Are you saying the Bishop wants to buy Sewale Cottage, too? But why? No, do not answer! It is not our business, and I was foolish to ask. Of course we will accept a bid from him. We are up to nineteen marks at the moment.'

'The Bishop does not want to buy it,' said Brownsley. 'He cannot – the King has frozen his assets. However, he wants it to remain in University hands and will be pleased if you accede to his request.'

'But we need the money for other things,' objected Langelee. 'And pleasing him is not one of our priorities, I am afraid. He may still be Bishop, but he is not here, and I doubt he will return.'

'Oh, yes he will,' declared Osbern hotly. 'And when he does, his enemies will be very sorry.'

'De Lisle has no enemies here,' said Michael, hastening to smooth ruffled feathers. 'And I am sure we can come to an arrangement that suits us all. Is that not so, Master?'

But Langelee's good humour had evaporated. 'We might. But then again, we might not. I do not take kindly to bullies, and anyone who tries to intimidate me can expect to be intimidated back.'

'I am glad you came when you did, Matt,' said Michael, after Bartholomew had mumbled some tale about the monk being needed at St Mary the Great, thus bringing the uncomfortable gathering to an end. 'I have always found Brownsley and Osbern rough company, and knew it was only a matter of time before they and Langelee fell out. They are too similar in their characters.'

'Perhaps Spynk and Danyell were telling the truth about the way they were treated by the Bishop's retinue. I know for a fact that Osbern and Brownsley are guilty of criminal behaviour, because they are the pair who have been searching Sewale Cottage – and probably digging holes in its garden, too.'

Michael gaped at him. 'Are you sure?'

Bartholomew nodded as he led the way to his own chamber, where Cynric was still poring over his Latin. 'So Margery had something the Bishop wants, and because they have not found it, Brownsley and Osbern have come to order Michaelhouse not to sell the place.'

'But *what* does the Bishop want?' asked Michael, frustrated. 'There is nothing left in the house, and I cannot see him being interested in doorknobs and hinges.'

'It must be because Sewale Cottage is cursed,' said Cynric helpfully. 'Margery died in it, see.'

'People have died in most houses, Cynric,' said Michael reasonably. 'And even if you are right, why should that matter to de Lisle?'

'Margery was a witch, and he probably thinks a bit of her magic will extricate him from his current difficulties,' explained Cynric. He spoke with absolute conviction. 'I doubt *God* will come to his rescue, him being a felon and all, so he intends to secure a different kind of help.'

Michael raised his eyebrows. 'And how did he find out about Margery's death when he is in Avignon? News takes weeks to travel those sort of distances.'

Cynric pulled a face that suggested this was an irrelevancy, so he did not deign to address it. Instead, he turned to something that lay on the table next to him. 'I finished searching her house this morning and I found this. I wanted to give it to you earlier, Brother, but decided to wait until the Bishop's louts had gone.'

It was a tome. Carefully, Bartholomew opened the ancient pages, and scanned them quickly. 'The title claims it is the *Book of Consecrations*, but it is not. I read some of that in Padua last year, and I remember the chapter titles. These are different.'

'How different?' asked Michael, bemused.

'Its sections were ordered around curses – curses using animals, curses using stones, curses using metals, and so on. But this is just a list of cures for chilblains and insect bites. Tulyet probably owns a copy of the real one. If you borrow it and compare the two, you will see I am right.'

'Where did you find it, Cynric?' asked Michael.

'Under a loose stair. I doubt anyone could have seen it in the dark – it was hard enough in daylight.'

Michael rubbed his chin. 'You may know this is not the real *Book of Consecrations*, Matt, but that does not mean Margery did. The fact that she kept it so cunningly hidden suggests she thought she had something worth protecting. And I do not think she could read anyway, so how would she have known what it contained?'

'And this is what Brownsley and Osbern were after?' asked Bartholomew doubtfully. 'I do not see the Bishop being interested in remedies for chilblains *or* a compendium of curses.'

'He will not want the remedies,' agreed Cynric. 'But I imagine he might find the curses useful. Do not forget that he is in exile, while dozens of his enemies tell tales about him to the King.'

'No,' said Michael firmly. 'I do not believe it.'

'Do you really think this book is why so many people want Sewale Cottage?' asked Bartholomew, not sure what to make of it all. 'Spynk, Arblaster, the canons and Dick?'

'Well, it does strengthen our theory that everything is related to witchery,' said Michael. 'Arblaster, and Spynk – and some canons, too, I am sorry to say – attend covens. *Ergo*, curses will be of great interest to them. Yet I still think we are missing some detail . . .'

'We are missing more than a detail,' said Bartholomew tiredly. 'I understand nothing.'

'Then let us review what we know chronologically,' suggested Michael. 'First, we had Margery Sewale unearthed. We know she was a witch, and Mother Valeria drew a magic circle on her doorstep. Margery carefully hid her false *Book of Consecrations*, and left Michaelhouse everything she owned.'

'Then goats were stolen from Bene't College,' said Bartholomew. 'Heltisle is concerned because the thefts stopped at the mystical number of seven. Arblaster has seven black goats and I think Barnwell Priory does, too, but neither has made any effort to hide them, so perhaps this is irrelevant.'

'Next, there was Danyell, who died of a seizure, but who lost his hand to Mother Valeria after he was dead,' continued Michael. 'He was interested in witchery, and so was his friend Spynk.'

'Spynk said Danyell was carrying a brick under his arm when he left their High Street lodgings,' said Bartholomew. 'That is odd, is it not?'

'Why?' asked Michael. 'He was probably going to do some business – masonry business.'

'It is odd because Danyell had been complaining of

381

chest pains, and Spynk said he intended to visit Mother Valeria, for a cure. Why was Danyell toting a stone around, when he probably felt very ill?'

'But he never reached Valeria,' mused Michael. 'She said she did not see him.'

'She *said* she did not see him,' repeated Cynric meaningfully.

'I believe her,' said Bartholomew. 'Why would she deny that he visited her, but admit to chopping off his hand? And he did die of a seizure – I do not think there is anything suspicious about his death.'

'Could you be wrong about that?' asked Michael.

'I could, but I am fairly sure I am not.' Bartholomew continued with his analysis. 'Danyell and Spynk fell foul of the Bishop, and travelled to London to complain about him. Spynk was interested in Sewale Cottage, and was killed in its garden. He arrived in Cambridge shortly before Ascension Day.'

'And Margery was buried on Ascension Day,' added Michael. 'Along with Goldynham and Thomas. All three have been hauled from their graves.'

'I am beginning to see a pattern,' said Bartholomew. 'We have been assuming that all these events are connected to the Sorcerer, and there are strong reasons to support that. But perhaps we are wrong.'

'Explain,' ordered Michael.

Bartholomew marshalled his thoughts. 'We know Osbern and Brownsley searched Sewale Cottage on several occasions. We also know that Spynk, Arblaster, Barnwell and Tulyet are all eager to purchase the place. I believe Tulyet's reason for wanting it, but the others I distrust. They know something is secreted there, and *that* is the reason they want to buy it.'

'The *Book of Consecrations*,' said Cynric, waving it in the air.

Bartholomew shook his head. 'It cannot be that.'

'Why not?' asked Michael. 'If people believe it contains powerful magic, then perhaps it is worth more to them than money. Although, I still do not think the Bishop . . .'

'Because Dick has a copy of *Consecrations* and, apart from Goldynham who wanted to destroy it, no one has tried to take his. It is no secret that he owns it: Goldynham probably told others about him having it, and Tulyet may have done, too. If it is the book that is attracting these buyers, then someone would have tried to purchase, borrow or steal Dick's. And no one has.'

'Goldynham wanted the Sheriff's copy because he intended to destroy it?' asked Cynric.

'Valeria said so. Perhaps he was afraid of what might happen if Dickon got his hands on it.'

'He has a point,' said Cynric worriedly. 'Perhaps I will steal it from the Sheriff's house, then, because Dickon will be a lot more dangerous than the Sorcerer in a few years' time.'

'So what were they looking for, if not Margery's book?' demanded Michael, ignoring him. 'I said it might be hidden treasure, and you told me I was wrong.'

'But now we know the Bishop is involved, it seems logical to assume money is at the heart of it,' said Bartholomew. 'He is unlikely to be interested in anything else.'

Michael grimaced at the verdict on his master's morals, but did not argue.

Cynric looked from one to the other. 'So,' he concluded, 'all this time, you thought the raids on Sewale

383

Cottage were something to do with the Sorcerer, but now you think they are not?'

The physician nodded. 'He *is* gathering his resources for some sort of play for power, but I do not think it has anything to do with whatever is going on at Sewale Cottage.'

'So we now have two cases to solve,' said Michael heavily. 'And we cannot say which is the more important, because we still do not really know what is hidden in Margery's house.'

'Which will you deal with first?' asked Cynric. 'Sewale Cottage or the Sorcerer's matters – the murders, the goats and the exhumations?'

'The Sorcerer stabbed Carton and may have exhumed those bodies,' said Michael with more conviction than Bartholomew felt was warranted. 'Perhaps he killed Thomas, too. So, we shall begin with the goats. Maybe they will lead us to this wretched warlock – hopefully before tomorrow night.'

Bartholomew trailed after the monk as he walked to Bene't College. It was late afternoon, and the warmest part of the day. People wilted, their enjoyment of the balmy weather vanished long ago. Tempers were frayed, and Bartholomew was sure the heat was responsible for some of the insults he heard bandied back and forth as folk began to declare their support for the Sorcerer or the Church. He knocked on Heltisle's gate, but there was no reply. Michael gave it a shove, more in frustration than in an attempt to enter, and was astonished when it swung open. The porters' lodge was deserted, and the only sign of life was a chicken scratching in the dirt.

'I did not like the mood of that crowd earlier,' said

Michael. 'Supposing some of them came here and attacked Heltisle for what he said about Isnard? We should make sure he is all right.'

Bartholomew followed him across the yard, but the hall was empty. The only person they found was a servant, who was sleeping under a bench. He shot to his feet when he became aware of the monk looming over him.

'The students are at a lecture in Peterhouse,' he gabbled. 'And all the Fellows have gone with them, except Master Heltisle, who is in the walled garden, reading.'

The monk set off towards the arbour, but Bartholomew stopped him. The hall had been pleasantly cool, and he was suspicious of the boy's claim that Heltisle would go to relax outside. He pushed the monk behind him and walked first, drawing his dagger as he did so.

'What are you doing?' demanded Michael, alarmed by his reaction. 'Heltisle is reading. Scholars do it all the time, I am told, although *we* have scant opportunity for such pleasures these days.'

'There is something odd about this. Stay behind me – unless you have a dagger of your own?'

'Certainly not. I am a man of God. However, I shall grab a stick if you think we might need it.'

Bartholomew led the way to the garden, where their approach was shielded by trees. He heard the bleat of a goat and reduced his speed, cautioning the monk to move stealthily. It was a waste of time; Michael was far too fat to be creeping anywhere. He tiptoed along like a hippopotamus, sticks and dried leaves crunching noisily under his feet.

Heltisle was lying in the grass when they found him. At first, Bartholomew thought he was dead, but he stirred when Michael touched his shoulder. There was a gash on the back of his head, and nearby was a branch. Someone had clubbed him, and the book that lay next to him suggested he had been taken unawares. Bartholomew helped him to sit, holding his arm when he reeled.

'I was attacked,' breathed Heltisle, when he had regained his senses.

'What were you doing out here in the first place?' asked Michael. 'It is like a furnace, and most folk are looking for somewhere cool to lurk.'

'I like the heat,' replied Heltisle. 'I have a skin condition that benefits from it, so I often bask. It is the cold I do not like. But who did this to me? I am in my own College!'

Bartholomew nodded through the trees, where he could just see Younge and his minions at the far end of the enclosure. Their attention was on the College goats, and they had not noticed what was happening around their fallen Master. 'One of them, I should imagine.'

Heltisle was shocked. 'But they are my loyal servants.'

Bartholomew thought otherwise. He watched the porters for a moment, then beckoned Heltisle and Michael to stand with him behind a sturdy oak, indicating that they were to remain silent. Michael complied readily enough, but Heltisle had to be convinced by a jab from the monk's elbow. The Master's jaw dropped when he saw Younge grab one of the goats and tie its legs together. The animal objected vociferously, but Younge was deft, and had clearly done it before. In moments, he had the creature trussed up. Then he dragged it to the nearest wall, and made a stirrup of his hands. One of his cronies stepped into it, another passed him the helpless animal, and it was quickly lobbed over the top of the wall. A voice on the other side indicated someone was there to receive it.

'And that solves the mystery of the missing goats,' said Michael, amused. 'Younge waits until everyone is out, then he and his cronies work together to spirit the animals away.'

'But it cannot . . .' stuttered Heltisle. 'I do not . . .'

'Matt is right to say one of them hit you, too,' Michael went on. 'Although I am sure they will be terribly solicitous when they "find" you and declare that intruders were responsible.'

Heltisle was white-faced. 'Younge has been with me for years, and I have never had cause to doubt him before. You must be mistaken.'

'Then let us put him to the test,' suggested Michael. 'Go and lie down where you fell, and we shall see what happens.'

Heltisle opened his mouth, but then closed it again, confused and uncertain. He was prone on the ground by the time Younge and the others left the garden; Bartholomew and Michael hid behind the tree. Most of the porters did not even stop to look at the Master as they passed; Younge waited until they were out of sight before kneeling next to him and grabbing his shoulder.

'Master Heltisle!' he shouted, all anxious concern. 'What happened? Did you see your attacker?'

'Who said I was attacked?' asked Heltisle coolly.

Younge was nonplussed. 'There is blood on your head . . .'

'There is blood on the *back* of my head,' corrected Heltisle. 'Which you cannot see, because of the way I am lying. I repeat: how did you know I was attacked?'

'Because the thieves who took the goat must have hit you.' Younge was becoming flustered.

'And how do you know a goat has been stolen?' pressed Heltisle. 'I am sure you did not count them before coming to see if I was dead. *Ergo*, you must have guilty knowledge of—'

Younge gave up his efforts to salvage the situation and drew his dagger. His voice became hard and angry. 'We took a few goats. So what? Bene't can afford it. But you have guessed too much, Heltisle. Your death can be blamed on these elusive thieves.'

He raised his arm preparing to plunge the blade into his Master's chest, and Heltisle released a monstrous shriek. Bartholomew leapt forward and grabbed the porter's hand. Younge twisted, and flicked out a leg that sent the physician sprawling. Then one of Michael's fists connected with Younge's chin, and he dropped as if poleaxed. Bartholomew crawled towards him, afraid the blow might have been too vigorous. But Younge was still breathing, although a lopsidedness to his face showed that his jaw was probably broken.

'I trusted him,' breathed Heltisle, shocked. 'And he was ready to kill me.'

'I will fetch my beadles,' said Michael. 'I assume you want him and his cronies locked up?'

Heltisle nodded weakly. 'But Bartholomew can fetch the beadles, while you stay here. Younge may wake up and I would rather have you protecting me than him. You were the one who felled the villain, while Bartholomew's so-called intervention almost saw me stabbed.'

'Not deliberately,' objected Bartholomew. 'He was too quick for me.'

'So you say,' sniffed Heltisle.

*

388

Fortunately, Beadle Meadowman happened to be walking along the High Street when Bartholomew emerged from Bene't College, and immediately took charge of the situation. He rounded up his colleagues and they went *en masse* to arrest the porters. People grinned as Younge and his henchmen were marched towards the gaol, and there were a lot of catcalls and jeers about comeuppance for surly manners. Heltisle was left with no staff, but help came from an unexpected quarter.

'I cannot see the University in trouble,' said Isnard, speaking loudly enough to ensure Michael would hear. 'I shall stand in until suitable replacements can be found – hopefully fellows more polite than the last lot. Of course, I cannot stay long. My loyalties lie with Michaelhouse.'

'You are just after the contents of their latrines,' said Heltisle accusingly. 'Like that heathen Arblaster. *He* wants dung for sinister reasons.'

'What sinister reasons?' asked Bartholomew, wondering whether basking in the sun for the benefit of his skin had left Heltisle a little deranged. 'It is used to fertilise fields.'

'It is also used in rituals that attract Satan,' countered Heltisle. 'Younge told me.'

'Well, there is a reliable source of information,' said Michael scathingly. 'Is that why you charged Isnard with being a necromancer this morning? Because he is keen to procure some dung?'

'And the fact that he has a penchant for dozing in cemeteries,' Heltisle mumbled. But the bargeman had just offered to do him a considerable favour, so he shot him an ingratiating smile. 'It was nothing personal, and it transpires that I may have acted on inaccurate intelligence. You must forgive me.'

'All right,' agreed Isnard cheerfully. 'But *you* must remember that without dung there would be no crops, no vegetables in the garden—'

'Do not talk to me about gardens,' muttered Heltisle, ushering the bargeman inside his College. Isnard paused just long enough to ensure Michael was watching.

'Perhaps I will let him back in the choir,' said the monk with a sigh. 'I do not think I can stomach much more of this obsequiousness.'

He turned to make his way back to Michaelhouse, and Bartholomew followed. The physician glanced at the sky and was relieved to see the sun beginning to dip as evening approached. He was exhausted, and wanted no more than to sit in the conclave with a cup of cool ale. It had been days since he had had an opportunity to relax with his colleagues, although he hoped William would not be there.

'It will be dark in a few hours,' said Michael. 'And whilst we have explained some of our mysteries, we are a long way from solving the most important ones. We do not know the Sorcerer's identity, who exhumed Thomas, Margery and Goldynham, or who killed Carton, Thomas or Spynk.'

'Do you think the Bishop's men killed Spynk? They were near his body, after all.'

'It is possible, but their presence in the garden might have been coincidence, and I would rather not challenge them until I have solid evidence of wrongdoing.' Michael threw up his hands in sudden despair. 'I am at my wits' end with this damned business – and I am tempted to take the opportunity for a good night's sleep, on the grounds that we will almost certainly not have one tomorrow.'

They reached Michaelhouse, but before Bartholomew

could take more than a few steps towards the sanctuary of his room they became aware of a rumpus taking place in the conclave. Michael grimaced.

'I hope Langelee has not invited Osbern and Brownsley in there. I do not want them in the inner sanctum of my home – my refuge from the world.'

They walked up the stairs, and entered the conclave. Langelee was standing by the window with a goblet in his hand. Wynewyk was next to him, while Suttone poured wine from a small cask. The atmosphere was happy and convivial, and William was the only Fellow not present. All attention was on a slight, dark-haired man who sat beaming affably at everyone from the Master's favourite chair.

'Clippesby!' Bartholomew exclaimed in delight, greeting the last of Michaelhouse's Fellows with genuine affection. Seeing him home again was the best thing that had happened all day. 'What are you doing here? You are not supposed to be back until September.'

'Did you come because I am due to give an important sermon tomorrow night?' asked Suttone, looking flattered. 'It is to the Guild of Corpus Christi, and I thought I might expound on the plague.'

'Actually, I came because of Carton,' replied the Dominican, smiling shyly when Michael grasped his shoulder to express his own pleasure at the wanderer's return. 'I thought you might need me for teaching, especially when I heard Mildenale has given his innate oddness free rein.'

'Oddness?' asked Michael warily. Clippesby was generally acknowledged to be insane, and had been incarcerated several times for peculiar behaviour, so it was unsettling to hear him accusing someone else of being strange. 'You are not saying that just because he is a Franciscan, are you?'

Clippesby shot him a reproachful look. 'I have never denigrated anyone for the colour of his habit. I am not William. And I am not Mildenale, either.'

'Yes, you have always been reasonable,' acknowledged Langelee. 'We are lucky to have you, because I doubt any other Dominican would have put up with William all these years. I am just glad you have not had to endure the last month, because he has grown much worse.'

'He has fallen under Mildenale's spell,' explained Suttone, going to refill Clippesby's goblet. '*Mildenalus Sanctus* has been whispering poisonous thoughts in his ear, and William is too stupid to dismiss them for the nonsense they are.'

'Mildenale has always been extreme,' said Wynewyk. 'We should have tried to keep him away from William, because with hindsight, it was obvious what was going to happen. William's foray into more serious fanaticism is partly our fault.'

'You would not think he needs our protection,' said Langelee. 'But you are probably right. Just because he has strong opinions does not mean he has a strong mind to go with them.'

'I knew Mildenale was dangerous,' said Clippesby. 'Not just to my fellow Dominicans, but to the whole town. So I applied for a sabbatical leave of absence specifically to travel to Blackfriars in London, and warn my Prior-General about him. I intended to come home as soon as I had delivered my message, but he kept me there. He said I needed a rest, although I cannot imagine why. I was perfectly healthy.'

'Does he know you are mad?' asked Langelee bluntly. 'That might account for it.'

'I am not mad,' said Clippesby mildly. 'It is the rest of you who are lunatics. However, I did interrupt my interview with the Prior-General to greet a hen, while his cat was a fascinating fellow. Unfortunately, not everyone appreciates the importance of being polite to God's smaller creatures. Including him, it would seem.'

'Right,' said Michael briskly, before they could go too far down a route that was sure to leave them all perplexed. Even Bartholomew did not understand all the peculiar workings of Clippesby's mind. 'What did your Prior-General say when you told him about Mildenale?'

'That he should be monitored before any action was taken, to assess the extent of the danger he poses. I assumed he would choose me to keep him informed, but he appointed Carton instead.'

'Carton?' asked Bartholomew. 'But he is a Franciscan, and . . .' He trailed off, thinking about what he knew – that Thomas had been suspicious of Carton, because the Franciscan convent in London had been flooded on the date of his alleged ordination. *And* Carton had been party to building plans in the Dominican Priory, something a member of a rival Order should not have known. The answer was suddenly blindingly clear. 'Carton was a Black Friar!'

Clippesby nodded. 'Since he was fifteen years old. But the Prior-General said the best person to obtain Mildenale's confidence would be another Franciscan, not a man from a different Order. Pretending to be a Grey Friar cannot have been easy for Carton, and it was a brave thing to have done.'

'He was uneasy, though,' said Bartholomew. 'He wore an amulet to protect him.'

'Yes, he did,' said Clippesby, nodding. 'A holy-stone, which he told me was imbued with great power against the Devil and wolves. He was a bit superstitious, but a good man, for all that.'

'Lord!' exclaimed Suttone suddenly. 'This means we have buried him in the wrong cemetery!'

'I do not think it matters,' said Clippesby. 'The Franciscans are decent men, and will not mind a Dominican among them.' He looked around, and saw his colleagues were not so sure. 'But I can talk to Prior Morden and arrange a transfer, if you think it is necessary.'

'I do,' said Michael firmly. 'We do not want him excavated and tossed in the street when the two Orders are next at each other's throats. In fact, we had better retrieve him as soon as possible.'

'Clippesby's news explains a great deal,' said Langelee, holding out his cup for more claret. 'Carton was always particular about privacy, and hated his students rifling through his belongings. It was because he really did have secrets.'

'One secret was that he owned books popular with Dominicans,' said Bartholomew, recalling what he had found when he had checked the contents of the man's personal library. 'Some expounded the Black Friars' stance on Blood Relics – which he probably told Mildenale and William he was going to burn – and on the way to Barnwell Priory last week he forgot he was supposed to be a Franciscan and started arguing the "wrong" side of the debate.'

'He was very devout,' said Langelee. 'I never believed he lied about taking holy orders, despite Prior Pechem pestering me to look at the documentation about it. And he only denounced Dominicans when pressed by one of his so-called cronies. That must have pained him, but he would have had to do it or risk exposure. Being a spy is not easy; it takes more skill than you imagine.'

'What about the guide to witchery he owned?' asked Michael of Clippesby. 'And his enthusiasm for watching covens with Cynric? Just how superstitious was he?'

'The Prior-General has ordered all his friars to keep an eye on any superstitious activities they happen to come across,' explained Clippesby, 'so learning that Carton monitored covens comes as no surprise. Meanwhile, he probably collected this witchery guide to burn – to "prove" to Mildenale that he was serious about stamping out heresy. Unfortunately, his more recent letters to the Prior-General showed he thought he was losing Mildenale's trust.'

'You arranged for him to come here in the first place,' recalled Langelee. 'You wrote asking if we would make him a commoner. Then we elected him a Fellow.'

'That was not supposed to happen,' said Clippesby. 'He was able to worm his way into Mildenale's confidence when they were commoners together, but maintaining the friendship was difficult once he was promoted.'

'So *that* is why the situation with Mildenale began to deteriorate,' said Michael in understanding. 'Carton's control over him started to slip. It coincides with when William fell under Mildenale's spell, too.'

'Precisely,' said Clippesby. He looked sad. 'When I read Carton's missives to our Prior-General and realised what was happening, I decided I had better come home. Unfortunately, I have arrived too late to save Carton's life.'

'Do you think that is why he was killed?' asked Bartholomew uncomfortably. 'Mildenale found out that one of his most trusted allies was actually a Black Friar?'

Clippesby regarded him soberly. 'It is possible. However, suspicions are not evidence, as Brother Michael is in the habit of saying. You will need proof before you accuse him.'

Chapter 11

It was still light when Bartholomew went to bed that night, but he fell asleep almost immediately, and was difficult to rouse two hours later when Cynric came to inform him that he was needed at the castle; Tulyet had engaged in a furious skirmish with the Huntingdon Way robbers, and two of his men had been hurt. Still not fully awake, the physician traipsed to the great fortress in the north of the town. Darkness had fallen at last, although there was still a hint of colour in the western sky, and bats were out in force, feasting on the insects that had proliferated in the unseasonable heat.

'We got one,' said Tulyet, watching him suture a wound in a soldier's abdomen that would almost certainly prove fatal. Mercifully, the man was unconscious, and knew nothing of what was happening or the physician would not have attempted it.

'One what?' asked Bartholomew, his attention more on his work than the restlessly pacing Sheriff. Tulyet walked stiffly, suggesting he had not escaped the encounter unscathed, but he had brushed aside concerned questions.

'One of the robbers,' snapped Tulyet. 'What else have

we been talking about since you arrived? They swooped down on us at Girton, not a mile from the castle, if you can believe their audacity! They were there before we could muster our defences, and then they were gone, leaving these two injured and Ned Archer dead. They were so fast – I have never seen anything like it.'

'This is the first time you have fought them?' asked Bartholomew, trying to concentrate on his patient and Tulyet at the same time. They were alone in the room, and he sensed his friend's need to share his frustration and shock – and the importance of not doing it in front of the men who were waiting for him to lead them out again as soon as the horses were ready.

Tulyet nodded. 'Until now, I have only seen the aftermath of their attacks, because they are gone long before my patrols arrive. But this was a carefully planned ambush, and we were found lacking.'

'When you say you "got" one of the robbers, what do you mean exactly? Is he dead? Does he need medical attention?'

'He is sitting in my prison with a smug smile on his face, assuring his guards that he will be free within a week. He says he has powerful friends who will not let him rot in gaol.'

'I do not suppose he has a bushy beard, does he? Or is abnormally large?'

'No – he is a grey-headed fellow of average height. He is well-dressed, though, and asked for a psalter to pass the hours. However, I did spot a bearded man during the ambush, and I saw one who was unusually large, too. The thought crossed my mind that they might be the pair you say have been renting Refham's forge. The attack was not far from the place, after all.'

'Brownsley and Osbern,' said Bartholomew. 'The Bishop's bailiff and hawker, respectively.'

'De Lisle is behind all this mayhem?' Tulyet stopped pacing to gape at him.

'He is in Avignon,' said Bartholomew evasively, loath to accuse a high-ranking churchman of heinous crimes to a royally appointed official. 'How can he know what his retinue does in his absence? However, Brownsley told Michael he is on his way to Ely, to raise money for the Bishop's living expenses. Perhaps this is an easier way of doing it than collecting taxes.'

Tulyet stared at him. 'A man called Osbern le Hawker was responsible for theft and damage that cost Spynk a thousand pounds, while one named Brownsley terrorised Danyell. And this is the pair you say you fought – twice in the house I want for Dickon, and once when they attacked Refham?'

Bartholomew nodded. 'Michael identified them when they came to order us not to sell Sewale Cottage. Now you know why they are so formidable. They are no mere louts – they are men who have engaged in criminal activities for years. But I cannot imagine de Lisle ordering them to do it.'

'No, but he might have told them he was in desperate need of money.' Tulyet's face was grim. 'This helps, Matt. Now I know what I am up against, I shall adapt my plans accordingly. Michael can come to the castle later, to see if he can identify the grinning villain who sits reading his psalms.'

'I cannot see how this connects to the Sorcerer,' said Bartholomew. He was about to rub his eyes when he remembered his hands were covered in blood. 'Brownsley and Osbern want something from Margery's house –

and I suspect Michael is right to think it will be money, given what they have been doing on the Huntingdon Way.'

Tulyet began to re-buckle the armour he had loosened. 'If de Lisle was at Ely, I would have no hesitation in suggesting *he* is the Sorcerer. But even he cannot manage that sort of thing from Avignon, so I predict you are looking for someone else. I doubt it is any of his henchmen, though, not if they are concentrating on terrorising the highways.'

'You are going out again already?' asked Bartholomew, watching him pick up his sword.

'Fresh horses should be saddled up by now. How is my soldier? Will he live? He has been with me for years and I do not want to lose him.'

'We will know in the morning,' replied Bartholomew, reluctant to tell the truth when his friend was about to do battle with some very dangerous opponents. He did not want him distracted by grief.

Tulyet nodded. 'I will try to be back in time to help you with the Sorcerer, but I cannot make any promises – I *must* catch these robbers before they murder any more innocent travellers. I am afraid you may have to tackle this warlock on your own.'

Unsettled and unhappy, Bartholomew left the castle. As he passed All Saints, he saw shadows flitting in the churchyard. It was not the same sort of gathering he had witnessed the previous night, and there was no laughter and song. Instead, people seemed to be moving with grim purpose. The tower door stood open, and two men were struggling to manhandle something through it. Others carried bowls or sacks. Bartholomew watched for a moment, and decided these were the Sorcerer's more dedicated disciples, busily making preparations for his début. His unease intensified when he realised it was now Saturday morning, and that whatever the Sorcerer planned was going to take place that night.

When he reached Michaelhouse, it was time for morning mass. Michael was missing, and Cynric said he had been patrolling the Market Square for much of the night. Apparently, Mildenale and William had assembled a group of devoted Church followers there, and their frenzied sermons had resulted in Clare College being attacked. Bartholomew was not the only one who had noticed Spaldynge's declining mental state, and William claimed it was because Spaldynge was the Sorcerer.

'Then Brother Michael sent beadles to All Saints, with orders to break up the coven,' added Cynric. 'But most folk like the All Saints witches – a lot more than they like Mildenale and William – so the beadles did nothing when they arrived. They just told the participants to be discreet.'

'Were you there, too?' asked Bartholomew, suspecting Michael would have sent someone he trusted. Unfortunately for the monk, Cynric was not wholeheartedly on the Church's side.

The book-bearer looked furtive. 'I might have been. But then I was seized by a sudden notion that those two villains might be in Sewale Cottage again, so I went to find out.'

'I see.' Bartholomew was too tired to remonstrate with him for failing to follow Michael's orders. The near-sleepless night was already taking its toll, and he hoped he would have the strength to face whatever was coming that day.

Clippesby took the morning mass, and his presence

401

was a bright flame in an otherwise cheerless occasion. William and Mildenale were notable by their absence, and Langelee said neither had been home all night. Bartholomew looked around and tried to remember when St Michael's had last seen such a small gathering; even during the plague they had mustered a bigger turnout. Clippesby performed for just Bartholomew, Langelee, Suttone, Wynewyk and Deynman.

As soon as the service was over, Cynric was waiting to say the physician was needed at the castle again. Inexplicably, the soldier with the lesser wound was dying, while the other had woken up and asked for something to eat. It was mid-afternoon before Bartholomew was able to return to the College. As he had missed breakfast and the midday meal, he was very hungry. He went to the kitchens in the hope that Agatha would take pity on him. He was not surprised to find Michael there, complaining that pea soup was hardly the kind of fare that would give a man the strength needed to fight a powerful villain like the Sorcerer.

'How do you know he is a villain?' asked Agatha, standing with her hands on her hips and declining to let the monk into the pantries. 'You do not know who he is, so he might be a saint.'

'He is a witch,' said Michael impatiently. 'He exhumes corpses, and is responsible for all the trouble that is currently affecting the town.'

'No, he is not,' argued Agatha. 'The Church is doing that. They are the ones making the fuss – men like *Mildenalus Sanctus* and William. And Thomas, when he was alive. And even Eyton, selling his protective charms and scoffing honey as if there is no tomorrow. The Sorcerer is not the villain here.'

Michael regarded her reproachfully. 'Witchcraft is not a bit of fun, Agatha. It is dark, dangerous and offensive to God. I do not mean the kind that Margery practised – the healing kind. I mean the sort that involves goats, blood and corpses. The Sorcerer may seem like a friendly alternative to orthodox religion, but I suspect people might discover tonight that he is something else altogether.'

A cold chill passed down Bartholomew's spine. Agatha regarded Michael in silence for a moment, then stood aside to let him pass. He had unsettled her, too.

'Do not eat the pork,' she called after him. 'It was covered in maggots this morning, and I have not had the chance to rinse it off yet. It will be all right when I disguise the flavour with a few onions.'

Bartholomew felt queasy just thinking about it, and had to force himself to swallow some bread and cheese. The cheese was rancid, and made him gag. Michael did not seem to care, and crammed his mouth so full that his cheeks bulged.

'Is there honey in that pot?' he asked, almost indecipherably, although that did not stop him from adding yet more to his maw. 'It is one of Barnwell's receptacles.'

The honey was much nicer than the cheese, and Bartholomew smeared it liberally on his bread, hoping it would mask the taste of mould. And perhaps it would shield him from evil, too, as Eyton claimed. Deciding he needed all the protection he could get, he ate more.

'Did you talk to Mildenale last night?' he asked eventually, sitting back and watching Michael scrape the jar with a spoon. 'Cynric said you were obliged to stop him and William from preaching.'

'They had gone by the time I arrived,' replied Michael.

'But not before their sermon caused a mob to descend on Clare and smash its windows. Ironically, fanatical Franciscans are the most powerful weapon the Sorcerer owns at the moment – their sermons are driving people right into his arms. I spent all morning hunting for them, but they are probably resting somewhere, sleeping off their busy night.'

'Clippesby was right to report Mildenale to his Prior-General; as usual, he showed more foresight than any of us. We have only just realised how dangerous Mildenale is, but he saw it months ago.'

'When the mob failed to find Spaldynge, they set their sights on Mother Valeria. There is a rumour that they will catch and hang her today.'

'She has left the town,' said Bartholomew, relieved. 'She packed all her belongings, and—'

'Unfortunately, that is untrue. She was seen only this morning. Foolish woman!' Michael sounded as exhausted and dispirited as Bartholomew felt.

'What do you want me to do?' asked the physician, determined to prevent the Sorcerer from turning his town into a battlefield. 'I am at your disposal – unless I am needed by a patient.'

'All our investigations have condensed into two simple issues: the Sorcerer and his plans, and the odd business at Sewale Cottage. Everything else – the murders of Carton, Thomas and Spynk, the exhumations and so on – relates to them.'

Bartholomew was not so sure. 'We thought Bene't's missing goats were connected to the Sorcerer, but they were just a case of theft. Perhaps—'

'There is no time for debate, Matt. I will continue my hunt for the Sorcerer, while you take Sewale Cottage.

I want you to go to Barnwell and demand to know why the canons are prepared to pay such a handsome price for it. Do not let them fob you off with claims that it would make a good granary, because we know that is a lie. You *must* learn what they want from it.'

It was a tall order, given that they had met with scant success so far. 'Can we not leave this until tomorrow? The Sorcerer is the more important of these two enquiries, because of what he plans to do tonight. It would be better if I helped you here, and we go to Barnwell in the morning—'

'We *think* the two issues are separate,' snapped Michael. 'But we cannot be sure – one of the people who wants the house may be the Sorcerer, do not forget. And there is the fact that it was the home of a witch. You *must* come back with answers. I cannot overemphasise how important this is.'

Bartholomew was daunted by the task he had been set. 'The canons have not been very forthcoming so far—'

'Then talk to Arblaster first. Tell him what we already know, and *demand* the truth from him.'

'If we are right about Sewale Cottage housing some kind of secret, then it is possible that Spynk was killed by one of the other bidders – namely the canons or Arblaster. Or by the Bishop's men.'

Michael nodded soberly. 'So you will have to be careful. Take Cynric with you.'

Cynric was nowhere to be found, and there was no time to hunt for him. In an effort to do as Michael ordered, Bartholomew even allowed Langelee to saddle him one of the College nags, knowing it would be quicker than travelling on foot. He climbed inelegantly on its back, and set off at a lively trot, faster than was safe in a town where the streets were full of carts, pedestrians and other riders.

He sensed a familiar tension in the air, and noted the way people gathered in small knots. He had seen it before, and recognised the scent of trouble. Churches had either closed their doors, or they had opened them for the faithful to be regaled with speeches condemning witch-craft. As he passed one chapel he heard someone shouting about burning Mother Valeria's hut. He reined in and listened for a moment, but it was not Mildenale's voice that was ranting, nor William's. It was some other fanatic in a habit, and he was disconcerted to see the place was bursting at the seams. The Church was tired of being the underdog and was beginning to fight back. In the distance, he thought he saw a flash, and wondered if it was lightning.

People regarded him oddly as he rode by. Some crossed themselves and looked away, as if afraid to catch his eye, while others winked and wished him luck. When Isnard did it, Bartholomew jerked his horse to a standstill.

'Luck for what?' he demanded sharply.

'For tonight,' replied Isnard. 'You will make your grand appearance. Are you saying it is not you, then? I confess I was sceptical when Mildenale told me it was, because you have never seemed that well organised to me. And not that interested in accruing power, either.'

'Mildenale is telling people I am the Sorcerer?' Bartholomew was appalled.

'William keeps saying it is unlikely, but Mildenale ignores him. Personally, my money is on Spaldynge. Well, it is on him literally, if you must know, because Eyton is running a sweepstake. I had to choose between you, Spaldynge and Canon Podiolo. It was not an easy decision, I can tell you.'

Bartholomew did not wait to hear more. He jabbed his heels into his pony's sides and urged it into a trot. When he approached the ramshackle bridge that spanned the King's Ditch, he saw a crowd had gathered, and could tell by the way they looked at him that Mildenale's rumour had reached their ears. Spaldynge was among them, and yelled something hostile. Bartholomew coaxed his horse into a gallop. Scholars, soldiers and traders scattered in all directions as he bore down on them. Several howled curses, but then he was across the Ditch and on to the Causeway. He kicked the horse into a full-out run, risking life and limb as it pounded along the hard-baked track. The beast stumbled once and he almost fell, saving himself only by grabbing its mane. It snickered in terror, but he spurred it on again. It still seemed a long time before the roofs of Barnwell Priory came into sight.

He decided to follow Michael's advice and tackle Arblaster first. The dung-merchant was one man, whereas the canons were rather more numerous, and questioning them would put Bartholomew inside an enclosure from which escape would be difficult. He would visit the convent only if Arblaster could not – or would not – provide the answers he had been charged to find.

The stench of manure was hot and strong in the dry, still air, and he coughed as he slid off the horse. He hammered on Arblaster's door, and saw, as he waited for a reply, that the dung-master's goats had white feet. He wondered why he had not noticed before that they could not be Bene't's animals. The door was opened by

Arblaster himself, but there was no welcoming smile this time. He stood aside for the physician to enter.

'Twenty marks,' he said flatly. 'But that is as high as I can go, because it is all I have left.'

'What is wrong?' asked Bartholomew, taking in the man's pale face and red-rimmed eyes.

Arblaster slumped against the wall. 'Michaelhouse has given its latrines to Isnard, and I think the canons are going to offer twenty-one marks for Sewale Cottage. Damn them! It was my last hope, but *they* will get it, and I shall be ruined. Jodoca has gone to talk to them. She says she has every hope of success, but Mother Valeria has cast a spell to bring me bad luck, so I am not confident.'

Bartholomew was confused. 'You only own twenty marks? But I thought you were rich.'

'I *was* rich – until the heatwave struck. But I need rain and *warm* weather for composting, and this unseasonable furnace has damaged my wares.'

'Why does Sewale Cottage represent your last hope?' asked Bartholomew. He saw Arblaster's head snap up sharply; the man realised he had said something he probably should not have done. 'We know something is secreted there, something a number of people want. What is it?'

Arblaster gave a bitter laugh. 'If I told you, Michaelhouse would refuse to sell it, and then even that frail hope would be gone.'

'We are not going to sell it anyway,' lied Bartholomew. 'So you may as well tell me.'

Arblaster eyed him searchingly, then drew a dagger from his belt. 'You are the Fellow who is not in step with the others – the one who has different views about what is going on. Perhaps *you* have worked out that there is more to Sewale Cottage than meets the eye, but your colleagues will not have done, and you have probably not remembered to tell them. If I kill you, I may yet be saved.'

Startled by the sudden change in the man, Bartholomew took a step away, but Arblaster moved faster, and the physician found himself hurled against the wall. The knife was in the dung-master's right hand, and Bartholomew used both his to try to keep it away from his throat. Unfortunately, a life of hauling manure had rendered Arblaster hard and muscular, and the blade began to descend.

'All the Fellows know something is hidden,' Bartholomew blurted, hoping he did not sound as desperate as he felt. 'They are searching for it as I speak.'

'You are lying,' said Arblaster contemptuously, as the knife moved inexorably towards the physician's neck. 'And you are not even very good at it.'

'What will they find?' gasped Bartholomew, resisting with all his might. It was not enough. 'Money? Jewels? Books?'

'Something that was brought here.' Arblaster braced himself for the fatal stroke as the blade touched bare skin. 'You will die not knowing, I suppose.'

Bartholomew knew he was not strong enough to prevent Arblaster from gashing him, and he also knew he was wasting valuable energy by trying. He forced himself to release the dung-merchant's dagger hand, and drove his fist into the man's stomach instead. It earned him a cut neck, but it also caused his opponent to drop the knife in shock. Unfortunately, the advantage was only momentary, and Arblaster managed to snag the physician's tabard as he started to run away. Both men fell crashing to the ground. Bartholomew fought valiantly, but it was not long before Arblaster had him pinned down. The dung-master glanced behind him, looking for the weapon, but Bartholomew managed to kick it away with his foot. And then they were at a stalemate: Arblaster could not kill Bartholomew without his blade, but the only way to reach it was by letting the physician go.

'Cynric will be here soon,' gasped Bartholomew, aware that it was hopeless to struggle, but unable to stop himself. 'You may as well let me up.'

'As I said, you are a dismal liar.' Arblaster leaned all his weight on the physician in an effort to subdue him. It worked; Bartholomew could barely breathe. 'But Jodoca *will* come, and then I shall kill you. Damn this sun! If it had not been so hot, I would never have tried to get Danyell's . . .'

'Danyell?' gasped Bartholomew. Despite his predicament, answers started to come to him in a series of blinding flashes, so clear that he wondered why he had not seen them before. Was it really necessary to be engaged in a death struggle before his wits were sharp enough to work properly?

Arblaster watched him, a half-smile on his face. He eased himself into a more comfortable position, one that was not crushing the life out of his captive. The physician still could not move, but at least he could breathe. 'You do not need me to explain – you have worked it out for yourself at last.'

'On the night of his death, Danyell went out,' said Bartholomew, hoping an analysis might distract Arblaster into letting down his guard. 'He carried something with him, which Spynk thought was a stone – a sample to

410

show a potential client. But it has always seemed odd to me that he should have been considering business when he probably felt very ill. I think he had what everyone is looking for. He hid it in Sewale Cottage, and intended to see Mother Valeria as soon as he had finished, to buy a cure from her. He died before that could happen.'

'I saw him.' Arblaster's expression was distant as he remembered. 'I was coming home from buying a spell from Valeria myself, and I spotted movement in the shadows. I did not want to be seen in that part of the town at such an hour, so I hid. Danyell entered the house with a box – which *may* have looked like a brick from a distance – and he left without it some time later. And then I heard a conversation between him and those two men.'

'What two men? Brownsley and Osbern – one huge and the other bearded?'

'The Bishop's louts,' agreed Arblaster, glancing towards the door. Bartholomew suddenly realised that while he was talking in an effort to distract Arblaster, so Arblaster was encouraging the discussion to occupy his captive until Jodoca could hand him his dagger. 'And we all know that anything involving de Lisle is going to be shady. So, I listened and I learned.'

'Learned what?'

'Despite Danyell's obvious terror – he was on his knees, gasping for breath before they even started questioning him – he was defying them. I could not hear everything, but I caught mention of digging holes. But then Danyell clutched his chest, and that was that – he was dead. The Bishop's men were furious. They dumped his body on the open ground opposite, then they broke into Margery's house.'

Bartholomew thought about it. Danyell had been terrorised by Brownsley in Norfolk, and meeting his tormentor in a dark street must have been more than his failing heart could stand. Brownsley's anger suggested Danyell had died without telling him what he wanted to know. He had, however, surmised that the box had been hidden inside Sewale Cottage, which explained why he and Osbern had expended so much energy searching it.

'What is in the box?' asked Bartholomew. Arblaster glanced at the door a second time. When Jodoca did appear, what would she do? Help her husband commit murder? Or talk sense into him?

The dung-master looked as though he was not going to answer, but shrugged when he saw it was a way to prolong the discussion. 'Treasure. What else can lead men to such lengths?'

'So, you knew about it because you overheard this discussion, while Spynk would have known because Danyell confided in him – or in Cecily, his lover. But what about the canons? How do they come to be in on the secret?'

'I do not know,' replied Arblaster. 'And I do not care.'

The fact that he had some answers filled Bartholomew with hope, and he knew he needed to brief Michael as soon as possible. He pretended to sag in defeat, encouraging Arblaster to relax his grip. The dung-merchant fell for the ploy – it was hard work pinning a man to the ground, and he was grateful for a respite. As soon as the weight eased slightly, Bartholomew mustered every ounce of his strength and brought his knee up sharply between his captor's legs, following it with a punch to the side of the head. Arblaster slumped to the ground, and Bartholomew rolled away, staggering to his feet as fast as he could. He ran to the kitchen for rope, and quickly bound Arblaster's hands and feet, not liking the notion of the man regaining his senses and trying to finish what he had started. He had just tightened the last knot when Arblaster opened his eyes.

'Jodoca!' he screamed, flailing furiously. 'Help me! He is getting away!'

Suddenly, Bartholomew recalled what Arblaster had said about his wife earlier – that she had gone to 'talk' to the canons at Barnwell. 'What is she doing?' he asked uneasily.

Arblaster struggled harder. 'She should have persuaded the canons to withdraw their offer by now. She is rather good at it, as Spynk can attest. She is more determined than me. I was ready to give up, but she told me to have faith. She will see us through this.'

'Jodoca killed Spynk?' asked Bartholomew incredulously. 'I do not believe you.'

'She will get you, too,' vowed Arblaster, writhing violently, although it was clear he was not going to escape. 'She will not appreciate what you have done to me. Jodoca!'

Bartholomew raced outside, climbed on the horse again and spurred it towards the convent. He realised he should have seen days ago what had happened, because all the clues had been there. Of course Danyell had been inside Sewale Cottage – his body had been found near it, and the cottage had been broken into that night, first by Danyell himself, and then by Brownsley and Osbern. Danyell must have chosen the place because he had been told that its sole occupant was recently dead, and he had assumed he would be able to conceal his box without being disturbed. He was a mason, so rearranging stones would have been a simple matter for him.

But why had he decided to hide his treasure, when most men would have taken it home with them? The answer to that was clear, too: Danyell had seen the Bishop's men lurking around – or perhaps he had heard talk about the robberies on the Huntingdon Way – and knew it would not be safe in his possession. No doubt he had also heard that Michaelhouse planned to sell the house, and his ultimate intention was to purchase it himself – or perhaps do it with the help of Spynk and Cecily.

Bartholomew frowned as he rode. Had Jodoca really killed Spynk? He supposed she might have been in Sewale Cottage's garden that night. The third shadow had not been with Osbern and Brownsley, so it was possible that Spynk had been lured there with promises of gold and found himself with a blade in his back instead. It was certainly one way of ensuring he did not make Michaelhouse another competitive offer. He frowned more deeply. Except, of course, that Cecily was probably the driving force behind the purchase, in which case Jodoca had taken the wrong life.

He reached the priory and flung himself out of the saddle to pound on the gate. He glanced up at the sky. It was an odd colour – a sickly yellow-blue he had never seen before, and the marshes were eerily quiet. There was no answer from the canons, so he hammered again, then jumped in alarm when the gate was suddenly hauled open by Podiolo. The infirmarian was carrying a broadsword, and Bartholomew leapt away, unused to seeing clerics wield such enormous weapons.

'We have suffered a murderous assault,' Podiolo

shouted angrily. His amber eyes looked sinister in the evening sunlight. 'But like Fencotes, I was not always a monastic, and I learned swordplay when I was a gold-smith in Florence – I am ready to defend myself and my brethren, so be warned.'

'Jodoca attacked you?' asked Bartholomew, edging back further when Podiolo waved the weapon closer than was comfortable. He had never seen the man so agitated.

'Jodoca?' echoed Podiolo, gaping at him. Then he frowned. 'Yes, of course it was – someone small and agile, but strong, and too short to have been a man. Jodoca! Who would have thought it?'

'What did she do?'

'She went after Fencotes with a dagger. Prior Norton fended her off, but she is still at large. I cannot imagine what Fencotes has done to annoy her.'

Bartholomew followed him to the infirmary, where the canons formed a protective phalanx around their fallen comrade. Lay-brothers clustered at the door, and Bartholomew thought that if any robber should want to attack another part of the convent and make off with the silver, now was a perfect time. Even as the thought came into his head, he wondered whether that was Jodoca's intention. Arblaster said they had lost every-thing. Did she intend to recoup their losses? Start a new life in another town, funded by monastic treasure, since Danyell's property was unavailable?

'It was Jodoca,' Podiolo announced, as Norton came to greet them. 'Bartholomew identified her.'

Norton's eyes bulged in horror. 'But she is a woman! And she was intent on murder – I could see it in her every move. She might have killed me, too if I had not screeched for help.'

'She was loath to tackle twenty of us, so she ran off,' explained another canon. 'We have no idea where she went, which is why we are here, all crowded together. There is safety in numbers.'

'How is Fencotes?' asked Bartholomew, stepping towards the bed. 'Did she harm him?'

'He is more alarmed than hurt,' said Norton. 'But I am glad you are here. Podiolo is no physician.'

'No, he is not,' agreed Bartholomew, knowing from Fencotes's grey, sweaty face that there was more wrong than just fright. It should have been obvious, even to the most inexperienced practitioner, that Jodoca's blade had struck home, and that the old man had received a wound that was likely to be mortal. 'Where are you hurt, Fencotes?'

The elderly canon gave Bartholomew a weak smile, but did not answer.

'Be careful what you say,' whispered Podiolo. 'It took us a long time to calm him after the attack. The only way we managed in the end was by promising to buy Sewale Cottage. At any cost.'

'He believes Sewale Cottage will be a good investment for our future,' added Norton. 'And that we will benefit in the long term, even if we pay over the odds now. Personally, I disagree, but we shall do what he says, to make him happy.'

'Arblaster told me what is hidden in Sewale Cottage,' said Bartholomew, kneeling by the bed and addressing the patient. The old man was icy cold, even more chilled than his usual grave-like temperature. 'I know why you are so determined to have it.'

'What are you talking about?' demanded Norton. 'It is just a house. Tell him, Fencotes.'

'The physician is right,' whispered the old man. He looked strangely at peace. 'There is a great box of treasure buried there – enough to swell our coffers for years to come. Or perhaps you will use it to help the poor. It does not matter, only that Barnwell has it.'

Norton was appalled. 'But great boxes of treasure do not fall from Heaven, and they are nearly always tainted. I am not sure whether we should take it.'

'It will be yours if you buy the house,' whispered Fencotes weakly. 'And you *will* buy the house, because you have promised. You swore on the Bible.'

'I did,' said Norton, his eyes so wide that Bartholomew wondered whether he would ever be able to close them again. 'But you should have told me the truth. I do not like being tricked.'

Gently, Bartholomew turned the old man over; blood had pooled on the mattress beneath him. Like Carton and Spynk, Fencotes had been stabbed in the back. Norton and the others gasped their horror, and the Prior looked accusingly at Podiolo.

'How could I see that when he was lying on it?' objected Podiolo defensively. 'Besides, you told me Jodoca had been repelled before she could inflict any damage.'

'Heal him, Bartholomew,' cried Norton, distraught. 'He is my oldest friend!'

'I cannot.' There was no cure for a wound in such a place, and to attempt one would cause the patient needless pain. It was kinder to let him die in peace.

'Stabbed in the back,' mused Podiolo. He still held his sword, and seemed less shocked by Fencotes's condition than his colleagues. Was it because he was an infirmarian, and so inured to such sights? Somehow, Bartholomew did not think so, and he edged away from him, unnerved

417

by his proximity. 'Like Carton. Does that mean Jodoca murdered him, too?'

'I think so,' replied Bartholomew, relaxing a little when Norton indicated with a wave of his hand that Podiolo was to put his weapon away. 'I know she killed Spynk, because her husband just told me.' He turned back to Fencotes, but the old man was fading fast, and Bartholomew did not want to hasten his end by demanding what might be a lengthy explanation. 'If I describe what I think happened to Carton, will you nod, to tell me if I am right? You do not need to speak.'

Fencotes inclined his head, so Bartholomew began.

'Carton was a Dominican, ordered to disguise himself as a Franciscan by his Prior-General, and sent to watch a dangerous fanatic. An unexpected promotion meant he began to lose control of Mildenale, which, being a conscientious man, distressed him deeply. When he was left alone in your chapel, he was seized by the urge to pray.'

'That amulet *was* his,' interrupted Podiolo. 'I have thought about it, and I remember seeing it around his neck. It is a powerful one, and should have protected him from evil.'

'But Carton's feelings about such items were ambiguous,' Bartholomew went on. He gestured to the one that was just visible around Norton's throat, and several other canons furtively hastened to conceal theirs. 'Just like many men, I imagine.'

'I always remove mine before I pray,' said Norton sheepishly. 'I only wear it when I am outside the sacred confines of our chapels.'

'Which is exactly what Carton did,' said Bartholomew. 'He took it off, then lay on the floor in the pose of a penitent, with his arms out to either side. Fencotes found

418

the charm later, between two flagstones. And what happened next is partly my fault. Cynric and I told Jodoca what Carton had come to do here. So, she and her husband engineered an excuse for her to leave their house, and she hurried to see what could be done to prevent the negotiations.'

'She stabbed him where he lay?' breathed Norton, appalled.

Bartholomew nodded. 'I thought he might have been killed by a tall man, because the wound was high. But the wound was high because she inflicted it when he was on the ground. I made an erroneous assumption, and it left Jodoca free to kill again.'

Fencotes opened his eyes. 'You cannot blame yourself for what Jodoca did,' he whispered. 'And you cannot blame yourself for Thomas's death, either. Carton knew it was suspicious, and tried to tell you several times that your medicine was not to blame. He even gave you a packet of powder, in the hope that you would think poison had killed him. He did not want you agonising.'

'I do not understand.' Bartholomew experienced a lurch of misgiving. 'Carton did not confess to killing Thomas, did he? Because Thomas was on the verge of exposing him as an impostor?'

'No,' said Fencotes firmly. 'I knew Carton was a Dominican – he confided in me because he needed a confessor, and felt he could not go anywhere else. He spent a lot of time here, unburdening himself and praying with me.'

Bartholomew recalled having been told that before, and had been surprised. Yet it made sense: Carton could not have visited the Dominicans for solace, because that would have endangered his mission, and he could hardly go to the Franciscans. But Barnwell was well outside the town, and Carton could have talked to Fencotes without fear of being seen or overheard.

'Carton thought Mildenale murdered Thomas,' Fencotes was saying, 'because Thomas kept asking awkward questions. He had no real evidence, but he knew Thomas's death was not your fault.'

'But why did Jodoca kill Carton?' asked Podiolo. 'Spynk and Fencotes, I understand, because they were competing for the house, driving up the cost between them. But Carton was not going to buy it.'

'No, but he took messages back and forth,' replied Fencotes. His voice was weaker now. 'And he wanted it to go to a convent, not a layman. He was going to persuade Langelee to sell it to us.'

Norton looked at the old man. 'Now there is only one question left. How did *you* know about Danyell's treasure? Did he confide in you, too?'

Fencotes sighed, a whisper deep in his chest. He did not have many moments left, so Bartholomew answered for him. 'Fencotes came late to the monastic life, and before taking his vows, he lived in Norfolk. Danyell came from Norfolk, too.'

'He was kin,' breathed Fencotes, barely audible. 'He came to me when he thought the Bishop's men might steal his treasure. I told him Margery Sewale's house was empty.'

'He hid it well,' said Bartholomew. 'Osbern and Brownsley have been hunting for days with no success, and he has even foiled Cynric.'

Fencotes gave the ghost of a smile. 'That is why we must buy the house, because it may take weeks to find. Masons know how to build decent hiding places.'

420

'You looked, though,' said Bartholomew, thinking of another small fact that had not made sense at the time. 'I treated you for injuries that were inconsistent with the fall you claimed to have had. You went to Sewale Cottage, to see if you could uncover it for yourself.'

'You are a clever lad,' breathed Fencotes, closing his eyes. 'I felt the hoard was slipping away, and wanted to see if I could find what others could not. But Danyell was too good, even for his old uncle.'

Bartholomew left the canons to give Fencotes last rites, and went outside. There was a breeze for the first time in weeks, but it was hot and stale, like something blown in from a desert. It made everything feel old and dry, and in the distance he thought he heard thunder. Was a storm on the way? Would it break the heatwave and usher in cooler weather? It was not long before Norton and Podiolo came to join him. The Florentine had drawn his sword again, and did not seem inclined to give it up.

'Will you tell Langelee our offer for Sewale Cottage is now twenty marks?' asked Norton. 'I know Arblaster offered twenty, too, but you will not want *his* money, not after what Jodoca did to Carton.'

'He probably does not have it, anyway,' said Bartholomew. 'Not if he is ruined.'

'He has it,' said Podiolo. 'I saw him counting it last night when I went for a walk. But that is the full extent of it. I heard him say so to Jodoca.'

Peering through other people's windows in the dark was odd behaviour for a monastic, but Bartholomew was too tired to think about it. He collected his horse and started to ride home. He was vaguely aware of someone on the Causeway ahead of him, but the sun was in his eyes and he could not see clearly. By the time he realised it was Jodoca, it was too late to do anything about it. She was on a sturdy white pony, and there were saddle-bags behind her.

'There you are,' she said, reining in. 'I understand you had a talk with my husband.'

Bartholomew was not sure whether to ride away from her as fast as his horse would carry him, attempt to make her his prisoner, or simply talk. He decided he should arrest her, but was obliged to revise his plans when he realised he had lost his dagger – he supposed he had dropped it during the scuffle with Arblaster. Jodoca, however, did have a knife, and she looked as though she was ready to lob it. And at such short range, she could not miss. Even so, he started to rummage in his bag for one of the several surgical implements that could double as a weapon.

'Raise your hands where I can see them,' she ordered immediately, seeing what he was doing. Her pretty face was cool and determined, and he reminded himself that here was a woman who had already taken three lives. 'Make no mistake, Doctor, I will kill you if you do not obey me.'

Reluctantly, he did as he was told. She edged her pony closer to him, cutting off his chances of escape with every step. The Causeway was too narrow for him to pass her, and the time it would take to turn his horse around would see a blade in his back for certain. He wished he had paid attention to the road, instead of reviewing the mysteries he had just solved.

'I want the answer to one question,' said Jodoca, when she was sure she had him in a position where he posed no danger. 'Tell me the truth, and I will let you go.'

He did not believe her. 'You want to know if you succeeded in killing Fencotes?'

She grimaced. 'What I actually wanted to know was whether the canons had recognised me – whether it is really necessary to leave Cambridge. Your reply implies that they did, and that it is.'

'They know you murdered Spynk and Carton, too. Stabbing me will not make your secret safe.'

'So my best option remains flight. Still, I managed to remove a few items of value from the canons' chapels when they were preoccupied with Fencotes. Those silly men are easily diverted.'

Bartholomew regarded her askance, amazed she should be so casual. 'Does it mean nothing that you have murdered three men?'

She gave the question some serious consideration. 'I just wish I had done it sooner, before Spynk and Fencotes started to drive up the price of Sewale Cottage. If I had, it would have been mine by now. I thought Michaelhouse would refuse to treat with Barnwell after one of your scholars was killed in its grounds, but I underestimated the power of greed.'

'You think Michaelhouse is greedy?' Bartholomew was astounded by her hypocrisy.

'Your colleagues have no scruples whatsoever.' She grinned suddenly, the beaming, sweet smile that had seen her voted the most attractive lady in Cambridge by his students. It was difficult to view her as a cold killer who stabbed men in the back. 'You think I should feel remorse for taking a life in a House of God. How naïve! I am a coven member, and such places hold no meaning for me.'

'Not all coven members feel the same way – your husband among them. Many still pray on Sundays, because they are confused by what they are being told – pulled by the Church one way and the Sorcerer the other.'

'Weaklings,' she said in disgust. 'I suffer from no such indecision. When you and your book-bearer told me what Carton had come to do, I decided to put an end to it.'

'I know,' said Bartholomew. 'The convent was virtually deserted, with most of the canons in their dormitory, and you guessed Norton would take Carton to the chapel, because it is cool. When you arrived, you saw Carton lying on the floor, praying, while Norton fetched him wine.'

Jodoca's expression was a little distant. 'It was all so easy. And then I went home and nursed my poor husband back to health.'

'And Spynk? I suppose you asked him to meet you in Sewale Cottage at midnight, perhaps with promises of recovering the box together.'

She smirked at him. 'That is exactly what I did, although I had no intention of sharing, of course. Unfortunately, the Bishop's henchmen arrived, too, and I realised my plan was not going to work. But then you appeared, and considerately created a diversion for me. While Spynk gaped at the spectacle, I stabbed him and escaped. Do you know where Danyell's hoard came from? Originally?'

'He brought it from London. Perhaps it came from work he had done—'

She laughed derisively. 'How could such a massive sum belong to a mason? It is the Bishop's money, extorted from some hapless victim, no doubt. His retainers were taking it to Avignon, but—'

'But Brownsley and Osbern were in London at the

same time as Danyell, and Danyell stole it from them.' Bartholomew was beginning to see a lot of answers now. 'He and Spynk fled north, and the Bishop's men tracked them. Brownsley said they had come to raise more funds . . .'

'But what he really meant was that he was in the process of retrieving what he had lost to Danyell's sticky fingers. So, now you know why Brownsley and Osbern have been searching so assiduously. They are afraid of getting on the wrong side of that dangerous Bishop. You have been very slow in reasoning all this out, whereas I put the clues together almost immediately.'

'Yes, but you had the benefit of knowing what Danyell said to the Bishop's henchmen. I did not.'

Jodoca grinned at him. 'Ride on, Doctor. We shall not meet again.'

Bartholomew declined. 'You will not kill me as long as I am facing you. You only stab in the back.'

She tightened her grip on the knife with a careless shrug. 'Only because it seems more humane, but we can go for a frontal shot, if that is what you prefer.'

Bartholomew braced himself. Was this where his life would end? On a dusty causeway in the marshes, stabbed by a ruthless killer? He glanced up at the sky, and wondered who would look after his patients. Somewhere off in the distance came another low growl. There would almost certainly be a storm later, and he was sorry he would not live to see cooling rain refresh the parched earth at last.

'Praying?' asked Jodoca. Her smile was mocking. 'Why? Your God cannot help you now. Close your eyes – you will find it easier.'

'There will be no more killing,' said Podiolo, stepping

out from the bushes at the side of the road and brandishing his sword. There were four lay-brothers at his heels, all armed with bows. 'Put up your weapon, madam. Defy me and we will shoot you.'

'You followed me?' asked Bartholomew, as he rode back to Cambridge with Podiolo sitting behind him. The horse was not pleased by the additional weight, but the physician was grateful for the canon's reassuring presence – and his sword. Jodoca might not be at large to harm anyone else, but he had not forgotten the mood of the town when he had left it, or the fact that people probably resented the way he had thundered across the bridge. Podiolo's weapon might make them think twice about delaying him with remonstrations when he returned. And he was sure Podiolo could be trusted now: if the Florentine had wanted him dead, he would not have stopped Jodoca from lobbing her dagger. Or would he? Uneasily, Bartholomew began to reconsider.

'Yes,' replied Podiolo oblivious to the conflict about him that was raging in the physician's mind. 'After you had gone, it occurred to me that she might want to know whether she had been identified as Fencotes's assailant. So I assembled a posse.'

'Thank you.'

'Prior Norton should have her husband in custody by now, too,' added Podiolo. 'Brother Michael can collect them tomorrow, after he has quelled this brewing battle between Church and Sorcerer. Do you mind going a little faster? I do not want to miss anything.'

'You want to take part?' asked Bartholomew, wondering which side Podiolo was going to choose. He might be a monk, but he was also an alchemist with a dubious reputation, and might go either way.

Podiolo laughed. 'Life can be dull in a convent, and I had forgotten how much I enjoy a skirmish. I shall represent the Augustinian Order in this fight against evil.'

'And what is evil?' asked Bartholomew warily. 'The Sorcerer with his cures for warts, or the fanaticism of men like *Mildenalus Sanctus* and William?'

But Podiolo only laughed a second time. Bartholomew tried to twist around to look at him, but could not see his face. He remembered what Isnard had said: that Podiolo was one of the men most strongly suspected of being the Sorcerer. Could it be true, and Bartholomew was about to aid his rise to power by giving him a ride into town? He was not sure what to think, and wished he was not so tired.

'The weather is breaking at last,' said Podiolo, when there was a flicker of lightning. It was bright in the dusky sky, and made Bartholomew wince. 'Just in time for the Sorcerer's midnight ceremony.'

Bartholomew tried to analyse his words, but could not decide whether he applauded the magician's ability to control the climate, or whether he hoped it would rain on the fellow's ceremonies.

'We should hurry,' he said, trying to make the reluctant nag move more quickly. It galloped a few steps, then settled back into the ambling pace it preferred. 'I have been away too long already.'

'That is what I have been trying to tell you,' said Podiolo. 'At this rate we will get there next week.'

When the horse stopped to eat some grass, Bartholomew slid off, grabbed its reins and hauled it towards the King's Ditch bridge. At last, it seemed to

427

sense the urgency of the situation and launched into an ungainly trot that forced him to run to keep up with it. Podiolo bounced inelegantly on its back, and the physician saw there was someone in Cambridge who was a worse rider than he.

'Who is the Sorcerer?' asked Podiolo. His words came in breathless bursts as he tried to keep his balance. 'I have asked around, but he has kept his identity very quiet.'

'I have no idea,' said Bartholomew. 'What about you?'

'No, it is not me,' said Podiolo, misunderstanding. 'Although I understand people have been saying it is, because of my interest in alchemy. Personally, I suspect someone like Heltisle, who is strong and arrogant. Or perhaps Chancellor Tynkell, because he is tired of standing in Michael's shadow.'

They were silent for a while, Bartholomew panting hard as he tried to find his stride. He forced everything from his mind, concentrating only on reaching the town as quickly as possible.

'God and all his saints preserve us!' exclaimed Podiolo suddenly, grabbing the reins and hauling on them for all he was worth. The horse came to an abrupt stop, and he struggled not to fall off. Bartholomew, who had been lagging behind, collided heavily with it, making it snicker nastily. The bridge was deserted – the soldiers had apparently abandoned their duties, and were nowhere to be seen. It meant one of two things: that Tulyet had called them away because he needed them for something else, or they had gone to take part in the mischief that was unfolding. Neither possibility boded well.

'What?' Bartholomew asked testily, wishing he had remained on the horse and let Podiolo go on foot. The run had sapped his energy and he was not sure he had the strength to go much further.

'Is that Goldynham?' Podiolo leaned forward in the saddle, peering into the gathering gloom. 'I heard his body has been wandering around the town at night.'

Bartholomew followed the direction of his gaze, and saw the prankster's pale cloak and fluffy hair. 'Not again,' he groaned. 'I do not have time for this now.'

Podiolo did not seem as discomfited by the notion of a walking corpse as Bartholomew felt he should have been. 'What shall we do?' the canon asked. 'There is no point in killing him with my sword, because he is dead already. Perhaps we should pretend we have not noticed him – although he does seem to be looking at you rather intently.'

Bartholomew stepped out from behind the horse and saw that Podiolo was right. It was dusk, but the light was better than it had been on previous occasions, and he was able to see a pair of very wild eyes beneath the halo of white curls. And then he knew exactly who was responsible for the prank.

'Do not play games, Spaldynge,' he called, alarmed that the Clare man should be losing his sanity in so disturbing a manner. 'Not tonight. Someone might decide mobile cadavers are unwelcome in Cambridge – you could be harmed.'

'Spaldynge?' echoed Podiolo in astonishment. He narrowed his eyes. 'So it is!'

But Spaldynge was not ready to concede defeat. He ducked into the undergrowth, so he was less visible, and began his peculiar hissing. 'You let me die, physician. Your medicine failed to save me.'

'Enough,' said Bartholomew irritably. 'Goldynham was not my patient – he was Rougham's. I never went anywhere

429

near him during his final illness, so you have picked the wrong corpse to imitate. You should have chosen Margery or Thomas.'

Podiolo dismounted, and moved towards the bushes, sword at the ready. 'What a fraud! He is wearing unspun wool for hair, and his cloak is not gold, but old yellow linen.'

Spaldynge tried to run away, but Bartholomew moved to intercept him. With a grimace, Spaldynge ripped off the wig. 'How did you know?' He sounded more disgusted with the physician for seeing through his disguise than ashamed of himself for playing such a trick.

'It was obvious,' lied Bartholomew. 'Each of your previous appearances occurred shortly after I had met you, or when you might have seen me pass your College. You went home, collected cloak and hair, and waited for me to come back.'

'You have never made a secret of your dislike for *medici*, either,' added Podiolo. 'And this is the act of a bitter, spiteful man. Even so, I am surprised you would sink so low.'

'You run an infirmary, Podiolo,' sneered Spaldynge. 'So of course you will take Bartholomew's side. You are as bad as each other.'

'Actually, I know very little about medicine,' said Podiolo, revealing lupine fangs in a cheerful grin that caused Spaldynge to back away uneasily. 'I am much more interested in alchemy.'

'You are the man who whispered at me in the church-yard, too,' Bartholomew continued. 'Doubtless that was your original plan, but then you thought Goldynham offered better potential.'

Spaldynge laughed unpleasantly. 'And it worked. I would have sent you mad eventually.'

'In this climate of superstition and witchery?' asked Podiolo, before Bartholomew could tell Spaldynge he had never been fooled by the disguise. 'Do not be an ass! People have been reporting all manner of unearthly happenings for weeks. Look at Eyton. He saw Goldynham coming out of the ground, and it did not render *him* insane. Besides, you are the one who is losing his mind. Just look at yourself!'

Spaldynge regarded him with a burning dislike, and Bartholomew suspected the canon might have placed himself in line for some unpleasant remarks in the future. 'Just stay away from me,' the Clare man snarled, starting to move away. 'Both of you.'

'I am going to inform your Master about you,' Podiolo called after him. 'Bartholomew may be too gentlemanly to tell tales, but I am a Florentine. You will be sent away in disgrace.'

'You would not dare,' sneered Spaldynge, but when he glanced back at the Augustinian there was real unease in his eyes.

'I would,' said Podiolo. 'However, I *might* keep silent if you tell us the identity of the Sorcerer.'

Spaldynge swallowed hard. 'But I do not know it.'

Podiolo shrugged. 'Then your Master is going to hear some interesting—'

'No!' cried Spaldynge, realising the canon was serious. 'I am telling the truth. I have no idea who the Sorcerer might be – I swear it on my plague-dead kin.'

Podiolo grimaced. 'Then we shall have to find something else for you to bribe me with. How about telling

431

us where Mildenale is? He is missing, and Brother Michael wants a word with him.'

Spaldynge licked dry lips and looked positively furtive. 'What makes you think I would know?'

'Because his speeches led defenders of the Church to attack your College last night, and I doubt you were willing to overlook such an affront. You will have hunted him down, ready to exact revenge. Tell me where he is hiding, and I will keep your unsavoury piece of play-acting to myself. However, if you lie, I will see you banished from Cambridge for ever.'

Spaldynge swallowed; Podiolo clearly meant what he said. 'He is in the shops owned by Mistress Refham,' he whispered, looking at his feet. 'The buildings Michaelhouse wants to buy, and that have been promised to *Mildenalus Sanctus* as a hostel.'

The streets were busier than usual, considering it was growing dark, and Bartholomew supposed those people not waiting for the Sorcerer to make his appearance could sense the brewing change in the weather; it made them restless. As before, they gathered in knots, although they were bigger than when he had left, more like gangs. It was unusual to see scholars and townsmen in the same clusters, and he found it disconcerting. It was like a civil war, where it was not clear who was the enemy. Prior Pechem was with a group of butchers, telling them the Devil planned evil work that night, while Eyton was selling charms and gobbling honey as if there were no tomorrow. Perhaps, Bartholomew thought grimly, for some folk, there would not be. He saw Meadowman, and asked whether Michael had had any luck in uncovering the identity of the Sorcerer. The beadle's expression was grim.

'Not as of a few moments ago, and he is getting desperate. He has not managed to track down Mildenale, either, although the man has certainly set his fires burning.'

Podiolo sniffed the air. 'I smell no fires.'

'I mean the fires of heresy,' explained Meadowman impatiently. 'Small pockets of fanatics, all yelling that everyone will be damned unless they go to church. Father William was leading one in St Michael's churchyard, and his followers threw stones at me when I tried to break it up.'

'William threw stones at a beadle?' asked Bartholomew uneasily. It did not sound like the kind of thing the friar would do, even in his more rabid moments.

'Not him – his disciples. He tried to make them stop, but they called him a witch-lover. There are dozens of these little demonstrations, and Brother Michael thinks they might be more dangerous than whatever the Sorcerer is planning. We are trying to break them up, but as soon as we put down one, another springs up somewhere else.'

'They are centred around churches?' asked Bartholomew.

Meadowman nodded. 'And chapels and shrines. We do not have enough men to cover them all, but he says we must try. Can I borrow your horse? It might lend me more authority.'

His face was pale with worry as he rode towards the Church of the Holy Sepulchre, where shouting could be heard. Someone was bawling the words of a mass, although it did not sound like a very holy occasion. It was accompanied by defiant cheers and whoops.

'Shall we tackle Mildenale ourselves?' asked Podiolo. 'Or find Brother Michael?'

'Find Michael. What is Mildenale thinking, to set the town afire like this? He will drive people into the Sorcerer's arms, not encourage them into the churches.'

'He has encouraged enough into churches,' said Podiolo soberly, nodding towards All Saints-in-the-Jewry as they hurried past. Lights burned within, and someone in a pulpit was wagging a finger at a far larger congregation than ever assembled on a Sunday.

Bartholomew asked passers-by for the monk's whereabouts, but received so many different answers that it was clear Michael was dashing all over the place in his attempt to gain control of the situation.

'We will never find him,' he groaned, after scouring the High Street for the third time.

'Then we must look in these shops for Mildenale ourselves,' determined Podiolo. 'It will save time, which is of the essence, as I am sure you will agree.'

Wearily, Bartholomew followed him back along the High Street, but skidded to a stop when someone lobbed a stone at him. It struck his medical bag, where it clanged against the childbirth forceps inside. The muted ringing was peculiar enough to make his would-be attacker turn tail and flee, screeching something about satanic regalia.

The Refham houses were dark and quiet when they arrived in St Michael's Lane. The shutters were closed on the windows, and the doors were locked.

'Mildenale is not here,' said Podiolo, disgusted. 'We have wasted yet more time.'

'Not necessarily,' said Bartholomew, trying to think clearly. 'We should look inside, to see if he really has been using one of these shops as a hideout. Or perhaps he left something here that may tell us where he has gone.'

'Shall I kick down the door?' asked Podiolo, brightening at the prospect of action.

'No,' said Bartholomew, wishing the Florentine was a little less bellicose. 'One of the back windows has a broken shutter.'

He led the way along an alley that was so narrow he was obliged to walk sideways. It led into a dirty yard, which had three windows. He stepped up to the nearest, grabbed the wood and pulled as hard as he could. It dropped off its rusty hinges and crashed to the ground. Podiolo laughed his delight.

'This is fun! I must keep company with you more often – I have not committed burglary in years.'

Bartholomew climbed through the window, and when he paused halfway to catch his breath, Podiolo gave him a shove that sent him sprawling, then scrambled in after him. There was a lamp on a shelf, which the Florentine lit while the physician took in the chaos of scrolls, parchments and books that lay around them. There was a makeshift table and two stools, and everything suggested someone had been busy there. Bartholomew picked up one of the texts. And then another.

'I doubt these belong to Mildenale,' he said in confusion. 'They are all about the occult.'

'So they are.' Podiolo frowned. 'However, Carton told me *he* was gathering heretical texts to burn. Is this Carton's collection, do you think?'

Bartholomew shook his head. 'These are different.'

'Here is a handbook for witches,' said Podiolo, picking up a black tome that was wrapped in cloth and leafing through it. 'How strange it should be here, in a place where Mildenale clearly likes to work.'

Bartholomew sat on a stool and tried to organise his

tumbling thoughts. 'That particular book *was* in Carton's collection, although it went missing recently. Does that mean Mildenale took it? Or are we basing too much on Spaldynge's intelligence? There is nothing to prove Mildenale was here.'

'I disagree,' said Podiolo, squinting at the manual in the dim light. 'Here are marginal notes written in Mildenale's hand – I would recognise that scrawl anywhere. However, it looks as though he has been studying it, not merely reading it. Furthermore, the ink has faded on some of his annotations, which suggests this book has been in his possession for a considerable length of time.'

Bartholomew picked up a text that was lying open on the table. It was entitled *The Book of Secrets*, and was adorned with a black pentagram. 'Mildenale was carrying this the other day,' he said. 'He claimed he was going to burn it, although he was also carrying books he said he was going to put in his new hostel's library.'

'I think he lied to you about that,' said Podiolo. 'It looks to me as though he has been *reading* it.'

'I do not understand any of this,' said Bartholomew, beginning to be overwhelmed.

'I do,' said Podiolo grimly. He held the witches' handbook aloft. 'This manual belonged to Mildenale, and Carton stole it from *him*. And do you know why? Because Carton had a mortal terror of heretical texts, and must have thought it too dangerous a thing to leave in Mildenale's hands.' He grabbed another book. 'And here is a copy of a treatise by Trotula, a woman healer Carton abhorred. It is in Mildenale's writing.'

Bartholomew struggled to understand what the evidence was telling him. 'Deynman heard Mildenale arguing with

436

Carton – Carton wanted to burn these books, but was waiting until he had enough for a good blaze, while Mildenale wanted them destroyed immediately . . . no! Mildenale said *he* would destroy them immediately, and demanded that Carton hand them over. Carton refused.'

'In other words, Mildenale wanted them first – to read them or make copies. But Mildenale is a fanatic who claims to despise everything to do with heresy. Why would he bother to replicate such tomes?'

'For the same reason he collected those, I suppose,' said Bartholomew, pointing to a shelf on which sat an assortment of dried frogs, black candles and glass pots.

Podiolo went to inspect them. 'I have been an alchemist long enough to recognise satanic regalia when I see it. These are items used to summon the Devil.'

'Mildenale is a witch?' Bartholomew shook his head in bewilderment. 'But he is the Church's most vocal supporter!'

'He certainly gives that impression,' said Podiolo soberly. 'But the contents of his lair suggest otherwise.'

Bartholomew's mind reeled. 'I still do not understand what—'

Podiolo grabbed his arm. 'Neither do I, but we must tell Michael as soon as possible.'

Chapter 12

The streets were almost completely dark as Bartholomew and Podiolo left Mildenale's lair, and people were out with torches. There was an atmosphere of expectation and excitement that reminded Bartholomew more of Christmas than of violence to come. It was eerie, and he was not sure what it meant, which was disturbing in itself. He met his brother-in-law, who was standing outside his house with his apprentices.

'We are waiting for the Sorcerer to make himself known,' Stanmore explained when Bartholomew shot him a questioning glance. 'Midnight cannot be more than three hours away, and we are all keen to see who he is. Langelee tells me it is the Chancellor, but I disagree. I suspect Tulyet.'

'Dick?' asked Bartholomew in disbelief.

Stanmore nodded. 'He commands authority, and the Sorcerer will not be a weakling. Are you all right, Matt? You look exhausted.'

'I need to find Michael.'

'I saw him waddling towards St Mary the Great a few moments ago. Did you see that smoke in the north earlier?

438

That was Mother Valeria's house going up in flames. Isnard says she was in it at the time, and that she died screaming some dreadful curses.'

Bartholomew gazed at him in shock, but before he could express his revulsion at such a vile, cowardly act, there was a sudden flicker of lightning that had the apprentices cooing in wonder.

'Here it comes,' said one, barely containing his glee. 'The Sorcerer is readying himself for his performance, and I do not think we will be disappointed.'

'Lightning is a natural phenomenon,' said Bartholomew, knowing he was wasting his time but unable to stop himself. 'It happens when there is a storm brewing.'

'The Sorcerer said he was going to end the heatwave,' said Stanmore. 'Thank God he has made good on his promise. The only person who likes it is Heltisle of Bene't College, but he has always been a little odd. However, he does have a commanding presence. Perhaps *he* is the Sorcerer.'

The apprentices cheered when there was a second flash of lightning, and the novices from the nearby Carmelite priory joined in. The Carmelites were known for brawling with townsmen, and Bartholomew braced himself for trouble. But there was some good-natured back-slapping, a few jockeying comments, and the friars went on their way. Once again, the physician was confused by the allegiances that seemed to be forming between groups that were usually sworn enemies.

'This promises to be an interesting night,' said Stanmore, rubbing his hands together with a grin. 'Although we shall go indoors if the clerics make trouble.'

'The *senior* clerics,' corrected one of his boys. 'The junior ones are all right – it is only old bigots like William and *Mildenalus Sanctus* who are making a fuss. They were preaching against the Sorcerer earlier, and some folk foolishly believed what they were saying.'

'Mildenale has been preaching today?' demanded Bartholomew, rounding on him. 'Where?'

The boy took a step back, startled by the urgency in his voice. 'I saw him this morning.'

'Have any of you seen him tonight?' pressed Podiolo. 'This is important.'

As one, the apprentices shook their heads.

'I have not seen him for hours, which is surprising,' mused Stanmore. 'I would have thought this would be a good time for him to spout. Of course, once he starts, the inclination of any decent man is to believe the exact opposite of what he says. He does the Church more damage than good.'

'The same goes for Father William,' said the boy. 'I saw him at St Bene't's, about an hour ago. He was harping on about fire and brimstone, which has always been his favourite subject.'

'I saw him, too,' said Stanmore, 'although I thought he spoke with less vigour than usual. He is—'

But Podiolo had grabbed Bartholomew's arm and was tugging him towards the High Street. They kept to the shadows, so as not to be waylaid by any of the little huddles of people who were out. Most were quiet and kept to themselves, and the only loud ones tended to be led by priests. These brayed about sin and wickedness, and their followers were dour and unsmiling.

When they reached St Bene't's, the churchyard was full of people. A fire was burning near the still-open pit of Goldynham's grave, and folk were singing a psalm. Bartholomew did not find the familiar words comforting,

440

because there was something threatening about the way they were being chanted.

'I hope they have not taken to cremation,' said Podiolo uneasily. 'They may believe the rumour that Goldynham wanders at night, and decide that reducing him to ashes is the best way to stop him.'

'No,' said Bartholomew in distaste. 'They are burning books.'

He pulled away from Podiolo and marched towards William, who was at the centre of the commotion. The friar was holding scrolls in his hands, brandishing them in the air. Others were yelling encouragement. Bartholomew recognised a few Franciscans from the friary and half a dozen Fellows from Bene't, although Heltisle was not among them, and neither was Eyton.

'The flames are the best place for these ideas,' William bellowed. 'This one says the Blood Relic at Walsingham is sacred and should be revered. Such theology is filth!'

His supporters stopped cheering and exchanged puzzled glances. 'Actually, Father, the shrine at Walsingham belongs to *our* Order,' said one. 'So the Blood Relic there *should* be revered.'

'Oh,' said William, blinking his surprise. He stuffed the scroll in his scrip. 'Perhaps we had better save that one, then.'

Bartholomew tugged him to one side. 'What are you doing?' he whispered fiercely.

'Burning books for Mildenale,' replied William, freeing his arm imperiously. 'I have always wanted to do it, but Michaelhouse would never let me. But why are you here? Mildenale told me you would be up at All Saints, preparing to step into power as the Sorcerer. Of course,

I would not be surprised to learn he is wrong. You have never *really* seemed the type to—'

'Where is Mildenale now?' demanded Bartholomew.

'I have no idea. He told me to carry on here, and show folk that the Church is a force to be reckoned with. He ordered me to burn all these books, but I decided I had better look at them first. Unfortunately, I keep finding ones that should not be here. Such as this scroll.'

'And this?' demanded Bartholomew, snatching a tome from the friar's left hand. 'Aristotle? How can you say that is heresy? You have been using it to teach your first-years for decades.'

William grimaced, then lowered his voice. 'Actually, I am coming to the conclusion that Mildenale is a bit of a fanatic, and I question my wisdom in following him. And, between the two of us, I find my delight at book-burning is not as great as I thought it would be. Some of these texts are rather lovely.'

'Go home, Father,' said Bartholomew quietly. 'You do not belong here.'

There was more lightning as Bartholomew ran to St Mary the Great, Podiolo still at his side. He heard a low growl of thunder, too, still in the distance, but closer than it had been. The storm was rolling nearer, and Bartholomew thought he could smell rain in the air. Or perhaps it was wishful thinking.

'I cannot get the town's measure tonight,' said Podiolo. 'It does not feel dangerous, exactly, but there is something amiss. The atmosphere is brittle. Do you know what I mean?'

Bartholomew knew all too well. People nodded at him as he passed, some appreciatively, and he hoped they

442

did not hold him responsible for the impending change in the weather. Others scowled. He did not like either, and was relieved when he met Suttone, who neither grinned nor glared. The Carmelite was wearing his best habit, and his hair had been slicked down neatly with water.

'Where are you going?' asked Bartholomew, surprised to see him looking so debonair.

'To treat the Guild of Corpus Christi to a sermon about the plague,' replied Suttone. 'Surely you cannot have forgotten? I have been talking about it all week.'

'At this time of night?' asked Podiolo. 'And you are going in the wrong direction. Guild meetings take place in Bene't College. I know, because I have been to celebrations there in the past.'

'I commented on the late hour, too,' said Suttone. 'But I am to speak after a conclave, and these affairs can go on for some time, apparently. They changed the venue, too. It is to be held in All Saints-next-the-Castle.'

'I thought that was where the Sorcerer's coven was supposed to be meeting,' said Podiolo in surprise. 'Are you set to address a horde of witches, then? If so, then the plague is a suitable topic – just as long as you do not plan on telling them how to bring it back.'

Suttone pursed his lips. 'I am reliably informed that no witches will be there. Their messenger was Mildenale, and he told me All Saints was chosen because it has no roof, and so will be cooler.'

'And you believed him?' asked Bartholomew incredulously. 'A fanatic, whose sole aim these last few days has been to make trouble?'

Suttone was offended. 'He told me that there have been misunderstandings, but that he and Michael had spoken, and all has been resolved.' He leaned forward conspiratorially. 'Although asking me to orate in All Saints is an odd thing to do, given that it feels like rain. We shall be drenched, and this is my best habit. Perhaps I should say an indisposition prevents me from attending. What do you think?'

Bartholomew tried to see how the situation could be turned to their advantage. 'I think you should go, but ensure you say nothing that smacks of the kind of bigotry favoured by Mildenale. He has made people think badly of the Church, and you have an opportunity to rectify that. Can you do it?'

Suttone smiled. 'Of course. I shall use the plague to demonstrate my points.'

He set off up the High Street. Bartholomew watched him go and wondered how much of his carefully prepared lecture would ever be heard.

'Mildenale,' he said softly. 'He is the Sorcerer.'

Podiolo's expression was sombre. 'Yes, I rather think he is. He has deceived us all by pretending to be so avidly on the side of the Church. Of course, it was his very fervour that drove folk towards the Sorcerer. And he clearly lied to Suttone about All Saints.'

'Then we must hurry,' said Bartholomew, as he began to race towards St Mary the Great. 'I sense time is running out fast.'

The physician was relieved when he and Podiolo reached the church unscathed. The monk was in the nave, issuing urgent orders to the beadles who dashed in and out with messages. Cynric was with him, his dark face alight with excitement.

'I still have not found *Mildenalus Sanctus*,' said the monk when he saw Bartholomew. 'And nor have I learned the Sorcerer's identity. But you were a long time. What happened?'

Bartholomew leaned against a pillar while Podiolo gave a precise and almost accurate account of all that had transpired. The physician was exhausted, and the atmosphere of electric anticipation was doing more to drain his flagging reserves of energy than shore them up. His head ached, and he could not remember a time when he had been more weary.

'So the killer of Carton, Spynk and Fencotes is no longer at large,' said the monk in relief. 'Thank God! That is one less thing to worry about.'

'There are a number of things you no longer need to worry about,' said Cynric, to be encouraging. 'You solved the mystery of Bene't's missing goats, and you know Mother Valeria was responsible for the blood in the font and stealing Danyell's dead hand. All you have to do now is defeat the Sorcerer and discover why Margery, Thomas and Goldynham were excavated.'

'I know the answer to the last question,' said Bartholomew, forcing himself to stand upright. 'Danyell hid the treasure he stole from the Bishop on the night before Ascension Day.'

'We know that,' said Michael impatiently, when he paused. 'What is your point?'

'That all three exhumations were of people who were buried on Ascension Day. We suspected from the start that it was not the work of witches, because there were no signs of ritual, mutilation of corpses, or theft of grave-clothes. I think Brownsley and Osbern are the culprits, because they thought Danyell might have hidden the treasure in one of those graves.'

'That is one of the least convincing theories I have ever heard you devise,' said Michael scathingly.

'Then think about it logically, Brother. Brownsley and Osbern had a discussion – a confrontation, if you prefer – with Danyell before he died. Arblaster overheard it. He said Danyell mentioned *digging holes*. The Bishop's men later did dig holes in Margery's garden, but they hedged their bets and searched other holes, too – graves.'

'He is right,' said Cynric, when the monk continued to look dubious. 'All three of those graves were dug before Ascension, and were left open overnight. It is entirely possible that Danyell might have put his treasure in one – and what a perfect hiding place! No one would ever think of looking there.'

'Osbern and Brownsley did,' remarked Podiolo dryly.

Michael was thoughtful. 'The bodies *were* pulled clean out, as though someone was making sure there was nothing underneath them.'

Bartholomew nodded. 'So, now you have solved that case, too, Brother. You can tell your Bishop to deal with Brownsley and Osbern, because I am sure he will not want their antics made public, not with so many other accusations dangling over him.'

But Michael shook his head. 'The Sheriff can arrest them, and de Lisle can take his chances in the lawcourts. I am tired of defending a man who is transpiring to be such a rogue.'

'Very wise,' said Podiolo. Bartholomew could not tell if he was being sarcastic or approving.

'Brother!' called a beadle urgently, hurrying down the aisle towards them. 'People are beginning to flock towards All Saints-next-the-Castle.'

'Of course they are,' said Bartholomew, bemused.

'That is where the Sorcerer's coven meets. Bowls and potions have been prepared, and his disciples were working hard there yesterday.'

'But my intelligence indicates the Sorcerer will appear *here*, at St Mary the Great,' argued Michael. 'Cambridge's biggest and most important church. All Saints was a ruse, designed to keep me up the hill when the real action will be in the town. Why do you think I am here?'

'Intelligence from whom?' demanded Bartholomew.

Michael paled suddenly. 'Oh, Lord! It was from Heltisle – but he had it from Mildenale.'

'Yet more evidence to suggest *Mildenalus Sanctus* is not as holy as you thought,' said Podiolo crisply. 'He has been fooling you for months – and fooling Carton, too.'

'But not Father Thomas,' said Bartholomew. 'He was a nosy, inquisitive sort of man, as we saw over Carton's ordination. I suspect he discovered something about Mildenale, too – or perhaps he just started asking questions. Either way, Mildenale decided to silence him. He lobbed a stone at Thomas in the High Street, and when that did not kill him, he broke his neck as he lay on his sickbed.'

'And let you bear the blame for his death,' said Cynric angrily. 'You gave Thomas a sedative, which probably *was* the right medicine in the circumstances, but he let you think you had killed him. He is a ruthless fellow, and I shall not mind plunging my sword into his gizzard tonight.'

Another beadle tore into the church, bringing news that supporters of the Church had set some of the market stalls on fire. As he spoke, a flash of lightning blazed through the church, before plunging it into darkness again. Several beadles crossed themselves. Podiolo touched something that hung around his neck, then began to press the messenger for details about the chaos in the Market Square. While he did so, Michael grabbed the physician's arm and hauled him to one side.

'Your Florentine friend seems very eager for me to think Mildenale is the Sorcerer,' he said in a fierce whisper. 'Why is that?'

'We have more than enough evidence to prove it,' said Bartholomew, although he understood the monk's reservations about Podiolo – the canon had outlined their findings in a strangely gleeful manner. 'Mildenale has been clever – using William, Thomas and Carton to turn folk against the Church, deliberately encouraging them to preach unpopular messages. And he certainly has an interest in the occult. You only need to glance inside his lair to see that.'

Michael's expression was grim. 'Well, we shall have answers tonight one way or the other, because something is about to happen. I do not want Podiolo with me, though. He can stay here with Meadowman.'

'I would rather lend my sword to defeating Mildenale,' objected the Florentine, when Michael began to issue orders.

'I need someone to guard *this* church,' said Michael, in a tone that indicated it would be futile to argue. He turned to Bartholomew. 'We must stop at Dick Tulyet's house on our way to All Saints. I heard he has abandoned his robber-hunt for the night, and I need to know what he plans to do – it would be a pity if we got in each other's way.'

'I would be careful of the Sheriff if I were you,' said Podiolo sulkily. 'Do not forget his father was a diabolist. Tulyet may not be the Sorcerer, but there is nothing to

448

say he is not a servant. After all, he has done very little to stop Mildenale, has he? He has spent most of this week away from the town, on the pretext of chasing highwaymen.'

With the Florentine's warning ringing in his ears, Bartholomew forced himself to follow the monk out on to the High Street.

Michael set an unusually brisk pace to Tulyet's house and Bartholomew struggled to keep up with him. The lightning was coming more regularly now, and the accompanying growl of thunder seemed almost continuous. The gathering storm lent more urgency to a situation that already felt desperate, and Michael was virtually running by the time they reached Bridge Street. When he knocked on Tulyet's door, both he and Bartholomew were hot, red-faced and panting.

'You look terrible,' said Tulyet, looking from one to the other. So did he. Lines of exhaustion were etched deeply into his face and his clothes were thick with dust.

'Well?' demanded Michael. 'What is going on?'

'A contingent of fanatics from Holy Trinity – led by Mildenale – hanged one of the Market Square crones earlier. He told me it was his duty to God, and was wholly beyond reason.'

'Did you arrest him?' asked Michael, appalled.

'I intended to, but he disappeared while I was battling with his followers. I do not care if he is a priest – and a man from your own College. I shall see *him* at the end of a rope for this.'

'I will not stand in your way.' Quickly, Michael told him all they had learned.

Tulyet's eyes were wide with shock by the time he had

finished. 'So all that remains is to prevent Mildenale from seizing power as the Sorcerer – ostensibly a benign healer of warts and an attractive alternative to the Church, but in reality something quite different.'

'And you can arrest Brownsley and Osbern for digging up graves, too,' said Michael.

Tulyet gave a tight smile. 'I caught them breaking into Sewale Cottage earlier, and they are both in the castle gaol. They confessed to losing the Bishop's treasure in London, and tracking it here. They fully expect to be released with no more questions asked, but de Lisle no longer holds that sort of authority with me. They will answer for their crimes before the King.'

'Brother Michael!' came an urgent voice from along the hall. It was Tulyet's wife. 'Come quickly. Dickon has something to tell you.'

'Later, madam,' snapped Michael, uncharacteristically rude. 'There is no time for trifles.'

But Mistress Tulyet was insistent. 'Please. You will want to hear what he has to say.'

She beckoned them into the kitchen, a massive stone room with a gigantic fireplace. Dickon sat at the table reading a book by lamplight. Bartholomew glanced at it. It was the *Book of Consecrations*.

'Are you sure he should have that?' he asked uneasily. 'A book of curses is hardly suitable material for a boy like him . . . I mean a boy so young.'

'It is a book on religion,' protested Tulyet, startled. 'It has a religious title.'

'What did you want to tell me, Dickon?' demanded Michael, unwilling to waste time on Dickon's education when he had a villain to unmask. 'Hurry! There is not a moment to lose.'

450

'Tell him what you told me, Dickon,' coaxed Mistress Tulyet, while Tulyet examined the book with growing horror. 'About Margery Sewale – what you saw when you happened to glance through her back window.'

She had chosen her words with care, but it was clear Dickon had been spying. He had done it to other neighbours in the past, so the revelation came as no surprise. 'I saw her saying spells with her two friends,' Dickon replied. 'The man with the roses and the Saint from Michaelhouse.'

'You mean Mildenale?' asked Bartholomew, not sure whether to believe that the gentle Margery would spend time with an unpleasant man like the friar, whether he was the Sorcerer or not.

'The three of them,' said Dickon, watching his father put the tome on the highest shelf in the kitchen, well out of his reach. 'They are the Sorcerer.'

'He is making no sense,' said Michael, heading for the door. 'And I need to catch Mildenale before anyone else dies. We will talk to Dickon tomorrow.'

'Wait!' shouted Dickon, eyes dark with anger that someone should dare treat him dismissively. 'The Sorcerer is *three* people – Mistress Sewale, the Saint and the Rose-Man. They worked *together* to make their spells. I heard them lots of times.'

Michael turned to face him. 'Three people,' he repeated.

'Three people,' repeated Dickon. He pointed at the *Book of Consecrations* with a grubby finger. 'Three is a special number for witches. I just read about it. Of course, they are only two now Mistress Sewale is dead. They made her die quicker than she should have done.'

'How do you know?' asked Bartholomew, hoping he

was not about to learn that Mildenale had laid murderous hands on a sick woman, as well as on Thomas.

'Because you ordered her to sleep,' replied Dickon. 'But the Saint and the Rose-Man made her get up to help them with their spells. Towards the end, she told them they were taking things too far, and was sad. She said she felt guilty, which is why she left all her things to Michaelhouse – she thought your prayers would keep her out of Hell. I heard her telling her priest that, before she died.'

Mistress Tulyet was shocked. 'You eavesdropped on a confession?'

Dickon grinned, unrepentant. 'It was her fault for leaving the window open. And a bit later, I heard the Saint tell Mistress Sewale that he was not sorry they had a dalliance all those years ago. What is a dalliance?'

'Lord!' breathed Michael. 'Margery and Mildenale were lovers? Who would have thought it? I suppose it must have happened thirty years ago, when Mildenale was here to help establish Michaelhouse, and Margery would have been a young woman. Still, it explains why a benevolent witch and a fervent friar should have sought out each other's company.'

'My father told me about Margery's skill with spells,' said Tulyet. 'I was under the impression she did not practise much any more, though. Mildenale must have encouraged her to take it up again.'

'She was angry about it,' said Dickon, struggling to follow what they were saying. 'She did not like dark magic, and kept telling the Saint and the Rose-Man it was wrong. Maybe that is why they made her work when she should have been in bed. They *wanted* her dead.' His eyes gleamed at the notion of such wickedness, and Bartholomew watched his reaction uneasily.

'Who is the Rose-Man?' asked Tulyet. 'This is important, Dickon. We must know his name.'

'If I tell you the answer, can I have the book back?'
asked Dickon slyly.

'Give it to him,' ordered Michael. 'Just keep him away
from bats, frogs and black cats for the rest of his life.'

Reluctantly, Tulyet retrieved the tome and handed it
over.

'I do not know Rose-Man's name,' said Dickon,
snatching the book and darting to the other side of the
table. His plump face was the picture of innocence. 'You
said you wanted an answer, and that is it: I do not know.
He always kept himself covered.'

Tulyet went with Bartholomew and Michael when they
left his house. The lightning was flashing every few
moments now, and the thunder was a constant growl.
Bartholomew could smell sulphur in the air, and
wondered whether it was from the brewing storm or the
Sorcerer mixing potions. They joined the stream of folk
who were heading for the dark, massy block of the castle
and the little church that huddled in its shadow. As in
the town centre, there was an atmosphere of excited
anticipation.

'Mildenale and this Rose-Man have been cunning,'
said Tulyet. 'Our soldiers and beadles are scattered all
over the town trying to quell little riots, and we do not
have the troops to storm All Saints and bring the festiv-
ities to a standstill.'

'But we must do something,' cried Michael, appalled
to think they were helpless. 'A lot of people see the
Sorcerer as some genial fairy who cures warts. However,
Mildenale has killed to achieve his objective, and God

453

only knows what this damned Rose-Man has done. These hapless fools think they are going to see some pretty display of sparks and a bit of coloured smoke, but I have a feeling something infinitely more sinister is in the offing.'

'But why would Mildenale and the Rose-Man harm anyone?' asked Bartholomew tiredly. 'These people have done nothing to warrant their violence. On the contrary, they are ready to serve—'

'You are missing the point,' interrupted Tulyet curtly. 'Folk will be more afraid of "the Sorcerer" if they know he has the power to kill and maim. And fear is a potent weapon – this pair do not intend to hold Cambridge in their sway for a night, but for a good deal longer.'

'Then we cannot let them succeed,' said Michael firmly.

'No,' agreed Tulyet. 'But we should stay hidden, and away from trouble, until we have assessed what we are dealing with. Follow me.'

He led them at a rapid clip along the wide lane that led to Chesterton village, and then doubled back, to approach All Saints from the east. Everyone else was coming from the west, so they were able to reach the grave-yard without being detected. The excursion sapped more of Bartholomew's energy, and the storm was not helping. The air was so hot and still that he could not seem to draw enough breath into his lungs; Michael and Tulyet were also wheezing and sweaty by the time they reached their objective. Together, they crept past the charnel house, and reached the great window of the chancel. A single voice could be heard within, and it was familiar.

'Suttone!' exclaimed Bartholomew, startled. 'He is giving his speech after all.'

'Mildenale is using him to entertain the crowd until he is ready,' surmised Michael. 'I suspect he would have

454

preferred the incisive wit of Peterhouse's Suttone, because I doubt our Suttone will keep this rabble amused for long. They are already murmuring their impatience.'

'The place is overflowing,' whispered Tulyet, peering around a buttress. 'There have not been this many people in it since it was built.'

'And aggressive men like Refham have been stationed outside,' added Michael. 'They have almost certainly been ordered to exclude anyone who might cause problems – such as us. I doubt we could get inside, even if we wanted to.'

Bartholomew climbed on a tombstone to look through the window. The chancel, lit by dozens of lanterns, had been decked in greenery, and a score of minions were making last-minute adjustments to the décor. He was startled to see Eyton among them. A number of amulets hung around the priest's neck; an acolyte of the Sorcerer he might be, but he was still taking no chances.

Bartholomew was amazed to recognise some of the faces in the nave – the Chancellor, Paxtone, Isnard, friends from other Colleges and hostels. He saw that Michael was right about Suttone: the Carmelite's lecture was not what folk had been expecting, and they were growing restless. Even Paxtone looked bored, and as a physician, he was usually fascinated by anything to do with the plague.

'Perhaps Mildenale is not coming,' said Tulyet hopefully.

'He will come,' said Michael. He winced when an especially vivid streak of lightning bathed the church in an eerie, dazzling light. 'How could any magician refuse such an evening for his début? It will rain soon, and he will bask in the credit for having caused it.'

'He must be getting ready somewhere,' said Bartholomew, climbing down. 'Dressing up, or whatever these people do when they make their grand entrances. Is there a crypt?'

'It collapsed last year,' said Tulyet. 'They will not be down there. However, they might be in the charnel house.'

'Of course!' exclaimed Michael, whipping around to look at it. 'Thick walls, no windows, a decent roof. Someone anticipated that it would come in useful and has taken care to maintain it.'

'Who is the Rose-Man?' mused Tulyet, as they made their way through the long grass. 'We know it is not the Chancellor, because I just saw him standing in the nave. The same is true of the Mayor, too.'

'I think we may be about to find out,' whispered Michael. 'Someone is in the charnel house. I am surprised we did not notice sooner.'

A low, sinister chanting emanated from within. Tulyet glanced at Michael and Bartholomew, raising his eyebrows to ask if they were ready. They nodded, so he drew his sword, then dealt the door an almighty kick. It flew open and cracked against the wall. Giving the occupants no time to think, he was inside like an avenging angel, sword at the ready. Michael followed more sedately, but Bartholomew hesitated, although he could not have said why. He remained outside.

'Mildenale,' said the monk pleasantly. 'Fancy seeing you here.'

Bartholomew shifted his position so he could see inside the charnel house, but still made no move to enter. Mildenale was wearing a dark gown with five-sided stars painted on it; it looked cheap and garish, like something

456

a travelling player might use. It had a hood, which shielded his face, but the physician could see his gleaming eyes and a strand of lank black hair. He wore his attire with a confidence that suggested it was not the first time he had donned it.

'What do you want?' he demanded, more annoyed than alarmed at the interruption. 'I am busy.'

Michael moved deeper into the hut, while Tulyet sheathed his sword. 'I have come to tell you that there will be no grand ceremony tonight,' said the monk. 'You are under arrest, for the murder of Father Thomas.'

Mildenale's smile was lazy and insolent. 'That was Bartholomew's fault. And if you accuse me, everyone will think you are just trying to exonerate your friend. No one will believe you.'

Michael declined to let the man's arrogance rile him, and began to prowl, looking in bowls and prodding pipes and mirrors with a chubby forefinger. 'We know exactly what you have been doing. Carton was employed to watch you, because the Dominicans saw you as a serious danger.'

Mildenale's expression was arch. 'Me? All I have done is tell folk to be wary of evil.'

'In such a way that you drove them straight into the Sorcerer's arms,' said Tulyet. He became businesslike, wanting the affair done with as soon as possible. 'We know about Margery – an old lover whom you used for your own ends, hastening her death as you did so – but who is the third member of your unholy triumvirate? You may as well tell us, because we will find out anyway.'

But there was something about Mildenale's smug carelessness that made alarm bells jangle in Bartholomew's mind, and he began to have grave misgivings about the wisdom of assaulting the charnel house. Mildenale had

457

set guards on the church, so surely he would not have left himself open to attack? The physician eased to one side, and tried to see whether anyone else was inside the building – someone who might even now be preparing to launch an ambush of his own. And with Senior Proctor and Sheriff out of the way, the town was infinitely more vulnerable. He could see no one, even when lightning flooded the hut with a blinding brightness. The thunder that accompanied it this time was so loud it hurt his ears. From the church, several cries of alarm interrupted Suttone's monologue.

'I shall not betray the only friend I have here,' said Mildenale evenly, clasping his hands together. He did not look heavenward, though: his eyes were fixed firmly on Michael and Tulyet. 'How did you know about Margery? Did Dickon tell you? The little brat was always spying on her. I wanted to cast a spell on him, but she would not let me. I was fond of her, but she was too weak for what I have in mind, so it is just as well she died when she did.'

'Then tell me why you betrayed your Church,' said Michael coldly. He gestured at the friar's exotic garb. 'This is not right.'

The whole situation was not right, thought Bartholomew, becoming increasingly convinced that something was about to go horribly wrong. Instinctively, he backed away from the door, still trying to work out what it could be. Alarm and exhaustion had transformed his wits to mud, and he could not think clearly. As he moved, his foot plunged into a rabbit hole, and he lost his balance. He fell backwards, landing neatly between two graves with enough of a thump to drive the breath from his body. For a moment his senses reeled, and all he could do was stare up at the sky. A distant part of his mind noted that there were no stars, and he supposed thunderclouds had rolled in. Almost immediately, another long flicker of lightning illuminated them, dark and heavy-bellied with rain. He thought he saw something else, too: a pale face not far from the charnel house. But then it went dark again and he was no longer certain.

By the time he had eased himself up on to one elbow, Mildenale had crossed his arms and was leaning against the wall, gloating. 'No one listened to me as a Franciscan, so perhaps they will listen now,' he was saying. 'We took the idea from the Hardys and old man Tulyet.'

'My father?' asked Tulyet, startled. He had been advancing on Mildenale, but mention of his kinsman made him falter. 'What does he have to do with this?'

'He made a potion to help him predict the future, but he was not as good a diabolist as he thought, and managed to poison himself. John Hardy and his wife met a similar fate when they tried it, too.'

'And you are better, I suppose?' Michael made no effort to disguise his contempt.

'I am. People have too much freedom, and it has led them down a dark path. I intend to terrify every man, woman and child in this miserable town, and force them to live their lives as *I* see fit. If they refuse, they can expect "the Sorcerer" to come and punish them. It is for their own good.'

He began to pace restlessly, moving closer to the door. There was another shimmer of light from the sky, and this time Bartholomew was certain a second person was watching from the shadows – someone dressed in the same kind of cloak as Mildenale. Bartholomew could only suppose it was the Rose-Man. He strained his eyes in the ensuing darkness, trying to see whether the fellow had a weapon.

'You criticise people for following evil ways, and yet you are a magician,' said Michael in disgust. 'I think there is a hiccup in your logic here, Mildenale.'

'I am different,' said the friar. 'I am not bound by the same constraints as others, because I know how to control dark forces. I have been reading about them for years. And yes, Brother, I did kill Thomas when he tried to stop me. Like William and Carton, he was supposed to support my work, not hinder it. He was a casualty of war – regrettable, but necessary. The same goes for you, I am afraid.'

'Is that so,' said Michael coldly. 'What do you plan to do? Turn us into toads?'

Mildenale reached the door. 'You will find out later. I cannot be bothered with you now.'

Suddenly, he was out in the churchyard, and the Rose-Man darted forward to slam the door closed behind him. Then both leaned against a nearby tombstone. The monument had not been there on Bartholomew's previous visits, and he realised it must have been moved recently. It fell with a crash against the door, blocking it far more effectively than any key.

'There,' said Mildenale, regarding it with satisfaction. 'That should keep them quiet until we have finished. And then we shall set the place alight, so they will never tell anyone what they have reasoned. I told you my plan would work.'

'Where is the physician?' demanded the Rose-Man. 'He was with them earlier.'

Bartholomew held his breath when they began to hunt for him, daggers drawn, and only the fact that he had fallen between two graves saved him from discovery. Fortunately, it was not long before Mildenale informed his accomplice that their quarry must have gone inside the church, and that they should not waste any more time on him.

'There will be plenty of opportunity to dispatch him later,' he added as they walked away. His last words were drowned by the loudest thunderclap Bartholomew had ever heard, and the flickering light from above made the pair look as though they were walking in jerks, like puppets.

As soon as they had gone, Bartholomew hauled himself upright and hurried towards the charnel house. Michael and Tulyet were yelling and hammering furiously, but thick wood and thunder muffled the racket they were making. He heaved with all his might, but the stone did not budge and he knew he would never be able to move it without help. It needed a team of men, preferably ones armed with levers.

'Matt?' came Tulyet's voice. 'Is that you out there? Fetch soldiers from the castle. Hurry!'

Bartholomew set off along the path that led to the gate. He started to run, but the path was treacherously uneven and he had not taken many steps before he went sprawling. His timing was perfect, because the lightning suddenly turned night into day for several long moments and the uncut grass concealed him as Mildenale and the Rose-Man paused by the tower door to give the cemetery a long, sweeping look. Had he been standing, they would certainly have seen him.

He raised his head and watched them. They leaned close together, and there was a brief flash of light as Mildenale lit a lamp. Bartholomew tried to think clearly.

Why were they using the tower door, rather than the main entrance at the end of the nave? It occurred to him that they might be about to set the whole thing alight, with their followers inside it, but dismissed the notion as insane. Why should they want their disciples incinerated? Gradually, it dawned on him that it might be intended as a demonstration of the Sorcerer's strength. As Tulyet said, fear was a powerful weapon – and people would certainly be frightened if they knew the Sorcerer was willing to perpetrate such dreadful atrocities.

His suspicions were confirmed when Mildenale nodded to Refham, who closed the great west door then disappeared into the darkness: the blacksmith's duties were done, and he was no longer needed. And the people inside the church were trapped.

There was no time to fetch soldiers to release Michael and Tulyet. Limping now, Bartholomew stumbled towards the tower door, intending to do all he could to prevent them from carrying out their horrible work. He paused for breath at the bottom of the stairs, then gasped in alarm at the sudden weight of a hand on his shoulder.

'Easy!' whispered Isnard. 'It is only me.'

Bartholomew sagged in relief. Isnard would help him tackle Mildenale and the Rose-Man. Then he realised that the bargeman would not be very good at climbing spiral stairs on crutches, and that the noise he made would warn the villains of their approach. Bartholomew closed his eyes in despair when he saw he was still alone.

Isnard jerked his thumb over his shoulder, towards the main body of the church. 'Master Suttone is giving all sorts of touching examples about the sacrifices made by friars during the plague. I did not want anyone to see me weep, so I slipped outside to compose myself. But they seem to have locked the doors, and I cannot get back in—'

'Michael and the Sheriff are trapped in the charnel house,' interrupted Bartholomew. 'Go to the castle and fetch soldiers to free them. Hurry! The lives of a great many people depend on you.'

Without waiting to see whether the bargeman would do as he was told, Bartholomew began to climb the stairs. They were uneven, and the stairwell was pitch dark. He ascended slowly, wincing each time his shoes crunched on a twig, or his groping hands caused the friable masonry to crumble. After what seemed like an age, he reached the top, trying not to breathe too hard and alert them to his presence. Mildenale and the Rose-Man were standing by the window that looked into the nave; the physician recalled how he had used it to spy himself. He could hear Suttone, still preaching the sermon he had told the Carmelite to give. A cold dread gripped him when he realised that if anything happened to Suttone, then it would be his fault.

The chamber had changed since Bartholomew had last been there. More scaffolding and winches had been erected near the window, and bowls were brimming with liquids and powders. Mildenale was busily setting some alight, while the Rose-Man stood near the ropes and pulleys, ready to lower them into the church.

'*Venite Satanus!*' Mildenale bawled, startling Suttone into silence. Immediately, acolytes in the nave doused the lanterns, and the church was plunged into total darkness. There was a gasp of awe from the congregation. 'Come, Satan! I conjure you, Lucifer!'

As he yelled, Mildenale touched his lamp to more of the bowls, and the Rose-Man sent them swinging into the nave on the rope pulleys. Smoke belched, black and reeking. People began to cough. One of the bowls fizzed with an orange light and released a spray of sparks on to the heads of those below. Someone screamed. Lightning jagged, illuminating a nave that was full of eerily shifting mist, and the accompanying thunderclap seemed to shake the very foundations of the building.

'*Diabolo diaboliczo Satana shaniczo!*' yelled Mildenale. '*Venite* Paymon, Egim and Simiel—'

'That is enough summoning,' murmured the Rose-Man. 'We do not want the entire population of Hell to arrive – we might not have room to accommodate them all.'

In the nave, the onlookers were suddenly not quite so happy to be watching the Sorcerer's arrival. There were cries that they could not breathe, and Bartholomew could hear them thumping on the door, clamouring to be let out. It would not be many moments before panic set in, and then there would be a stampede. People would be crushed as they tried to reach an exit or clamber through the windows.

Mildenale looked disappointed to be cut short. 'Are you ready, then?' he asked.

The Rose-Man nodded, and stepped towards a long piece of cloth that dangled from the roof. At first, Bartholomew did not understand what it was for, but then he saw it had been treated with some substance, probably a compound that would make it burn. He followed its route with his eyes, and saw it snaked towards the dead ivy that formed the roof. The dry leaves would go up like kindling, and then what remained of the rafters would follow. It was time to act. He grabbed a piece of broken wood from the floor, then burst into the chamber with no more thought than that he had to prevent the Rose-Man from touching the cloth with his flame.

'Stop!' he yelled.

The Rose-Man whipped around at the sudden intrusion, and Bartholomew saw his face for the first time, stark and bright in another blaze of lightning. He was the handsome fellow who had loitered on the edge of the crowds that had gathered to watch the antics of Cambridge's various fanatics – the man who wore a rose in his hat. Yet there was something about him that scratched another part of Bartholomew's memory, something about the eyes . . .

But Mildenale did not give him time to think about it. He lunged at the physician with a dagger, then fell back with a bruised arm when the physician scored a lucky jab with his length of timber.

'Kill him!' screamed the Rose-Man. 'Do not dance with him!'

Hissing with pain, Mildenale advanced again. Bartholomew swung the wood a second time; it was rotten and flew into pieces on impact. But it was enough to make Mildenale jerk away, and as he did so, his foot shot through a hole in the floor. He fell awkwardly and began to shriek in agony, causing more alarm to the people milling in the nave. Then his cries were drowned out by the most violent thunderclap yet, and the lightning flickered like a spluttering lantern, almost continuous. The storm was directly overhead now.

With a sigh of exasperation, the Rose-Man drew a

knife from his belt and advanced on the physician. And it was then that Bartholomew recognised the glittering eyes.

'Mother Valeria!'

Bartholomew was not sure whether it was the shock of recognising the witch that drove him to his knees, or the fact that an explosion suddenly rocked the building. He saw surprise flash across Valeria's face – it was not something she had planned. In the brief silence that followed, he heard people screaming that a churchyard tree had been struck by lightning; then the resulting blaze began to shed its own unsteady glow through the nave windows. Panic seized the Devil's disciples – there were more howls of terror, and a concerted rush for the door that saw some of them trampled underfoot. Bartholomew turned his gaze back to the woman who stood in front of him.

'Of course it is me!' sneered Valeria, regarding him with rank disdain. 'I am the most powerful witch in Cambridge, so who else did you imagine the Sorcerer to be? Fool!'

Bartholomew jerked away from her blade, managing not to be run through only because Valeria was forced to tread warily on the crumbling floor. He tried to rally his reeling senses. 'You are a man?'

She looked startled, then rolled her eyes. 'You saw me out in the town. I forgot. No, I am not a man, although I am tall enough to pass for one. No one knows that, though, because my clients only ever see me sitting, hunched over my cauldron with my false nose and false chin. Just as they expect me to be.'

'You kept your leg covered when I wanted to examine

it,' said Bartholomew, automatically focusing on a medical matter. 'And you always wear gloves. You are no more than thirty summers . . .'

'My skin would have betrayed me as somewhat younger than the hundred years I claimed, and I could not be bothered to apply pastes and powders every time I needed a remedy from you.' Valeria smiled, and there was pure malice in the expression.

'There were rumours that you were growing weak—'

'Do I look weak to you?' she demanded.

Bartholomew glanced at Mildenale; the friar had extricated himself from the hole, and was gripping his ankle, face contorted with pain. But it would not be long before he pulled himself together and rejoined the affray. Bartholomew knew he should be concentrating on disarming Valeria before he was outnumbered, but he could not stop himself from asking questions.

'Why are you doing this? What have these people done to you?'

'It is time for me to ascend to another level.' Valeria seemed oblivious to the mounting chaos in the nave below, and to the storm raging outside. 'No one can make curses like me, but people are stupid. They come to whine about unfaithful lovers and demand charms for making money, but they do not give me their respect. Well, they will give it to me now.'

'Warts,' said Bartholomew tiredly. 'The Sorcerer is said to be good with warts. So are you.'

She smiled her malevolent smile. 'I am better with other things – such as summoning demons to let these ridiculous people know who is in charge. But why did you become involved? I told you to stay away from me – from the Sorcerer. Why did you not listen? I would

467

have spared you. Now I cannot. Deal with him, Mildenale. I have other business to attend.'

Without waiting for her accomplice to reply, she turned back towards the cloth and her lantern. Bartholomew hurled himself across the chamber, aiming a kick at Mildenale as he went, and wrenched her away. She yelped as she twisted her bad knee, and then they were rolling across the floor, clawing and scrabbling at each other like wildcats. She was strong, and he struggled to keep her hands away from his eyes. He discovered that her long fingernails were one thing that had been real – and that they were determined to do him harm. Then more lightning forked, so close he thought he could hear it tearing it way towards the ground, and the air was full of the stench of smoke and sulphur.

He was vaguely aware of Mildenale crawling towards the cloth, and knew he would not be able to stop him as long as he was fighting Valeria. He tried to throw her off, but she was a resourceful opponent. First she flicked powder in his face that burned his eyes and made him choke, and then she stabbed his arm with a fragment of wood. He was losing the battle, and Mildenale had almost reached the cloth. Below, the terrified screams from the nave were growing louder and Bartholomew could hear Valeria laughing at him through the thunder. She thought she had won.

Then came the sound of footsteps pounding up the stairs, and he heard Michael's distinctive pant. The monk burst into the chamber, Tulyet and Isnard behind him.

'Enough,' roared Michael, striding forward to haul Valeria away from the physician. 'It is over now. Desist!'

But Valeria was not so easily dissuaded. A slash of her

468

claws forced Michael to release her, and she raced towards the window, grabbing the lamp at the same time.

'No!' cried Bartholomew, as she reached for the cloth.

Michael stormed towards her, but the floor was unequal to such a load. It began to disintegrate. The monk gritted his teeth and forced himself on and, just when the flame was a finger's breadth from the cloth, he managed to seize Valeria and fling her backwards. But he was in trouble. Planks were crumbling beneath his feet, and in desperation he clutched at the tangle of cords. Bartholomew darted forward to save him, but it was too late. With a howl of alarm, the monk toppled out of the window and was left dangling high above the nave.

Jerking the ropes had set off a chain reaction. Sparks flew, and there was a burst of dazzling green light that made the people in the nave look up and howl their terror. The flames illuminated the black smoke Valeria had released earlier, and it illuminated the monk hanging above them.

'No!' shrieked Valeria, crawling towards the window. Her voice was all but drowned by the next thunderclap. 'He has ruined everything! *I* am supposed to descend in a flurry of sights and sounds, not him!'

'You were going to set the church on fire,' yelled Bartholomew, desperately trying to work out which of the ropes would allow him to haul Michael to safety. 'And incinerate—'

Valeria rounded on him with such violence that he recoiled. 'Of course I am not going to burn the place!' she screeched. 'Why would I do that? I want people in awe of me, not dead.'

'You have locked the doors,' Bartholomew began. 'And—'

469

'So no one will be able to leave before the grand finale,' she screamed, exasperated. 'I have been a witch long enough to know folk are easily panicked, and I did not go to all this trouble to have them scurry out like frightened rabbits before they have seen the best parts.'

'It was all her idea,' said Mildenale, stabbing a finger at his accomplice. He winced when lightning lanced into his eyes. 'I tried to stop her—'

'Liar,' Valeria snarled. 'You are the one who has goaded the town into this frenzy, not me.'

'I have seen something like this before,' said Isnard, ignoring them both as he inspected the ropes. And before Bartholomew could stop him, he had set the lamp to the cloth. A wheel began to turn.

'No!' howled Valeria a second time, hurling herself at the bargeman. Tulyet intercepted her and held her in so tight a grip that she was unable to move.

Fascinated, Bartholomew watched machinery grind into action, and saw the swinging monk lowered gently to the nave floor in a fabulous display of smoke, sparks and fumes. Michael staggered slightly when he landed, then hurled the ropes away, as if he imagined he might be hauled back up again if they remained anywhere near him. And then it began to rain. First, there were just a few drops, which made small dark circles on the stone floor. Then there were more.

'Brother Michael,' said Suttone from the chancel, maintaining an admirable calm. 'There you are. I was just telling everyone how you worked so tirelessly to give last rites during the Great Death.'

'Is *he* the Sorcerer, then?' asked Eyton. He looked disappointed. 'I thought it was going to be the Sheriff.'

'There is no Sorcerer,' said Michael tiredly, glancing

470

up as the rain intensified. 'There is nothing but tricks and superstition. Go to the tower and look for yourselves. You will see the bowls and powders that were used to create this nasty little display.'

Then the heavens opened. Slowly, fear and confusion gave way to delight, as folk raised their hands to catch the precious drops, turning their faces skywards to let them be bathed in clean, cooling rain. The Chancellor and Heltisle performed a jigging dance together, and Suttone dropped to his knees to say a heartfelt prayer. Cynric did the same, although he did so while clutching one of his amulets.

'It is true,' said Eyton, returning a few moments later. Tulyet was with him, holding Valeria firmly by the arms, while Isnard had subdued Mildenale with the help of the Sheriff's sword. 'It was all a trick, said to have been put in motion by this lady, who claims to be Mother Valeria.'

'That is not Mother Valeria,' said Cynric with great conviction, eyeing the young woman with open disdain. 'Mother Valeria is a *real* witch.'

Epilogue

'I have decided to let Isnard back in the Michaelhouse Choir,' said Michael. 'I was impressed by the way he used his crutches as levers to rescue us from the charnel house, and I think such ingenuity should be rewarded. Do you?'

'I do,' said Tulyet. 'He saved the entire town that night with his quick thinking. Had he gone to the castle to fetch soldiers, as Matt had ordered, there would have been deaths for certain.'

It was a week after the incidents that had culminated in All Saints-next-the-Castle, and the monk, Bartholomew and Tulyet were sitting in Michaelhouse's orchard, using a fallen apple tree as a bench. The Fellows often used the place when they wanted peace and quiet, and it was pleasant that day. The searing heat had passed with the storm, leaving cloud-dappled skies and a more kindly sun.

'Dickon has apologised again for biting you, Matt,' said Tulyet after a while, although Bartholomew doubted the boy had done any such thing. 'And to encourage him to keep his word, I have given him a proper sword.'

'Christ, Dick!' exclaimed Bartholomew, appalled. 'Now he will stab me instead!'

'I will disarm him before you arrive,' said Tulyet stiffly. 'Besides, it was part compensation for having taken the *Book of Consecrations* away from him. I read it last week, and decided it is not the sort of thing that should be in any Christian home.'

'What did you do with it?' asked Bartholomew uneasily. Dickon was resourceful, and might find a way to get it back again.

'I gave it to Deynman,' replied Tulyet. 'For the Michaelhouse library. It will go some way towards restoring the books that Mildenale ordered William to burn.'

'Langelee has sent William on a sabbatical leave of absence as punishment for that particular episode,' said Michael, tactfully not mentioning that it was not the sort of tome that should be available for students. Perhaps Langelee would sell it – there were plenty of folk who would pay handsomely for such a volume, and Michaelhouse was always eager for ready cash. 'And Prior Pechem has arranged for him to serve the time in a remote Fenland hospital. That should keep him out of mischief for a while.'

Bartholomew turned his thoughts to what had happened on the night when everything had come to a head. 'When you pitched out of the window on those ropes, I thought you were going to fall to your death.' He shuddered. It was not a pleasant memory.

Michael chuckled. 'So did I, but it was all very stately. Once I realised I was in no particular danger, my chief concern was that someone might look up my habit.'

Bartholomew regarded him askance. 'We had Valeria

and Mildenale trying to kill us, and you were worried about your dignity?'

Michael adopted a prim expression. 'A man without dignity is a man with nothing. How can I command respect if the entire town knows intimate details about my nether-garments?'

'I do not think anyone was very interested in those,' said Tulyet. 'Most were more concerned with the fact that they had been promised the Sorcerer – a denizen of Hell, no less – and what they saw descending through the fire and smoke was the University's Senior Proctor.'

'I should have fined the lot of them,' said Michael dourly. 'But people are like sheep in matters of faith. They believe whichever noisy fanatic comes along and tells them what to think.'

'Not all of them, Brother,' said Bartholomew. 'At least half the crowd were just curious. Isnard, for example – he told me ages ago that he was uncomfortable with sorcery, but he went to All Saints because he did not want to be the only one who had missed out.'

'I agree,' said Tulyet. 'Even people who had declared their support for the Church could not resist slipping in for a look – men like Heltisle, Eyton and Prior Pechem.'

'Heltisle,' said Michael with rank disapproval. 'How I dislike that man! Did you know he has been unable to recruit any more porters? He and his Fellows are obliged to do gate duty themselves, which serves them right for giving Younge so much freedom.'

'He paid in other ways, too,' said Tulyet. 'He lost seven goats – it would have been eight if you had not caught Younge stealing the last one – and goats are expensive.'

'What will happen to Mildenale and Valeria?' asked

Bartholomew, not very interested in Bene't College's financial losses.

'Mildenale has claimed benefit of clergy, which means he is unlikely to hang,' replied Tulyet. 'He says Valeria was the one who led him and Margery astray, threatening to expose their ancient dalliance unless they did as she ordered. Meanwhile, Valeria is saying the whole episode was Mildenale's idea, and she was powerless to resist.'

'How did Valeria find out what Mildenale and Margery did in their youth?' asked Michael. 'They were very discreet; no one I have spoken to knew anything about it.'

'According to Mildenale, Margery confided in a fellow witch – a woman she thought was a friend. She misjudged Valeria.'

'Poor Margery,' said Bartholomew sadly. 'Perhaps they did hasten her end, because their plans for the town's future would have filled her with horror.'

'Both Mildenale and Valeria deny intending to burn the church,' Tulyet went on. 'But I know a lie when I hear one. They *were* going to set it alight, then threaten a cowed population with a repeat performance if it showed signs of disobedience – whether people were living the kind of lives Mildenale deemed suitable, or not paying proper homage to the power-hungry Valeria.'

'They were certainly going to raze the charnel house with you inside it,' said Bartholomew. 'I heard them discussing it.'

Tulyet's expression was grim. 'Even if their plan had succeeded, their partnership would not have lasted. Both wanted to be in charge, and each would have worked to undermine the other eventually – just as they are turning on each other now.'

'We were wrong about so many things,' said Michael, after another silence. 'We thought everything was connected to the Sorcerer – the exhumed corpses, the blood in the font, the goats. But they were nothing of the kind.'

'They were all quite separate incidents,' mused Tulyet. 'Danyell's theft of the Bishop's money precipitated a chain of events that drew Michaelhouse and Sewale Cottage into contact with Spynk, Arblaster and Jodoca, and the canons of Barnwell. And then with Osbern and Brownsley.'

'And you,' added Michael. 'You wanted the house, too.'

'I heard the canons paid twenty-five marks for it in the end,' said Tulyet. 'For that price, they are welcome to it, although I understand they have had no success in locating the treasure.'

'Nor will they,' said Michael. 'Cynric searched the place from top to bottom before we made the sale, and he says the hoard is not there. I cannot imagine what Danyell did with it, but it will never be Barnwell's. All Fencotes's machinations were for nothing.'

'I heard Cynric ripped up the floor in his determination to find it,' said Tulyet. 'And you were obliged to lay new tiles before you sold the cottage. Was that not expensive?'

Michael smiled. 'Refham put them in for us, free of charge, to make amends for trying to deprive us of his mother's bequest. We have you to thank for that, Dick. Tell Matt what you did. It was announced at the last Fellows' meeting, but he never listens to anything that happens in those, and I can see from his bemused expression that this one was no different.'

Tulyet grinned. 'A number of people complained that Refham had cheated them, and when I searched his house for evidence of his crimes I found his mother's will. It was made when she was in sound mind, and was witnessed by three priests from Ely. In it, she expresses her desire that Michaelhouse should have those shops for the price of a shilling.'

'A shilling?' echoed Bartholomew in surprise.

'A nominal fee,' said Michael smugly. 'So, we have the property we wanted, and Refham gets virtually nothing. And he was obliged to lay us a nice new floor into the bargain.'

Bartholomew thought uncomfortably about Mother Valeria's spells. Had the cursed stone she had buried really brought about the blacksmith's plunge into financial disaster? Still, at least she had not managed to kill him.

'Did you hear he is dead?' asked Tulyet.

Bartholomew gazed at the Sheriff in shock. 'What?'

'He tried to leave the town, because Michaelhouse was not the only one after him for compensation,' Tulyet explained. 'He put all his worldly goods in a cart, and left for Luton after dark one night. Unfortunately, the last of the Bishop's men were still at large, and a cart loaded with valuables was far too attractive a prize for them to ignore. He and Joan were killed during the skirmish.'

'I doubt that made him happy,' muttered Michael.

'And the Bishop's retainers?' asked Bartholomew. 'Where are they?'

'In my prison, although a few managed to escape. Perhaps they will go to Avignon, to see if de Lisle can use them there. I hope he will be sensible enough to decline their services. Will you try to raise money for him, Brother? He is in desperate need of funds, and you are one of his favourites.'

Michael's expression was troubled. 'I would have done, but the antics of Brownsley and Osbern – and the testimonies of Danyell and Spynk – have unsettled me. I see now that de Lisle *has* used underhand tactics to amass wealth, and I dislike the strong intimidating the weak.'

'So do I,' said Tulyet. 'He claims he knows nothing about what his retainers have been doing, but I am not so sure. They raised a lot of money from their crimes, and he is not stupid. He must have guessed it was coming from somewhere suspect.'

Eventually Tulyet left, and Michael breathed in deeply of the scented summer air. 'I am glad term has started. We have Clippesby back, and we are rid of William for a while, so things are improving.'

'Not everything,' said Bartholomew sadly. 'I am sorry Carton is dead.'

'So am I. Still, at least he lies in the right cemetery now – Clippesby arranged it yesterday. I wish he had told us what he had come do; we might have been able to help. It is a pity Jodoca killed him – and a pity Mildenale killed Thomas, too. Still, at least your conscience is eased: it was not your sedative that ended Thomas's life. And I understand Paxtone and Rougham have changed their minds, and say you were right to have given him a potion that would calm him.'

'Medicine is not an exact science, Brother. There is more magic in it than you might think.'

John Brownsley knew he was dying, and he blamed the Bishop. He had been a loyal servant for years, but a single careless moment had seen Danyell slip into the London tavern where he was staying and steal the box of coins intended for Avignon. The hoard had contained a fortune – eighteen hundred and five silver shillings and nine gold coins, all packed into a specially made casket. The coins had been raised from revenues imposed by the Bishop, and Brownsley had collected them personally. It had not been pleasant work, because not everyone could pay – and more than one family would starve that winter because he had insisted on taking what was due.

After the theft, Brownsley had tracked Danyell and his friend Spynk all the way to Cambridge, where he had managed to corner the man. Danyell had freely admitted to stealing the box, but had stubbornly declined to say where he had hidden it. The stupid man claimed it was his revenge on the Bishop for terrorising him in Norfolk. And then Danyell had just clutched his chest and died, although neither Brownsley nor Osbern had laid a finger on him. It had taken several searches of Sewale Cottage, but Brownsley had located the hoard in the end. It had been buried near one of the walls in a specially made recess. It was neatly and cleverly done, as he would have expected from a talented mason like Danyell.

It was a safe place, so he had left it where it was, intending to collect it later. He knew the Bishop would be delighted, not only with the brimming box, but with the additional revenue collected by his colleagues along the Huntingdon Way, too. But then everything had turned sour: he and Osbern had been arrested, and Cambridge's Sheriff had crushed their gang of henchmen.

Brownsley had not been worried at first, because de Lisle had always rescued him in the past, pulling strings, passing bribes and having words in ears. But this time, the Bishop had not bothered. Castle prisons were unhealthy places, and Brownsley had caught a fever. He had seen such sicknesses before, and knew this one was going to kill him.

His original plan had been to claim the hoard as soon as he was released, and take it to Avignon. But the Bishop had not helped Brownsley, so Brownsley did not see why he should help the Bishop. The box could stay where it was, and good luck to it. Perhaps it would bring a smile to someone's face in the future. He wondered why the book-bearer had not seen it when he had searched. The Welshman was supposed to be observant, so why had he failed to see the clues?

Brownsley closed his eyes, and supposed he would never know.

Historical Note

In October 2000, a remarkable discovery was made in Cambridge. Some 1,805 silver pennies and nine gold nobles or half-nobles were discovered near the corner of Chesterton Lane and Magdalene Street. The silver coins date from around the time of the plague (1348–1350), while the gold ones appear to have been laid on top of them by about 1355. The coins were in an iron-studded wooden chest, which had been placed in a hole near a wall. It seems that the hole was then sealed with a stone, and the room overlaid with a new clay floor. Whether the home improvements were carried out specifically to hide the money, or whether someone just took advantage of a convenient situation will probably never be known.

The hoard would have been a fabulous amount of money in the fourteenth century – perhaps enough to pay an agricultural labourer for six years. Why it was deposited, and by whom, is not known, although it is likely that its owner had every expectation of reclaiming it, but never had the chance. Whoever hid the money probably lived in the house where it was buried, either as its owner or as a tenant. Barnwell Priory is known to have owned property in the area, and records show the building was occupied by one Margery Sewale in the 1450s. The coins and a reconstruction of the chest are on display in the Fitzwilliam Museum in Cambridge.

The Prior of the Augustinians at Barnwell in 1357 was Ralph de Norton. The convent was wealthy and respected, and hosted kings, archbishops and high-ranking nobles. Henry Fencotes was one of its canons in the late fourteenth century, while the Italian Matteo di Podiolo was at the Cambridge convent by 1359.

The Master of Michaelhouse in 1357 was Ralph de Langelee, and his Fellows probably included Michael de Causton, William Gotham, John de Clippesby and Thomas Suttone (who had a namesake – Roger Suttone – at Peterhouse). Edmund Mildenale was a Fellow at the College's foundation in 1324; he was rector of East Bradenham church in Norfolk during the plague, and lived on until at least 1361. Not much is known about Roger de Carton, except that he was a Michaelhouse Fellow in 1359.

Like most Colleges, Michaelhouse was keen on acquiring property, especially the land and buildings that adjoined it. In the 1340s or 1350s, its scholars were either given or purchased three houses (or shops) from Joan Refham. Her husband had died during the plague, and it was possible that the arrangement included the College's priests chanting prayers for his soul. The houses stood on ground now belonging to Trinity College, and were later called St Catherine's Hostel.

Bene't College (now Corpus Christi) was founded in 1352 with donations from two town guilds: St Mary and Corpus Christi. Its first Master was Thomas Heltisle (or

Eltisley); Sir John Goldynham and John Hardy were among the first benefactors. William de Eyton was rector of St Bene't's Church in the early 1350s, and later went to South Pool in Devon.

Prior William Pechem ruled the Cambridge Franciscans after the plague, and one of his friars was named Thomas of Irith, who was ordained as a deacon in 1354. Bukenham was a University proctor in the 1330s. Robert Spaldynge was a member of Clare College, and records show he engaged in dubious activities (a fictional account of these is given in *To Kill or Cure*).

It is almost impossible to imagine the impact of the Black Death on the medieval world, but contemporary evidence suggests people reacted very differently to the threat of its return. Some clung even more firmly to the Church, and tried to live reformed lives. Others turned to more ancient gods to protect them, and it seems there was an increase in witchcraft and paganism. Gatherings are thought to have taken place in the churches that were abandoned after the plague-deaths of their congregations; one such chapel was All Saints-next-the-Castle. However, the distinction between magic and religion was still quite blurred in the 1350s, and many people would have been perfectly happy to go to church on Sunday and visit a witch on Monday.

The Bishop of Ely – the Dominican and papal favourite, Thomas de Lisle – was a complex and contradictory man. He was elected to his See in 1345, and almost immediately launched into a bitter feud with a merchant called Richard Spynk. Spynk plied his trade in Norwich although he owned property all across Norfolk and was one of its richest inhabitants. Spynk decided

Norwich's defensive walls needed refurbishing, and not only paid for much of the work, but gave a lot of his time to oversee the project, too. All was going well for Spynk until he met Ely's new prelate.

De Lisle, along with a band of henchman that included his keeper of parks at Downham (Osbern le Hawker), is said to have besieged Spynk at his various properties 'threatening [Spynk's] life and threatening him with mutilation of his members and capture and incarceration of his body, so that for fear of death he dared not go out'. The relentless attack is said to have cost Spynk almost £1,000 in lost cattle and other goods, as well as damage to his houses and assaults on his staff.

This was not the only crime de Lisle was accused of committing. In the 1350s, he was charged with being complicit in at least sixteen charges of theft, extortion, receiving stolen goods, abduction, arson, cattle rustling, assault and eventually murder. One complainant was the King's cousin, Blanche de Wake, and another was John Danyell, who claimed he was terrorised by de Lisle's steward, John Brownsley. In the winter of 1356, alarmed by the evidence massing against him, de Lisle fled to the papal court in Avignon. He never returned to his native country and died in 1361.

Was such a high-ranking churchman guilty of these crimes? The consensus seems to be that he was unlikely to have soiled his own hands, but that the attacks might well have been carried out on his orders or with his tacit agreement. Money was scarce after the plague, and landowners were often ruthless in getting it where they could. In regard to the Spynk case, de Lisle argued that the cattle he took were in lieu of money he was owed.

Spynk denied it, but the court found in favour of de Lisle anyway, and the matter was eventually forgotten – although probably not by Spynk. The later charges laid against de Lisle by the various other complainants probably left Spynk thinking, 'I told you so.'